THE DARK EARL

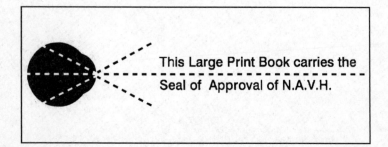

This Large Print Book carries the
Seal of Approval of N.A.V.H.

THE DARK EARL

VIRGINIA HENLEY

THORNDIKE PRESS
A part of Gale, Cengage Learning

GALE
CENGAGE Learning·

Detroit • New York • San Francisco • New Haven, Conn • Waterville, Maine • London

GALE
CENGAGE Learning·

LIBRARY OF CONGRESS CATALOGING-IN-PUBLICATION DATA

Henley, Virginia.
    The dark earl / by Virginia Henley.
      p. cm. — (Thorndike Press large print basic)
    ISBN-13: 978-1-4104-4530-8 (hardcover)
    ISBN-10: 1-4104-4530-5 (hardcover)
    1. Aristocracy (Social class)—England—Fiction. 2. England—Social life and customs—19th century—Fiction. 3. Large type books. I. Title.
PS3558.E49634D36 2012
813'.54—dc23   2011041266

Published in 2012 by arrangement with NAL Signet, a member of Penguin Group (USA), Inc.

Printed in the United States of America
1 2 3 4 5 6 7 16 15 14 13 12

For my beautiful great-granddaughter
Aireanna Lillian Henley

ACKNOWLEDGMENTS

I am indebted to the following historical and biographical sources, which provided a wealth of information on Victorian England's society, monarchy, government, and noble families, including the Hamiltons, Ansons, Lambtons, and Montagus.

- Scott Crosier: *John Snow: The London Cholera Epidemic of 1854*
- Nicholas Culpeper: *Culpeper's Complete Herbal*
- Lord Frederick Spencer Hamilton: *The Days Before Yesterday*
- Lord Holland: Memoirs of the Whig Party, 1854
- John Pearson: *Stags and Serpents*
- J. Preest: *Lord John Russell*
- Charles Spencer: *The Spencers*
- R. Turner Wilcox: *The Mode in Costume*
- *Burke's Peerage, 107th edition:* Charles

Mosley, editor
- *Britannica* online encyclopedia

PROLOGUE

Staffordshire, England
Summer 1842

"It's the most *enchanting* house I've ever seen in my life!" Lady Harriet Hamilton stood enraptured before the magnificent Georgian mansion known as Shugborough Hall. Eight soaring Doric columns dominated the central portico, and graceful pavilions had been added to either side. "Is Father going to buy it?"

"No, no, Harry. Shugborough Hall isn't for sale. Only the contents are being auctioned," Louisa, Duchess of Abercorn, informed her eldest daughter. "Your father intends to buy books and paintings today."

A wave of deep disappointment swept over the young girl as she gazed at the hall with longing. *I wish you were mine!* She spoke to the house as if it were a living thing that could hear her thoughts.

The duchess turned and addressed her

daughters' governess. "Mary, keep a close watch on Lady Beatrix. I suppose I shouldn't have brought her. A six-year-old will be bored to tears at an auction sale."

"I shall watch them like a hawk, Your Grace."

"Oh, you needn't put a leading string on Harry. She knows how to comport herself. Houses hold a fascination for her. You know she has an inquisitive mind that soaks up everything like a sponge."

When Mary took hold of Lady Beatrix's hand, the child stuck out her tongue at her sister. Lady Harriet, however, didn't even notice. She had eyes only for Shugborough and her curiosity knew no bounds.

Thomas Anson felt a burning humiliation as he watched people begin to arrive for the auction sale. The nobles who would swallow up the entire possessions of his ancestral home had insatiable appetites for the valuable collections that had been acquired by his forebears, and the seventeen-year-old heir was helpless to prevent this desecration.

Every member of the *ton* knew that the profligate excesses of his father, the Earl of Lichfield, had brought about his financial collapse. His gambling addiction was no secret, and the entire contents of Shugborough Hall needed to be auctioned to meet the earl's disgraceful debts, which now totaled seven hundred thousand pounds.

Thank God Mother has been spared the shame of being present. The Countess of Lichfield had packed up the exquisite collection of Chinese porcelain and carried it off to their town house in St. James's Square because she adamantly refused to part with it.

Thomas was relieved his older sisters lived in remote counties. All were married and their husbands' good names shielded them from this scandal, which was the talk of London.

He resented with every fiber of his being parting with Shugborough's treasures, and was consumed with a feeling of impotence that he could do nothing to avert the estate's defilement. *Well, almost nothing,* he amended. As a token protest, he had removed a few precious horse paintings by John Frederick Herring and George Stubbs and secretly hidden them away in one of the outbuildings. Thomas realized he was holding a small painting by John Wootton, of the racehorse *Victorious* that had won at Newmarket in the last century. He surreptitiously slipped from the house and hurried

11

across the velvet lawn toward the pale blue and white Chinese pagoda.

When he entered the building, he stopped dead in his tracks. The red lacquered door to the storage room on the back wall of the pagoda stood open, and the slim figure of a female, her back to him, stood inside.

"What the devil do you think you're doing?" he demanded curtly.

At the sound of his voice, the female swung about to face him, and he realized with relief that she was only a child who could not possibly be more than nine years old.

Lady Harry stared at the dark youth with curiosity. Both her parents were dark, as was she, but this fellow was as swarthy as a Gypsy. Suddenly her green eyes widened.

"I needn't ask what you're doing. 'Tis obvious you are stealing!"

Thomas Anson took immediate offense, because that was *exactly* what he was doing.

"You cheeky little bitch. You have no right to be here poking your nose into every nook and cranny of this estate."

"I have as much right to be here as you. My father is here to buy paintings — perhaps those very paintings that you are stealing!"

"I happen to be Lord Lichfield's son. Our family *owns* these paintings."

"Piffle! Lichfield's heir?" She looked pointedly at his black hair and dark complexion. "More likely you're a stableboy stealing the family blind."

Thomas drew himself up to his full height and summoned an air of authority. "You need your arse tanned. Get the hell out of this pagoda before I take you across my knee."

Harriet stiffened. "My father is the Duke of Abercorn. If you lay a finger on me, he will have you thrashed within an inch of your miserable life."

Miserable, indeed. His mouth quirked with amusement. "Since your father is the Duke of Abercorn, and my father is the Earl of Lichfield, we are at an impasse."

Harry's eyes sparkled with secret enjoyment. "A duke's daughter trumps an earl's son any day of the year." She glanced back at the horse paintings she had discovered hidden behind the door. "They are so lovely, you cannot bear to part with them."

He was amazed that such a young girl could be so perceptive. "If I can bear being Lichfield's son, I suppose I can bear anything."

She heard the mocking bitterness in his

voice. "I won't say a word," she promised.

He nodded his head in thanks, far more grateful than he dared put into words.

"Thank you so much, James, for buying the first editions of Rousseau. I know they were expensive, but the thought that I own *Émile* fills me with *joie de vivre*." Louisa, Duchess of Abercorn, stood on tiptoe and kissed her husband's cheek.

"I bought the entire library. The books on architecture and art are for you, Harry. You'll appreciate them when you are older," her father declared.

"I shall appreciate them now if they have pictures of houses and explain how they are designed." Her eyebrows drew together as she thought of Lichfield's son. "We didn't bring the books back with us to London. You don't think they'll get stolen, do you, Father?"

"Whatever has put such an absurd notion into your head? They are bought and paid for. The auction will go on for at least another week. When it's over, we'll send the wagons to transport everything we have acquired."

"They are auctioning the furniture day after tomorrow." Louisa fanned herself with the Shugborough auction catalogue. "I saw a pair of brass-mounted Regency armchairs I wouldn't mind for the library."

Harry's face lit up. "If you're going again, promise you will take me with you?"

Her mother smiled her assent. "Shugborough made quite an impression on you. I think on Thursday we'll leave Beatrix at home with Louisa Jane and baby James."

The assembled crowd filled the elegant reception rooms and spilled into the long gallery. The bidding on Shugborough Hall's furnishings was fast and furious, and Harry slipped away unnoticed through the vast kitchens, then made her way outside. She skipped across the velvet lawns, and stopped before each white marble statue. She recognized Venus, but it was the male statue close by that held her attention the longest. The name carved on the pedestal of the young god was Adonis. *He is superb!* As her eyes admired his naked limbs, she wondered if all males looked like this without their clothes. *Silly, only gods are this perfect.*

Harry passed the Chinese pagoda and entered a structure that was called the *Tower of Winds.* As she gazed at the magnificent sculpted black marble centaurs, Harry thought she could hear music. She cocked her head to listen, and then broke into a smile of delight — it was the summer wind wafting through the diamond-shaped holes that had been specially designed into the tower walls.

Harry heard the thunder of hooves and ran outside to watch a rider gallop like a fiend toward the river. It was the dark devil she had encountered before, astride a black hunter. It was obvious that he was still angry and she surmised he could be dangerous, but this didn't stop her from admiring him. *He looks exactly like a centaur!*

She wandered over to a high wall that had an arched wooden door at its center. She turned the iron ring on the door and allowed it to swing open. She found herself in a walled garden complete with a cascading fountain and a profusion of scented flowers. Enchanted, she sat down on a rustic bench to watch the birds splash in the water. The fragrant jasmine and honeysuckle attracted myriad bees and butterflies.

All at once, a sparrow hawk swooped down. Fearing for the little birds, she flapped her arms to scare it off. It flew a short distance away and spied a little green snake. It took the snake in its hooked beak and was about to carry it off. Harry screamed and ran toward the hawk. It promptly dropped the snake and flew off with a screech of protest.

With relief, Harry watched the little green snake slither to safety, and her heart filled with joy. "I love this place," she murmured. "Shugborough is —" She searched for the right words, then smiled. "Absolute perfection!"

Thomas Anson didn't return to the hall until the afternoon light faded and dusk had begun to fall. He hoped that all the vultures who had descended earlier would have taken wing by now. He dismounted and led his horse into the pasture behind the stables. He slipped off the saddle, hoisted it to his shoulder, and headed toward the tack room. When he heard his father's voice coming from the stables, he stopped and waited, hoping he would leave. The contempt he felt was like bitter gall in his mouth.

His ears pricked up when he heard the name *Ranton*. This was his father's nearby sporting estate, complete with racing stables, where the nobility, including the prime minister and certain lesser members of the royal family, came to indulge their bloodlust by shooting game and gambling away their fortunes.

His father's voice ordered, "Wait until close to midnight. Make absolutely sure nobody sees you. The paraffin is stored in the stone outbuilding next to the stables."

Paraffin? Christ Almighty, he's arranging to burn the place down. Thomas's gut knotted. *Curse the swine! He has Ranton insured for a half million.*

He quietly retraced his steps back to the pasture, resaddled his horse, and headed toward Ranton. He covered the miles swiftly and by the time dusk turned into full darkness, he had reached the estate. He entered the stables, where a dozen Thoroughbreds were housed in box stalls. He slipped a bridle onto the first horse and led it outside.

The head groom questioned his actions. "What are ye about, m'lord?"

"All the animals are to be moved to the meadow." He knew he could not tell the stable hands the ugly truth. "Father's orders. Be quick about it."

Thomas ran to the kennels, where the buckhound hunting dogs were housed. He opened the gate wide, picked up a dog whip, and lashed it a few times to make sure the animals cleared off. After he was sure they were safe, he made his way toward the house. Ranton had originally been an abbey; its tower dated from the fifteenth century. He found the head gamekeeper eating supper in the kitchen with the house-keeper.

"Mrs. Barlow, I want you to assemble the servants," he said urgently.

"Bless yer heart, m'lord, there's only me here. All the staff was transported to Shugborough to help with the auction sale."

He sank down onto a kitchen chair with relief. "I want you two to clear out when you've finished eating."

"Whatever for?"

"For reasons I can't explain. Just make sure you don't sleep here tonight."

The two people at the table exchanged a knowing glance.

"And by the way, if anyone asks, you haven't seen me. I haven't been here today."

Before Thomas had ridden five miles back toward Shugborough, he could see flames lighting up the sky. He reined in his mount and stared at the orange glow with horror.

The depraved swine did it. He actually paid someone to have it burned down. God rot his stinking soul!

The hall was in darkness when he arrived home, as if it were peacefully sleeping. He encountered no one as he made his way to his bedchamber. When he opened the door, he found the room empty, and he realized that even his bedroom suite had been sold.

Thomas Anson stretched out on the floor and folded his arms behind his head. Hatred and loathing consumed him. Dread formed a lump in his throat that almost choked him. It was fear his father would order the torch be put to this house too. But gradually, his love for Shugborough Hall surrounded him and overcame all else. *If it takes me a lifetime, I will restore everything that has been taken from you today,* he promised the house faithfully. *Once you are mine, I will restore you to absolute perfection!*

CHAPTER ONE

Hampden House, London
June 1854

"*Oh, bugger and balls!* Sometimes I wish we were back in Ireland." Lady Harriet Hamilton removed the second hat she had tried on and flung it across the room. "Living in London is far too repressive. I have no freedom to do anything."

Her sister Lady Beatrix laughed. "It hasn't curtailed your swearing."

Harry joined in her laughter. "Nor my wagering, or flirting, or roaming about the city unescorted." She looked in the mirror and wrinkled her nose. "It's these bloody fashions set by the queen. They are hideous!"

"You're nineteen, going on twenty, so you can't possibly go bareheaded."

"Well, I abso-bloody-lutely refuse to wear a bonnet. They make me look like Old Mother Hubbard." She was totally unaware that her long dark hair and pale green eyes gave her a rare and striking beauty.

The Duchess of Abercorn swept into her daughters' bedchamber. "Aren't you ready yet? I usually insist on being fashionably late, but today that's out of the question. Victoria and Albert are officiating at this grand opening of the second Crystal Palace, and we cannot insult the queen by being tardy." The Duke of Abercorn was Prince Albert's *groom of the stole,* and for the last eight years had also been his friend and confidant. "This official opening, which marks the beginning of the Season, has already been delayed a month because the male statues were considered too shocking for the queen's sensibilities." She gave a sardonic laugh. "Since Victoria has had eight children, I'm sure she's more than familiar with *male parts.*"

"It is utter desecration to ruin beautiful statues by chopping off their genitals and replacing them with fig leaves," Harry said with disgust.

"Oh, the fig leaves were subsequently considered too offensive, so now they've draped all the statues with cloth."

Harriet and Beatrix rolled their eyes.

"Do you think Prince Teddy will be there?" Jane, who was seventeen, asked with apprehension.

"Of course he'll be there. He's the heir to the throne and his doting parents think the sun shines out his arse," her mother replied. "What's he done now?"

"When we were at Windsor last week, he touched my breast," Jane declared.

"But he's only thirteen," Harry said.

"What the devil does age have to do with it?" her mother asked. "He's a male, and already randy by the looks of him. Don't be alone with him, darling, or he'll have your drawers off."

"Royalty has its privileges," Harry quipped.

"Too bad he isn't a bit older," Beatrix said with a wink. "If you play your cards right, you could end up a princess."

Jane blushed. "You are a devil, Trixy!"

"All three of you are devils. What's the holdup here?" their mother demanded.

"Harry refuses to wear a bonnet," Trixy complained.

"Well, I should think so," the duchess declared, plucking the decoration from one of the discarded hats. "Pin this bunch of cherries into your hair. Always remember, we don't *follow* fashion; we *set* it." She touched the crimson ostrich feathers on her own hat to prove her point.

When the fashionably gowned quartet emerged onto Green Street, they found sixteen-year-old James waiting by the phaeton. He opened the carriage door for the ladies. "I'm sitting on the box with Riley. Your crinolines leave no room for me."

"Just don't let your new top hat blow away," his mother warned.

James shut the door. "I wish you had let me take the train. It lets you off at the main gate to the palace grounds."

"The railway was built to accommodate the masses. There will be such a crush of hoi polloi today, you wouldn't be able to breathe," the duchess declared with a shudder.

"I'll ride the train with you later in the week, James," Harry offered. "I rather like the hoi polloi."

James climbed up beside their driver. He turned, winked at Harry, grinned at his mother, removed his hat, and held it in his lap for safekeeping.

"You have a tender heart, Harry. I put it down to the time your father was the lord lieutenant of County Donegal and the ruinous rains came. One end of Ireland to the other became a vast wasteland of putrefying vegetation. I took you with me on my mercy visits to the poor, and you've championed

24

the downtrodden ever since."

"I'm following in Uncle Johnny's footsteps." Lord John Russell, the Duchess of Abercorn's half brother, had served a six-year term as England's prime minister until two years ago.

"Our family has decidedly bad timing. Johnny had been in the House of Commons thirty-three years before he became prime minister. Ireland hadn't had a chance to recover from the tragic potato famine when he took office."

"But he was still able to do lots of good things," Harry reminded her mother. "Not only did he abolish the Corn Laws, but he was able to limit the working hours for women."

"Oh, let's not talk politics, Harry. The Season officially opens today and it's supposed to be a celebration," Trixy declared.

"Every other year, the Season opens in May. That's another delay we can blame on Her Gracious Majesty," Harry said with disgust.

"Speaking of celebrations, I don't understand why I can't make my debut with Harry and Trixy. Think of the expense it will save if we all have our Season together."

"Since when did you start caring about expenses, Jane?" her mother asked dryly. "A

25

coming-out ball tells society that the young ladies making their debut are ready for marriage. Since Harriet and Beatrix are only a year apart, they are having their Season together."

"But I'm seventeen. I don't want to be left out," Jane pleaded.

"You're hardly out of the schoolroom. It would be scandalous of me to throw you onto the marriage market. Just be happy that I will allow you to attend their ball."

Harry poked Trixy in the ribs with her elbow. "D'you hear that? We are to be thrown on the marriage market. Sold to the highest bidder, I warrant."

"Sounds like an exciting adventure to me," Trixy teased. "A guinea says I get more proposals than you."

"Marriage proposals, or the other kind?" Harry asked.

"Don't jest. You'll get plenty of both," their mother warned.

"You shock my sensibilities. Society's morals have changed since the decadent Regency era, when you came of age, Mother. Gentlemen today treat ladies as if they were saints. They want their females to be pure and innocent, and will do everything in their power to protect them from being tainted by the wicked world." Harry gave a mock sigh. "Queen Victoria has taken all the fun out of everything."

"Rubbish! Gentlemen may pay lip service to the *pure and innocent,* but in reality nothing could be further from the truth. Beneath the facade of respectability, lust and licentiousness lurk. The male of the species will take advantage of any opportunity."

Harry winked at her sisters. "Is that what Father did?"

Lady Lu smiled her secret smile. "None of you would have been born if he hadn't. The last thing I wanted was a child."

Harry's eyes widened in surprise. "How did he persuade you?"

"He promised that if I gave in to his passionate advances, he would give me a girl." Her wry gaze swept over her daughters. "If I'd known he would give me *three* daughters in a row, I might have resisted."

The Hamilton sisters laughed. Their mother had always said outrageous things and she encouraged them to follow in her footsteps.

When they arrived at Crystal Palace Park, there was already a crush of carriages. Riley drove the phaeton as close to the front entrance as he could manage, and the Hamilton family alighted and made their way

27

inside to await Her Royal Highness Queen Victoria and Albert, her prince consort.

They made their way past the series of ornamental fountains and ascended the dais built especially for the ribbon-cutting ceremony. Within minutes, the royal family came into view with its retinue of attendants.

Harry's glance was drawn to her father, who walked directly behind Albert. Not only was Abercorn taller, but he was far handsomer in her opinion, since the prince consort's hair had receded alarmingly. She watched her parents exchange an intimate glance. *They are still in love with each other. That's the kind of marriage I want.*

As Queen Victoria delivered her speech, extolling the Crystal Palace as a showplace for the industrial, military, and economic superiority of Great Britain, Harry's mind wandered back to the summers at Barons Court, their Irish estate. Vivid memories of her father rowing her mother across the fairy-tale lakes or taking her up before him on one of his Arabians filled her head. *He's still wooing her after twenty years of marriage.* Harry sighed. *How utterly romantic!*

Her thoughts were brought back to the present when she saw young Prince Teddy edging close to her sister Jane. Harry murmured to her brother, "Teddy can't keep his hands off Jane. When you get him alone, thump him on the nose."

He whispered back, "I may be reckless, but I'm not raving mad. Teddy will be *king* one day. It pays to have friends in high places." He glanced at fourteen-year-old Princess Vicky. "It must run in the family. The Princess Royal can't keep her hands off my private parts."

"Well, I'll be damned!" Harry exclaimed in utter shock.

"We declare the second Great Exhibition open to the public." Victoria cut the ribbon and the throng cheered, "God save Our Gracious Majesty!"

The fountain water jets suddenly rose up over a hundred feet in the air. The spectacle caused the crowd to step back, and only the privileged spectators on the front row were anointed by the spray.

Harry lost no time making her getaway. But as she left the dais, she paused before Prince Teddy and smiled sweetly. "I dreamed about you last night, Your Highness. You touched Jane's breast, and I shoved you on your arse!"

It took him a moment to gauge her meaning; then he threw back his head and laughed with glee. "That's why I didn't touch yours, Harry."

She shook her fist at him and hurried off, eager to see the fantastical displays that had been brought from around the world. An entire wing of the glass building had been divided into courts depicting the history of art and architecture from ancient Egypt through the Renaissance. Harry drank it all in, moving slowly so she could appreciate the fine details. She stopped to look at a display of extinct animals from around the world. She stared at some ugly green creatures made of plaster.

A deep voice from behind her said, "They are called *dinosaurs*. Do you like them?"

Harry turned around to see who addressed her. The gentleman was tall and extremely dark. There was something vaguely familiar about him that stirred her memory, and suddenly she was swept back to Shugborough, the mansion that had stolen her heart more than a decade ago. She could even smell the jasmine and honeysuckle. "I would call them monstrosities," she drawled. "I much prefer *centaurs*."

Their eyes met, and held. "So, you know who I am."

"And you, obviously, are aware of my identity."

Green eyes stared into pewter as the male and female took each other's measure. Harry saw a man in his late twenties. Though handsome, his features were stern and unsmiling. He carried himself with a great deal of unbending pride, and had an animal magnetism that was fatally attractive.

"I think it unwise to wander about alone in this crowd. May I escort you back to your family, my lady?"

"You arrogant devil!" She laughed in his face. "I would be offended if you weren't so ridiculous. I do not conform to the rigid rules of propriety, my lord!"

He looked pointedly at the cherries adorning her hair. "It is evident that your upbringing has been remiss. Your father should have taken you across his knee."

"And tanned my arse? If I remember correctly, that's what you threatened to do the last time we met."

It was clear the young beauty was mocking him. She had been outspoken as a child; now she was downright brazen. Thomas Anson was tempted to take her by the shoulders and shake the insolence from her. He clenched his fists to keep his hands from violating her.

Anson possessed a supreme air of author-

31

ity that rubbed Harry the wrong way. She threw him a contemptuous smile and turned away. Before she had taken a dozen steps, she came face-to-face with D'Arcy Lambton, the young Earl of Durham. He was the grandson of Lord Earl Grey, and a close family friend.

"Hello, Harriet. You look ravishing today."

"D'Arcy." She gave him her hand and he took it to his lips.

"Did you know they have a circus set up in the center transept?" He pointed in the opposite direction. "Oh, there's my friend Thomas. Come, let me introduce you to him." He led her toward Anson, and greeted him warmly. "Allow me to present Lady Harriet Hamilton. . . . This is my good friend Thomas, Lord Anson."

The corners of Harry's mouth lifted with amusement as she offered Anson her hand.

He took it stiffly, and bent his mouth to her fingers.

"You're supposed to kiss it, not bite it," she warned with a gurgle of laughter.

"You know each other?" D'Arcy asked with surprise.

"Thomas and I have been acquainted for years. We once conspired to steal some paintings together."

D'Arcy laughed. "I warrant they were

valuable. Thomas is an authority on art."

Anson glared at her with disapproval. "You are incorrigible," he muttered.

"Flattery, begod!" Harry teased.

"Harriet and I are going to take a look at the circus. Why don't you join us?"

"Oh, yes, please do," she urged. "I hear they have a tightrope walker."

Anson accepted immediately. Since he knew her invitation was insincere, it gave him perverse satisfaction.

Harry, flanked by the two handsome lords — one fair, the other extremely dark — made her way through the crowd to the center transept. Trumpets blared, followed by a drumroll, and as everyone raised their eyes, they saw a man ascending a narrow metal ladder. He didn't stop until he reached a dizzying height; then he took a firm grip on a long, thin pole and stepped out onto a high wire that was almost invisible. The crowd below gave a collective gasp.

"His name is Blondin. If he walks the tightrope successfully, it will make him famous," Thomas predicted.

"A guinea says he doesn't make it all the way across!"

D'Arcy coughed uncomfortably. "Thomas doesn't make wagers. He is opposed to any kind of gambling on principle."

Harry felt her cheeks flush. She knew she had made a faux pas. Instead of apologizing, she said recklessly, "Surely when a male wagers, it shows courage."

Thomas's features hardened. "And when a female wagers, it shows vulgarity. As a matter of fact, I find this entire display rather vulgar."

"If you are referring to Blondin's tights, I think they display his manhood magnificently."

It was D'Arcy's turn to flush.

Harry gritted her teeth. There was something about the dark devil that made her behave outrageously. She saw Anson's eyes narrow. The look of censure he gave her was threatening. *If we were alone, he'd shake me until my teeth rattled.*

Harry slipped her arm into D'Arcy's, using him as a shield. "Did you receive your invitation to our ball? The guest list was extremely selective, but since you are an earl, we made an exception in your case," she teased.

"You and Lady Beatrix are making your debut together. I assume you'll be spending the Season in London and won't be going to Barons Court until later in the year?" D'Arcy asked.

Harry sighed. "You assume correctly,

more is the pity. I miss Ireland."

"What is it that you miss?" Anson asked pointedly.

"I miss the people. They have an irreverent sense of humor. They are not straitlaced like the English, who worship at the altar of respectability."

"To the Irish, drinking and gambling are virtues," Anson said dryly.

"Indeed they are. I am grateful that they taught me to do both."

His dark eyes were filled with censure. "You revel in audacity."

"You have guessed my secret, my lord. Since I discerned your secret years ago, I warrant we are even."

A cry of alarm from the crowd drew all eyes upward, where Blondin swayed precariously, before he regained his balance.

"Oh Lord, I can't bear to watch. If he falls, it will make me ill. It's outrageous that a man is forced to do such things for money."

Anson's grim expression softened. "You've just revealed another secret. . . . You are tenderhearted."

"Yes, I do take pity on those less fortunate." Her green eyes glittered with mischief.

"So you may consider yourself invited to

my debut ball."

"I admit to being guilty of showing my disapproval, Lady Harriet, but surely such cruel punishment doesn't fit the crime."

She threw back her head and laughed. "You do have a sense of humor after all!"

CHAPTER TWO

"I'd like a colored sash on this presentation gown," Harry declared firmly.

"Out of the question," her mother said flatly. "White shows off your dark hair and green eyes to perfection. I don't hear Beatrix complaining about having to wear white."

"I know that white is flattering, but it's the *principle* I object to. It is unheard of to be presented to the queen in anything but pristine white, and that is precisely my point."

"I won't relent on this decision, Harry. Victoria's court has rigid rules. If you don't conform, it will reflect on your parents."

"The queen might censure *you,* but Father can do no wrong in Victoria's eyes," Harry teased.

"It would reflect badly on you too. Your virtue could be whispered about."

"How ridiculous that wearing white declares one's virtue. You're usually quite lenient about letting me make my own decisions."

"Too lenient!" Trixy declared.

"When was I too lenient?" the duchess demanded.

"When you caught her gambling with the Irish stableboys."

"I was grateful that gambling was the only thing she was doing with them," the duchess said dryly.

The modiste, who was doing the final fitting of the Hamilton girls' presentation gowns, looked shocked. Their mother quickly changed the subject. "You needn't wear the same gowns to your ball. If you are willing to risk your reputation, I'm sure Madam Martine will be only too happy to satisfy your craving for color."

"I have some lovely pastel blue organza, Lady Harriet."

"How bloody insipid!" Harry bit her lip when she saw the stunned expression on the modiste's face. "Oh, I'm so sorry, madam. Please forgive me. I have a dreadful habit of speaking my mind."

"Blue organza sounds very pretty to me, madam," Trixy declared. "My sister is nineteen, *going on twenty,* and has the taste of an older woman."

"That was unkind. You know that Harry's debut was postponed because my dearest mother passed away." Georgina, Duchess of Bedford, had died the previous spring.

"Trixy's barb about my age completely missed the mark. At nineteen, I am a woman, while she and Jane are still girls."

"There's more to being a woman than turning nineteen, darling," her mother stated.

"I assume you are speaking of virginity, or lack thereof," Harry declared. "That's another unfair burden that makes the sexes unequal!"

Madam Martine almost swallowed the pins she held in her mouth.

"Come down from your soapbox, Harry." The duchess helped her daughter from the stool she was standing on. "I'm sure Madam isn't up to a lecture on *women's rights*. Just tell her what color you would like for your ball gown."

"Pale green with an emerald sash," Harry said without hesitation.

Her mother laughed. "You are Irish down to your fingertips. I'm sure your father will be delighted at your choice."

"Uncle Johnny! I'm so happy you will be attending our presentation to the queen this afternoon. Without you, it would likely be dull and depressing as a London fog!"

Lord John laughed. "You flatter me, Harry. But what makes you think it'll be dull?"

"Well, let's face it. A score of debutantes dressed in identical white, chaste as the driven snow, attending Victoria's Drawing Room, isn't exactly a bacchanalia."

"And what do you know of bacchanalia?" he teased.

"Nothing yet, but I'm hopeful my Season will rectify that."

"I wish I were being presented today," Jane said wistfully.

Johnny kissed her cheek. "Your time will come, Jane. And you won't have to share the spotlight with your sisters."

"But I like sharing things with Harry and Trixy. They make everything exciting."

The Duchess of Abercorn rolled her eyes. "Only an innocent could think one of Victoria's Drawing Rooms exciting." She picked up her fan. "I assume we are using your carriage, John. Pray lead the way."

"I love this Grand Staircase at Buckingham Palace." Lady Beatrix gazed at the royal portraits that had been built into the walls.

"I much prefer Windsor Castle." Lady Harriet's crinoline swayed precariously as she ascended the marble steps. "Its ancient walls are steeped in history."

The Hamiltons joined the other debutantes who were being presented at today's Drawing Room and Harry marveled at the excited twittering of the young ladies. Since her father was Prince Albert's groom of the stole, and she was a frequent visitor, she did not hold the royal family in awe as the other debutantes did. As she looked about, she decided that Trixy's white gown flattered her dark coloring, but the fair-haired girls looked washed-out. The females were all shapes and sizes, from scrawny to lumpy.

Harry spied her friend Lady Emily Curzon-Howe, who had lovely chestnut-colored hair. "I think it tiresome that we must all wear white."

Emily whispered behind her fan, "White flatters you and me, but Lady Augusta Seymour looks like an unmade bed."

"That's rather cruel, but I was thinking the exact same thing," Harry murmured.

When the chamberlain opened the door to the throne room, everyone filed in and waited politely for their turn to be acknowledged by the queen.

Harry sighed with relief when her father arrived. She gave him a radiant smile, and the Duke of Abercorn bent and kissed her

41

brow, then kissed Beatrix. James Hamilton was a loving father who doted on his daughters.

Abercorn murmured his thanks to his brother-in-law Lord John for accompanying his ladies to Buckingham Palace. He then watched proudly as his eldest daughter walked down the throne room and made her curtsy before the queen.

"Lady Harriet, we are delighted to welcome you to our Drawing Room. Your gown is lovely. The Duchess of Abercorn's fashion sense is incomparable."

"Thank you, Your Gracious Majesty." Her Season had begun at long last.

When all the debutantes had been presented, everyone was free to mingle and partake of the refreshments. Harry joined her family. "The queen complimented my gown and Mother's fashion sense."

"Victoria's manners are always perfect," her father declared. "She's after your mother for her *Mistress of the Robes*."

The duchess rolled her eyes and gave a delicate shudder.

James laughed before turning to his daughters. "Are you ready for your ball?"

"Yes. Harry and I can't wait. Are you coming home tonight, Father?"

"I am, my dear." James spoke to his wife. "I'm tired of sleeping alone, aren't you?"

Louisa gave him a sideways look. "What makes you think I'm sleeping alone?"

Harry smiled at their banter. *Mother holds him in the palm of her hand. They act like lovers. That's the kind of relationship I want.*

James Hamilton greeted Richard Curzon-Howe, who had been lord chamberlain to the late Queen Adelaide. He stood with his daughter Emily, from his first marriage. Abercorn was always amazed that the aging earl had been able to attract such a young second wife.

Lady Abercorn greeted Lady Curzon-Howe and felt a twinge of compassion for the young Irish beauty. The ladies had coordinated the dates of their debutante balls.

Lady Emily drew close to Harry and whispered in her ear, "I want you to formally introduce me to your brother."

"Are you sure? He's only sixteen," Harry informed her.

"What the devil does that matter? He's extremely handsome and someday he'll be a duke of the realm."

Harry approached her brother, with Emily in tow. "James, I'd like you to meet Lady Emily. She'll be at our ball tomorrow night."

Harry winked. "Seems she's attracted to younger men."

Emily smiled. "It runs in the family. My father wed a lady not much older than I."

James took her hand to his lips. "How fortuitous. I'm raving mad about older women. I shall claim the first dance tomorrow night."

Harry said dryly, "A match made in heaven. I shall give you some privacy."

She joined her mother, who was in conversation with Lord John.

"May I rely upon you to bring our sister Rachel to the ball? If everyone sees she is held in high esteem by her family, it will put an end to the scandalous gossip about her." When Rachel was born, the rumors were rife that the famous artist Edwin Landseer had fathered her. The speculation had begun again when Georgina, Duchess of Bedford, passed away.

"Poor Rachel was absolutely devastated when she heard the rumor. But I believe the fact that she still resides at Campden Hill with the family's blessing has done much to quell the gossip," John assured her. Lord John and his wife, Fanny, lived next door to Campden Hill in Kensington, at Holland House. Lady Holland had left it to him in her will, perhaps because Johnny had been like a son to her, or more likely because she detested her own daughter-in-law.

"Rachel is such delightful company," Harry declared. "Will you please invite her to stay with us for a few days after the ball?"

"Of course. Rachel has such a happy disposition. John, tell her to bring enough clothes for a fortnight. 'Tis a pity that she is still unwed. It always falls to the last daughter left at home to look after the mother, and Rachel dutifully dedicated herself to Mother the last few years. I'll try my hand at matchmaking while she's in London."

Harry saw that Prince Albert was making a beeline toward her mother. Lady Lu attracted admirers from grooms to princes. Harry knew that where Albert went, Victoria followed, so she took Johnny's arm and led him toward the refreshment table. "There's something I want to ask you. I believe Thomas Anson is a member of Parliament. What can you tell me about him?"

"Thomas is the member for Lichfield, Staffordshire. His father, the Earl of Lichfield, was also a politician until his health gave out. Like me, Thomas is a Whig."

"Surely you can tell me more than that."

Johnny eyed her with speculation. "Well,

let's see. He's dark, handsome, thirtyish, unwed, an art expert. He'll inherit his father's earldom, but no fortune, I'm afraid."

"He'll inherit Shugborough Hall."

Johnny hid his glee. He knew of Harriet's passion for houses. "Viscount Anson is a very serious, no-nonsense sort of man. He doesn't suffer fools gladly. I warrant he's far too sober and straitlaced for you, Harry."

Indeed! Thomas Anson is direct, assertive, and utterly self-assured. He delivers his reprimands in a clipped tone. "I invited him to my ball, in spite of the fact that he thoroughly disapproves of me, and makes no bones about it."

"I thought D'Arcy Lambton was at the top of your list of suitors."

"Oh, he is. Absolutely! The Earl of Durham owns Lambton Castle."

"Have you ever seen the castle?"

"No, but I've seen it in paintings. It was designed in the style of a Norman stronghold. I can't wait to visit it."

"It's built on the site of a more ancient castle known for its legendary dragon. You must ask D'Arcy about it."

"How fascinating! I love legends. Ireland is steeped in them. I shall ask him about the dragon tomorrow night at the ball."

■ ■ ■ ■

The following day, the Hamilton ladies greeted John's wife, Fanny, and Lady Rachel. They arrived in the afternoon with ample time to dress for the ball.

"I'm so glad you'll be staying with us for a while, Rachel. I'm dying to hear what you are planning to write in your next book." Harry picked up Rachel's hatbox and they headed up the stairs to the guest wing.

"Why don't you share the guest chamber with me? I need some good ideas, and two heads are decidedly better than one."

"That's a splendid idea." Harry had always been proud that her aunt penned romance novels, and was thrilled at the prospect of contributing to her next book. "We can also help each other dress for the ball. I hope your gown is ravishing. Mother has invited every eligible bachelor in London."

"Harry, need I remind you that I am a twenty-eight-year-old spinster?"

"Rubbish! You are a fascinating woman of the world and a redhead to boot. You simply *have* to marry, Rachel. An unwed woman has no more rights than a child. Once we are married, we can join the Married Women's Property Committee. They are doing their utmost to change the law so we can own property in our own right." Harry laughed. "First things first. We are going to have great fun, starting tonight."

"You are a marvelous dancer, Father." Lady Harriet, partnered by the Duke of Abercorn, opened the ball, while her sister Beatrix danced with their uncle Lord John Russell. "I chose to wear green for Ireland, even though it flaunts convention."

James smiled down at his daughter. "I'm surprised you didn't insist on the ancestral Abercorn crimson."

"Mother has dibs on that color, though I must admit she looks glorious in it."

"I predict that you and Beatrix will steal her thunder tonight, and she wouldn't want it any other way. I see she let you wear her emerald and diamond earrings."

"Yes, she's the most generous mother in the world."

"I predict it won't be long before you have your own jewels."

"By that, I take it you mean I will soon have a husband."

"I warrant there are at least a half dozen suitors here tonight, eager to steal you away from me."

"I'm looking for someone exactly like you, Father." She gazed up at him with genuine love and admiration.

"Oh, if your standards are that high, I shall be stuck with you forever," he teased.

"You're full of blarney. Go and dance with Trixy."

The Earl of Durham claimed the second dance with Lady Harriet.

"Have you been waiting for me, D'Arcy?" Harry's eyes sparkled with happiness.

"Longer than you think. I've been awaiting your debut for more than a year."

"I must think of a suitable reward for your patience," she teased.

"Your beauty is radiant tonight. Promise you'll let me escort you to supper later?"

"Only if you'll tell me about the Lambton dragon."

His blue eyes danced with laughter. "Legend has it that when he was a boy, my early ancestor John Lambton went fishing in the River Wear and caught an eel, which he promptly threw down the well. Years later, when he returned from the Crusades, he found the surrounding villages desecrated by a dragon that emerged from the well. It ate all the livestock and even snatched away small children. The villagers couldn't kill it because whenever they hacked off a piece of the dragon, it grew back."

"Whatever did Crusader John do?"

"He consulted with a wise witch, who advised him to cover his armor with spearheads, but she warned that once the dragon was dead, he would have to kill the first living thing he encountered, or his family would be cursed for nine generations and wouldn't die in their beds."

"A dragon *and* a witch. How fascinating!"

"When the dragon wrapped itself around him, it was mortally wounded by the spearheads. As he hacked off the pieces, they were washed away in the River Wear.

"After he killed it, his dog ran out to greet him."

Harry caught her breath. "Oh, no, he didn't?"

"No, he didn't have the heart to kill his dog, so for nine generations the Lambtons were cursed."

"Which generation are you?"

"I'm at least the twelfth, I believe."

Harry smiled. "So there is every likelihood that you will die decently in your bed."

He bent close to whisper, "Or indecently."

Her smile widened. "If you're lucky!"

The Duchess of Abercorn stared at a dark

male who had just arrived. She had no idea who he was and turned to her brother. "Johnny, who's that swarthy gentleman? I'm sure I didn't invite him."

"That's Thomas Anson. Harry invited him. He's the member for Lichfield."

"Good Lord! His father is the reprobate Earl of Lichfield. How does Harriet know him? I hope he isn't following in his father's footsteps."

"Thomas is the antithesis of his father. Viscount Anson is extremely principled. He was supportive when I was PM and I consider him a friend." John signaled and Thomas made his way across the ballroom.

Once the men exchanged greetings, Anson bowed before the duchess, who smiled and offered him her hand. He took it to his lips. "Your Grace, may I have the honor of this dance?"

"It would be my pleasure, Lord Anson." As they moved onto the floor, she examined his features. *He's as tall as my husband, but much darker. I wonder if the rumors about his mother are true.* Barbara Philips's father was a prosperous West Indian planter and because of his daughter's black hair and dusky complexion, it was hinted that she could be half-caste.

He is treating me with great formality. His

features are stern because he doesn't smile. He looks at least thirty. . . . I wonder why he isn't married. Lady Lu smiled up at Anson. "Are you a confirmed bachelor, my lord?"

Thomas hid his amusement. "I have nothing against marriage, Your Grace. I simply cannot afford the luxury of a wife. Every penny I earn goes toward buying back Shugborough's treasures and antiquities that were auctioned a decade ago."

"What a noble endeavor. I salute you, my lord."

"Noble perhaps, but the task I have set myself is gargantuan."

Gargantuan indeed. We bought Shugborough's entire library, along with paintings and furniture, and have no intention of selling them back to you. "Is your father well?"

Anson stiffened. "The earl's health is indifferent. He has been bedridden for more than a year."

"I'm so sorry. It must be a sore trial for your mother." *It's a wonder she hasn't poisoned the bastard by now. She was a great heiress when they wed, and Lichfield went through her fortune like a dose of salts.* "Lord John tells me you are a member of the House. How do you fare with the new coalition government? 'Tis a hodgepodge of

Peelites, Tories, Radicals, and Irish members."

"I must confess that as a Whig, I fared better under your brother's prime ministership."

"Then let us hope our present prime minister's term is a short one."

Anson's brows drew together. "Isn't Prime Minister Aberdeen your father-in-law, Your Grace?"

"Absolutely not! The Earl of Aberdeen is my husband's *stepfather.* The man is persona non grata in an Abercorn residence."

"Forgive me," he said gravely.

"Nothing to forgive, my lord. I'm sure you understand the inevitable clashes that ensue when opposite personalities are forced to live under one roof."

"Indeed I do, Your Grace."

Lady Lu spotted her sister Rachel and decided to introduce her to the viscount. Though he vowed he wasn't looking for a wife, the right female might convince him otherwise.

"Lord Anson . . . Thomas, may I present my favorite sister, Rachel?"

He bowed politely. "May I partner you in the next dance, my lady?"

The duchess wasn't the only one consider-

ing matchmaking. Harry was being partnered by an Irish friend of her father's, Lord
James Butler, whose older brother was the
Marquis of Ormonde. "Captain Butler, I'm
so pleased you are in London and could attend our ball."

"I have retired from the Seventh Foot,
Lady Harriet, though everyone still calls me
Captain. I'm in London to petition Queen
Victoria to approve fairs in Kilkenny."

"That shouldn't prove difficult. Father will
persuade the prince; then Albert will persuade Victoria. Tell me, Lord Butler, do you
like redheads?"

"Being Irish, I must admit that I find red
hair extremely attractive."

She glanced around the ballroom searching for Rachel. Her brows drew together
slightly when she saw her being partnered
by Thomas Anson. They were laughing
together and Harry felt a stab of envy. She
maneuvered her steps until they were next
to the other couple. "Since I believe in equal
rights for women, I'd like to cut in."

Rachel laughed at the audacity of her
niece, and smoothly moved toward Lord
Butler, who welcomed her with open arms.

Thomas Anson gave Harry a frown of
disapproval. After a moment's hesitation, he
did the polite thing and they began to dance.

"Have no fear. I've no great desire to dance with you, my lord. I simply wanted Lord Butler to partner Rachel."

"I thought you were collecting suitors."

"Oh, I am. But the captain is about forty — much too old for me, and he's a second son to boot."

"You have no shame."

She laughed up at him. "I am guilty of serial misbehavior."

He gazed down at her through narrowed eyes, assessing her. "You are deliberately hurling yourself against my principles. And enjoying yourself immensely."

Harry's mouth went dry. *My God, the dark devil is shrewd. He knows exactly what I'm up to.* The music stopped. "Thank you for the dance. Will you excuse me?"

"For now. Go forth and gather your suitors."

"I have so many," she teased. "There's William Montagu, Earl of Dalkeith. He is heir to —"

"Yes, I know. Heir to the dukedom of Buccleuch."

"And coming this way with purpose is Henry, heir to the Earl of Mount Edgcumbe."

"That would be robbing the cradle. Or doesn't age matter, so long as he —"

"So long as he was born with a silver spoon up his bum?" she finished outrageously. *Harry, you're trying to goad him into laying his hands on you.*

A male voice interrupted her exciting thoughts. "May I have this dance?"

She turned to find D'Arcy Lambton at her elbow. "Why, if it isn't the Earl of Durham," she declared, and threw Anson a triumphant smile.

Abercorn swept his wife into his arms. "I thought I'd better steal a dance, before the handsome Lord Anson claims you again."

Lu was surprised. "How do you know him?"

"Palace business. He is an associate of Whitfield Cox, the fine-art dealer. I recently procured a painting through him for Prince Albert."

"When I asked him if he was a confirmed bachelor, he told me he couldn't afford a wife because he was restoring Shugborough's treasures. If he hopes we'll sell back the paintings we bought from Lichfield, he'll be sadly disappointed."

"I saw you introduce him to Rachel. Tell the truth and shame the devil — you cannot resist matchmaking." His arm tightened and he stole a kiss.

■ ■ ■ ■

When Harry was dancing with Henry Edgcumbe, she realized that though he was a couple of years older than she was, because of Lord Anson's remark about robbing the cradle, Henry suddenly seemed exceedingly immature. *I think he would make a perfect suitor for Beatrix. After all, Edgcumbe will become an earl.* Harry smiled sweetly and began to extol her sister's virtues.

William Montagu, Earl of Dalkeith, claimed the next dance. He was the member of Parliament for Midlothian, Scotland, and a Tory like Abercorn.

"Will, even though you were educated at Cambridge, I can detect a delightful burr in your voice," Harry told him. Her eyes shone as she thought about Dalkeith Palace in Scotland, which his family owned. *Someday he will inherit his father's dukedom of Buccleuch.* "Will, I think Montagu House in Whitehall is the most magnificent mansion in London."

"If I persuade my mother to give an entertainment, will you promise to attend?"

Harry gave him a radiant smile. "I would love it above all things. Oh, I didn't realize this was a cotillion. What a pity we have to

57

change partners."

Leicester Curzon-Howe, Emily's older brother, smiled down at her. "I thought I'd never get a chance to dance with you."

Harry returned his smile. *Leicester is about twenty-five, but alas, he has two older brothers before him in line to inherit his father's earldom.* They got only halfway around the ballroom when the music again stopped so everyone could change partners.

"Lady Harriet." Lord Anson gave a brief bow and offered back her words from earlier. "Have no fear; I have no great desire to dance with you."

"For a man who scrupulously adheres to priggish Victorian values, you have a wicked sense of humor."

"You do amuse me," he admitted. "I cannot wait to see what outrageous thing you'll do or say next. With that in mind, would you allow me to escort you to supper?"

"I'm afraid I've promised that honor to D'Arcy." Harry gave him a teasing glance. "Perhaps I can fulfill some other desire?"

Thomas gave her a speculative look. "How about showing me your library?"

I'll be damned. . . . Does he want to see the books that used to belong to his family? Or does the dark devil want to get me alone?

"Follow me, and you shall see, an elephant's

nest up a rhubarb tree." She took his hand and led him from the ballroom.

The library was in another wing on the same floor. When they arrived, they found Harry's brother James sitting in a brass-mounted armchair with Lady Emily Curzon-Howe curled in his lap. The pair jumped up guiltily and hurried from the room.

Harry dropped Thomas's hand. "Speaking of robbing the cradle! Lady Emily is obviously following in her father's footsteps."

If Thomas was amused at her remark, he didn't show it. Harry watched him closely as he examined the myriad rows of books. His thick black curls were so tempting, she had an urge to touch them. His stern demeanor, however, seemed to forbid such intimacy.

His glance traveled over the volumes, taking inventory. "Some of these once belonged to my family. But I thought your father bought the whole library."

"He did," she confirmed. "Some of them are at Bentley Priory in Stanmore, quite a few volumes are at Campden Hill, Kensington, and the rest are in my father's library at Barons Court in Ireland."

Thomas Anson lifted his hand to touch a

book directly behind Harry; then their eyes met. "So, in spite of being in favor of women's rights, you have made up your mind to marry this year?"

"Indeed I have. When I marry, my very first act will be to join the Married Women's Property Committee."

His dark eyes filled with amusement. "Your very first act?"

The corners of her mouth went up. "Well . . . perhaps my second."

His acquisitive fingers moved from the books and hung suspended in the air.

The electricity between them was palpable. His animal magnetism was irresistible to Harry. She caught her breath as his fingers began to trail across her cheek. She moved against him in invitation. Harry felt his muscular arm sweep about her and when his mouth took possession of hers, she opened her lips. She gave in to temptation and threaded her fingers into his dark curls. The fragrance of jasmine and honeysuckle filled her senses. *Is it Thomas Anson that is sending these shivers of excitement through me? Or is it the thought of Shugborough?*

CHAPTER THREE

"What time is it?" Harry sat up in bed and stretched her arms over her head.

"You don't have to get up," Beatrix told her. "I wanted to tell you that Henry Edgcumbe kissed me last night!"

In the other bed, Rachel opened her eyes and yawned. "The ball didn't end until four this morning. Why is everyone awake?"

"Trixy cannot wait any longer to confide her secrets," Harry explained.

"D'Arcy escorted you to supper. Did he kiss you?" Beatrix asked breathlessly.

"As a matter of fact he did . . . more than once," Harry confessed. "I've accepted his invitation for a carriage ride in the park this afternoon."

"Oh, Harry! D'Arcy is courting you." Beatrix sounded positively envious.

"Well, he claims he's already waited a year." Harry spoke to Rachel. "How about you? Any secrets to confide?"

Rachel smiled. "I must admit I found Captain Butler very attentive."

"He told me he was mad about redheads." *That's only a slight exaggeration.*

"He told me when he is in London, he rides in Rotten Row at six every morning."

"Rachel, tomorrow we must rise early. Since Hyde Park is just across the road, we can easily be there by six. He wouldn't have told you he rides there unless he was hoping you would join him." *I wouldn't be the least bit surprised if Anson rides early. No afternoon carriages for the dark centaur.*

"I wouldn't want James to think I was chasing him," Rachel protested.

"*James,* is it?" Harry teased. "Does he know you write romance books?"

"I shall save that shock for when we know each other better."

"Did D'Arcy really kiss you more than once?" Trixy asked wistfully.

Harry thought of Thomas Anson. "Sometimes, once is enough."

Trixy sighed. "With D'Arcy, I suppose that's true. What will you wear for your carriage ride?" She couldn't keep the envy from her voice.

Harry knew that Trixy was longing for a serious courtship. "Good heavens, that's hours away. I shall think about it after lunch."

A young housemaid brought Harriet and Rachel breakfast trays.

"Thank you so much, Rose. When I've eaten, I'll come down to the kitchen and help you pack a basket for your family. There will be so much food left over from the ball, there won't be enough shelves in the larder to hold it all."

"That's so generous, Lady Harriet. My mum will be ever so grateful. My little sisters call you 'the Angel.' "

"How refreshing. My own sisters often call me 'the Devil.' "

"That's a thoughtful thing to do, Harry," Rachel said when the maid left. "Is her family very poor?"

"Yes, they have so many children. But the Fergusons are very clean. They don't live in a slum. They live on Broad Street in Soho. Mother passes along the clothes that we have outgrown. Rose visits her family every Saturday, and we make sure she doesn't go empty-handed."

Over toast and eggs, Harry and Rachel exchanged ideas for a book.

"I'd like to write about real people, but there's always the risk that they'd recognize

box opposite was a most beautiful lady — he fell in love with her at first sight. Imagine his surprise when he learned that she was his wife! He decided to woo her properly, and he was successful. Their marriage was so happy that they kissed and cuddled in public. They ended up with twelve children."

"Oh, that is such a romantic story. I shall incorporate it in my next book. Thank you for providing me with such a splendid plot, Harry."

When Lady Harriet stepped up into D'Arcy Lambton's phaeton, she was wearing primrose yellow with a matching parasol. She had contemplated pairing her outfit with a vivid black and white one, but decided it would draw too many eyes. Since she wanted the parasol only to hide behind when D'Arcy kissed her, the yellow was preferable.

"You always look lovely, Harry, but today you seem to be bathed in sunshine."

"That's exactly how I feel on this glorious day."

Hyde Park was busy. Not only was half of fashionable London riding in carriages, but throngs of ladies and gentlemen were strolling along the paths, hoping to see and be seen.

The Earl of Durham drove once around the park, greeting friends and acquaintances and allowing Lady Harriet to do the same. She caught a glimpse of her brother James riding with Lady Emily, before D'Arcy took a left turn and drove across the Serpentine Bridge into Kensington Gardens. He found a secluded path where the sunshine filtered through the leafy shade trees, and reined in his horses.

D'Arcy took Harry's hand and squeezed it. "At last, I have you all to myself."

She glanced right and left mischievously. "Are you sure no one is hiding in the bushes?"

He slowly stripped off her glove and took her bare fingers to his lips.

"We certainly want no witnesses to such wanton behavior," Harry teased.

"I'll give you wanton behavior." D'Arcy's arms swept about her and drew her close.

Harry shielded them with her parasol and then reached out to brush her fingertips along his blond mustache. She held her breath when he captured her lips in a stolen kiss.

When he withdrew his mouth, she gazed at him for a full minute. Her parasol cast him in a golden glow and she thought him almost beautiful, in an angelic sort of way. "You have inherited your grandfather's handsome looks. My grandmother always extolled Earl Grey's attractiveness. I warrant she was half in love with him."

"And could you follow in the incomparable Georgina's footsteps?"

"I believe I could be *half in love* without much persuasion," she teased.

He pulled her closer and demanded fiercely, "What good is half in love?"

"Surely half in love is better than not being in love at all? You're an earl of the realm with a castle. If you woo me in earnest, I'm sure you won't be disappointed."

D'Arcy kissed her again and Harry closed her eyes, enjoying the intimacy of his heated embrace to the full. When his hand reached for her breast, she pulled away. "Don't be greedy," she murmured. "If that's what you're after, it will take a little more wooing."

"I'm sorry, love. You drive me mad, and I've waited so long."

"School yourself to patience. 'Tis said that anticipation is half the pleasure."

"There you go with your *halves* again." He smiled ruefully. "I've decided to host a dinner party next week. The invitation will include all members of your family, of course. I'll invite some bachelors for your sisters as well."

"How lovely. Too bad there won't be dancing, since it's a perfectly legitimate way of holding me in your arms. Still, I shall look forward to your giving me a *private* tour of your grand residence on Carlton House Terrace." Harry pulled on her glove, indicating that their tête-à-tête in the carriage was over.

"Did you enjoy your afternoon drive, darling?" The duchess joined her family in the dining room for the evening meal. She made no bones about the fact that she thoroughly approved of a match between Harriet and the Earl of Durham.

"It was everything I hoped it would be," Harry said with a smile.

"Last night it came as a surprise that you had invited Thomas Anson. I had no idea that Lichfield's son was a friend of yours."

"He's D'Arcy's friend, not mine. I believe they were at Oxford together. He introduced Lord Anson to me at the opening of the Crystal Palace."

"Are you aware that his father is a debauched gambler who was disgraced by a financial collapse brought about by gargantuan gaming debts?"

"Completely aware, Mother. Lord Anson is the antithesis of Lichfield. I believe he is overly stern and moral, with an impeccable character, to make up for his father's reputation." *He's also extremely good-looking, with black curly hair and pewter eyes that sometimes glitter silver.*

"It's something that is never spoken of in polite society, but Lichfield's wife is the daughter of a wealthy sugar planter in the West Indies, and it's whispered that she could have native blood."

"But only whispered in *impolite* society, I take it," Harry teased. *That would certainly explain the devil's swarthiness.*

Rachel laughed. "Well, thanks very much, Lu, for trying to palm him off on me last night."

"I did no such thing," the duchess protested.

"Of course you did," Harry contradicted her mother. "But I came to the rescue and took him off Rachel's hands immediately by switching partners so she could meet the dashing Lord James Butler."

"Rachel . . . you are blushing!" her sister said with delight.

"Oh please, say it isn't so. There is nothing so unbecoming in a redhead. Screamy-colored hair is bad enough without having screamy-colored cheeks to match."

"I have it on good authority that Lord Butler adores red hair," Harry declared.

Lady Beatrix interrupted. "William Montagu, Earl of Dalkeith, danced with me more than once last night."

Jane, who had been quietly captivated by the conversation, said, "Oh, I think William Montagu is *divine*. His Scots burr sends shivers up my spine."

"Thank heavens our brother James is dining out with Father tonight. He'd never let you live that one down," Harry told her. "He'd follow you around teasing you about kilts, sporrans, and haggis until you ran from the room screaming."

"Thank heavens he's still at an age where teasing his sisters amuses him. All too soon he'll think himself so grown-up, he'll avoid you like the plague."

"Before I forget, may Rachel borrow your mount, Mother? We'd like to go riding in the park tomorrow." Harry didn't divulge it would be at the crack of dawn.

"It isn't even light yet," Rachel said. "Are you sure we should do this?"

"Absolutely sure. Fortune favors the bold. It will give you a chance to be alone with Lord Butler. I shall make myself scarce as

70

soon as you meet," Harry assured her.

"You are very generous."

"On the contrary, I'm quite selfish. I have an ulterior motive. A certain male acquaintance of mine might just be in the park at such an ungodly hour."

When the pair arrived at the row, dawn was breaking. Galloping horses thundered by them, mounted by gentlemen intent upon their morning exercises. It wasn't long before a man drew rein beside them and tipped his hat.

"Lady Rachel . . . Lady Harriet . . . what a pleasant surprise," James Butler declared. "Would you care to join me, ladies?"

"I think my horse picked up a stone. You two go ahead and I shall catch up with you," Harry urged. She winked at Butler to let him know it was a ruse.

She watched them gallop off, side by side, then proceeded with a slow canter. She examined each of the male riders who passed, and smiled serenely when they tipped their hats. It was a quarter of an hour before the horseman she'd hoped for reined in beside her.

Lord Anson did not tip his hat. "Surely you're not riding here alone at this hour?" he demanded.

"I would love to tell you that I am, simply

to ignite your outrage, but alas, such is not the case. I came with my aunt Rachel. By coincidence, we encountered an admirer of hers, so I'm giving them a little privacy."

"Their meeting was accidentally on purpose, no doubt."

"As was ours, perhaps."

Pewter eyes looked into green. "I don't ride here often. Rotten Row is too tame for me. I like to ride farther afield."

"I enjoy a good gallop myself," she hinted.

"Would you care to join me tomorrow on a ride to Richmond?"

"I thought you'd never ask. Can we ride alongside the river?"

He nodded his assent. "Meet me at Cumberland Gate — same time." This time he did tip his hat, and galloped off on his black hunter.

Harry watched him. *If I narrow my eyes, man and horse merge into one.* She thought over their encounter. *He totally disapproves of me, yet he wouldn't have made the assignation if I didn't intrigue him.* She smiled her secret smile.

"You were right, Harry. Riding in the row this morning was a brilliant suggestion."

Rachel hung her habit in the wardrobe, and donned a day dress.

The corners of Harry's mouth turned up. "The idea came to me in a vision."

Rachel sat down at the writing desk. "I want to jot down your romantic suggestions for my next book. I'm still shocked at the idea of anyone having to marry to settle gambling debts. I don't know much about gaming — I suppose I should do some research."

"Oh, I'll teach you how to gamble and wager. It's great fun," Harry assured her.

"Charles James Fox ran his own gaming hell. In Regency times, it was not considered decadent. It was all open and aboveboard. Even Almack's had a gaming room upstairs."

"Since Victoria came to the throne, the middle class is hell-bent on reforming public morality. At all costs we must be protected from the Seduction of Gambling."

They heard someone whistling a merry tune. "It's James. I'll ask him to bring us some cards." Harry went to the door and hailed her brother. "Bring us some playing cards, and some dice if you have them."

In a few minutes, James returned with both. "If there's any betting, let me in on it."

"I'm going to teach Rachel how to play cards and wager. It's too bad there are no gaming hells anymore. We need to do research for a book, and White's has always prohibited females."

"White's is dull as ditchwater these days. It's just a political club," James remarked. "There are, however, private hells." He waggled his eyebrows suggestively. "All exclusive and hush-hush of course."

Harry's eyes widened. "You devil, you've been holding out on me! You haven't actually visited one, have you, James?"

He riffled the cards in his hand. "As a matter of fact —"

"Oh, you *have!*" Harry cried. "Who took you to such a place? Where is it? You must take Rachel and me."

"I went with John Montagu, William's younger brother. It's at a house right here in Mayfair, and *no,* I won't take you."

"*Where* in Mayfair? And unless you want Father to know what you've been up to, you assuredly *will* take us."

James threw his sister a look of desperation. He regretted opening his mouth. "It's a private establishment, known as Hazard House. If I take you, you'll both have to disguise yourselves with masks. If anyone learned I'd taken my sister to such a place, I'd be blackballed from polite society."

Harry's eyes sparkled. "I'll wear a mask

and something theatrical and everyone will assume I'm your mistress! Oh, even better, I'll get a red wig and Rachel and I can be *twin demimondes.* Only think what that will do to blacken your reputation!"

"That would bring us unwanted attention. It would be better to wear something inconspicuous," Rachel suggested. "In any case, I must first learn how to play."

"Very well. We'll put it off until next week, and in the meantime, I'll teach you everything you need to know."

Harry arose at five and donned her new emerald green riding habit.

Rachel roused and asked sleepily, "Wherever are you going?"

"It's far better that you don't know. That way you can give a truthful answer if anyone asks." Harry opened the door quietly and tiptoed from the room.

In the stable, Harry told Riley she would saddle Amber. His look told her he was wise to her shenanigans, but she was grateful he kept his warnings to himself.

When she reached the park, the first glimmer of light penetrated the darkness. Lord Anson and she arrived at the same time, which obscured the fact that she was eager.

"I admire promptness. I find it a rare trait

in a female."

And I warrant you know many females. "I pride myself on my rare traits." She fell in beside him and they trotted through the park to the south exit.

"One of which, I assume, is riding about London at the crack of dawn."

"There's no traffic at this hour. It's infinitely safer." They trotted their mounts past Ranelagh Gardens on their way to the river.

"That depends upon whom you encounter," he said flatly.

A frisson of excitement spiraled through her. "You needn't warn me that you can be dangerous. I've known that since the first time I laid eyes on you."

He turned his head to look at her. The first rays of sun revealed that Harry was not wearing black, but emerald green, a color that matched her eyes. "You look radiant."

That's a compliment. I shall return the favor. "And you look like a centaur astride your black hunter. What's his name?"

"Victorious."

"You didn't name him to honor the queen," she said flatly.

"You are quite perceptive . . . something I've known since the first time I laid eyes on *you*. I named him after a racehorse that won at Newmarket in the last century."

Her eyes widened in comprehension. "*Victorious* was one of the paintings you swiped from Shugborough!"

"I didn't *swipe* it. I *saved* it from the vultures."

Vultures like my family. "Do you still have it?"

"I do. In time, I intend to restore all Shugborough's treasures."

"That is so admirable." Harry hesitated, then confessed, "I fell in love with Shugborough that day."

In unison, they began to gallop. As they passed Syon House, she called out, "Did you ever see such a monstrosity in all your life? Its history is ancient, and its interiors are reputed to be magnificent, but the exterior is square, squat, and profoundly ugly."

As they galloped past the next mansion, Anson asked, "We won't pass it today, but have you ever seen Osterley Park?"

"Yes. Its white columns are graceful, but they are at serious odds with the red brick."

"A marriage made in hell," he jested.

A phrase that jumps to mind when you think of your parents. "What was it Horace Walpole said about its ornate drawing room?"

"He said it was worthy of Eve before the Fall."

Harry threw back her head and laughed. "He was such a witty sod!"

They galloped through Kew Gardens and followed the Thames as it curved down toward Richmond, and the pair slowed their pace to enjoy the lush view. "There's no one about. How would you like to ride hell for leather?"

"I saw you do it once." *You looked like a centaur.* She gave him a wistful glance. "I'd love to, but I don't want to hurt my palfrey."

"I'll take you up before me, unless you are afraid." He knew it would goad her into doing it.

"You're on! I'm afraid of neither man nor beast." She dismounted and tied her horse's reins to a tree. Then she strode to his side and raised her arms.

He lifted her before him, intending to let her ride sideways, but she put her legs astride, never heeding that the slit in her riding skirt tore open to accommodate her.

"Ready?" he whispered in her ear, as he pulled her body between his thighs.

"Ready!" she cried, and he dug in his heels.

They thundered through the park as if his hunter had been struck by lightning. He felt her hair stream backward, and brush against his cheek. She felt his cock pressing against her bum. The sensation of the wind rushing past her, and Anson's hard thighs gripping her, gave her a feeling of exhilaration she'd never experienced before.

As they galloped back to her mount, Thomas made the decision to stop at an inn so they could refresh themselves before they returned to London.

He drew rein. "I wouldn't dream of inviting you into an inn if they didn't have a lovely private garden at the back. I'm sure you are in need of sustenance."

"Can you hear my belly rolling?" she teased.

He dismounted in one fluid motion and held up his arms. She came down to him, ignoring her torn skirt and exposed legs. He set her feet to the ground, but his powerful hands held her against him for a long, drawn-out moment.

Thomas Anson is attracted to me. The wooing has begun!

A hostler took their horses, and side by side they walked around to the back of the inn. Thomas opened a gate and they entered a walled garden.

"Oh, it is delightful! I don't know how you found it, but it reminds you of the walled garden at Shugborough."

Thomas felt surprise. "You remember the garden?"

"Absolutely! Whenever I think of it, I smell jasmine and honeysuckle."

They sat at a rustic table and a mob-capped maid came to serve them. Thomas ordered a hearty breakfast of ham, sausage, eggs, lamb kidneys, and a jug of ale. *That's hardly a meal for a lady.* "What would you like?"

"I'll have the same and some fried bread." Harry rolled her eyes and licked her lips.

Thomas thought perhaps she was being facetious, but when the food came, Harry reached for the bread and tucked right in. He poured her a mug of ale, which she drank without hesitation. He almost smiled. "You have a strong man's appetite."

Harry wiped her mouth on her linen napkin. "And not just for food."

No, you have a hunger for excitement and an appetite for the finer things of life. I own something you desire — Shugborough. Your family owns something I desire. Thomas cautioned himself: *She is an outrageous minx. It could be a match made in hell.* He took her hand, pressed his lips to her wrist, and felt her pulse beating wildly.

Chapter Four

"Harry, you are extremely lucky!"

"That's skill, not luck, Rachel," Harry corrected as she collected the pile of halfpennies the girls had bet in their afternoon card game in the drawing room.

"It's due to all the practice she's had," Beatrix informed Rachel. "When we are in Ireland, she plays daily with the stable hands. She's learned all the tricks of the trade."

"You mean she cheats," Jane said sweetly.

"Only when I've exhausted every other means," Harry pointed out.

"Then you must teach me how to cheat," Rachel said.

"Anyone can cheat. Getting away with it is what I must teach you. Watch closely." Harry dealt the cards slowly. "Tomorrow I'll show you the intricacies of casting dice."

That evening, Harry and Rachel began to

dress for Lady Emily's debutante ball.

"I'd never met the Curzon-Howes before. The earl's wife doesn't look very old."

Harry laughed. "She isn't. Anne is only a couple of years older than I am. The earl is a lot older than his second wife, but he's still randy. Gave her a son before they'd been wed a year, then quickly added another son and a daughter. Lady Emily does whatever she pleases. Her stepmother is too busy with her own children to know or care what Emily is up to."

"Isn't the countess Irish?"

"Yes — her maiden name was Gore. She's from Kilkenny, the same county as James."

"They must know each other, then," Rachel surmised. "Do you think Lord Butler will be there tonight?"

"I shouldn't be at all surprised."

"In that case, I'll wear my turquoise gown. It's far more flattering than the gray."

There was a sharp rap on their bedchamber door. "Can you speed it up, Harry? We're already over an hour late," young James complained.

"What the devil's your hurry? It's only a debutante ball." Suddenly it dawned on Harry that her brother was itching to get his hands on Lady Emily. She winked at Rachel. "Better be discreet about fondling Emily. She has an older brother who could plant you a facer."

"Ha! Leicester Curzon-Howe is no match for me. I take boxing lessons, y'know."

The Earl and Countess of Howe, along with Lady Emily, who had greeted their guests in the entrance hall of their Grosvenor Square mansion, had moved on to the ballroom by the time the Hamiltons arrived.

As she invariably managed to do, Lady Lu drew every eye when she made her entrance. Tonight she was wearing fuchsia silk with diamonds blazing at her throat. Her three daughters and her younger sister, who were also exquisitely gowned, added to the impressive tableau.

"He's here!" Rachel murmured happily as she spotted Lord Butler.

"Go forth and conquer," Harry whispered.

D'Arcy Lambton hurried across the ballroom. "I've been waiting hours. Where have you been, Harry?"

"Teaching Rachel how to cheat at cards. I come by it naturally, but would you believe that some females are most inept when it comes to deceit?"

"I warrant you get away with it only because you are beautiful."

"That's blatant flattery. You must have an

ulterior motive."

"I do. I want to wed you and bed you — not necessarily in that order."

"Then you'd better get in line, Lord Durham."

Harry was deeply disappointed that Thomas Anson had not been invited. She hadn't really expected him to be there, but she had kept a faint glimmer of hope alive until she had searched the entire ballroom with her eyes. *The night will seem endless.*

"James, the night seemed endless until you arrived." Lady Emily led her partner to the refreshment room, and lifted a glass of champagne to his lips. Then she placed her mouth where his had been and finished the wine. She licked her lips. "I can taste you."

James felt his cock lift its head and lengthen.

Emily knowingly glanced down at the bulge in his trousers. "If I told you that you had a manly body, would you hold it against me, Jamie?" she whispered provocatively.

His cock hardened.

"I'm warm, and growing hotter by the minute," she murmured.

James felt his erection buck.

"I think we'd both feel better if we got some fresh air. Why don't we take a stroll in the garden?" She reached into her décolletage and produced a key to the private Grosvenor Square garden.

"Won't you be missed, Emily? . . . It's your ball?" James wondered if he could walk.

"Balls can be such fun." She stroked the key across the swell of her exposed breasts. "I'd like to play with yours, Jamie."

"And I'd like to play with yours, my beauty." *I'll walk if it kills me!*

There was such a crush of guests — all arriving in the supper room at the same time — that the young couple was able to slip down the stairs and out the front door unobserved.

Emily unlocked the garden gate, took James's hand, and led him beneath a chestnut tree.

He pulled her into his arms, and dipped his head to capture her mouth in a hungry kiss. She opened her lips and he slid his tongue inside to experience his first French kiss. It was so arousing, he pressed her back against the tree trunk and rubbed his hard cock against her soft belly.

Emily slid her hand down between their bodies to caress his erection. "You are so big, Jamie. Is this your first time?"

He had too much male pride to admit it, and allowed her to open his trousers and

85

take his cock in her hand.

"It would be a shame to waste it, don't you think?"

"I do indeed." He pulled up her voluminous skirt and was both shocked and thrilled to find that she was naked beneath her gown. James rubbed his erection back and forth between her legs, and his thumb caressed her mons.

Emily began to gasp. She thrust against him, and then cried out her release.

James felt rampant. He opened her cleft with impatient fingers and was about to thrust inside her, when she pulled away.

"No, James! I can't let you spill your seed in me."

"I can't stop now!" he groaned in an agony of need.

"I'll take care of you, Jamie." She dropped her skirt. "Let me have your coat."

It seemed an odd request, but he removed it and handed it to her.

Emily dropped it onto the grass and sank down before him on her knees. She licked the head of his cock, circled it with the tip of her tongue, and then she drew the hard length of him into her mouth and began to suck.

James had never known such ecstasy existed. "Don't stop," he gasped, as he held her head captive. When his climax came, it was so hard he shuddered for a full minute.

Emily tucked his limp cock back into his trousers, and then she helped him into his coat. "Let's go back up. I fancy some strawberries with that cream I just had."

"You go ahead. We shouldn't show up together." *This time I know I'll find walking next to impossible.*

As he staggered up the last few steps of the elegant staircase, Harry spotted him.

"No wonder you went out for some fresh air. I know it's unusual for me, but I've never been so bored in my life."

James gave his sister a serene smile. "There's a first time for everything, Harry."

The following evening, Harry joined Rachel in the library. "Here is the book you wanted to read."

"I'm thrilled you have Wollstonecraft's *Thoughts on the Education of Daughters.*"

Harry handed her a second book. "We also have *A Vindication of the Rights of Woman*. I can't believe you've never read them. They are required reading for every female. Mary Wollstonecraft firmly believes that the physical desirability that society imposes on us is the means by which male domination enslaves us." Harry winked. "I personally believe it is the other way about." She picked up a book from the desk and carried it to a deep-cushioned, brass-mounted library chair.

"What are you reading?" Rachel asked.

"It's a brand-new book that just arrived. It's by Barbara Leigh Smith: *A Brief Summary in Plain Language of the Most Important Laws Concerning Women.*"

"Leigh Smith? I've never heard of her."

"Her father built the school for the poor in Vincent Square. I persuaded Father to donate money, and when I took it round there, I met Barbara. Her father deeded the school to her, but he has to hold it in trust, since women are not yet allowed to own property. She and her friends meet every Friday in Langham Place to discuss women's rights. She holds open house through the day and into the evening. I've joined the crusade, and promised to sign all their petitions. It won't be long before things change!"

"Oh, I'd love to meet her. Though my writing must be frivolous compared to hers."

"I beg to differ. There is nothing frivolous about love and romance. They are at the heart of every woman's dreams. Barbara is very Bohemian. I warrant she would totally approve of us visiting Hazard House for an evening of gaming."

The pair read in silence for a half hour; then Harry threw back her head and laughed. "Listen to this. Barbara and her friend traveled about the Continent wearing blue-tinted glasses and unconventional short skirts to show off their legs. She wrote a poem about it." Harry recited:

Oh! Isn't it jolly to cast away folly,
And cut all one's clothes a peg shorter
(A good many pegs) and rejoice in one's
    legs
Like a free-minded Albion's daughter?

Harry looked up from the book. "Rachel, we must get ourselves invited to a masquerade ball so we can wear costumes that show off our legs."

"Victoria wouldn't be amused."

"Oh, you've put your finger on a most entertaining solution. We'll wear short skirts to the queen's annual Bal Costume at Buckingham Palace!"

When the invitations arrived from D'Arcy Lambton, Earl of Durham, for the dinner party at Carlton House Terrace, they included Louisa, Duchess of Abercorn, her sister Rachel, all three of the Hamilton daughters, and young James.

"Durham never fails to do things correctly, etiquette-wise, that is," Lady Lu declared as they prepared to leave for the dinner.

"Perhaps that comes from his late mother, Elizabeth. After all, she was lady of the bedchamber to Queen Victoria." Harry slipped on her cloak and picked up her fan.

"More than likely it was because she was Earl Grey's daughter. It will be like old times. I remember dining at Earl Grey's town house when I was a girl and he was the prime minister," the duchess recalled. "He outlived D'Arcy's parents and left Carlton House Terrace to his grandson."

When the five ladies stepped into the phaeton, the duchess spoke to her son. "James, I'm afraid you'll have to ride with Riley again."

"Don't give it a thought. I much prefer it to being smothered by crinolines, or skewered by whalebone," he added irreverently.

When the carriage arrived at Carlton House Terrace, D'Arcy was waiting outside to greet them. Etiquette dictated that he offer his arm to the duchess to escort her upstairs. Fortunately, his friend Thomas arrived on foot from the Ansons' nearby town house in St. James's Square. He was just in time to offer his arms to Lady Harriet and Lady Rachel. Young James Hamilton parodied his action and with an amused grin escorted his sisters Beatrix and Jane.

Harry could feel the powerful muscle in Lord Anson's forearm. She squeezed it with her hand, sending him a secret signal that no one else was privy to. When he glanced down at her, she covered her mouth with her fan to conceal her amusement. She felt him squeeze back, telling her to *behave* herself, and this time even her fan couldn't hide her bubbling laughter.

Upstairs, Durham's majordomo, Fenton, took the ladies' cloaks and ushered them into the drawing room, where two liveried footmen offered the guests champagne from Georgian silver trays.

With sparkling eyes, Harry immediately picked up two flutes, and waited for Anson's expression to change to disapproval. When he kept a straight face, she handed one of the glasses to Rachel and the other to Beatrix. She took two more, knowing his dark glance was riveted on her. When she handed one to Jane, she saw his black eyebrows draw together. She blithely sipped her own champagne. "What?" she asked.

"Jane's too young to be drinking," he murmured.

"What do you expect, when I set the example?"

"I expect no better, truth be told."

"Do you enjoy being the arbiter of young girls' morals?" she teased.

"No, but I quite enjoy being the arbiter of yours."

"It's a full-time job," she warned.

"I think I'm up to it."

D'Arcy joined Harriet and Thomas.

"It was most thoughtful of you to invite Captain Butler and Will Montagu," Harry said with a grateful smile.

"Ah, and here comes Henry Edgcumbe. I attempted to match every lady with a dinner partner of her acquaintance."

"That was so considerate. Poor old James will be the odd man out."

"Not at all. I shall place him at the foot of the table as cohost."

William Montagu and Henry Edgcumbe joined the group. Each had brought a glass of champagne for Lady Harriet.

Oh dear, I have four men vying for my attention. Trixy and Jane will hate me. Harry held up her glass and smiled at the two young lords. "I'm sure my sisters would love some champagne."

D'Arcy spied his chance to remove her from the others. "Harry, how about that tour I promised you?"

She glanced quickly at Anson and saw the silver flash of his eyes. Harry waved her fan languidly. "That is so thoughtful of you, D'Arcy. Why don't we invite Mother to join us? She remembers dining here when your grandfather was prime minister. I'm sure it will bring back fond, nostalgic memories for her."

For a moment D'Arcy looked stunned. Then his sunny good nature returned. "I'll have a word with Her Grace and be right back."

Montagu and Edgcumbe sought Harry's sisters, and she found herself alone with Thomas. "D'Arcy is never ill-humored when things don't go his way."

His smile was rueful. "That's because things have always gone his way."

There's an understatement. At twelve years old, D'Arcy was already an earl of the realm, with a castle and a fortune at his disposal.

D'Arcy returned with the duchess. Harry took his arm and the trio went off to explore the elegant Carlton House Terrace residence before dinner was served.

"This was your mother's private sitting room," the duchess declared. "I've always loved this chamber, with its painted ceiling." She looked pointedly at Harry. "Any lady could be happy here."

They moved on to the library, where portraits of D'Arcy's father and grandfather hung. "It's easy to see why Elizabeth fell in love with John Lambton. I warrant he was one of the handsomest men in England. You have inherited your father's good looks. . . . Don't you think so, Harry?"

"Absolutely. I believe D'Arcy was touched by the angels." *His golden hair and blue eyes truly give him the look of an archangel.*

The earl's majordomo appeared at the library door.

"Dinner must be ready. Shall we repair to the dining room, ladies?"

Each place setting had a card printed with the name of a guest, and the diners took their places. D'Arcy sat at the head of the table, with Harry on his right, and the duchess on his left. Thomas was seated between Harry and Beatrix, and Henry Edgcumbe was paired with Jane. Across the table, Will Montagu sat next to the duchess, and Rachel was paired with Captain Butler. Young James sat at the foot, opposite D'Arcy.

Though the setting was formal, the company was anything but, and the conversation flowed freely, along with the laughter.

Though Harry listened attentively to D'Arcy, all her senses focused on the dark lord who sat beside her. On an impulse she nudged his foot with her own and smiled when she felt him nudge back, though his full attention seemed focused on Trixy.

I wonder if things are never what they seem on the surface. I must tell Rachel to write a scene where a secret flirtation is carried on under cover of the tablecloth. Harry deliberately dropped her napkin, and when Thomas retrieved it, their hands touched.

The Earl of Durham had spared no expense on the dinner he served to his guests. The soup was lobster bisque laced with cream and sherry. Next came an artichoke salad with goat cheese, lemon, and black olives. The first entrée was wild Scottish salmon, and when that was cleared away, plump roast partridges were served. A different imported wine was poured with each course, and the main dessert was a luscious traditional English trifle, followed by a wheel of warm, melting Brie cheese and fresh fruit.

"You have a dainty appetite, Lady Beatrix," Thomas remarked when he saw the tiny amount of food she consumed.

Her eyelashes fluttered prettily. "Please call me Trixy, my lord."

He watched Harry dip a rusk into the Brie and sigh with repletion as it melted in her mouth. "You have a voracious appetite."

She gave him a saucy sideways glance. "And you know what that suggests."

"It suggests that you are an outrageous baggage," he murmured.

Harry felt inordinately pleased with his response.

Her mother watched the byplay across the table, then spoke to D'Arcy. "You are a perfect host. We would love to entertain you at Hampden House. Promise you will accept if I invite you to dinner?"

"I would be most honored, Your Grace."

"Oh, no formalities, please. Call me Lu."

On the carriage ride home, the duchess did not bring up the subject of Thomas Anson. She did, however, announce that she intended to reciprocate D'Arcy's hospitality and invite him to dinner. Then she changed the subject to William Montagu. "I adore Will's Scottish brogue. He spent the entire dinner gazing across the table and then told me that all my daughters were bonny lassies."

Jane spoke up. "I wish I'd been seated next to Will. He makes my pulses race."

"What's wrong with Henry Edgcumbe?"

her mother asked.

"Well, nothing, except he spent most of his time conversing with Trixy."

"Can I help it if men find me irresistible?" Trixy teased. "Lord Anson told me I had a dainty appetite. Gentlemen notice these things, Jane."

Harry smiled her secret smile.

Later, at home, Harry beckoned her brother into the guest chamber she was sharing with Rachel. "I spoke with Will Montagu tonight about you and his brother visiting Hazard House. I told him that next time Rachel and I intended to go."

"How could you, Harry? I told you that in confidence."

"Don't worry, James. Will told me he would be only too happy to accompany us. The whole thing will be a lark. Make your plans with John and Will and let us know which evening you decide upon."

When Harry and her young aunt were abed, she asked Rachel if her relationship with James Butler was progressing.

"I can't believe how well we get along. It's as if we've known each other for years."

"I can see that the Irish rogue is attracted to you, but is the feeling mutual?"

"Oh, yes. He fair takes my breath away."

"Splendid! Then it is a full-blown court-ship," Harry declared. "Isn't it amazing the things that can be accomplished at a simple dinner party?"

Rachel laughed. "Nothing about the Earl of Durham's dinner was simple."

"No. It was delightfully complex. I was invited to the theater tomorrow evening. I agreed to go only if the captain invited you. So you can expect a note in the post from him in the morning."

"Oh, Harry, that was clever. So D'Arcy is definitely courting you?"

"I suppose he's trying. But I'm going to the theater with Thomas Anson."

CHAPTER FIVE

"Darling, I fail to see the attraction. When you can have your pick of escorts such as the Earl of Durham, or Montagu, who's heir to the dukedom of Buccleuch, why would you choose Thomas Anson?" the duchess asked her daughter.

"The attraction is physical," Harry explained, rolling her eyes in mock ecstasy.

Her mother laughed. "Well, there is that, if you like the dark, dominant type."

"*You* obviously did."

"Well, who could resist James Hamilton? But be warned, Harry. Anson has to work for a living, and he told me himself he couldn't afford the luxury of a wife."

"Don't worry, Mother. I don't expect him to propose marriage."

"That's precisely why I *shall* worry," she said dryly.

"What could possibly happen when I'm in the company of my maiden aunt?"

Rachel found it difficult to keep a straight face. They heard the doorbell. "Oh, they're here." She pulled on her evening gloves and picked up her cloak.

The two gentlemen awaited them downstairs in the entrance hall. When they stepped outside, Harry saw that Lord Butler had brought his carriage. She waited until he helped her young aunt inside before she spoke. "I'm sure you'd rather spend the evening alone with Rachel. I have no intention of playing gooseberry."

The two men exchanged a speaking glance before Butler jumped into the carriage.

Harry tucked her arm into Anson's. "Why don't we walk to the corner and hail a hansom cab?"

"Is this charade to deceive your mother?"

"It is quite impossible to deceive Lady Lu; I've tried often enough. When she asked me what my attraction to you was, I told her quite frankly that it was *physical*."

"You thoroughly delight in being precocious."

"I freely admit it. Are you complimenting me, or censuring me?"

"And pray, what is the difference? When I censure you, you take it as a compliment."

She squeezed his arm. "If I am such a sore trial, why are you courting me?"

"You are the daughter of wealthy nobility." He paused, then added almost reluctantly, "And you are the most attractive, maddening female in London."

"You seem completely dispassionate; then suddenly you say something that gives it the lie."

"My dispassion is a mask. I assure you, my life has been deeply affected by my emotions. I simply don't display them."

"You pride yourself on being in control — of both others and yourself. I wonder what it would take to make you lose that rigid control."

Thomas hailed a hansom cab and helped Harry inside. He took the seat opposite her, so he could see her face in the glow of the lamp. "If you persist in your outrageous behavior, you may find out," he warned.

She ignored the warning. "Are you taking me to the Royal Surrey Theatre in Blackfriars to see *The Widow and Her Wooers*?"

He refused to be baited. "No, I chose a play that would appeal to someone who champions the poor and believes in equal rights for women. I'm taking you to the Pavilion in Piccadilly to see *Oliver Twist*."

Harry's face was suddenly transformed. Her provocative expression vanished and was replaced by a soft, radiant look as if her heart were melting. "Oh, that is so perceptive of you. *Oliver Twist* is the perfect choice."

During the first act, when Harry got a lump in her throat, she felt Thomas take her hand. During the second act, when a tear rolled down her cheek, he wiped it away with his thumb. When it was over, she was crying openly and he pressed his linen handkerchief into her hand. "Oh, I don't know when I've enjoyed myself so much."

When they left the theater, Thomas said, "Come on, I know just what you need."

He took her down Piccadilly to Swallow Street and led the way into an oyster bar. He ordered her champagne and oysters, and he asked for the same, but with ale.

Oh dear, the only oysters I've eaten have always been decently breaded. Can I do this without embarrassing myself?

When the oysters came, Harry sipped her wine and watched her companion, and then she followed his lead to the letter. After a shake of pepper, a dash of vinegar, and a squeeze of lemon, she proceeded to lift the half shell and tip the raw oyster into her mouth. She held her breath and swallowed. Then she laughed, feeling excessively proud of her accomplishment. She repeated the process nine times, and then looked at him with round eyes, as if to say, *Please help me.*

Thomas grinned. "You've never had raw oysters on the half shell before, have you?"

Harry shook her head.

He took the three that remained before her. "You are a brave woman."

When they left the café, Thomas hailed a hansom cab, but this time he sat next to Harry. He knew the ride from Piccadilly would not be a long one, so he decided to make the most of it. Slowly, he removed her evening glove and took her fingers to his lips. When she seemed to enjoy the intimacy, he slipped his arm about her and drew her close.

He dipped his head and when his mouth covered hers, she opened her lips to welcome his kiss. His embrace tightened and he kissed her again. This time he brushed her lips with his tongue, and he felt her shudder. His kiss deepened. He drank from her mouth, which was hot and sweet with passion.

Thomas felt his cock, which had already hardened and lengthened, begin to pulse.

He was both surprised and pleased at how splendidly uninhibited her response to his kisses was. His imagination took flight, picturing her beneath him, naked, in his bed.

He curbed his desire. He wanted far more than a quick fuck in a carriage.

Harry's senses were filled with the male scent of him and the taste of him. She felt the slow, hot glide of his lips along her neck and moaned softly. Her arms stole around his back and she felt the powerful muscles beneath his coat. She tried to imagine what it would feel like if her naked breasts were pressed against his wide chest, and desire flared in her like wildfire spreading through her veins.

The carriage slowed, and it took her a moment before she became aware of anything but Thomas Anson. When he eased his arms from around her, she gazed up into his dark eyes and sighed. "Oh, I was right," she said softly. *"It is physical."*

Thomas Anson lay awake for hours contemplating his evening with Lady Harriet. Only a month ago, he had had a vile argument with his ailing father about marriage.

"You'll soon be thirty. It's more than high time you found a wife! You'll need a rich heiress for the upkeep of Shugborough," his

father had said.

Thomas sneered. Losing Shugborough's treasures hadn't stopped his father from gambling. Until he'd fallen ill a couple of years ago, he'd been out every night indulging his addiction at Brooks's and other London clubs. *"You want me to follow in your noble footsteps — marry an heiress and squander her fortune. Marriage doesn't appeal to me, and after watching yours all my life, is it any wonder?"*

"You and your sainted mother want me dead!" he shouted. *"You look down your nose at me, you arrogant young swine, but when I'm gone, you'll be in for a rude awakening. All the expenses will fall on your shoulders — then we'll see how you cope, Lord Bloody High-and-Mighty!"*

Thomas had left the chamber before he helped his father to meet his maker. He vowed that the last thing he would do was follow his father's orders to marry. Shortly after that, he had attended the opening of the Crystal Palace and encountered Lady Harriet Hamilton.

Thomas thumped his pillow and laughed at himself. *How bloody ironic.* He wanted nothing more than to fly in the face of his father's demands, but his inner voice was now urging him to open his mind to the possibility of securing Harriet Hamilton in marriage.

Both her parents came from noble families of the highest distinction. Abercorn held titles in England, Ireland, and Scotland, and her mother, Lady Louisa Russell, was the daughter of the venerable Duke of Bedford. Abercorn had abundant wealth and property in three countries. Added to this was the enticing allure of the possessions that had once belonged to Shugborough.

A picture of Harry came full-blown into his mind. *There's no denying she is a rare beauty. Though she can be precocious beyond bearing, she simply needs taming.* Remembering the taste of her kisses, he felt his cock begin to stir. *I warrant she would be rewarding in bed.*

Toward morning, Thomas awoke in a panic. He had had his recurring nightmare that Shugborough was on fire. He threw back the covers and ran to the window, drenched in fear. Only then did he realize he was in London, and he had been dreaming. He returned to bed, but was determined to stay awake so his nightmare would not return.

In the morning, as Thomas was about to leave the town house in St. James's Square, his father's attorney, Martin Fowler, arrived.

Another summons from the querulous old devil. It's the third this month. No point in questioning Fowler. The man isn't even civil.

Thomas bade him a curt "Good morning" and departed. He was on his way to Whitehall. Before things went further with Lady Harriet, he intended to see Abercorn and get his permission to court his daughter. Her father might want no connection with Lichfield's son, and Thomas had too much pride to sneak around behind his back.

James Hamilton was a member of the Queen's Privy Council, and Thomas Anson, familiar with the Parliament buildings, made his way to the Privy Council offices. He presented his card to the clerk and asked to see Abercorn.

After a few minutes' wait, Hamilton came out to greet him and took him into his office. "It's good to see you, Lord Anson. You're here on a matter of business, I take it." Hamilton handled the business affairs of Prince Albert, who was the force behind moving the Crystal Palace from Hyde Park to a permanent location. It was a showcase for Britain's manufactured goods, which were superior to those of most other countries, and Abercorn negotiated the contracts and handled the reams of paperwork connected with the enterprise.

"Thank you, Your Grace. It's more of a personal nature than business."

"Then have a seat and make yourself comfortable."

"It is no secret that my father, the Earl of Lichfield, accrued enormous debts due to an excessive lifestyle and an addiction to gambling."

Abercorn steepled his fingers and listened attentively.

"For some time, he has been in ill health and has perhaps a year left. I am heir to the earldom and Shugborough, but I will inherit no wealth. Though earning money is frowned upon for a gentleman, you are aware that I have a business arrangement with Whitfield Cox to augment my salary from Parliament."

James Hamilton made no comment; he knew there was more to come.

"I would like to pay court to Lady Harriet, but will not do so without your approval."

Abercorn smiled. "My dear fellow, I have no objection. You are not your father. But it is Harriet who must decide if she wants you for a suitor. She has a mind of her own, you know."

"Indeed she has, Your Grace."

"I find it admirable that you have been so

frank about your prospects. There is no shame in business." His eyes twinkled. "Shugborough is quite an enticement."

Yes, she'll get to live at Shugborough, and in the marriage contract, I'll negotiate that the library and the paintings be returned to where they rightfully belong.

"I'm a little nervous," Rachel confessed to Harry as they rang the doorbell at Langham Place.

"No need. The women will welcome another advocate with open arms."

It was Barbara Leigh Smith herself who opened the door and ushered them inside to join suffragists Emaline Davis, Frances Cobbe, and Millicent Fawcett, among others, who were talking up a storm in Barbara's sitting room.

"I want you to meet Lady Rachel Russell, who writes women's romantic fiction and has actually had her books published," Harry said with pride.

"In a man's world, that is a rare accomplishment," Barbara declared. "Welcome to Langham Place, Rachel."

"Thank you so much. Harriet is presently reading your book, and has promised to let me have it the minute she's finished."

Barbara was not wearing a crinoline

beneath her calf-length skirt, and the tattoo of a butterfly was clearly displayed on her ankle. Rachel's eyes widened in shock. Harry's eyes narrowed with envy.

"And what are *you* reading?" Emaline Davis asked Rachel.

"Wollstonecraft's book on the education of daughters."

"I champion *higher* education for women. It is outrageous that neither Oxford nor Cambridge permits women to enroll. We could have our own college — we don't have to rub shoulders with the male nobs and snobs."

Harry laughed. "I warrant the men would want to rub more than shoulders!"

The women joined in the laughter. "No doubt we could teach them a few things," Emaline declared. "I'm going to draw up a petition, so you two young women can sign it before you leave."

Before the afternoon was over, they spoke not only of women's rights but also of the plight of poor children, and the squalid state of London's slums and the unsanitary conditions rife in certain sections of the city. Before they left, Harry and Rachel enthusiastically signed their names to a half dozen petitions.

When the pair left, Harry decided to stop

at a shabby row of establishments near London Bridge. She found what she was looking for next door to a cats' meat shop.

"This is a tattoo parlor," Rachel pointed out.

"Yes, I know." She pushed open the door and made the bell jangle.

Rachel followed Harry inside. "You're not going to get *your* ankle tattooed?"

"Of course not. What would be the point of that? No one would ever see it!"

"Harry, perhaps you should think this through. A tattoo is not something to get impulsively."

Harry brushed aside Rachel's protest.

The man inside showed Harry a book of designs and she scrutinized them thoroughly before shaking her head. Then suddenly she knew exactly what she wanted.

"A little green snake!"

Rachel looked as if she might faint.

"Where do ye want it, m'lydy?"

Harry held out her hand and pulled up her sleeve. "Can you put it around my wrist like a bracelet?"

"Fer a guinea, I can put it round anythin' ye fancy."

Harry pictured it around her thigh, and then her breast. "The wrist will do nicely."

When the artist had finished his masterpiece, she held up her arm and admired the tattoo with great delight. Once outside the shop, however, she began to have misgivings.

"I'll have to keep it covered up until I am brave enough to display it to the world." Her wrist still throbbed in pain, but she knew that the hurt would be worthwhile, and she was content that the little green snake would be with her forever.

The Duchess of Abercorn had decided to accept only the most exclusive invitations during her daughters' Season. There was no way she would ever decline an invitation to a ball thrown by Charlotte, Duchess of Buccleuch, at Montagu House in Whitehall.

On the day of the ball, Lady Lu cast a worried glance at her eldest daughter, who was wearing a jacket. "Are you cold, Harry? I hope you're not coming down with something." She placed her hand on Harriet's forehead.

"No, of course I'm not cold. I've never felt better. I just happen to think this jacket flatters me. I came to beg a favor. Do you think I could borrow one of your bracelets? I particularly like that broad gold cuff you got last Christmas."

"The cuffs are a pair. You must wear both

to make a fashion statement." The duchess unlocked her jewel chest and handed her the bracelets. "I might as well leave it unlocked — when your sisters see the cuffs, they'll embark on a treasure hunt."

Later, when Rachel and her niece were dressing for the ball, she noticed that Harry put on the cuffs before her gown. "No one knows yet?"

Harry shook her head. "I'm such a coward." She lifted her arms and waved them about. "It doesn't show, does it?"

"No, it is well hidden. You are not a coward, Harry, but you are extremely impulsive. Sooner or later —"

"Yes, I know, Rachel. But I much prefer *later* rather than *sooner*."

"Act in haste and repent at leisure."

"Oh, you sound just like Grandmother."

"I should," Rachel replied dryly. "I lived with her for twenty-eight years."

"I have absolutely no regrets about my tattoo. I adore my little green snake. I simply have to choose the right time to reveal it without shocking everyone's cockerocity."

"You stole that word from me," Rachel said with a smile.

"Who better to steal from than a *wordsmith?*"

Harry's sisters came into the bedchamber. "How do I look?" Trixy asked anxiously.

"You look very pretty," Harry assured her. "White and peach are perfect colors for a brunette. And, Jane, I can't believe how grown-up you look tonight."

"Thank you. I think it's because I'm wearing Mother's earrings. My pulse is racing like mad, just thinking about going to Montagu House."

"Perhaps you're like me — cannot decide if it's the *manse* or the *man* that excites you."

"Oh, it's definitely Will Montagu," Jane admitted ingenuously.

"Are you ready, ladies?" their mother called from the foot of the central staircase.

Harry, in a gold and white tissue gown, led the way down.

"Your father will meet us at Montagu House. It's only a few steps from his Privy Council office." Her glance swept over her daughters. "I must say the Hamilton ladies will turn every male head tonight. I pity the other females who have accepted Charlotte's invitation. James, just see if Riley has brought the coach around."

At Montagu House, an upstairs chamber had been assigned as a dressing room for

female guests. The Duchess of Abercorn paused dramatically at the top of the grand staircase surrounded by her daughters. Above her was a large stained-glass dome that was brilliantly lit to show off its magnificence.

"I am counting on one of you to become the Countess of Dalkeith and future Duchess of Buccleuch. That way, I shall be able to visit Montagu House on a regular basis and descend this staircase with the dramatic flair it deserves."

Harry paused beside her mother and watched with amused eyes as the gentlemen in the ballroom below gathered and stared up in silent admiration at the tableau of feminine pulchritude. Then they descended the staircase together.

Harry curtsied to the Duchess of Buccleuch, who stood waiting to greet her guests. Though she knew that Lady Charlotte was approximately the same age as her mother, she looked at least ten years older. *I put that down to serving as Mistress of the Robes to Victoria for five years.* "Your Grace, thank you for your lovely invitation."

William Montagu stood with his mother to greet their guests, while his father, the duke, stood to one side in conversation with three other men. Will took Harry's hand and brought it to his lips. "Welcome to Montagu House, Lady Harriet."

She winked at him and murmured, "If you do this to Jane, she will faint with excitement."

"If you promise me the first dance, I'll ask Jane for the second," he bargained.

"Done!" Harry moved on quickly so her sisters could have at him.

Abercorn was one of the men talking to Buccleuch. She curtsied prettily to her host and stood on tiptoe to kiss her father. "Did you hear the one about the Irishman and the Scot who walked into a tavern and —"

Walter Montagu, whose brogue was far thicker than his son's, threw back his head and roared with laughter, while her father's eyes twinkled at her jest.

"She's a right saucy lassie, James. If I were ten years younger, I'd be chasin' her."

"And I'd let you catch me, Your Grace."

Abercorn greeted his wife. "Hello, darling. You look ravishing tonight."

"Does that mean you'll be coming home with me?" she asked with mock alarm.

"Would that be inconvenient?" he teased.

"Well, you know what the French say: *Marriage is so difficult, it takes three to make it work.*" Lady Lu wafted her fan. "Ah, here comes Lansdowne. . . . I've promised the

116

marquis the first dance."

Harry exchanged an amused glance with her father. Lansdowne was at least seventy.

When the music began, Will Montagu claimed his partner.

"Have you set the date yet for our visit to Hazard House?"

Will nodded. "Aye, keep Thursday of next week open. Our brothers John and James will join us. I take it Lady Rachel will be coming? Do you think I should invite Captain Butler?"

"No, please don't. It might give him a disgust of her if he thought she frequented gaming hells. We are trying to do it on the quiet, Will."

Before the dance ended, she saw Lord Anson arrive, and she felt her heart do a little flutter. "There's Thomas. Thank you for inviting him."

"I had to insist, over Mother's reservations. She considers Lichfield beyond the pale. But when Father backed me up, she retreated with grace." He waggled his eyebrows. "She'd die of shock if she found out we planned to visit Hazard House. But of course, she has no notion that such places even exist."

When the dance was over, Thomas Anson walked a direct path to her and asked formally, "May I have the next dance, Lady Harriet?"

"You may, my lord, but please call me Harry. I love the way Will rolls the *r*'s in *Harriet,* but it sounds hideous when anyone else says it."

"You don't care for your name?"

"It would be wicked of me to say I hated it. My father's mother was Harriet. She died shortly after my parents were married. My parents wanted to honor her memory. Can I do less?" She smiled softly. "But I do prefer *Harry*."

"*Harry* suits you," he said grudgingly, "though it's not very ladylike."

" 'What's in a name?' " she quoted merrily. " 'That which we call a rose by any other name would smell as sweet.' "

"Juliet."

"Romeo!"

"Would you like me to reject my family name?" he asked solemnly.

"Deny your father and be newly baptized as my *lover?*"

"That is most provocative — of course, that's precisely why you said it." Pewter eyes met green. "Try to behave yourself, Harry."

"Oh, if you insist . . . I shall try my utmost."

"Before anyone else asks, may I be your

supper partner?"

She leaned into him and smiled. "I would have turned anyone else down."

When they danced, she noticed that he held her at a respectable distance. Though she guessed he would prefer to hold her close, Thomas observed all the conventions.

Myriad adjectives describing his behavior danced through her head in time to the music.

You are ever respectable, responsible, principled, honorable, upright, moral, strict, straitlaced, and far too rigid. But I wonder if you are totally incorruptible? I shall have great fun finding out.

When the dance ended, D'Arcy was waiting for her. Though the two males greeted each other warmly, Thomas glanced into her eyes before he relinquished her to his friend.

As the music began, D'Arcy's smile reached his blue eyes. "I received your mother's invitation to dinner next week. Thank you for reminding her."

Harry had forgotten about it. She held her breath. *Please don't let it be Thursday.*

"Mother usually reserves Wednesday for dinner guests. I hope that isn't inconvenient?"

"Not at all. Dinner with you would take

precedence over any other invitation."

The adjectives that describe D'Arcy are opposite those for Thomas: affable, pleasant, friendly, sociable, jovial, extremely easygoing, and filthy rich.

"May I escort you to the supper room later?"

"I'm sorry, D'Arcy. Thomas already asked me."

For an instant his laughing blue eyes turned dark. Then he smiled. "That's what I get for being late to the ball."

"Why don't you ask Trixy?"

He nodded happily. "I shall."

Harry danced next with her father, then the Duke of Buccleuch, the Earl of Winterton, and young Henry Edgcumbe. Between dances she stopped to chat with her mother and Rachel. "Why don't you invite James Butler to dinner next Wednesday?"

Rachel blushed prettily. "A delightful idea," her sister said. "I don't know why I didn't think of it myself." She glanced at Harry with speculation, but kept silent.

Harriet danced a second time with Will Montagu and when the music stopped, they found themselves next to their mothers, who were exchanging pleasantries about court.

Lady Charlotte looked upon Lady Lu's

daughter with approving eyes. "It goes without saying that the lady who marries my son will be invited to become Mistress of the Robes to Our Gracious Majesty."

The look of alarm was visible on Harry's face. Without sounding facetious, the Duchess of Abercorn said smoothly, "A lofty aspiration for any young lady."

No ball at Montagu House was complete without a Scottish reel. Since Will had promised to partner her sister Jane, Harry took D'Arcy for her partner. They'd danced strathspeys before. Whenever Victoria gave a musical evening, she delighted in Scottish dancing. The ladies always ended up laughing because crinolines were not best suited to Highland Flings.

"D'Arcy, you should host a Scottish dance, where all the men must wear kilts."

"And what about the ladies?" he teased.

"I'll wear a kilt if you will. My great-grandparents were the Duke and Duchess of Gordon." She raised her eyebrows. "A scandalous couple, by the way."

"I got some of that newfangled photographic equipment on display at the Crystal Palace. They take images of people, called photographs, that are amazingly lifelike."

"Then I shall take a picture of you wearing a kilt — knobby knees and all!"

"That isn't what I had in mind, and well you know it, Harry," D'Arcy chided.

"Shame on you. A lady's limbs must be covered at all times. Our bodies are temples and not to be used for physical exertion, or to be put on display to please gentlemen."

"Pull my other leg, Harry. It's got bells on it."

When Thomas arrived to escort her to supper, he found the pair rollicking in laughter.

She linked her arm through his. "I was trying my utmost to behave myself."

He gave her a grave look. "You are deceiving yourself."

She bent close and whispered, "Yes. I do it all the time."

As the guests were migrating to the supper room, Thomas held her back, and then led her out onto one of Montagu House's balconies. "Fresh air will banish your giddiness."

Trixy saw the pair leave, and caught up with D'Arcy while she had the chance.

Harry bent far out over the balcony above a garden. Thomas didn't try to stop her, but drew close. When she straightened, he enfolded her in his embrace and his mouth took possession of hers. Her arms slid about his neck and clung for long minutes.

Harry withdrew her lips. "You seem to be in a hurry."

"I have to be. You are surrounded by earls and future dukes who are eager to steal the marriage prize from me."

"They'll first have to surmount the obstacle of my father."

"I've already asked him if I may pay court to you, and he has no objections."

"Hell and Furies! You *are* in a hurry. I believe I can smell jasmine and honeysuckle. When is this marriage to take place?"

"He told me it was for you to decide if you want me for a suitor. And though it was totally unnecessary, he informed me that you had a mind of your own."

"I rather like being wooed. I believe it would be prudent to wait until the end of my Season before I decide."

"You don't know how to be prudent. It isn't in your nature to be prudent. You are impulsive and reckless, and need a firm hand to protect you from yourself."

"And you are offering your firm hand? What makes you feel so cocky? Keeping your hand in your pocket all day?" she taunted outrageously.

He ignored her vulgar words. "I'm not offering for you yet. A decent amount of time should be given to escorting you about. Then, if you are amenable and your family reconciles to the idea, we will proceed to negotiating the marriage contract."

Harriet suddenly went still. "You are serious."

"Always."

"We'd make a very odd couple. One serious, one frivolous; one *strait*laced, the other indecorous; one strict and stern, the other disobedient."

"Opposites are said to attract."

Harry shook her head thoughtfully. "The attraction is the *challenge* we symbolize to each other." *You want to tame me . . . and I want to make you wild.*

"Will you come to the Crystal Palace with me on Friday? I know there are many exhibits we would both enjoy."

"Such a respectable assignation," she teased. "Surrounded by crowds there is little chance of indiscretion."

"If I promise to do something indiscreet, will you come?"

"Since I'm so impulsive and reckless, how can I resist? I'd like to go by train. Let's meet at the station at ten."

CHAPTER SIX

"Hello, D'Arcy. Whatever have you brought?" Harry asked. The two dinner guests had arrived at Hampden House within minutes of each other.

"This is the photographic equipment I was telling you about." He saw Rachel and Lord Butler. "Hello, Captain. After dinner, I shall take a photograph of you and Lady Rachel. The images are absolutely lifelike."

The talk prior to dinner was all about the Crystal Palace and the amazing inventions on display there.

"Abercorn has spoken of little else for the past two years," the duchess declared. "Prince Albert decides what should be on display, and Abercorn has to do the donkey work to get it done. I'm weary of the subject."

At dinner, D'Arcy was seated between Harriet and Beatrix. Facing them were Lady Rachel and Lord Butler. Her brother,

James, partnered Jane.

The duchess skillfully turned the conversation to the Earl of Durham's property. "Harry has a fascination for stately historic houses. Do tell us about your castle, D'Arcy."

"Lambton was built on the same site as a castle from a century earlier. It was originally erected as a fortress against the wild inhabitants of the north, I warrant. It's built on a hill overlooking the lovely river and the wooded Wear Valley, where I hold the annual pheasant shoot. Lambton is fashioned after a Norman castle with a vast, high-ceilinged great hall."

"What a marvelous chamber for entertaining," the duchess declared. "The Earl of Durham will be expected to marry a lady who will be a worthy chatelaine, and a charming hostess for the numerous guests you will entertain at the castle."

D'Arcy smiled at Harry before he answered her mother. "Absolutely. I must confess that I have ambitions to one day become the lord lieutenant of County Durham."

Trixy's heart was in her eyes as she hung on to his every word.

"That's marvelous, D'Arcy," Harry said. "Did you know that Father was the lord lieutenant of County Donegal in Ireland?"

"Yes, my ambitions were stirred by Abercorn. Perhaps sometime in the future we can discuss the duties and qualifications required in that post."

"The main qualification for lord lieutenant is money to burn," Lady Lu said dryly.

Harry patted D'Arcy's hand. "Then Durham has found its man."

Trixy sighed, imagining herself a countess.

The duchess turned her attention to Lord Butler. "James, do tell us about Kilkenny Castle and your famous collection of Ormonde paintings."

"Well, not to fault Lambton, but Kilkenny is an *authentic* Norman castle, built in the thirteenth century to defend the medieval town of Kilkenny."

It was Rachel's turn to listen transfixed.

"The castle has round towers at its four corners and an interior courtyard. The Butlers of Ormonde have lived there for five hundred years. The collection of paintings is vast in number."

"Ireland holds a very special place in my heart. Rachel, when the Season is over, you must come and stay with us at Barons Court," the duchess invited.

"Oh, thank you! I would love it above all things." Her glance met Lord Butler's before her lashes swept down to conceal the hope in her eyes.

"You must all come and visit us at Kilkenny when you return to Ireland."

"Why, thank you, James. We will take you up on your generous invitation." The Duchess of Abercorn again turned her attention on D'Arcy Lambton. "Wouldn't it be wonderful if you could take some photographs of your castle and the places around Durham? I'm sure Harriet would be fascinated to see them."

"Oh, D'Arcy, you must. I've seen a painting of your castle, but a photograph would be an exact reproduction."

"Yes, I will certainly take photographs. Of course, I won't be visiting Durham until the Season is over." His generous mouth widened into a smile he bestowed on Harry.

He means until my Season is over. He makes me feel special — I can do no wrong in his eyes. There is absolutely no denying D'Arcy's attraction. Harry's thoughts strayed to Thomas Anson and she smiled inwardly. *I can do no right in his eyes.*

After dinner, D'Arcy began to set up his photographic equipment in the drawing room. Harry's brother, intrigued by the paraphernalia, insisted on helping. Lady Rachel was placed in a chair, with Lord Butler standing behind her.

D'Arcy cautioned, "Don't be alarmed. I have to create a flash of light so your image can be captured." He took a small bag and sprinkled some black powder onto a hand-held device. "When I say *ready,* I want you both to smile and hold absolutely still."

"What is this black stuff?" young James asked.

"Gunpowder," D'Arcy murmured quietly.

"Jolly good! Let me hold it for you." James's eyes sparkled at the thought of danger.

When D'Arcy was ready to pull the cord attached to the box he held, he said, "Ready," and nodded to his assistant.

James set a lit taper to the gunpowder, and the flash and puff of smoke made Rachel's eyes widen to the size of saucers.

"Oh dear, I'm going to look a fright!"

Standing behind her, Captain Butler dropped a kiss on top of her head. "That would be impossible, my dear."

D'Arcy was beaming from ear to ear. "That's all there is to it. Now I'd like to take a photograph of you, Harry."

Immediately, James made a suggestion. "Why don't we take a photograph of both of you? Show the captain how to pull the cord, and I'll do the flash-of-light thing again."

Harry smiled mischievously at D'Arcy. "You sit in the chair and I'll stand behind you." Posed thus, she thought wickedly, *I rather like the dominant position!*

"Oh, the flash really is startling!"

D'Arcy turned and looked up at her. "You look as if you have stars in your eyes. Will you come for another carriage ride on Friday?"

"Oh, I'm sorry. Thomas Anson is taking me to the Crystal Palace on Friday. I talked him into taking me on the train."

"Then you must come on another day. I won't take no for an answer, Harry. We don't have to go to Hyde Park. I'll take you anywhere you'd like to go."

"That's very generous of you, D'Arcy." *You really do have a lovely disposition.*

The following evening, when Will Montagu arrived, ostensibly to escort Lady Harriet and Lady Rachel to the theater, the Duchess of Abercorn greeted him warmly. "It's extremely thoughtful of you to include James in your plans. You will undoubtedly have a good influence on him, and will keep him from running with a riffraffy crowd as sixteen-year-old males are wont to do."

Will flushed slightly. "It's my pleasure, Your Grace."

When Harry and Rachel came on the scene, they were wearing dark cloaks over their gowns. Both had pulled back their hair in a severe style and donned a hat with a veil that partially obscured their features.

"Why the incognito?" the duchess asked. "You look as if you're on a secret mission."

"We are," Harry declared. "We don't want our other suitors to gnash their teeth with jealousy because we are attending the theater with the Earl of Dalkeith. When you sit front row in the Montagus' theater box, the eyes of the world are upon you."

"Mmm, that's something you usually thrive on, Harry," the duchess pointed out.

"Yes — everyone remarks how much I take after my mother."

"Flattery will get you everything." She raised her voice. "James, where the devil are you? Surely you know it is déclassé to keep ladies waiting?"

Her son arrived, out of breath from rushing. "Sorry!" He almost laughed out loud when he saw Harry and Rachel, but his sister lifted her veil and gave him such a militant look, he sobered immediately.

When the conspirators climbed into the Montagu carriage, they found John Montagu waiting for them. "I gave Angus directions to Hazard House and bribed him with a guinea to keep his mouth shut."

"Ye witless sod! I already gave him five quid," Will declared.

Harry almost choked with laughter. "Speaking of money" — she looked expectantly at Will — "Rachel and I don't have much."

"Don't worry, lass. I'll bankroll both of you."

"Thank you, my lord. Never again will I allow anyone to insinuate the Scots are tighter than bark on a tree." Harry felt Rachel kick her for the blunt insinuation, and it sent her off into another peal of giddy laughter.

The carriage hadn't gone too far before it pulled up in front of a tall house on Half Moon Street. When Will helped Harry to alight, she stared up at the dark facade, marveling that it had no distinguishing features that made it stand out from its neighbors in the row. *It looks like a respectable home, not a gaming hell.*

At the front door, a porter held out his hand and when Will put something into it, they were welcomed with a bow. The party ascended to the second floor, which consisted of four brilliantly lit gaming rooms. The tall windows were covered by heavy drapes that prevented the lights from spilling out into the street.

The first room was for ombre and faro card games, the second for baccarat and chemin de fer. A third room held small dice tables to accommodate the hazard players. The fourth had a roulette wheel at one end and a long dice table at the other.

"We are not the only females," Harry noted, as the group toured the rooms.

"No, but we are likely the only ladies," Rachel whispered.

Most of the males were unaccompanied, but it was obvious that the few females who were escorted by gentlemen were mistresses rather than wives.

"Oh, I want to play roulette. How exciting!"

Will Montagu bought a quantity of chips and handed some of them to Harry and Rachel. Harry placed her bet immediately, but Rachel waited for Will to make his choice before following his lead. Young James and John each placed their bets and the croupier spun the wheel, and then spun the ball in the opposite direction. After it slowed, the ball dropped into the pocket of 6 red.

"I won!" Harry was elated.

All the men had chosen black as they usually did, and placed their bets on uneven numbers. "Whatever made you choose six red?" Will asked.

"I was born on the sixth and red is the ancestral Abercorn color, of course."

He shook his head. "That would only make sense to a female."

"Don't be too superior — you lost!" Harry continued to bet on red, while the men stuck to black. Rachel changed her course, deciding to follow her niece's example rather than Will's. When James's and John's luck did not change, they wandered off to one of the cardrooms.

Harry had beginner's luck and her pile of counters kept growing. Finally, Will steered them over to the dice table. "Would you like to have a go at shooting dice?"

"I'd *love* to, but the table is divided into three and I'm not sure how to bet."

"Well, I'll place the wagers and you can throw for me. Remember to use only one hand and the dice must hit the wall at the opposite end of the table." Will handed her the dice and she blew on them before shooting them down the table.

"Where did you learn to do that?" Will asked.

"In Ireland. It's our stableboys' favorite

pastime."

"I'd like to look around and observe the various card games. I'm here to do research, not to actually gamble," Rachel reminded Harry.

"Good idea. Will must play his favorite card game and we'll watch." She shook her head in wonder as they walked. "Fortunes must be won and lost in these rooms."

He pointed to a staircase at the end of the room. "Actually, high-stake games are held up there in a private room."

"Can we go and see?"

Will shook his head. "I'm afraid not. They only take place on Friday night. Besides, the owner of Hazard House is extremely selective in the men he allows upstairs. Only inveterate gamers are invited. 'Tis rumored they can use a private entrance at the back if they don't want their identities known."

Harry was fascinated. "Have you ever been up there? Do you know the owner?"

"No, I've never been invited. The man has a rather black reputation. I've seen his ravishing female partner — she runs the place. Her fatal beauty lures men to wager deep. 'Tis said that if a man gets in over his head, she gifts him with a silver bullet. The tales are legendary . . . though I don't know how much truth they contain. I don't come

here often — I'm just an occasional punter."
He sat down at the faro table and the ladies
hovered to observe the play.

"Rachel, when you write the part of your
story where the two older men gamble, the
ravishing assistant must serve the loser a
silver bullet on a tray. Then, rather than kill
himself, he offers the winner his daughter
in marriage. You must have it take place in
a private room where they've insisted on
concealing their identities. And you must
portray the sinister owner of the gaming hell
as the *Knave of Clubs* because of his black
reputation."

"Harry, they were real historical people,"
Rachel pointed out. "They must have been
extremely wicked to settle their bet by marrying their offspring."

As they went to another cardroom to look
for James and John, Harry observed the
gamblers closely. There was a great deal of
laughter, but she noticed that both the men
and women drank almost continuously, and
though the mood seemed frivolous and
merry, it was a facade. Permeating the
pretense of gaiety was an atmosphere of
cynicism tinged with desperation.

James looked up at his sister. "My pockets
are to let. John's in queer street too."

"Well, to be truthful, Rachel and I have

seen enough. Let's go and find Will."

The young men looked extremely relieved.

On the way home, Harry thanked the Montagu brothers sincerely. "It was a great adventure. One I shall remember always. You were very generous to indulge us, Will. I'm sorry we dragged you away at such an early hour."

"It was my pleasure, ladies," he said with a wink. "I was happy to disabuse you of the notion that we Scots are tighter than bark on a tree. As to the early hour, it gives me time to drop in at White's."

"Can I come too?" James asked eagerly. "After we take my sister home, of course."

"Of course. Midnight is far too early for sixteen-year-old reprobates to retire."

The trio of males departed the carriage outside number 11 St. James's Street and William dismissed their driver. When they entered White's, the porter bade Montagu a good evening and, assuming the pair of younger men were Montagu's guests, did not ask for proof of membership.

"Montagu, good to see you." D'Arcy Lambton greeted his friend warmly, and then exchanged a jest with young James Hamilton about the gunpowder.

James grinned. "John and I are going to

the smoking room — our pockets are to let."

"Don't blow yourselves up," D'Arcy advised. He turned to Montagu. "The whiskey is on me. How about a game of écarté?"

They sat down at a small gaming table for two and Will dealt the cards. "What's this about gunpowder?"

"I bought photographic equipment, and gunpowder is required to provide a flash. I was invited to dinner at the Hamiltons' last night, and took some photographs."

"Getting your feet under Lady Harriet's table, I take it."

"I am. I've waited a year for Harry to make her debut."

Will looked amused. "She is a high-spirited lass, and daring beyond belief."

"What's she been up to?"

"Talked her brother into taking her to Hazard House tonight. I went along to make sure she and Lady Rachel didn't get into trouble."

D'Arcy gnawed on his lip for a moment, then grinned. "That's part of her attraction. She'll make me a very amusing wife."

"So you intend to offer for her?"

"Absolutely." He glanced across at Montagu. "What the devil's so funny?"

"What makes you think Harry will say *yes?*"

"Because she'll become the Countess of Durham and live in a castle."

"She has more than one suitor, y'know. I could make her the Countess of Dalkeith and the future Duchess of Buccleuch, and then there's Thomas Anson, to name two."

"With Lichfield for a father, Anson doesn't stand a chance. He has no wealth and dabbles in *business,* for God's sake."

"That's a rotten thing to say. Thomas is our friend."

"Come on, Montagu. It's not just his father. There's the gossip about his mother."

Will's eyes narrowed. "You're a muckraker. You're also very cocksure, Lambton. Would you care to make a wager about these nuptials? Say a hundred guineas?"

"Let's make it two hundred!" Drink had made D'Arcy reckless. He summoned one of White's attendants. "Fetch the betting book."

D'Arcy decided to walk home, since White's wasn't far from Carlton House Terrace. He questioned the wisdom of what he and Montagu had done. It wasn't the wager that worried him, and certainly not the money involved. It was the fact that it was recorded in White's betting book for the entire world to see. It would be more than humiliating if

Harry could not be persuaded to become his countess.

D'Arcy dismissed his doubts, but when he retired, he found that sleep eluded him.

It's true that Montagu will be a duke some-day, but Harry seems ambivalent toward him. He hasn't been invited to dine at Hampden House either, as I have. My family's longtime connection with Harry's gives me a great advantage over Montagu. My grandfather Earl Grey was an intimate friend of theirs. The Duchess of Abercorn makes no secret about wanting me for her son-in-law.

Reluctantly his thoughts turned to Thomas Anson. *He poses far more of a threat than Will Montagu. I don't understand why Harry is attracted to him when he never hides his disapproval of her. Perhaps baiting him is just an amusing game to her.* He smiled in the dark. *What you learned tonight is ammunition to win the battle. Anson has such abhorrence toward gambling it would kill his attraction for her if he found out where she spent the evening.*

At nine o'clock the next morning, D'Arcy made his way to Buckingham Palace Road and planted himself outside the railway station. The best part of an hour went by before he spotted Thomas coming south.

140

He walked briskly toward him, and pretended to see Anson at the last moment. "Hello, old man, where are you off to?"

"I'm meeting Lady Harriet at the train station. We're visiting the Crystal Palace today. Is that where you're going, D'Arcy?"

"No, no, nothing so exciting. I'm off to the palace on a matter regarding Durham."

"Your responsibilities to your county are no small matter. It's a good thing you have influential connections at the palace."

"I'm amazed Lady Harriet has the stamina to go traipsing about the Crystal Palace when she was out gambling till late in the night."

Anson's black brows drew together. *"Gambling?"*

D'Arcy rubbed his nose. "Ah, damnation, I've let the cat out of the bag. Don't breathe a word, but I ran into Montagu around two this morning at White's. . . . Said he'd escorted Harry to that gaming hell Hazard House."

Harriet Hamilton hummed a merry tune as she left the Palace Gardens and strolled past the Royal Mews on her way to the train station. She lifted her face to the warm sun, happy that she was alive on this glorious summer morning. *I'm glad I left my parasol at home. I certainly won't need it inside the Crystal Palace.*

She had chosen a new dress of mauve silk embroidered with purple violets for her outing with Thomas. Anticipating the heat of the crowds both on the train and inside the glass building, she had left off her cloak and, in place of a hat, had pinned back her dark curls with silk violets.

Harry glanced up and down Buckingham Palace Road in case her escort was waiting for her outside the building. *We agreed to meet at the train station, so I assume he'll be inside.* She smiled at the people who were entering the station beside her, some of them with children who seemed just as excited as she was today.

She stopped and allowed her gaze to travel about the crowds, searching for Thomas.

She spotted him at the far end. His tall figure and head of thick, curly black hair were easy to pick out of the throng. She lifted her arm and waved gaily, and her heart did a little jig of happiness as he recognized her and began to stride toward her.

She noticed that he wasn't smiling. In fact, his features were hard, his expression grim. When he drew close, she realized that he was angry.

As he reached out powerful hands and grabbed her shoulders, Harry knew she was mistaken. He wasn't angry. He was consumed by fury.

"Did you go to a gaming hell last night?" he demanded. His black eyes burned into her. "Answer me, damn you!" He shook her. "Did you go to Hazard House?"

"Take your hands from me, Lord Anson!" she spit.

He removed his hands from her shoulders, but his expression was still threatening.

She raised her chin. "Yes, I did, and I shall go again anytime I please!" Her anger was so hot she couldn't control it, and she raised her hand to slap his face. She felt him grab her fingers before they made contact. Her sleeve fell back and revealed her secret.

Anson looked down in horror. "What the hellfire is that, mistress?"

"It's a bloody tattoo — what do you think it is?" she cried defiantly.

"You defiled your body with a *tattoo?*" he ground out in disbelief.

"Not just a tattoo — but a *snake!* It goes all the way around my wrist — see?" Harry waved her arm in front of his nose.

"Why can't you act like a lady? You deliberately flaunt yourself so you'll be the center of attention."

"It's the perfect accessory for frequenting a gaming hell! Wouldn't you agree?"

People around them had stopped to stare, and they were quickly attracting a crowd.

He took a firm grip on her hand. "Swear to me you will never go to Hazard House again. I forbid it!"

"Forbid? Forbid?" She began to laugh, but there was no mirth in it. She snatched her fingers from his. "Don't raise that all-powerful hand to me, Anson, or use that arrogant, dominant tone as if you were my lord and master. You will never own one small part of me." She drew herself up to her full height. "Good-bye . . . and good riddance!"

CHAPTER SEVEN

That was disastrous. I handled it so badly.
Thomas Anson was furious with himself for
alienating Lady Harriet. *I know damn well
she has a mind of her own. I should have
known she would bolt the minute I tried to
control her.*

Thomas headed toward Whitehall. He was
the member for Lichfield and had constitu-
ency matters to attend to before Parliament
closed next month. *D'Arcy Lambton will step
into my shoes the minute he knows there's
trouble between Harry and me.* Suddenly
Thomas had a revelation. *D'Arcy already
knows! We didn't meet by accident today. It
was a deliberate plan. He met me for the sole
purpose of telling me that Harry had visited a
gaming hell last night. He knew it would be
like waving a red flag in front of a bull.*

When Thomas arrived in Whitehall, he
picked up the papers he needed. Then he
went into the pub where the members

gathered for lunch. Will Montagu frequented the place almost daily and today was no exception. "Hello, Will. Mind if I join you?"

"It would be my pleasure." Will hailed a waiter.

"I ran into D'Arcy this morning. He couldn't wait to tell me that you took Lady Harriet to Hazard House last night."

"Damnation, I knew I shouldn't have told him. Harriet and Rachel were just having a lark and I went along to make sure they were safe." Will hesitated. "Look, I know you think D'Arcy is your friend, but he'll thwart you from wooing Harry any way he can. He is determined to make her his wife."

"What makes you so certain?"

"He wagered me two hundred guineas that she would become the Countess of Durham. It's in White's betting book."

Thomas masked his anger. If D'Arcy truly cared for Harry, he would never besmirch her by making wagers about her. *Putting her name in White's betting book was a swinish thing to do.* A fierce surge of protectiveness for Harry rose up in him. He wanted to shield her from harm, guard her from being hurt. He cursed his own stupidity for alienating her. How could he protect her when she wasn't even talking to him?

Will changed the subject and they discussed things they must do before Parliament closed for the month of August. Montagu represented the borough of Midlothian, and Thomas knew he worked hard for his Scottish constituents.

Thomas was in a somber mood when he arrived home. He'd had high expectations for his visit to the Crystal Palace with Harry. Instead, his morning had turned into a disaster.

He picked up his post from the hall table and opened what looked like an invitation. It was from Lord John Russell and his wife, Fanny. They were hosting a surprise birthday party at Holland House for his sister Louisa, Duchess of Abercorn.

"They have no idea that Harry and I are now estranged." He went to the library intending to politely decline. *That's the coward's way out. If you want her, have the courage to fight for her. D'Arcy has taken the attitude that all's fair in love and war, so fight fire with fire, and beat him at his own game.* His mood lightened considerably.

Within a half hour, Thomas was back to being somber. A knock on the library door brought a footman with a summons from his father. Thomas took the stairs two at a time and entered his father's bedchamber.

He saw that his father's face was bloated and mottled red. A few papers were strewn about the bedclothes.

"It's more than halfway through the London Season. I want to know if you've lined up a wealthy marriage prospect yet."

"As a matter of fact, I have not," Thomas said coldly.

"Just as I thought. You need something that will prod you to action." Choler made his face almost purple. "I intend to change my will!"

"Again?" Thomas asked with contempt.

"Yes, again! It will stipulate that if you have not wed an heiress before I die, you will forfeit Shugborough."

Thomas hung on to his temper, though mention of Shugborough, so dear to his heart, always made him feel vulnerable. *Do you never tire of these threats?* "The law of primogeniture will prevail. As your heir, I will automatically inherit. It is British law."

"With the help of my attorney, I've come up with a way to circumvent you, unless you wed money." Lichfield's breathing became labored. "I will swear out and sign an affidavit that you are to be disinherited."

Thomas recoiled. "Your thinking and your threats are twisted. An affidavit to disinherit

148

me would only bring worry and unhappiness to Mother, and you've brought her enough sorrow."

"You can prevent the sorrow. If you take a wife whose wealth can restore Shugborough, I will instruct my attorney to burn the affidavit."

Thomas felt his jaw clench like a lump of iron. *Why do you hate me so much? Is it because you suspect I know your shameful secret, that I know you burned Ranton for the money?*

Thomas was not overly worried. An affidavit to disinherit him would carry little weight with the court. The laws of primogeniture would prevail. But it pained him that his father was seeking revenge against him, which in turn would hurt his mother.

"I don't believe I have much to worry about. You are too cantankerous to die."

Thomas made his way back to the library and accepted the invitation to attend the Duchess of Abercorn's surprise birthday celebration.

"Johnny is throwing Mother a surprise birthday party on Tuesday," Harry informed Rachel. "He does it annually, so I doubt it will be a stupendous surprise."

"Since I always open Campden Hill to the

guests that day, it will put an end to my stay in London."

"I'm sure Johnny and Fanny will have invited Lord Butler. They take a great interest in Mother's matchmaking."

"Well, Johnny does, at any rate. He's well aware of your preference for Thomas Anson over your other suitors."

"Oh, that's all off," Harry said casually.

"Whatever happened?" Rachel asked with concern.

"Nothing happened. Isn't it a woman's privilege to change her mind?"

"So D'Arcy is back in favor?"

"He was never *out* of favor," Harry insisted. "The Earl of Durham has been waiting for over a year to pay court to me."

"Well, your mother will be happy, but perhaps Beatrix's nose will be out of joint."

"I feel awful that Trixy has developed feelings for D'Arcy, but she has always known he has a *tendre* for me."

"Well, I suppose I'd better start packing my things. I've truly enjoyed sharing a chamber with you, Harry. It's been great fun."

"Oh, let me help you, Rachel. I've enjoyed it too. Don't be surprised if I come and stay with you at Campden Hill. I find your company far more stimulating than Trixy's."

"D'Arcy, I've been hoping you'd pay me a call." Harry gave him a warm smile.

"Don't you remember, Harry? I promised you a carriage ride."

"Of course I remember. You said it didn't have to be Hyde Park — you promised to take me anywhere I'd like to go. And the place I'd like to go is Campden Hill, in Kensington."

"Such a coincidence. I just got an invitation from Lord John, who's hosting a birthday fete for your mother on Tuesday at his house in Kensington."

"How lovely. We can attend it together if you like." She watched his eyes kindle. "I'll just see if Rachel is ready."

D'Arcy looked at her blankly. "Rachel?"

"Yes. We are taking her home to Campden Hill. It is right next door to John's house, and the gardens run together. We use both places for the birthday celebration."

"But I thought we could be alone, Harry."

"And so we shall. On the way back, there will be just the two of us. It will take at least an hour. That's fifty minutes longer than propriety dictates a young debutante should be alone with a gentleman." She winked.

"I'll go and get my parasol."

On the way back from Campden Hill, D'Arcy was surprised when Harriet asked if she could take the reins. "I don't think you'd enjoy it," he said repressively.

"Of course I will. I've driven in Ireland since I was a child, and some of the roads are in a dreadful state."

"Harry, this isn't a donkey cart. It's my brand-new phaeton and my best grays."

"I shall take that as a yes. You are amazingly generous, D'Arcy."

Though he wasn't best pleased, he decided he might be able to take advantage of the situation. He stopped the carriage, handed her the reins, and climbed in the other side. He moved close beside her and placed his arm about her. "You'll need my strong arm in case they bolt. I shall take that as a yes. You are amazingly generous, Harry."

Her lips twitched. *Two can play that game.* She drove sedately until they reached a long, flat stretch of road. "Hang on, D'Arcy!" She slapped the reins sharply, and let the horses have their head. The matched pair sprang forward in tandem, galloping as if Old Nick were on their tails. "Hell for leather — nothing can compare!"

The Earl of Durham did not appreciate

anyone taking control. That it was a female who did so, and moreover one he intended to make his wife, was anathema to him. He took the reins from her and forced the horses to slow from a wild gallop to an easy trot.

Harry had high spirits, and rather than reprimand her, he decided to manipulate her.

"On the way to Campden Hill, I thought I detected a bit of a limp in the carriage horse on the right. A mad gallop could injure him."

Harry was immediately contrite. "Oh, I am so sorry. What a thoughtless creature I am. Perhaps he picked up a stone. Do let's take a look at his hoof."

They climbed out of the phaeton, and while Harry held the horse's bridle and stroked his nose, D'Arcy took a cursory look at his hoof. "Ah, yes, it was a stone."

He hid his amusement as she climbed into the passenger seat like a penitent. He took the driver's seat and picked up the reins.

"Go slowly, D'Arcy, and I'll watch his gait."

"If you move over close to me, you'll have a better view."

She obeyed him immediately.

From now on, I'll handle you like a filly.

Harry watched the horse closely for about a mile. "I don't detect a limp now."

"No, nothing to worry about; he's right as rain."

"Thank heavens." She smiled up into his blue eyes. "Tell me about your County of Durham. What is it like?"

This will be tricky. Don't sully her ears with the grim reality. "Durham has some of everything — lush green countryside, many dales and valleys, and it's steeped in history."

"It sounds lovely."

"Durham Cathedral stands on a high, narrow hill, surrounded on three sides by the River Wear and its tree-covered banks. It holds the ancient tomb of Saint Cuthbert."

"He died defending us against the Vikings. How valiant he must have been."

"Durham also boasts the ruins of Barnard Castle, built in the twelfth century."

"Oh, I love castles."

"You will certainly love Lambton Castle. It's almost new. It was built by my father and he spared no expense making sure it boasts every modern convenience. Ancient castles may have atmosphere, but I'd hate to live in one of the damn things."

"How very unromantic of you, D'Arcy," she teased.

"Oh, I can be romantic." He slowed the horses. "Especially with a lady as lovely as you in my arms." He drew her close and captured her mouth in a sensual kiss. He indulged in three or four while she was in a giving mood, and then held her at arm's length as his avid glance swept over her. "I'll tell you one thing — the people of Durham will think you a goddess stepped down from Olympus when you become their countess."

"You are rather taking things for granted, D'Arcy Lambton," Harry said archly. "You will have to woo me and win me before I become your Countess of Durham."

"Stop teasing. Even the Duke and Duchess of Abercorn want me for their son-in-law. What sort of engagement ring would you like?"

"I don't want to be engaged. I want to be betrothed and have a betrothal ring . . . but not until the end of the Season. It's not far off. Do you suppose you can make me fall in love with you by then, D'Arcy?"

"End of the Season? Don't you think that's a colossal waste of time? If we make the formal announcement, we could be tucked up snugly making passionate love tonight." His hand moved down to cup her breast.

"You are a silver-tongued devil," Harry

mocked. "How can any lady resist you?" She peeled his hand from her breast and placed it on the reins. "It's clouding over. I would consider it extremely gallant if you could get me home before it rains."

"Your wish is my command, Harry, but if you make me wait until after we are married, I shall keep you abed for a week."

"Only a week?" she teased. "I thought earls of the realm were voracious."

"I'll show you voracious!" He pulled her hard against him.

She held out her hand for a raindrop. "You'll show me a soaking if you don't hurry."

Harry shook the rain from her drenched parasol, and the housekeeper, Mrs. Foster, stood it in the entrance hall to dry. Then Harry ran upstairs to the bedchamber she shared with her sisters so she could change her clothes.

"I'm glad you're back." Trixy unfastened the buttons on the back of Harry's dress. "I've been waiting to ask you a question. Do you think it would be too forward of me to ask D'Arcy Lambton to be my partner at Mother's annual birthday party?"

"Of course it wouldn't be too forward of you." Harry stepped out of her dress. "It would, however, be a complete waste of time. This afternoon, I asked D'Arcy to partner me." She took a dress from her wardrobe and slipped it over her head.

"Damn you, Harry! I thought that Thomas Anson was wooing you."

"Well, he tried, but he didn't succeed."

"Well, I think it's inconsiderate and decidedly shallow to collect all the eligible bachelors like you were gathering a bunch of dandelions, and then toss them aside one by one because they don't match your dress."

"You are mixing your metaphors, Trixy," she teased lightly. "It is your Season too — you are perfectly free to *gather your rosebuds while ye may.*" Harry changed into slippers. "I have to decide what to give Mother for her birthday. I'll see you at dinner."

When Harry left, Jane commiserated with Trixy. "It doesn't seem fair that all the young men are so bedazzled by Harriet, they don't even look at the rest of us. Do you think it's because she is the oldest?"

"No, it's because they wear blinkers. They are blind to what's around them. Men want what other men want. Haven't you noticed that at an auction they all bid on the same horse?"

"We have to have a plan for the birthday

party. Trixy, I will sing your praises to D'Arcy Lambton, if you will tell William Montagu how much I admire him."

Beatrix began to laugh. "Oh, wouldn't it put Harry's nose out of joint if one day you became the Countess of Dalkeith, and lived at Dalkeith Palace?"

"I don't really care about besting Harry," Jane confided, "but Will Montagu has stolen my heart, and I cannot stop daydreaming about him."

"In that case, it sounds like a good plan to me. I shall direct Will Montagu's attention to you, and you must sing my praises to D'Arcy Lambton."

The two girls clasped hands, crossed their hearts, and made a secret pact.

"This is so delightful. I want to thank Johnny and Rachel for giving me a surprise party every year. My birthday wouldn't be the same if we didn't celebrate it at Kensington. I also want to thank all the guests for accepting the invitation."

The duchess spoke on the verandah of Holland House, with the ladies gathered to one side, and the men on the other congregating about the duke and Lord Johnny.

Harry was surprised to find Thomas Anson in attendance. She immediately sought him out and challenged him. "What are you doing here?"

"I was invited by Lord John."

"You cannot be my partner today. I am with D'Arcy Lambton."

"I wouldn't dream of asking you, Lady Harriet. I am partnering another."

"Oh." Harry was discomfited and felt like a fool. "Forgive me," she said stiffly.

"There is nothing to forgive." He smiled warmly. "Though I am no longer courting you, I see no reason why we can't be friends. Do you?"

You are being extremely civilized. I hadn't expected it of you. "No reason at all, since we've known each other for so many years."

James Hamilton raised his hands. "As always, the first event will be a race across the lake. The exercise will work up an appetite for lunch. I apologize for the manmade lake. It cannot compare to our chain of natural lakes in Ireland, but it will have to suffice. Seek out your partners, and head down to the rowboats."

Harry turned away from Thomas and spotted Lambton. "Hurry, D'Arcy!"

"What's the point?" he drawled. "Your father always wins. He was a champion oarsman for Oxford University."

Thomas overheard D'Arcy and it spurred

him to compete. He grabbed Trixy's hand. "Will you be my partner?" They were running to the rowboats before she found breath to answer. Rachel and James Butler beat them to the first boat, but Thomas and Beatrix were far ahead of the Duke and Duchess of Abercorn.

Jane was breathless with excitement when Will Montagu offered to share his boat with her, and young Henry Edgcumbe invited Lord John's wife, Fanny, to be his partner.

Once they were on the lake and the actual rowing began, Abercorn pulled into the lead, and his daughters urged their partners with raucous shouts of "Row faster!" in a competitive desire to beat their father.

Thomas Anson put his back into the effort and pulled on the oars. He was pleased when he shot past Captain Butler, who looked to be in top physical shape. At the halfway point, three of the rowers were even — Abercorn, Thomas, and D'Arcy.

Harry was filled with excitement. "We can win this race, D'Arcy!"

"No, I want your father to win. Once we are married, I want him to recommend me for lord lieutenant of Durham, and he won't if I make him look bad."

D'Arcy, there is no way you could make the magnificent Duke of Abercorn look bad.

By sheer dint of will, Thomas Anson began to pass Abercorn. Trixy was beside herself with excitement at the prospect of winning. When their rowboat pulled ahead of her parents' boat, she stood up and shouted encouragement to Thomas. "Go! Go! Go!"

As it shot forward, Trixy lost her balance, then her footing, and over the side she went with a splash and a scream. She went under, bobbed up with arms flailing, and then went under again.

Immediately, Thomas removed his shoes and dived into the lake. From behind, he firmly grabbed her beneath the arms, and swam with her to the closest bank. He dragged her up onto the grass and knelt over the gasping, coughing Lady Beatrix. "Are you all right?"

When she nodded and spluttered, he sat her up and slapped her on the back. By this time, Abercorn had reached the end of the lake. He jumped from his rowboat and sprinted toward his daughter.

"Well done, Anson." He lifted his daughter's chin and looked into her eyes. "Damnation, Trixy, I've taught you better than to stand up in a moving rowboat." He looked at Thomas. "She knows how to swim. I taught her myself."

161

"I think she swallowed too much water and it made her panic."

Trixy gave him a grateful look. "You were very gallant to dive in for me. I thank you with all my heart, Thomas."

He grinned at her. "If you are brave enough to get back in and trust me, I'll row you across the lake so you can go and put on some dry clothes."

Trixy laughed. "I would trust you with my life, Thomas."

On the way back across the lake, Trixy confided in him. "Harry has treated you very badly. She didn't have the time of day for poor old D'Arcy when you started to pay court to her. Now she's doing the same to you, so she can become the Countess of Durham."

As Thomas listened to her, certain things began to dawn on him. *Trixy is infatuated with D'Arcy Lambton. When I began to court Harry, Trixy thought the way was clear for her to catch D'Arcy. She longs to be the Countess of Durham.* Thomas felt her pain.

My dearest Lady Beatrix, there is nothing I would like better than to see you become the Countess of Durham.

CHAPTER EIGHT

The Duke of Abercorn provided Thomas with some of his clothes while Anson's wet garments were laid out to dry. By the time they returned to the party, the gentlemen were bidding on the decorated picnic baskets of the ladies. The identities were kept secret until the auction was completed.

When Trixy's basket was bought by Will Montagu, and Jane's was procured by D'Arcy Lambton, the sisters exchanged a gleeful look, for here was their chance to fulfill their pledge and sing the other's praises.

As Trixy unwrapped a roast partridge for the Scot, she confided, "My sister Jane was in heaven when she shared your rowboat. She never stops talking about you, Will. She is infatuated with everything about you, especially your brogue."

Will laughed. "That's very flattering. Most young ladies are smitten by Montagu

House, rather than Montagu's heir."

Jane decided to make D'Arcy aware of her sister Beatrix by telling him her sister's innermost secrets. "I shouldn't be telling you this, but Trixy has lost her heart to you."

She took out a carafe of claret wine and poured him a large glass. "She was over the moon with happiness when Harry was being courted by Thomas Anson. She hoped that you would ask her to go for a carriage ride."

D'Arcy quaffed his wine and listened attentively.

"When Trixy found out that Harry had asked you to partner her today, she was devastated and gave Harry a setdown."

"Really?" He smiled lazily. "What did she say?"

"She told Harry that it was inconsiderate and decidedly shallow to collect all the eligible bachelors like she was gathering a bunch of dandelions, then toss them aside one by one because they didn't match her dress."

D'Arcy laughed. "Trixy is delightful. Harry does have a tendency to blow hot and cold. But she won't change her mind this time. She's met her match."

Jane's eyes widened. "So you intend to offer for her?"

"Absolutely. We already have an under-standing. Harry has agreed to a betrothal at the end of the Season."

Jane sighed. "It must be wonderful when two people fall in love."

Thomas Anson found himself paired with Rachel Russell. He decided it was his opportunity to learn a few things about Harry. "I heard you paid a visit to Hazard House last week."

"Oh Lord, I suppose everyone has heard by now. I needed to do research on gambling for one of my stories, so Harriet arranged for us to go to a gaming hell. It was a dreadful place; I couldn't get away fast enough."

"But Harry enjoyed it?"

"Oh no, not at all. But she is so generous. She arranged it for my sake."

"What sort of things does Harriet enjoy?"

"High on her list is championing women's rights. She is friends with Barbara Leigh Smith and the women suffragists who meet in Langham Place."

Thomas smiled. "Yes, I know she is interested in getting a bill passed so that women can own property."

"The causes she champions are much broader than that. She cares about the plight of poor children, and the squalid state of London's slums. She has just signed petitions to improve the unsanitary sewage that is rife in certain sections of the city."

"So, she is a champion of the downtrodden and follows the lead of her uncle Lord John Russell."

Rachel laughed. "Johnny is my brother."

"Yes, I know he is. He works tirelessly in Parliament. I admire him enormously." Speaking with Rachel made Thomas all the more aware that he had been too quick to judge Harry.

After lunch, Lady Lu announced a game of croquet. The ladies were thrilled; the men not so much, but they gallantly agreed to join in the game.

The Duke of Abercorn pulled Thomas aside. "How would you like to join me at the trout stream for a bit of fishing while the ladies play croquet?"

"That would suit me to a T, Your Grace."

Harriet and D'Arcy strolled arm in arm across the lawn toward the croquet hoops and mallets. Their eyes followed Abercorn and Anson as they headed toward the trout stream carrying fishing rods.

"Damnation! I was looking forward to a private word with your father. I shall need his help if I ever hope to be appointed lord lieutenant of Durham."

Harry stopped walking and looked up into his eyes. "Would you like me to ask him for you, D'Arcy?"

"Would you, Harry? I'm sure he would put in a good word for me if he knew I was going to be his future son-in-law."

"I haven't agreed to marry you yet, D'Arcy," Harry teased. "Of course I will ask him. Father will speak to Prince Albert — Albert will speak to Victoria, and voilà!"

D'Arcy pulled her to him and kissed her. "Voilà indeed!"

The birthday supper served at six was a veritable banquet. Prawns and lobster accompanied smoked trout. Roast game hens, stuffed with chestnuts, followed. Haunches of venison had been roasting all afternoon, and by the time it was served, the flesh was tender and the skin was a crackling, crispy brown. The vegetables were all grown at Campden Hill. Leeks, marrows, squash, and roasted apples decorated the meat platters.

Ale, cider, wine, and Irish whiskey were there for the taking, and the myriad desserts, from fruit tarts to gingerbread, were surpassed only by the magnificent two-tiered birthday cake decorated with roses.

After the meal, Lady Lu opened her presents. She made as much fuss over the simple handmade offerings of her younger children as she did the rope of magnificent black pearls from her husband.

Harry gave her a book that included all four parts of Keats's epic love poem *Endymion.*

"*'A thing of beauty is a joy forever'* — he could've been writing of you, Mother."

"Thank you, darling."

D'Arcy had framed a photograph he'd taken the night he'd been invited to dinner.

"D'Arcy, how thoughtful. Though it tends to disprove Keats's first line."

The last gift she opened was a delicately carved mother-of-pearl fan. "Oh dear, there is no card. But whoever it is from has exquisite taste and knows what will please a lady." She looked at Thomas Anson and wondered if the fan was from him.

Harry made an announcement. "Ladies and gentlemen, we are all invited next door, where Mademoiselle Rachelle will do a Mystical Tarot Card Reading for any who are brave enough to take a glimpse into their future."

Every last female present was eager and excited. The men dutifully followed them next door to Campden Hill, pretending a disbelief in all things mystical and total disinterest in predictions about their futures. They assured one another, however, that fortune-telling was good for a laugh.

Lady Rachel, wearing a Gypsy dress, head scarf, and golden earrings, sat in the drawing room at a table that was decorated with mystic paraphernalia. Before her were a crystal ball, an incense burner, tall candles, and tarot cards.

The lamps were turned down low and the guests took seats around the room. When the duchess arrived, she inquired, "Are you sure you wouldn't rather have a séance? They are the absolute rage these days."

Rachel spoke up. "Lu, if we have a séance, Mother will show up and point out all our shortcomings."

"Good Heavens, you're right. Her catalogue of complaints would be so long, we'd miss the fireworks display that Abercorn has planned."

"Since it's your birthday, would you like me to read your cards first, Lu?"

"Absolutely not. I don't need the tarot cards to tell me what's in my future. I have my own predictions. Before the year is out, I shall be planning at least two, and possibly three, weddings." She gave Captain Butler a speculative look. "After the Season, Abercorn will insist on an idyll to Barons Court in Ireland, and I'm sure you can all guess what happens nine months after an idyll."

Everyone laughed at her innuendo.

"By that, I take it you intend to outdo the queen?" Rachel remarked.

"I rather think it is Abercorn who is determined to outperform Prince Albert."

When the laughter died down, Rachel challenged, "Come on, which one of you is brave enough to go first?"

No one spoke up and the room fell silent. Finally, Harry stood up, and pulled D'Arcy after her. "Never let it be said that I am a coward!"

D'Arcy helped her into a chair at the table, and took the other one himself.

Rachel picked up the tarot cards and handed them to Harry. "Since there are so many here who would like a reading, we will use the *Celtic Cross* layout, which limits you to eight cards." She nodded to Harry. "Shuffle the deck, make a wish, and lay out the first four cards in a cross. Then place the next four over them in a diagonal cross."

Harry followed instructions and quickly laid out her eight cards.

"Your first card is the *Fool*." Harry's sisters giggled, and Rachel hushed them with a fierce glare. "This card means you have a choice in life. At the end of the path you choose lies a destiny. Trial and error brings wisdom. The choices you make determine whether you end up a wise woman or remain a fool."

D'Arcy took Harry's hand and squeezed it.

"Ah, your next card is the *Lovers.*"

"Bravo!" D'Arcy said with a grin.

Rachel continued: "On the surface, it represents young love, romance, courtship, and marriage. The man protects and the woman enjoys his security. On a deeper level, it is a struggle between love and lust. However, it is the female who determines the quality of the love relationship. The male merely responds. The woman leads; the man follows."

All the girls cheered.

Rachel picked up the next card. "The *Hanged Man.*"

"That sounds bad," Harry declared.

"Not at all," Rachel said firmly. "It has a humorous overtone. Please note there is nothing to show he is tied to the cross. He is standing on his head to shake up his brains. The card means you should suspend judgment and postpone plans. But always remember that you can free yourself anytime you wish. To achieve your desired goals, you must change the direction of your life."

"All the rest of my cards are *swords*. What does that mean?"

"*Swords* represent quarrels, anxiety, deception, and enemies. They also represent courage, a fighter for truth, and a defender of man's rights."

"You mean *woman's* rights," Harry corrected.

"Unfortunately, all these *swords* in your layout mean you won't get your wish."

Harry wrinkled her nose. "Now it's your turn, D'Arcy. Don't be a coward."

He winked at Rachel, shuffled the cards, and laid them out. "Do your worst."

"Your first card is the *Wheel of Fortune.* This means things will take a turn for the better. You will make constant progress in your life, work, and goals. It means getting ahead, and being in control. Though your fate will have unexpected twists and turns, this card means you will have an abundance of good luck."

Will Montagu laughed. "D'Arcy never has any other kind."

Rachel continued. "Your next card is the *Empress,* which means abundance in all things — health, crops, big business profits. The *Empress* opens the door to all earthly treasures and pleasures."

D'Arcy's grin stretched from ear to ear.

"All the rest of your cards are *pentacles,* which represent wealth, luxury, jewels, inheritances, property, castles, financial security, and money to burn."

Now all the men were laughing. "That's D'Arcy, all right. Wouldn't you know it?"

In the darkened room, Thomas Anson heard Lady Beatrix sigh with longing. He bent his head toward her. "Why don't you go next, Trixy? I predict your tarot cards will be good."

Harry and D'Arcy moved away from the table, and Thomas held a chair for Beatrix, sitting down beside her to lend her courage.

Trixy was eager and yet hesitant at the same time. As she shuffled and laid out the cards, her hands trembled.

Rachel picked up the first card. "Oh, the *Nine of Cups.* Trixy, that is the highest of all tarot cards. It means happiness, contentment, and fulfillment. It is the wish card, and anytime it begins a layout, it means you will get your wish."

Trixy gasped with joy.

Rachel continued. "The *Sun.* Trixy, I can't believe how good your cards are. This means a golden opportunity. It means attainment, success. You will have both material wealth and personal satisfaction." Rachel turned over another card. "Look at that — the *Three of Wands.* That is a time card. You will achieve your desires in a three — that could mean three days, three weeks, three months, or three years."

"Well, I hope it doesn't take three years!"

Rachel continued. "All your other cards are *pentacles* and, as you know, that means luxuries, jewels, property, and financial security."

"Thank you, Rachel, for telling my future, and thank you, Thomas, for giving me courage to have my cards read."

"If you want something, Trixy, you should go after it," Thomas urged. "The cards say you will achieve your desire in a three."

"Rachel did say I was sure to get my wish. Now it's your turn."

Thomas hesitated. He didn't believe in prophecy — he believed you made your own fate. But this was just a game. It amused Trixy, and he would be churlish to decline.

Rachel picked up the first card he laid out. "The *Magician.* This means you are your own man. It signifies self-mastery, self-control. It represents intelligence and confidence. You do not need the approval of others. When you set a goal, you will achieve it."

Rachel picked up the next card. "The *Chariot*. This often follows the *Magician*.

"It means your willpower and your mind are your only weapons for survival. You will achieve your goals only if you exercise self-discipline."

Rachel lifted the next card and she hesitated. Both she and Thomas saw that it was the *Death* card. He looked into her eyes and imperceptibly shook his head.

At that moment, Abercorn arrived. "There you are, Thomas. I believe your clothes are dry, and I was wondering if you'd like to give me a hand with the firework display."

Thomas had a horror of fire, but he firmly pushed it away. "It would be my pleasure, Your Grace." He placed the *Death* card facedown and got up from the table.

Abercorn waved his hand. "Enjoy your tarot card readings, ladies. By the time you are finished, we'll have the fireworks set up in front of the lake. I promise you all a fitting climax to a birthday celebration that will light up the sky."

An hour later, the guests emerged from the house and began to gather at the spacious gazebo that overlooked the lake. As they walked, some of them separated into couples. Will Montagu accompanied Lady

Jane, Captain Butler walked beside "Mademoiselle Rachelle," and D'Arcy Lambton strolled hand in hand with Harry. When Henry Edgcumbe fell in beside Trixy, she gave him a grateful smile.

Abercorn, with the help of Thomas Anson, had set up the fireworks so that they would go off consecutively, one after another, without pause. He'd bought them from the manufacturer that had created the magnificent pyrotechnics for the opening of the Crystal Palace, and felt confident the display would be twice as spectacular as the previous year.

He spoke confidentially to Thomas. "Much as I'd like to set them alight myself, I cannot deprive the gamekeeper of doing the honors. Hawkins has done it every year and I don't want to run the risk of offending him."

Thomas glanced at Hawkins, who stood at the ready with his lantern and long wooden tapers with sulfur tips. Thomas was relieved to see a row of stable hands with water-filled wooden buckets. "I think that's a wise decision, Your Grace. Shall we join the spectators?"

The crowd had now grown to include the indoor and outdoor staffs of both Campden Hill and Holland House. The Duke and

Duchess of Abercorn's younger children had been given permission to stay up late to watch the fireworks, and sat on the grass in front of their watchful nursemaids.

Abercorn joined his wife, and then he signaled Hawkins to start the show. As the first brilliant Roman candle shot into the air and filled the sky with a silver shower of stars, he slipped his arm about Lady Lu. "Happy birthday, darling."

She gazed up at him with adoring eyes. "You promised me skyrockets, and you've always kept your word."

Harry, standing near her parents, heard their loving exchange, and wished with all her heart that when she married, her husband would worship her with the same devotion her father lavished upon her mother. She felt D'Arcy's arm steal about her waist and draw her close. She decided not to pull away from him. *I believe D'Arcy truly loves me.*

Thomas began to watch the enraptured faces of the Hamilton children. It warmed his heart that their devoted parents had dedicated themselves to assuring their offspring had happy childhoods. He could not help but compare Abercorn's paternal care with the shortcomings of his own father. He vowed that when he had children of his own, he would be a loving parent.

Thomas glanced down and saw Beatrix smiling up at him.

"I'm sorry I spoiled your day by falling into the lake, my lord."

"Trixy, in no way did you spoil my day. You have been a delightful companion."

She gave him a skeptical look. "You are a good friend to say so."

"I mean it, Trixy. Would you do me the honor of allowing me to escort you to the queen's Bal Costume at Buckingham Palace next week?"

"Oh, thank you. I would be honored indeed, Thomas."

After the fireworks display, and before the guests thanked their hosts and departed, they enjoyed another piece of birthday cake and offered a final toast to Lady Lu. The family was spending the night at Campden Hill, and though the gentlemen had been offered accommodation for the night, they all graciously declined.

D'Arcy clapped Thomas on the back. "Why don't you drive back to London with me? I'd appreciate the company."

"I came with Montagu, but since you and I live so close, there will be no need to inconvenience Will if you'll drop me off."

When the stablemen harnessed Lambton's grays to his phaeton, he took the reins and Anson climbed up beside him. Thomas complimented him on his matched pair and waited for D'Arcy to bring up the subject of the Hamilton daughters. He was shrewd enough to know it was inevitable.

"You lucky devil, Thomas. That was an amazing opportunity to play hero to Trixy."

"Beatrix is such a delight. She is so fun loving and amenable and always ready to defer to a gentleman's wishes."

"Abercorn certainly seems to have taken a special interest in you."

"That was just his way of thanking me for going in the lake after his daughter. He's very fond of Beatrix. I enjoyed her company today — it was truly refreshing."

D'Arcy gave him a level look. "You mean refreshing after dealing with Harry."

Thomas flashed him a grin. "*You* said that — I didn't. But we both know that Harriet has a mind of her own, and could never be described as amenable."

"She'll settle down once she becomes a wife."

Thomas spoke with deliberate calculation. "I'm not so sure. Her main reason for marrying is because she'll have more rights as a married woman. She has joined the suffragists so she can crusade for women's rights."

"When she becomes the Countess of Durham, she'll have no time for that nonsense."

"No, she will be consumed by the plight of those who work in the Durham collieries. She'll take up the cause of the poverty-stricken miners. It is amazing that two sisters can be so different. Beatrix's only desire is to have a noble husband she can love and serve."

"You lucky dog, Anson. Will you offer for her?"

"Good heavens, no. We are just friends. Trixy has lost her heart to another."

"Do you think so?"

"I know so, D'Arcy. She never stops talking about *you*." He paused for emphasis. "It must be very gratifying to have both beautiful sisters eager to do your bidding."

"Good morning, Father. I thought I'd join you for breakfast."

The servant arrived with Abercorn's food. "What would you like, my lady?"

"I'll have exactly the same as my father, thank you."

"Harriet, everyone is still sound asleep. To what do I owe this honor?"

"I always enjoy spending time with you,

but to be brutally honest, I want to have a private conversation without the rest of the family interrupting."

"Ah, you have an ulterior motive. But I'll let you in on a little secret. Everyone in the world has an agenda."

Harry thought about it for a moment, and then smiled at the truth of his words. "I have some questions about the role of lord lieutenant. What duties does it encompass?"

"Lord lieutenants are the queen's representative in their county. They arrange visits for members of the royal family and they present medals and awards to industry on her behalf. They are responsible for law and order and to see that justice is carried out. For the most part, the lord lieutenant and his wife participate in social activities to promote a spirit of cooperation between the county's people and its industry."

"When you were lord lieutenant of Donegal, I don't remember any royal visits, or award presentations, or many social activities for that matter."

"That's because there were none. It was during the time of the tragic Irish potato famine. The entire populace suffered devastation. Your mother and I were hard-pressed to keep the people of Donegal from starvation."

"Did England pay for that, or did you use your own money?"

"I wasn't naive enough to expect the government to send money to Ireland. It has always been a poor country that contributed little to England's wealth." He strove to lighten his words with humor. "And your uncle Johnny didn't become prime minister until my two-year term was over."

"Why on earth would D'Arcy Lambton want to be the lord lieutenant of Durham?"

"Now I see the reason for your questions. Durham is a very different kettle of fish than an Irish county. England derives a great deal of her wealth from Durham."

"So you think D'Arcy could well afford to be its lord lieutenant? The appointment wouldn't reduce him to being a pauper?"

Abercorn laughed heartily. "Since D'Arcy Lambton is the Earl of Durham, he will grow wealthier with every passing year. England is the leading industrialized country in the entire world, and coal is its most important commodity. Only think for a moment — coal heats our homes; it is the fuel we use for cooking. Coal is used to run our factories, our railroads, and our ships. Every shovelful of coal helps to fill D'Arcy's coffers."

"Thank you so much for enlightening me.

You paint such a clear picture."

"So D'Arcy entertains serious ambitions to become Durham's lord lieutenant?"

"Among other ambitions."

"Such as?"

"He wants you for his father-in-law."

"So that's the way the wind blows." His brows drew together. "You know, Queen Victoria makes these appointments on the recommendation of her prime minister."

Harry's face fell. The present prime minister was Abercorn's stepfather, and there was neither love nor even civility between them. Then she brightened. "There is a way around that obstacle. If you recommend D'Arcy Lambton to Prince Albert, he will be sure to mention it to Her Majesty. Victoria strives to please her husband in every way."

"Did D'Arcy ask you to speak to me, Harriet?"

"Absolutely not. He was going to talk to you himself, but when I offered to speak to you on his behalf, he was extremely grateful."

"Has he asked you to marry him, Harry?"

"He hasn't formally proposed, because I've told him I won't give him an answer until the end of the Season. But he has referred to me as his future countess, and he insists our marriage is what you and Mother want for me."

"Harriet, your mother and I want you to make up your own mind when it comes to choosing a husband. The choice is yours, not ours. We want only your happiness."

"Thank you, Father. Your assurance means a great deal to me."

CHAPTER NINE

The family spent the day at Campden Hill and in the evening drove back to London.

Before Harry left, she visited with Rachel to bid her good-bye. "You must try to come to the queen's costume ball at Buckingham Palace next week. It will be so much more fun if we can both be there in our short skirts."

"As a matter of fact, I *shall* be attending. Lord Butler has invited me, and has offered to pick me up in his carriage. I don't know if I shall have enough courage to wear a costume with a short skirt, however."

"Well, to be truthful, I don't know what I'll be wearing either. But I know I'll have more fun if you are there. Bye-bye, Rachel. Thank you for making Mother's birthday celebration so special."

Two hours later, after their cook, Mrs. Gilbert, fed them some chicken broth with dumplings, the Hamilton sisters retired to bed. Their conversations centered about the tarot card readings that "Mademoiselle Rachelle" had provided.

"My cards were better than anyone else's, and moreover, I'm supposed to get my wish within a three!" Trixy could not hide her excitement.

"What do you think, Harry?" Jane asked. "Do wishes really come true?"

"Some do, I suppose. But my tarot cards were mostly *swords,* so I don't have much hope. I also got the *Fool* and the *Hanged Man.* I couldn't have received worse cards."

"Oh, Harry, they weren't all bad," Trixy reminded her. "You got the *Lovers!* I wish that I'd gotten that card. It must be the most exciting thing in the world to have a lover!"

Harry climbed into bed and thought about it. "The cards say that it is the woman who determines the quality of the love relationship. The man merely responds. There may be some truth in that."

In the middle of the night, Harry began to dream:

She was riding in an open carriage with D'Arcy. They were driving up to a beautiful castle that stood atop a green hill.

"Welcome to Lambton Castle, my love."

"Ahhh, it is even lovelier than I imagined. I

have such a passion for buildings, and this is an exact replica of a medieval castle."

"Wait until you see the interiors," he promised. He took her hand and helped her from the carriage. "When Father had it built, money was no object."

The great hall was spacious, its walls decorated with ancient swords and burnished armor. A long oak table, polished to a mirror finish and complete with twenty-four carved chairs, sat before a massive stone fireplace. The floor was covered with a thick Oriental carpet, and ironbound chests stood against the walls.

"What are the chests for?"

D'Arcy walked over and lifted one of the lids. "They are to hold all the gold coins I receive from selling Durham's coal."

Harry lifted her arms and twirled about with joy. Then she began to ascend a grand staircase. She looked behind and beckoned, making sure D'Arcy would follow. When she ran out onto the ramparts, he caught up with her and led her to the crenellated wall.

"I was saving it as a surprise, but I got word today that I have been appointed lord lieutenant of Durham."

"Congratulations, D'Arcy." She brushed her fingertips across his cheek and gazed into his blue eyes. "Without a doubt, you will be the *handsomest lord lieutenant this county has ever known."*

He slipped his arms around her and drew her close. "Harry, will you marry me?"

She lifted her arms about his neck and laughed up into his attractive face. "Yes, D'Arcy, I would love to be your wife and become the next Countess of Durham."

His lips captured hers in a long, sensual kiss. Then suddenly the air was filled with the cascading silver and gold stars of fireworks that lit up the dark sky. The castle pyrotechnics ended in a loud explosion.

It brought Harry out of her dream, and she sat up in bed with her heart pounding. Then she realized it was a loud crack of thunder that had awakened her. She got out of bed to close the window and stood staring at the flashes of lightning that lit up the sky. When her heart stopped racing, she remembered her dream. *D'Arcy asked me to marry him, and I said yes!*

"The theme for this year's Bal Costume is the Restoration period. I wager every male attending will be disguised as King Charles the Second," Harry declared.

"And every female will be Queen Catherine of Braganza," Trixy added.

"Well, certainly Queen Victoria will, but I

prefer going as the insatiable Barbara Castlemaine," the duchess jested.

"But that wouldn't be a disguise," Harry teased.

"Oh God, I'm turning into my mother! I just remembered that she went to a royal masquerade ball at St. James's Palace dressed as Barbara Castlemaine."

"Really? And who were you dressed as?"

"I blush to tell you that I was pretty, witty Nell Gwyn, complete with saucy red curls. I remember singing a very naughty ditty to your father — though he wasn't your father at the time."

"In your day, masquerade balls had one purpose in mind — dalliance. The guests were encouraged to wear risqué costumes, and indulge in flirtatious liaisons. Everyone wore masks to hide their identities, and the king and queen turned a blind eye, pretending it was all innocent fun and games," Harry declared.

"You have read too many books where these masquerades have been romanticized. My father totally disapproved. He said that licentious costumes led to licentious behavior, and, thinking back, he was quite right."

"But Queen Victoria's ball, in contrast, will be as exciting as a Sunday school dance. The guests will parade around the Buckingham Palace ballroom wearing ultrarespectable costumes. Exposed bosoms are considered scandalous. I swear, if any lady was daring enough to wear an *authentic* Restoration fashion, it would be the last royal ball she ever attends."

"Fortunately, costumes that represent other countries around the world are always acceptable. I have a fancy to dress as a Russian, since I have a flair for the dramatic."

"Mother, I warrant that's a perfect choice for you, and it has given me an idea for my own costume. No, Trixy, I won't tell you. It's to be a surprise."

Harry hurried from the room and went in search of her brother James. She found him in the library polishing the hilt on an old sword. "Don't tell me you've been challenged to a duel by Lady Emily's brother?"

James laughed. "It's for the costume ball."

"Let me guess. . . . You're going as a cavalier."

"How did you know?"

"What other disguise would any red-blooded young noble choose? I need your help regarding my own costume, James. But first I have to swear you to secrecy."

"You're going as Lady Godiva!"

"No, silly. It's just that Rachel and I made a pact to show off our legs at the queen's

Bal Costume. So I've decided to go as a Scottish lad."

"A Scottish lad? Good Lord, Harry, you never grow tired of shock and surprise."

"Remember the kilt you wore when we were invited to Balmoral? You were about twelve, so I think it will fit me."

"It must be up in the attic, unless Mother sent it home with Rose along with all my other clothes I've outgrown over the years."

"I doubt there'd be much call for kilts in Soho," she said dryly. "Let's go and look."

The pair spent the next half hour searching through trunks, and at last found what they were looking for.

"Yes! Just as I was hoping, the entire outfit is here — the black velvet jacket, the knee-socks, and, most important of all, the sporran!"

"Do you truly have enough nerve to wear that to the palace, Harry?"

"Only after I've shortened it," she said with a wink.

On the night of the ball, Harry's face was devoid of all powder and paint. She brushed her long black hair back smoothly and fastened it with a leather thong. She covered her eyes with a black mask, and then she placed a Gordon plaid tam-o'-shanter on

191

the side of her head, and pinned it to her hair so it wouldn't fall off.

When D'Arcy Lambton called for her at Hampden House, Harry made sure her evening cloak covered her costume.

D'Arcy was wearing a brocade coat, satin knee breeches, and a powered wig.

"Oh, you look marvelous. Your Regency outfit looks positively authentic."

"It should. It belonged to my grandfather Earl Grey." He stared at Harry's scrubbed cheeks and pulled-back hair. "You look like a boy tonight."

"That's precisely what I'm supposed to be. Will you be courageous enough to dance with me?"

"Since I'm privy to the secret that beneath your disguise there beats the heart of a passionate woman, I'll be courageous enough to do more than dance with you, sweeting."

"Let's hurry. I can't wait to see what costume Rachel will wear tonight."

At Buckingham Palace, when a footman took Lady Harriet's cloak, D'Arcy's mouth gaped open when he saw the short kilt and Harry's deliciously long legs exposed for the entire world to see. "Good God, Harry, you make me feel randy as a Regency buck!"

"Lucky you," she teased, then added with a wink, "Lucky me!"

They joined the circle to parade around the throne room. Harry received many disapproving stares over her daring costume, but she blithely shrugged them off. "By the way, I spoke to my father and told him you had an ambition to become the lord lieutenant of Durham."

"Good girl! What did he say?" he asked eagerly.

"He informed me that Queen Victoria makes such appointments upon the recommendation of her prime minister."

"So, do you think your father will recommend me to Aberdeen?"

"Not a chance. They dislike each other. Intensely!" Then she smiled. "Father will do better than that. I warrant he will speak directly to Prince Albert."

The reception rooms were crowded with people in costume. Everyone of consequence in London had accepted the prestigious invitation to the queen's Bal Costume at Buckingham Palace.

The parade music stopped, which was the signal for everyone to find a dance partner. D'Arcy hesitated about leading a Scottish lad onto the dance floor, and Harry was secretly enjoying his discomfort.

Will Montagu was partnering Jane, and when they saw D'Arcy and Harry, they stopped to chat. "Great minds think alike," Harry quipped when she saw that Montagu was in full Highland dress. "You must save me a dance, Will. It will set tongues a-wagging."

Jane looked aghast at her sister. "Harry, your knees are bare!"

"Aye. So are Will's. The only difference is that I put rouge on mine."

Harry watched the dancers whirl by and when the music stopped, she found herself standing beside the queen, who was garbed in a magnificent Restoration gown, sans the low neckline of course.

Victoria smiled at the Earl of Durham in his brocade coat and powdered wig. "How very elegant you look, Lord Durham." She glanced at the youth in the kilt. "And who is this young gentleman?"

D'Arcy cleared his throat. "It's . . . it's young James Hamilton, Your Majesty."

Harry's mouth fell open.

"James, of course! Forgive me for not recognizing you," the queen apologized.

Harry bowed low, and then quickly fell back into the crowd. "You were embarrassed to acknowledge me because I was showing my legs. You have the courage of a louse, D'Arcy Lambton."

"You forget yourself, Harry. That was Her

Gracious Majesty the Queen of England. It would have shocked her beyond belief if she'd recognized you flaunting your limbs."

"You are afraid I'd put your lord lieutenancy in jeopardy!" she teased.

"Nonsense! I was only thinking of your reputation."

"Go and get me a drink, and I will forgive you," she promised. In the crowd, Harry spotted Lord Butler. He was easy to recognize because he was wearing his brilliant captain's uniform with its shiny brass buttons. She made her way across the floor and was delighted to see that her adventurous aunt had found the courage to expose her legs.

"Well done, Rachel. Your doublet and hose turn you into a most fetching page boy. Would you believe it? When the queen asked who I was, D'Arcy introduced me as James! When I challenged him, he swore it was to protect my reputation. He's such a coward."

Rachel laughed. "Has D'Arcy seen your tattoo yet?"

"I'm afraid not."

"Ho! Now who is the coward?" she teased.

"Tattoo?" Captain Butler looked at Harry in disbelief.

Harry rolled her eyes. "Don't ask!"

"Where is D'Arcy?" Butler questioned.

"He went to get me a drink, but he must have gotten lost in the crowd."

"Here's Thomas and Beatrix. Oh, your gown is ultrafeminine, Trixy," Rachel declared. "You look so lovely, you make me wish I hadn't dressed as a boy."

Harry saw Anson's eyes sweep over her from head to foot. She also saw the amusement written there that he couldn't quite conceal.

Captain Butler ran an appreciative hand over the elaborate gold braid on Thomas's coat. "Is this the admiral's uniform of your famous ancestor George Anson?"

"It is indeed. Perhaps it's presumptuous of me to wear it, but he's the only Anson who ever achieved greatness."

"You never told me you had a famous ancestor," Harry said. "I'm curious as a cat."

"He became admiral of the fleet and won many great naval battles against the French. He circumnavigated the world, and captured ships laden with gold. He is the one who brought back the many treasures that once furnished Shugborough Hall."

The treasures your father sold to pay off his gambling debts.

"You are not being presumptuous when you wear his uniform, Thomas. You are honoring him." Green eyes met pewter and held for long, drawn-out moments.

Abercorn, dressed as King Charles, joined them. "Your mother is off dancing with Prince Albert, and I have just had the privilege of partnering our gracious queen. It appears my services are needed here, since one of my daughters is without a partner."

"D'Arcy went to get me a drink, but has obviously been waylaid." Harry raised her arms and her father led her onto the floor without a flicker of disapproval at her costume.

Halfway through the dance, Harry spotted D'Arcy, who was having an animated conversation with none other than Prime Minister Aberdeen.

"I can't believe it! D'Arcy is hobnobbing with your detested stepfather."

"Did you happen to tell him that it is the prime minister who recommends lord lieutenants to the queen?"

Harry looked up at her father as comprehension dawned. "I'll be damned."

"Don't be offended. It shows expedience and ambition — traits that will serve him well, both in business and in government."

"But he's fraternizing with the enemy. Shouldn't loyalty count for something?"

"Indeed it should . . . in a husband. But

you are not married yet, Harry."

As the dance ended, Abercorn waltzed Harriet over to the spot where Anson was standing. "Thomas, I shall leave my daughter in your capable hands." He turned to Beatrix and gallantly offered to partner her in the next dance.

"You need not dance with me, Thomas. If I'm perceived as a male, it may spark gossip, and if I'm recognized as a female exposing my limbs, it will shock sensibilities."

He raised his arms in invitation. "What are friends for?"

Harry smiled her acceptance and they moved onto the floor as the music began. The moment she went into his arms, she realized with alarm that she would have to put up her guard against his devastating animal attraction. Her physical response to him was potent. She took a deep breath and searched for a topic of conversation that would distract her thoughts from the overwhelming magnetism of the dark devil.

"You are the member of Parliament for Lichfield, Staffordshire. What is it like there?"

"It's quite lovely. Staffordshire is the heart of England. It's agricultural rather than industrial. Stafford, the town closest to Shugborough, is the main coaching stop between London and Chester. It's also the main route to the northwest and Ireland, so it is relatively prosperous. The railways skirted us in favor of Birmingham in the Midlands, so that is the town that has exploded in size and manufacturing. Lichfield, a few miles south of Shugborough, has a medieval cathedral reputed to be the loveliest in England."

Harry searched her memory. "I believe it has three spires."

"It has indeed."

"I remember from my visits to Shugborough." *I can smell jasmine and honeysuckle.* She closed her eyes and almost drifted into a romantic fantasy. A voice inside her head warned, *Stop it, Harry!* She opened her eyes quickly. *D'Arcy Lambton is far better husband material than Anson. Thomas is dominant and demanding, and if I became his wife, I would be so enamored, I would allow him to rule the roost. D'Arcy has such a pleasant, easygoing nature, he will allow me to have my own way and make my own decisions.*

Thomas continued with his description. "Lichfield is known for falconry, sheepdogs, heavy horses, and ferret racing."

A picture came full-blown in her imagination. "It sounds like —" She hesitated.

"Absolute perfection," Thomas murmured as the dance ended.

"There you are, Harry!" D'Arcy arrived with a glass of wine in hand. "I've been searching for you everywhere."

She smiled and took the wine. "I've been right here, all the time."

"I haven't had the pleasure of dancing with you yet." D'Arcy seemed torn.

"Would you feel better if I removed my mask and let my hair down?"

"I'd feel infinitely better, my love."

"Hold my wine." Harry unfastened her mask, removed the thong from her hair, and shook her tresses until they cascaded about her shoulders. Then she took back her glass and drained it. She turned to Thomas and placed the empty glass in his hand. "What are friends for?" she murmured outrageously, and was rewarded by the amusement she saw in his dark eyes.

As they danced the next three dances, D'Arcy was clearly enjoying himself. Holding her in his arms, he whispered intimate compliments, and when he held her at arm's length, he gazed enraptured at her legs. Then he would draw her close, and brush his hard thighs against hers.

The master of ceremonies announced that once more the guests must parade in a circle to show off their magnificent costumes, so that prizes could be awarded. After that, the supper rooms would be opened.

"Oh, Lord, the last thing I want to do is parade again. I've been gawked at enough for one night," Harry declared.

D'Arcy waggled his eyebrows. "Your wish is my command, lassie." He took her hand and led her from the ballroom. They zig-zagged through a throng of people, who all seemed to be going in the opposite direction. They finally found a chamber that was less crowded, and made their way out onto its secluded balcony.

D'Arcy enfolded her in his arms and captured her lips in a possessive kiss.

Harry began to giggle.

"What the devil is so amusing?"

"Forgive me, D'Arcy. It's your powdered wig. I feel preposterous being kissed by a man who resembles a fop."

"That is soon remedied." He swept the wig from his head and tossed it aside.

"That's better. The moonlight turns your hair to pale gold," Harry murmured. Unable to resist, she reached up and ran her fingers through his blond curls. This time, when his mouth sought hers, she opened her lips in invitation.

D'Arcy's hands reached beneath her kilt

and he caressed her bum with the palms of his hands. He pressed her forward into his erection and moaned deep in his throat.

"Harry, there's such a mob here, we could slip away to Carlton House Terrace and never be missed."

"D'Arcy, I can't. If I leave here and come to your house, you know very well what will happen."

"I can't wait any longer, Harry." He caressed the inside of her mouth with his tongue. "And why the devil should we wait? The Season will be over when Parliament recesses in August. In less than three weeks, we'll announce our betrothal." He took her hand and pressed it to his throbbing sex. "Don't be a cocktease, Harry. You can feel the state that I'm in."

Though she was impulsive and wildly curious about sex, she had more good sense than to give in to a randy male's sexual demands.

"Harry, if you love me, you'll come with me now."

"D'Arcy Lambton, what you are feeling isn't love — it is *lust*." She pulled away. "I want to wait. I can't — *I won't* — come with you tonight."

D'Arcy heaved a sigh of pure frustration. "You drive me mad, Harry!" He reached inside his brocade coat and took out a key. He slipped it into her pocket. "I'm trusting you with the key to my heart, as well as my house, Harry. I know you're daring enough to overcome your ridiculous Victorian scruples and come to me."

Harry slipped her arms about his neck and leaned into him until their mouths were almost touching. "It makes me feel very wicked to have your key tucked beneath my heart. Perhaps I am falling in love with you, D'Arcy. The temptation to turn up in your bed one of these nights is almost irresistible." She laughed. *"Almost!"*

Young James Hamilton was having the time of his life. *Dressing as a cavalier was the best decision I ever made.* Females pursued him relentlessly and some even lined up to dance with him. He didn't need to steal kisses; the young ladies offered their lips freely. At first, he tried to discern their identities beneath their disguises, but soon gave up.

James eagerly searched for Emily Curzon-Howe, but found it rather difficult because of all the different costumes. He was soon receiving so much attention that he stopped looking for Lady Emily.

When the master of ceremonies announced the second parade, James stood watching the circle of costumed masqueraders, and applauded when the prizes were handed out. His glance swept over each lady as he tried to decide which one he would partner next.

A young female in a white-feathered mask walked a direct path to him. "Jamie!"

"I've been looking everywhere for you." Pleased to finally encounter Lady Emily, he swept his eyes over her elaborate costume. "Your gown is lovely." He touched one of the glittering crystals that encrusted her shapely bodice. "I think you should have won a prize."

She took his hand, and he willingly followed her, hoping for his own prize. They went through French doors at the side of the ballroom that led out to a stone balustrade. The minute they were alone, she reached up to remove his eye mask. Then she opened her bodice to reveal her bare breasts.

"What do you think of these, Jamie?"

James was bemused. Clearly, the voice did not belong to Lady Emily. He raised his hand to remove her mask, and suddenly he was filled with horror. "Princess Vicky!"

The French doors swung open. Her Gracious Majesty the Queen of England, who had watched her daughter disappear from the ballroom, stared in outrage at the shocking scene before her. "Victoria! Seek your chamber immediately."

Young James Hamilton frantically searched the ballroom until he found his sister. "Harry, I'm in the most god-awful trouble!"

Early the next morning, Harry and her brother stood before their father in the library. "James is in the most god-awful trouble. You must help him, Father."

When his son told him what had happened, Abercorn was incredulous. "Are you telling me that the Princess Royal bared her breasts to you?"

"She did. And it's not the first time she's indulged in lewd behavior toward me."

"Meaning?"

James glanced at his sister. "Last time we were at Windsor, she put her hand on my groin, and . . . rubbed herself against my thigh."

"Why on earth did you go out on the balustrade with her?"

"I thought it was Emily Curzon-Howe."

"I see," Abercorn said quietly. "Well, since Queen Victoria caught you in such a compromising situation, you have no alternative but an abject apology. You will accompany me to Buckingham Palace this morning, and I'll try to get an audience for you with Prince Albert."

"But it was the queen who saw us." James was racked with misery.

"My dear boy, you cannot discuss anything of a salacious nature with Her Majesty. It is simply not done. The queen's outward demeanor is puritanical to a marked degree."

"Do you think she will have told Prince Albert?"

"I am certain of it. Victoria shares every thought with him and seeks his opinion on the most insignificant matters. I assure you, she will not consider Princess Vicky's welfare *insignificant*."

Young James squared his shoulders. "I warrant I have no choice."

Abercorn added a warning. "Your apology had better be sincere. You've been accepted at Oxford, but a word from the royal family could change that in an instant."

At Buckingham Palace, Abercorn bade his son take a seat and wait until he was summoned.

Then the duke entered Prince Albert's office, a chamber familiar to him. He waited until the prince had given his two secretaries instructions for the morning, and spoke only when they were alone.

"Your Highness, I have brought my son to apologize for the incident that happened last night at the Bal Costume. If you would honor him with a moment of your time, I would be indebted to you."

"Ah yes, the *unfortunate incident.* Show him in, Abercorn."

With trepidation, James followed his father into the prince's office and waited until Albert spoke first.

"Well, James?"

"Your Highness, I humbly beg your pardon for taking the Princess Royal out onto the balustrade last night. I am fully responsible for my disrespectful behavior and freely admit the blame is entirely mine. I give you my word of honor it will never happen again, sire."

Prince Albert gave him a rueful glance. "I accept your apology, Lord Hamilton."

Both Abercorn and his son waited for the prince to say more, but after a moment, they realized the audience was over.

"Thank you, Your Highness." Young James bowed his head and departed.

Prince Albert signaled Abercorn to remain. The queen's consort had few friends in the British aristocracy, and even fewer intimate confidants. He considered Hamilton one of them. "Come and sit down, James. Your son was most gallant to take the blame onto himself for the unfortunate incident last night."

"I expected no less, Your Highness."

"As you can imagine, Victoria and I discussed the matter for hours after the ball. We decided that we could no longer ignore Vicky's lack of restraint. Much to the queen's embarrassment, our oldest daughter is . . . *physically* . . . precocious. We have decided the best course is to arrange her engagement to young Prince Frederick of Prussia. Today I am issuing an invitation for him to join us at Balmoral."

"Forgive me, but an engagement at fourteen years old might raise eyebrows."

"We are aware of that, James. It will be a private engagement. We won't announce it to the public for at least two years."

"I am indeed sorry that my son caused you so much worry and concern."

Albert waved his hand. "We've known about Vicky's precocious behavior for some time. This has merely precipitated our future plans for the Princess Royal."

Abercorn bowed his head. "You are extremely understanding and generous, sire."

On the ride home, James thanked his

father for his help. "I appreciate all you do for me, Father. Thank heaven the matter is over and done."

"Not quite, James. You mentioned Emily Curzon-Howe. Reading between the lines, I take it you have an intimate relationship. If Earl Howe learns of it, the repercussions could be detrimental to your future — you'd be forced to offer for the young debutante."

James flushed.

"I think it advisable to find yourself an opera dancer."

Chapter Ten

"Whatever is amiss?" Harry stepped over the threshold of Barbara Leigh Smith's house on Langham Place and knew by the look on the face of the woman who opened the door that something was wrong.

"Go through to the sitting room," the woman said.

Harry could hear outraged voices, punctuated by the sound of someone sobbing, as she joined the eight suffragists gathered in the chamber.

Barbara said, "There's been another pit disaster . . . an explosion at Murton Colliery. Emaline's brother-in-law is one of the miners reported missing. She's going to Durham this afternoon to be with her sister. Word is that fourteen are dead and more missing."

"Durham?" Harry's hand went to her throat. "Murton Colliery is in Durham?"

Barbara nodded. "God rot the pit owners!

Have you any idea how many disasters occur every year? Yet still there are no safety measures taken to improve the deadly and dangerous working conditions of the coal miners."

"Bloody greedy owners!" Sarah Taylor shouted. "When the miners in these Durham pit villages try to band together to form unions, the owners crush them with savage beatings and even murders!"

"The men should go on strike and refuse to do such dangerous work," Harry said.

"How would they feed their children?" Barbara asked. "The only jobs available in the County of Durham are down the pit."

"It's tragic how many men are trapped every year in cave-ins, but it's heartbreaking to know some of them are just little lads."

"No, Sarah," Harry explained, "Parliament passed a law forbidding women or children to work in the mines. My uncle Lord John Russell worked tirelessly to get this law passed."

"You are naive, my dear. The mine owners ignore the laws. They still employ children as 'trappers.' They open and close trapdoors inside the mine tunnels to allow carts to pass through and to provide ventilation." Sarah pressed her lips together.

"But that's outrageous! Something must

211

be done," Harry declared. "I shall see that the members of Parliament are informed immediately."

"Politicians turn a blind eye to the dangers down the pit. There's flooding, and cave-ins, as well as firedamp gases that build up and cause massive explosions."

"A pit disaster means catastrophe for the families involved. If a miner is killed, his wife and children become destitute and are sent to the workhouse," Barbara explained.

"We are taking up a collection for Emaline to take to Murton."

Harry opened her reticule, and handed Emaline two guineas. "Take this. It's not much, but I shall get more and return as quickly as I can."

Harriet hailed a hackney cab and told the driver to take her to Carlton House Terrace. When the carriage stopped, she jumped out and asked the driver to wait. She was about to knock on the front door when she remembered that D'Arcy had given her a key. She pulled the key from her reticule and let herself in.

The Earl of Durham's majordomo was taken aback when he saw Lady Harriet Hamilton dash through the entrance hall and begin to ascend the stairs.

"It's all right, Fenton. I have my own key.

I do hope D'Arcy is at home."

"His lordship is in the library, my lady." He did his best to hide his disapproval.

She was quite breathless when she flung open the door and rushed inside the book-lined room.

D'Arcy stood up from his desk and strode to meet her. "Harry, my love. You decided to come!" He picked her up and swung her around with glee.

"Put me down! I'm not here for dalliance. I'm here on important business, D'Arcy!"

"Darling Harry, nothing is more important than dalliance."

She grabbed a lock of golden hair and pulled it hard. "Put me down this instant."

When he saw the incensed look on her face, he set her feet to the carpet. "What the devil is wrong?"

"D'Arcy, something dreadful has happened. There has been a mine explosion at Murton Colliery in Durham."

"It's all right, Harry. The village of Murton is in East Durham, miles away from Lambton. There is no danger that the castle will have been damaged."

"I'm not concerned about your *castle*. I'm worried about the men trapped down the pit. It's a terrible disaster. I hear that there are at least fourteen dead! D'Arcy, you must go to Durham immediately and do something."

"Where did you hear this news?"

"I went to a women's meeting in Langham Place. Emaline Davis's brother-in-law is one of the miners missing in the explosion. She's rushing up there to be with her sister this afternoon," Harry gabbled breathlessly. "You must do something!"

"Do what, my love? If the miners are dead, I cannot bring them back to life."

"No, no, of course not. But as the Earl of Durham, you must go and give the families moral support. They will need help . . . money . . . doctors . . . rescue workers. The women at Langham Place are taking up a collection to give to Emaline."

"Slow down, Harry. You are in a mad panic. You will make yourself ill." He led her to a chair and gently pushed her into it. "It is pointless for me to go rushing up to Durham every time there is an accident in a mine. I employ overseers and land agents at great expense to investigate these disasters. I have full-time secretaries whose job it is to send me reports, so it won't be long before I learn all the details."

"The conditions these coal miners work in are appallingly dangerous. Can you imagine working down a pit, hewing coal with a pickax all day, while floods and cave-ins and gas explosions threaten every minute you are underground?" She jumped up from the chair, unable to sit still. "The colliery owners are greedy swines who won't pay for safety measures."

"Harry, the colliery owners are the ones who provide jobs and pay the coal miners' wages."

"But when a miner is killed, his wife and children become destitute and they are sent to the workhouse. When a man loses his life down the pit, the owners should pay his widow compensation. As the Earl of Durham, you must go and speak to these owners and make them do the right and decent thing. It is your moral obligation, D'Arcy."

"Harry, I assure you I live up to my Durham obligations."

"But the destitute families need money," she pleaded.

He knew he must placate her. "When I get the reports, I'll send money. It has to go through the proper channels, or there's every probability it will fall into the wrong hands."

She placed her hands on his chest in supplication. "Promise me, D'Arcy! Promise you will send money the minute you get the reports?"

"Of course I promise. I would do anything to make you happy, Harry."

My God, this isn't about me. It's about the poor wretches in Murton. "I have to go, D'Arcy. I gave my word that I would return to Langham Place."

"I wish you wouldn't associate with these women." He stopped, knowing he'd said the wrong thing to a woman as headstrong as Harry. "I don't mean that. It's just that I can't bear to see you upset about perceived injustices. I wish you would leave it to us men to right the wrongs. These suffragists have no authority or power to change things."

Harry refused to allow her emotions to plummet into hopelessness. *The suffragists will never accept defeat and neither will I.* "I must go, D'Arcy."

She hurried outside and was relieved to find that the cabdriver had waited for her. "Please take me to the Parliament buildings in Whitehall. I'll get your money from my father."

"Who's yer father?" he asked out of curiosity.

"James Hamilton, the Duke of Abercorn."

He touched his cap. "Hop in, luv. I'll have ye there in a trice."

Harry rushed into her father's office. "There's been a mining disaster in Durham. My friends at Langham Place are taking up a collection. I need some money, Father."

Abercorn searched his daughter's face and saw that she was in earnest. "And how is the money to get to Durham?"

"Emaline Davis is traveling there this afternoon. Her sister's husband is missing in an explosion at Murton Colliery. I promised them I'd return with money."

"I can write you a bank draft. . . . I don't carry much cash."

"No, it has to be real money, Father. Give me whatever you've got."

Abercorn opened a flat leather case and counted out five tissue-thin Bank of England ten-pound notes. "Fifty pounds is a lot of money for a lady to carry around."

She snatched up the notes, and stood on tiptoe to kiss his cheek. "Thank you, Father. You are a lifesaver!" She rushed to the door, then turned and came back. "Sorry, but I also need money for my cabdriver."

He reached into his pocket and gave her a couple of guineas. He knew it would be futile to reprimand her for traveling about London on her own. "Be careful, Harry."

This time she knew the hackney-cab driver would be waiting, because he had every expectation of being paid. She showed him the golden guineas. "These are yours if you will take me back to Langham Place and wait for me again."

He grinned from ear to ear. "Hop in, yer ladyship." At a couple of pennies per mile, two guineas was more than a week's wages.

Barbara Smith opened the door. "Has Emaline left for Durham yet?" Harry asked. "I've got money for her!"

"Come in, Harriet. She's almost ready to depart. How much did you bring?"

"Fifty pounds."

"Good heavens, that's a fortune!" She ushered Harry into the sitting room.

Harry took the five Bank of England ten-pound notes from her reticule.

"We'll have to sew this money inside your petticoat, Emaline. It's the only way to keep you and the pound notes safe."

Barbara plied her needle and thread and sewed a cloth pocket inside Emaline's underskirt. Then she kissed her friend. "Go with God, my dear."

"I have a hackney waiting. I'll take Emaline to the coaching station."

"Bless you, Harriet Hamilton. What would we have done without you today?"

In the dining room at Hampden House,

Harry sat next to her father in silence. The mine disaster was unfit dinner conversation, but she was extremely grateful that he was spending the night at home. She drew strength from his comforting presence. When the meal was over, Harry followed him to the library and shut the door.

"You were so generous, Father. I thank you from the bottom of my heart for not questioning me."

"My dear, all I had to do was look at your face to see you were desperate."

"I should have come straight to you. Instead, I went to D'Arcy Lambton. As the Earl of Durham, I thought he would go rushing up there and make everything right."

"Harriet, you shouldn't have done that. Unwittingly, you thrust D'Arcy into a thorny predicament — damned if he did, and damned if he didn't."

"What do you mean?"

"First, let me explain a few things about the County of Durham. You are aware that it provides England with coal. There are scores of mines, and as a result, there is a great deal of *subsidence.* That is when the earth's surface collapses downward from being undermined. Many of the mines were opened long ago when careful planning and preventative measures were unheard of. When D'Arcy's father was created Earl of Durham, he inherited the land, and wherever large coalfields were discovered, he leased it to various colliery owners who put down shafts and opened up the mines."

Harry pictured miles of lovely green fields and rows of houses sinking and collapsing into deep, black holes.

"D'Arcy inherited all this when he was a boy, but had no say in anything until he came of age a few years ago. He cannot afford to antagonize the colliery owners, whose mines provide Durham and England with so much wealth. When he proposes measures that will improve the miners' working conditions, he must be diplomatic. He has to walk a fine line, and cannot be seen to take the side of the miners against the owners."

"I don't really see why not," Harry said stubbornly.

"He cannot go barging in there and throw his weight around simply because he is the Earl of Durham. The colliery owners would complain to the Crown. Moreover, if he angered these owners, they could shut down the mines — hundreds of men would be thrown out of work and their families would starve. There would be riots, Harry. As Earl of Durham it is his responsibility to ensure that things run smoothly."

"I see. Perhaps that's why D'Arcy wants to be appointed lord lieutenant, so he can have a greater influence on the coal industry."

"Being the queen's representative would certainly add to his power."

"Thank you for explaining, Father. Things are always far more complicated than they seem." Harry managed to smile. "D'Arcy promised me faithfully that he would send money to help with the disaster once he got the reports."

"You are tenderhearted, Harriet. Championing the downtrodden is a heavy burden for one so young. If you let it consume you, it will destroy your happiness."

When Harry left the library, she felt extremely restless. She wandered into the empty ballroom and stopped to gaze out a window. The gas lamps on the street below cast small circles of illumination, but their light did not reach across the road into Hyde Park, where the tall trees shrouded it in darkness.

Her heart was heavy. She could not shake off the thought of all the children who would be crying themselves to sleep tonight. As she left the ballroom, her feet carried her in the direction of the nursery. The events of the day inexorably drew her to check on her little sister and brother.

"They are asleep, Lady Harriet," the children's nursemaid informed her.

"I'm glad they're asleep, Mary. Thank you for watching over them so vigilantly. I won't disturb them. I'll just stand at the door and look at them for a few moments."

The nursery was shadowed, but she could see that the children were sleeping. Five-year-old Ronald was clutching a stuffed rabbit, and four-year-old Maud's dark curls against the white pillowcase brought a lump to Harry's throat. She remembered a prayer for hopeless causes that Mary, the Irish Catholic nursemaid, had taught her when she was a little girl, and she began to silently recite it:

Oh Holy Saint Jude, Apostle and Martyr,
Great in Virtue, and Rich in Miracles,
Near kinsman of Jesus Christ,
The faithful intercessor of all who invoke
    your special patronage in times of
    need,
To you, I have recourse from the depths
    of my heart,
And humbly beg you, to whom God has
    given such great power,

To come to the aid of the people in
   Murton, Durham,
And in return I promise to make your
   name known.

As she gazed at the well-cared-for children who were surrounded by love, the lump in her throat eased, and the heaviness of her heart lifted. She knew she had so much to be thankful for, she should be rejoicing.

Harry returned to the library to select a book. She needed something to distract her thoughts from again sinking into dark despair. She chose a book on architecture by Robert Adam and sat down in one of the brass-mounted library chairs. She began to read about Harewood House and studied a sketch of the gardens that had been designed by Lancelot "Capability" Brown. She could not help comparing the stately home to another that always lingered in her memory.

Her thoughts were interrupted when someone walked past the library door. She raised her eyes from her book as her brother backtracked and came in to join her.

"Harry, I heard something outrageous tonight that I think you should know."

"Hello, James. From whom did you hear

this shocking news?"

"From John Montagu. He told me that his brother Will and D'Arcy Lambton have a high-stakes wager about you."

She closed the heavy book with a thud. "About me?"

He lowered his voice confidentially. "It seems that D'Arcy bet Will two hundred guineas that Lady Harriet Hamilton would accept his proposal of marriage. They registered the wager in White's betting book."

Harry was stunned. "Insufferable swines!"

"I knew you would be livid. Not about D'Arcy making you the Countess of Durham — we all expect that — but to put your name in the betting book is unconscionable."

She shook her head wearily. This was all she needed to hear to finish off a day that had drained her emotions to the last drop. "Thank you for telling me, James."

Harry sat alone in the library. The last thing she wanted to do was go up to the bedchamber she shared with Beatrix and Jane. Her brother's words echoed in her head, intensifying her anger until she became incensed. Putting her name in White's betting book was a trifling offense when measured against the greater sin that D'Arcy

Lambton and Will Montagu had committed. She was devastated that young nobles could be so immature and irresponsible as to wager two hundred guineas to amuse themselves. She rocked back and forth in anguish. *Only think what those poor wretches in Murton could do with that money.*

A thought of Thomas Anson came unbidden. *He is right to condemn gambling. It is truly the scourge of the upper classes. How many fortunes have been lost because of gaming addictions? Anson knows firsthand what it is like to have his family's happiness destroyed by it.*

It was long past midnight when she went upstairs, quietly undressed, and slipped into bed. She lay there hour after hour, tossing and turning as sleep eluded her. Just before dawn, she finally fell asleep and began to dream. She awoke with a start and tried to recall the details of the dream as it began to fade. All she remembered was D'Arcy's laughing countenance and money chests filled with gold coins.

The end of her Season was rapidly approaching and she wished she could hold back time. From what James had said, she wasn't the only one who was expecting D'Arcy to propose and make her his countess. *I thought I was ready to say yes, but after yesterday's events, I need more time before I commit myself.*

Rose tapped on the bedchamber door before she entered. Then she came in, opened the drapes, and turned out the lamp.

Beatrix and Jane awoke and sat up in bed.

"Good morning, ladies. Would you like breakfast trays, or will you eat downstairs?"

"Nothing for me, thank you, Rose." Harry threw back the covers.

"We'll have breakfast downstairs," Trixy told Rose.

"I've decided to go and visit Rachel for the weekend."

"Harry, you can't! It's Saturday. Have you forgotten that we are invited to a musical evening at the Edgcumbes' tonight? It will likely be one of the last parties of the Season and everyone will be there."

"Yes, I had forgotten. But I want to see Rachel and I need to talk to Uncle Johnny about something important before Parliament recesses. Please offer my regrets to Lady Caroline."

"Harry, I wish you'd come. You can go and see Rachel tomorrow."

"No, my mind is made up. You will have Henry Edgcumbe all to yourself."

"But what about D'Arcy?"

"He will simply have to manage without me for once," Harry said firmly.

CHAPTER ELEVEN

"Thank you for letting me sit up on the box with you, Riley. The exhilarating ride was just what I needed this morning." Harry climbed down, not caring that her wind-blown hair looked like a wild blackberry bush.

"Harry, how lovely to see you." Rachel picked up her niece's luggage. "Riley, go to the kitchen and have some ale before you drive back to London."

"Thank ye very much, m'lady. Shall I come back for ye on Monday, Lady Harry?"

"Oh, no. Why don't you stay until at least Tuesday?" Rachel suggested.

"Yes, come back for me on Tuesday. Mother may need the coach in the morning, so come after lunch, Riley."

The trio went into Campden Hill and Riley made his way through to the kitchen.

Rachel's eyes were alight with curiosity. "To what do I owe the pleasure of your company, may I ask?"

"My visit is more likely to depress you than give you pleasure, I'm sorry to say, but you are so easy to talk to."

"That's only because I'm a good listener."

"Yes, that's exactly what I need."

"I'll order us some tea. On second thought, sherry would be better. Come into the sitting room and I'll pour us a couple or three."

Harry sipped her wine and sighed with appreciation. "Where do I start? With a confession, I suppose. I came to escape attending a musical evening being given by the Earl and Countess of Mount Edgcumbe, because D'Arcy Lambton will be there."

"Why do you want to avoid D'Arcy?"

"Because he will ask me to marry him, and I haven't made up my mind yet."

"Are you certain he will propose?"

"Absolutely. I found out that he bet Will Montagu two hundred guineas that I will accept his proposal of marriage. The fools registered the wager in White's betting book."

"What the devil is the matter with men? That's like the story I'm writing . . . a lady forced to marry because of a gambling debt!"

"Well, unlike your story, I'm not being

forced. But I honestly don't know whether to accept D'Arcy's proposal or postpone giving him an answer. That's why I'm avoiding him, until I make a decision. That, and the fact that I would make a scene when I kick his bloody shins for making wagers about me."

"You did right to come and visit me. It will give your temper time to cool, so that you can come to a rational decision."

Harry ran her finger around the rim of her sherry glass. "If only it were as simple as getting over my temper. It's far more complicated than that."

Rachel lifted the decanter. "Drink up, and I'll pour you another. I'm all ears."

Harry took a deep breath and plunged into the tragic story of the mine explosion. She described the scene at Langham Place and then she recounted her visit to D'Arcy.

"Hearing about such disasters scalds the heart. But it sounds to me like the Earl of Durham is in sore need of a countess."

"Oh, absolutely, Rachel. As Countess of Durham, I would take on the cause of improving the lives of the miners and their families, as well as crusading for safety measures down the pits."

"Then why do you hesitate?"

"Because I'm not sure that's what D'Arcy

would want his countess to do. I fear we would be constantly at odds. He hates that I associate with the women at Langham Place. He says the suffragists will never have the authority or power to change things, and I should leave it to men to right the wrongs."

"That's laughable. My brother has dedicated his life to righting wrongs, but men like Lord John Russell are few and far between."

"That's another reason I came. I need to talk to Uncle Johnny tomorrow."

"Harry, you don't give yourself enough credit. D'Arcy is in love with you. If you became his wife, he would be putty in your hands. Remember what the tarot cards say: *It is the woman who leads, and the man who follows.* A clever wife, who knows how to be subtle, makes most of the decisions in a marriage. You need look no further than your mother, or my mother, for proof of that."

"Father loves my mother deeply. He would do anything for her." Harry sighed. "That's the kind of marriage I hope to have."

"Marriage does give a woman power, and as Countess of Durham, you would have even greater power. And only think of the wealth that marriage to D'Arcy would bring."

"D'Arcy makes it plain that he is in love with me, and I am very fond of him. I can't put it off much longer. Next time he proposes, I will have to give him his answer."

"Harry, you know that most marriages are not love matches. And from my observation, even if they are, one partner always loves more than the other," Rachel said shrewdly. "It is far more preferable to be the one who is loved."

"You are a wise woman, *Mademoiselle Rachelle.* Just make sure that Lord Butler worships the ground you walk on before you agree to marry him."

"You'll be able to observe that for yourself. I invited him to dinner tonight."

"Oh, Rachel, I will be intruding on your privacy."

"Not at all. If you hadn't arrived, I would have had to ask my brother John and his wife to act as chaperones. Even though I'm a bit long in the tooth, it would be scandalous of me to entertain a gentleman if I were alone."

"Society's rules are utterly preposterous. I am often tempted to do something scandalous, and I warrant you are too. The closest we ever came was showing our legs at the queen's masquerade ball. How excessively daring of us!"

"What about your tattoo? That was certainly throwing caution to the wind."

"I've worn long sleeves ever since because I don't have the courage to reveal it."

"But at least you had the audacity to act on an impulse. I tend to live vicariously through the characters I write about, who often invite scandal. On paper, I am fearless."

"Tonight, as soon as dinner is over, I shall withdraw to the library so that you may spend the evening alone with the dashing Irish captain." Harry drained her glass. *"Amour toujours!"*

"Harriet has a passionate interest in great houses and castles, and never tires of hearing about them," Rachel told James Butler.

"Your family deserves a great deal of credit for restoring Kilkenny Castle to its original medieval appearance. Ireland has far too many ruins," Harry declared.

"So many deserted Ireland during the years of the famine, and numerous tenanted estates fell into rack and ruin. Kilkenny has over twenty thousand acres, but we managed to keep our tenants," he said proudly.

"What did you do differently from the

other Irish landowners?" Harry asked.

"We didn't collect rents from our tenants for a period of five years."

"Oh, James, that is so commendable." Rachel reached out to touch his hand.

They have eyes only for each other. Harry pushed back her chair. "I promised Father I'd search for some books he thinks might be in Campden Hill's library. I'm sure you'll both excuse me."

Lord Butler jumped up immediately. "Good night, Lady Harriet." His warm brown eyes told her how much he appreciated her thoughtful gesture of withdrawing. Now he and Rachel could enjoy a few hours of privacy.

Harry made her way to the library and lit the lamps. *There are so many fascinating books here, I could be occupied for weeks.* Her maternal grandfather, John Russell, the Duke of Bedford, had been a bibliophile and his favorite collection of botany books, with their colorful illustrations of magical herbs and plants, took up an entire library shelf — some were more than two hundred years old.

Out of curiosity, she searched for the books that her parents had bought at the Shugborough auction more than a decade ago. They had bought the entire library from William Anson, Earl of Lichfield, and quite a few of the books had found a home in Campden Hill's library.

Harry spied a book by Rousseau and took it from the shelf. It was a novel entitled *Julie, or the New Heloise,* written in 1761. A folded note fell from the book, which she opened and read.

This explains why Rousseau's books were in Shugborough's library. The author sent his hero on a fictitious voyage around the world with Admiral Anson, and when Rousseau came to England, he visited Shugborough Hall.

Harry speculated that Admiral George Anson had written the note a century ago. It said that Rousseau was delighted that Shugborough Hall Park was a place where wild animals were free from shooting and hunting. The knowledge warmed her heart.

A few lines of a Rousseau poem had been translated into English:

Oft let me wander, when the morning ray
First gilds thy groves and streams, and
    glittering towers,
And meditate my uncouth Doric lay . . .

Harry's memory flew back to Shugborough. She recalled the eight soaring Doric columns that graced the front of the enchanting house. Her fingers stroked the little green snake coiled about her wrist, as she smelled the jasmine and honeysuckle in the walled garden. Again she heard the music in the Tower of Winds and saw the magnificent sculpted centaurs. Harry shuddered. *I mustn't think of Thomas.*

She put the book back on the shelf and knew she must find something to read that would occupy her thoughts. She needed a novel that would divert her from the sadness of the Durham disaster, which still haunted her.

Harry glanced at the desk and noticed a book lying open. She picked it up and read the title: *The History of Tom Jones, a Foundling,* by Henry Fielding.

I can't believe my luck. I've heard about this ribald novel, but never dreamed I would ever get my hands on a copy. She turned to the first chapter and realized with glee that Rachel had underlined all the naughty bits. She sank down in a comfortable chair and began to read avidly. *"In a very few minutes they were both naked. . . ."*

At midnight, Rachel made her way to the library and found Harry engrossed in a book. "James just left. Thank you for giving us privacy. It was so generous of you."

Harry saw that Rachel's face was delightfully flushed, and guessed that her aunt was in love. "I have been thoroughly entertained reading about the wicked adventures of Tom Jones. Just reading the passages you underlined has enlightened me about the relationships between males and females. I intend to read it from cover to cover. I expect it will give me an invaluable education about human nature."

"The first time I read it, I was shocked to the core. But it is so titillating, I soon began to enjoy his adventures vicariously."

"I think it's rather sad that we can only enjoy them vicariously. Aren't you tempted to indulge in some of these naughty escapades with your virile captain?"

"Tempted beyond belief."

"Then why didn't you, Rachel? Tonight you had every opportunity."

"I held back because I hope that Lord Butler will ask me to marry him. However, if he has no intention of making me his wife, I would gladly become his mistress."

"Bravo! Henry Fielding would be proud of you."

Rachel shook her head. "Whatever would he have thought of Victorians?"

"He would have laughed till he peed himself. Fielding would have pointed out that virtue is its own punishment!"

"I was under the impression that when a bill is passed in Parliament, it becomes the law of the land. Why aren't laws obeyed?" Harry was sitting on the verandah of Holland House with her uncle.

"People do not change when we tell them they should; they change when their circumstances tell them they *must*. To which bill are you referring?" Lord John Russell asked his niece.

"The Mine Workers Bill that made it illegal for women and children to work down the pit. I've heard you mention how long it took to get it passed."

"You would think that women and children working in coal mines would be an abomination in any civilized society. But do you know what finally got enough votes to pass the bill and make the practice illegal?"

Harry shook her head.

"Puritanical outrage — not outrage over the heavy drudgery, or the danger, or the brutalizing environment for children, but outrage that some of the miners worked naked.

"Public decency was concerned that the

result of the sexes working together underground would increase the rate of illegitimacy."

"Society has peculiar ideas about what is moral and what is immoral, I'm afraid. When classical Roman sculptures must be draped for fear that they offend sensibilities, it shows how shallow our values have become."

"The government makes the laws, but they are often impossible to fully enforce. The colliery owners are greedy for profits. Inspectors are few and far between, and who is to know if they take bribes? The owners swear they obey the law and that no male younger than twelve is employed, but they continually pass ten-year-olds off as being older."

"How naive of me to think you could stride onto the floor of Parliament and demand that the law be enforced. I am only just learning about the County of Durham and how important coal is to England. A few days ago, there was a mine disaster. I learned about it from the women at Langham Place. I was horrified when they told me of all the dangers the miners face down the pit. I immediately confronted D'Arcy Lambton, fully expecting he would rush up there and do something for the workers."

"The Earl of Durham is caught between the devil and the deep."

"Yes, Father explained his position to me. D'Arcy hopes to be appointed lord lieutenant of Durham, which would give him greater authority. *If* he were so inclined to use it," Harry added uncertainly.

"Lambton is one of the wealthiest nobles in England. As lord lieutenant, he would be in a position to promote better safety standards in the mines, and raise the standard of living for the workers of Durham County."

"D'Arcy wants me to marry him."

He searched her face. "Will you accept his proposal, Harry?"

"I am persuaded that I should." She gave him a tremulous smile. "Just think of all the good I shall be able to do as the Countess of Durham, and I'll have even more influence as wife of the lord lieutenant. It is such a worthy cause — how can I even consider saying no to D'Arcy?"

"You are not asking my advice, so I hesitate to give it. But if you are in love, you must let nothing stop you, Harry."

"I am packing tonight so that we can go riding in the morning. Riley won't be here until after lunch." Harry pointed to the

book beside her bed. "May I borrow *Tom Jones*? I promise to take good care of him."

"Of course you may borrow the book. It will make you laugh out loud."

"I have so enjoyed my visit, Rachel. It has given me a much-needed respite from the social pressures of the Season. You have provided me with the peace and quiet I needed to come to a definite decision about marrying D'Arcy."

"Will you accept his proposal?"

Harry smiled. "Yes. You see before you the future Countess of Durham."

Rachel embraced her. "Darling, I wish you every happiness."

Harry set out her riding habit for morning and finished her packing. She undressed, got into bed, and reached for *The History of Tom Jones*.

Just before dawn, Harry began to dream.

She was standing on a pedestal being fitted for her wedding dress. Over a tight steel corset and lace-trimmed white muslin drawers, she was wearing three starched petticoats reinforced with whalebone. When her sisters helped her don the cream satin wedding gown, it had so many flounces and ruffles that it measured ten yards around.

"I would like something simpler."

"That's out of the question, Harry," her

mother declared. "You must have a magnificent wedding gown that befits the Countess of Durham. Your bridegroom is one of the wealthiest nobles in the realm. He expects us to spare no expense in providing you with an elaborate trousseau that will make you the envy of every lady in England."

The large chamber overflowed with dozens of ball gowns, and scores of day dresses. As Harry counted more than thirty pairs of shoes, a wave of guilt swept over her. "Such extravagance is immoral," she protested.

"Nonsense! You will be living in a castle. As Countess of Durham, you will be expected to entertain the nobility — perhaps even royalty. Your first event will be to act as hostess for the annual Lambton pheasant shoot. You and D'Arcy will preside over the banquet in the high-ceilinged great hall. This golden velvet gown, trimmed with sable fur, will be perfect for the occasion."

Harry recoiled. "I want Lambton Castle to be a place where wild creatures are free from hunting and shooting."

"When you become a wife, you must learn to be amenable to your husband's wishes. If you please him, he will shower you with jewels." Her mother opened a black velvet box that had arrived from her bridegroom an hour ago. "These diamonds are only the first of

many priceless baubles he will gift you with."

Harry threw her mother and sisters a pleading glance. "Would you mind leaving me alone for a few minutes? This is all so overwhelming."

The minute she was alone, the window flew open, and there stood Tom Jones. The wickedly seductive devil beckoned to her. He had an animal attraction that she couldn't resist, and without hesitation she gave in to the temptation. She tore off the wedding gown and petticoats, and climbed through the window in her muslin drawers.

When the rakish devil lifted her before him on his black horse, she cried, "Thomas, let's ride hell for leather!"

"Have you ever ridden *hell for leather?*" Harry asked Rachel as they led their mounts from Campden Hill's stables. The July morning had brought heavy dew that turned the cobwebs to brilliant diamonds. *I think I dreamed about diamonds.*

"No, I don't believe I have," Rachel replied, "but there is nothing to stop us."

"It is exhilarating beyond belief. Let's have a race!"

"I'm game. You set the course."

"Let's ride in a huge circle that encompasses Campden Hill and Holland House, and also the lake. The finish line can be the courtyard."

They both mounted and lined up their horses side by side. "Ready . . . set . . . go!" Harry cried, and they took off as if they were riding the wind. Each time she glanced across at Rachel, she saw that her young aunt was laughing, as her hair streamed behind her like a red banner. Harry knew that she could easily win the race, but she realized how much pleasure Rachel would feel if she reaped this small victory.

When they arrived back at the courtyard, they reined in and slowed the pace. Then they decided to ride around again, but this time at a canter so they could converse.

"The countryside is lovely around here. Riding in Ireland is one of the things I miss most. I suppose we are lucky that our London house overlooks Hyde Park, but for a good gallop, it cannot compare with Barons Court."

"Oh, I had the most marvelous dream about Ireland last night. Barons Court was so vivid. Mother was there and it was just like the last time we visited, except James Butler was with me. Georgina was quite taken with him."

"Of course she was. Grandmother adored handsome, gallant men, and they in turn worshipped at her altar. I've been trying to remember *my* dream. Fragments keep stealing back to me, but most of it has vanished into thin air. To be perfectly honest, I think I was dreaming about Tom Jones."

"You lucky devil! What were you doing? Were you the wench he was in bed with?"

"What were we doing?" Harry used Fielding's own words. "I could only describe it by the 'use of an expression too indelicate to be here inserted.' " They went off into peals of laughter.

After their ride, they stabled the horses, and walked through Rachel's herb garden outside Campden Hill's kitchen. "Look at how the mint is spreading. You must take some back to London with you."

While Harry picked the mint, Rachel gathered a large bunch of thyme and another of rosemary. The air was redolent with fragrance as they headed toward the kitchen door. "Oh, look. The lavender is in bloom. I shall steal some to slip into my luggage when I finish my packing."

"I have some muslin bags I made for just that purpose. I'll get you a couple."

By the time the pair had tied and wrapped the herbs, Harry realized the morning had slipped away. She grabbed the muslin bags of lavender. "I must be sure I packed everything — Riley could be here any moment."

"Take your time. I'll take him to the kitchen and feed him sandwiches and ale," Rachel promised.

"Thank you for offering, Riley, but I won't ride on the box this afternoon. I shall sit inside as befits a lady. I don't want to arrive in London looking like a wild hoyden."

Harry kissed Rachel good-bye. "Thank you for making my stay so enjoyable. My last few days have been delightfully calm and serene, and I'm sad to be leaving."

"Don't be sad, Harry. Think of the exciting time that is before you. I envy you."

As the carriage rolled along the road that led from Kensington to London, Harriet's serenity began to dissolve. She became somber as her head filled with thoughts of the disaster and the wretched existence of the coal miners and their families.

Her father's words echoed in her head: *Every shovelful of coal helps fill D'Arcy's coffers.* Then she remembered Rachel's words: *Only think of the wealth that marriage to D'Arcy will bring.*

Her spirits sank further with every mile that brought her closer to London, and it began to dawn on her that it was the thought of accepting D'Arcy's proposal of marriage that was stealing her happiness.

Harry recoiled. *Every penny of D'Arcy's wealth is earned on the backs of coal miners. It is blood money! I could never become the Countess of Durham. My conscience would never allow me to be happy for one single day, knowing the luxurious life I enjoyed came at such a horrendously high cost to the men, women, and children of Durham.*

She thought of D'Arcy and her stomach knotted. *How can I be so cruel to him?* She remembered Uncle Johnny's advice: *If you are in love, you must let nothing stop you.*

All at once, everything fell into place. "I'm not in love with D'Arcy Lambton!"

CHAPTER TWELVE

Harry glanced out the window and saw that they were in London. She opened her reticule and thrust in her hand, searching for the key D'Arcy had given her. When her fingers closed about it, she hammered on the carriage roof, just behind where Riley was perched. She felt the carriage slow and pull to the side of the street.

Riley jumped down and opened the carriage door. "What is it, Lady Harriet?"

"Before you take me home, I'd like you to stop at Carlton House Terrace."

Riley bit his lip. He knew very well she was going to D'Arcy Lambton's residence, but he was also under the impression that in the very near future she would be the Countess of Durham. "I'll have ye there in a trice, my lady."

As the carriage climbed Constitution Hill, Harry's mouth went dry with apprehension. "It's only fair that I tell D'Arcy right away.

It is thoughtless and cruel to keep him dangling," she said aloud. Her inner voice mocked her. *Tell the truth and shame the devil. You just want to get it over with, Harry Hamilton!*

Lady Harriet ascended the front steps, inserted her key, and unlocked the front door.

She anticipated Fenton's long, disapproving face. *I'll tell him I have to speak to D'Arcy about a personal matter and ask him to make sure we are not interrupted.*

As she crossed the entrance hall and reached the stairs, Fenton did not make an appearance. *I wonder if it's his day off? It seems strange that none of the servants are about.* Harry entered the drawing room and found it empty. She went down the hall to the library, but the book-lined room, with its large desk, was also empty.

Oh dear, D'Arcy must be out. My timing is dreadful. I feel like an intruder. As she withdrew from the library, she thought she could hear the murmur of a man's voice. She turned her head to listen, but when all that followed was silence, she thought she must have been mistaken.

The sound of a woman's laughter broke the quiet. It was so unexpected that Harry couldn't believe her ears. *D'Arcy is entertaining a female. Who the devil can it be, and where are they?*

The next time the laugh came, it trailed off into a giggle, and Harry followed the sound. Though she had never been in the wing that held the bedchambers, she knew where they were located from the tour he had given her on the night of his dinner party at Carlton House Terrace.

Harry paused outside a bedchamber and when she heard movement inside, accompanied by murmuring, she opened the door.

Her jaw dropped as she saw D'Arcy Lambton with a female in his arms. Both were stark naked. "Trixy!"

Harry's sister shrieked and burst into tears.

D'Arcy dropped Trixy onto the rumpled bed and grabbed his robe. "Harry, I can explain."

Harriet ignored him and focused on Beatrix. "Get dressed immediately." She turned and left the room. Her emotions were in turmoil, her thoughts were in disarray, and her pride lay in shards all about her.

D'Arcy hurried after her.

Harry's blazing anger forced her to quickly gather her thoughts.

When she reached the drawing room, she

held up her hand to silence him, and pierced him with a stare that pinned him to the spot. "You rapacious swine!" Harry was so furious she was panting. "How long has this been going on? My God, Trixy could be with child!" She took a deep, steadying breath. "Tonight, D'Arcy Lambton, you will present yourself to my father and ask him for the hand of his daughter Beatrix. You must insist that you do not wish to wait."

"Harry, please —"

Harry held up her hand to silence him. She raised her chin and issued her ultimatum. "Two weeks. If you are not married at the end of two weeks' time, I will personally see that you never, *ever* become the lord lieutenant of Durham."

They stared each other down, but it was not Harry who looked away first. She handed him his key. "I have no further use for this."

Beatrix, trembling, pale, and a little defiant, appeared at the drawing room archway.

Harriet said quietly, "Come. The carriage is outside."

The sisters descended the staircase and departed the house in silence. Once they were inside the carriage, Beatrix whispered, "I'm sorry I hurt you, Harry, but I'm madly in love with D'Arcy."

251

"You haven't hurt me, Trixy. I came to tell D'Arcy that I didn't want to marry him."

Harry saw a look of pity come into her sister's eyes, and she knew that Trixy didn't believe her. *She thinks I'm trying to save face.* Harry thought about what her family's reaction would be when D'Arcy Lambton made an offer for her sister. *Hellfire, they will all look at me with pity.* Her instincts told her that she must not repudiate D'Arcy. She knew that what had happened today must remain a secret. *I love Trixy. I don't want her to think that the only reason she got him was because I rejected him.*

The Duchess of Abercorn put her finger to her lips as she closed the bedroom door. Not until she undressed and got into bed beside her husband did she murmur, "I was rendered speechless tonight, which is a rare event for me."

"Lu, I have a confession to make. When young Lambton arrived after dinner and asked to speak with me privately, I dreaded him asking for Harriet's hand. When he asked my permission to marry Beatrix, a great weight was lifted off my chest. Harry is far too sensitive and tenderhearted to be wed to a happy-go-lucky, callous young devil like Lambton. On the other hand,

Trixy and D'Arcy seem an excellent match."

"Well, I'm extremely thankful that one of my daughters will become the Countess of Durham. But Harriet must be absolutely devastated."

James slid his arms about his wife and drew her against him. "I'm not so sure, darling. I don't believe for a moment that she lost her heart to him. As a matter of fact, I think she feels contempt that he doesn't do more for the working poor in his county."

"If you are right, then it is infinitely better that they don't marry. A wife should be able to revere her husband, and take great pride in him, not hold him in contempt."

James raised her chin with his fingers and looked into her eyes. "Do you revere me, Lady Lu?"

"At the risk of swelling your head, along with other prominent body parts, I must confess that I do." She licked her lips. "Will you reward me with a sugared mouse?"

"I will reward you with anything your heart desires."

She reached out to fondle his erection. "Damn you, Abercorn, you know I cannot resist such blatant temptation."

Harriet decided to ease the awkward situation by removing herself to the guest wing to sleep in the bedchamber she had shared with Rachel. Her emotions were in turmoil, and more than anything, she needed to be alone to think things through.

All her preconceived notions of D'Arcy Lambton being in love with her had been shattered into a million pieces. *The lecherous swine betrayed me!* The lump in her throat almost choked her. *Don't cry. Don't you dare cry, Harry Hamilton!*

Finding D'Arcy and Trixy in flagrante delicto had shocked her to the core. What she had witnessed today not only wiped away her trust in men; it had given her self-confidence a grievous blow. For the first time in her life, she felt unattractive, unloved, and unsure of herself. Lying alone in the darkness, Harry felt so vulnerable that her eyes flooded with tears.

Anger with herself was the only thing that saved her from sobbing her heart out. She dashed away her tears with impatient hands. *Stop feeling sorry for yourself. You've been saved from a loveless marriage.*

She threw back the covers, slipped out of bed, and crossed to the window. She stared into the darkness with unseeing eyes and vowed that no man would ever deceive or make a fool of her again. *In the future, I will never consider marrying any man unless he gives me absolute proof that he loves me, and I am sure that I love him in return.*

"I absolutely love my gown." Beatrix smiled at Madam Martine as she tirelessly pinned up the hem on the white satin wedding dress that measured ten full yards.

Harry sent up a fervent prayer of thanks that it was not she who would be wearing the nuptial monstrosity.

Their mother swept into the room. "That's a relief. St. George's Church is confirmed for the first Tuesday in August. The church has been reserved every day of the month, but since our wedding will be small, they can accommodate us in the afternoon."

"Isn't it amazing?" Trixy took off her veil and handed it to Jane. "Everything the tarot cards predicted has come true! It said I would get my wish in a three, and it will be just over three weeks from that night to my wedding day!"

"It's magical," Jane said with a heartfelt sigh. To spare Lady Harriet's sensibilities, it had been decided that her sister Jane would be Beatrix's maid of honor, and the seventeen-year-old was swept up in the romance of it all.

Harry thought of the tarot cards she had

drawn that night. *The* Fool *told me I had a choice in life, and that trial and error would bring wisdom.* A picture of the *Hanged Man* came into her mind. *It was right too. I was not tied — I could free myself at any time. It warned that to achieve my desired goals, I must change the direction of my life. There seems to be a profound truth connected with the tarot cards.*

"People are bound to gossip, so be prepared," the duchess warned her girls. "For one thing, the engagement will be scandalously short, and traditionally, it is the *eldest* daughter who is supposed to wed first."

"Mother, you are the one who has taught us that we *set* fashion; we don't *follow* it," Harry said dryly.

On the last day of July, Parliament recessed for the month of August. Thomas Anson gathered his papers together. He was looking forward to spending time in Staffordshire, touching base with his constituents. The gardens at Shugborough would be blazing with color and he couldn't wait to spend time at the estate that meant so much to him.

As Thomas was leaving the House, he saw William Montagu and stopped to bid him good-bye. "I suppose you'll be going to

Midlothian during the recess. Scotland should be lovely at this time of year."

"Yes, but I won't be able to leave until after D'Arcy's wedding. He has asked me to be his best man."

"Lambton is getting married?" Thomas felt his heart plummet to his feet.

"Surely he told you? Still, it's all been such a rush."

Red-hot fury almost blinded him. Thomas felt as if the walls were closing in on him, and suffocation was imminent. "I'm sorry, Will. I'm in a bit of a hurry. I'm off to Staffordshire tomorrow. Good-bye. I shall see you in September."

That son of a bitch beat me to the mark! Thomas cursed himself. *I knew damn well he'd ask her. But I thought she'd turn him down!* He strode along Whitehall, oblivious to the other pedestrians who crowded the busy thoroughfare. *Don't be an idiot, Anson. What young lady of fashion would turn down an offer to marry an earl of the realm? Especially an earl with an obscene fortune to lavish upon her.*

"Mother, will you be all right if I leave for Shugborough in the morning?"

"Of course. I will be perfectly fine. You mustn't worry about me, Thomas. Your

257

constituents will welcome you with open arms. And so they should, with the perquisites for Lichfield you manage to garner in Parliament."

"That's why they elected me. I'm just doing my job. I'll take the two paintings I procured recently and hang them back where they rightfully belong."

Barbara Anson laid down her fork and looked at her son. "Fowler was here again today. The narrow-eyed wretch turns up every week like clockwork. He visits more often than the doctor."

Thomas tried for a light tone. "Devious plotting with his attorney is one of the few things that brings Father pleasure. Try not to let it upset you." *I will make sure the depraved swine never hurts you again.* "While I'm away, you must let Norton attend to his needs. If you allow it, Father will run you ragged with his inconsiderate demands." *That's the other thing that provides him with perverse pleasure.*

The servant, who came into the dining room to clear the table, brought a message that the earl wished to see his son. Thomas had expected it. After a visit from Martin Fowler, he was always summoned.

Thomas had a heavy heart, and he climbed the stairs slowly, well aware that this encounter would do nothing to lighten his spirit. He entered the chamber, crossed to the bed, and looked unflinchingly into his father's pouched eyes.

"By any remote chance, are you in pursuit of the heiress we spoke of?" His words were labored and Thomas could hear wheezing inside his chest.

"Sorry to disappoint you, Father."

The old man smirked. "You are waiting for me to die." Speaking brought on a coughing spell, and Thomas poured him a glass of water. But when he proffered it, the bedridden man knocked it from his son's hand. "When that day arrives, you think your troubles will be over, but you are wrong, you arrogant young swine."

My mother's troubles will sure as hell be over.

"Fowler was here today. Let's see how the laws of primogeniture help you when my signed affidavit is read with my Last Will and Testament."

The maggots are already eating your brain.

"It swears that you are illegitimate."

Thomas recoiled. "You are insane! That is a deliberate lie. How can you bring such shame to Mother?"

"You, and you alone, can prevent the shame. As promised, if you take a wealthy wife before I die, Fowler has orders to burn the affidavit."

Thomas felt his gut knot. He clenched his fists to prevent his hands from choking the life from the monster. "If you declare me a bastard, who, pray, will be your *legitimate* heir?"

Lichfield sneered. "My firstborn child, your sister Anne Frederica. She's the only one I'm sure I fathered. Her husband, Lord Elcho, has plenty of wealth to lavish on Shugborough."

For the first time since he was a boy, the cold finger of fear touched his heart.

The thought of losing Shugborough was unendurable to him. Thomas closed his eyes and gathered his strength. *No power on earth will wrest Shugborough from my hands. I hereby vow to keep it in my possession, or die trying.*

"Thank you for inviting me to ride with you, Father." Harry was truly grateful for the opportunity to be alone for a private conversation.

"I anticipated that Hyde Park would be practically deserted on the first day of August." The bond between Abercorn and his firstborn child was special. "You did the right thing, Harry, deciding not to marry

260

D'Arcy Lambton."

"Yes, I know." She threw him a grateful smile. "It finally dawned on me that I didn't love him. Now, of course, I realize that he didn't love me either. That was rather hard to swallow. But in truth, I've had a miraculous escape from a loveless marriage."

"I sensed that you were not totally devastated over his asking Beatrix to become his wife, but I know that something is bothering you."

"Oh, Father, you are so perceptive. It is my conscience. It's playing merry hell with me. I feel like I have shirked my duty toward the hardworking people of Durham. My heart is heavy over their plight, and I could have done so much good if I had become the Countess of Durham."

"I recommended Lambton for the lord lieutenancy, and before Prince Albert and Victoria left for Balmoral, he told me that the queen had agreed."

Harry reined in and came to a halt. "Oh, Father, you did that for my sake!"

"I did, but thinking about it, I warrant Lambton's appointment can be a good thing. It could spur him to take on some responsibility. He has no father or grandfather to guide him, so as his father-in-law, I thought I might take on the role."

"That's a splendid idea. If you can badger him into bettering the lives of the poor people of Durham, my conscience won't prick me so relentlessly."

"Working for a royal prince has taught me to be a diplomat. Badgering gets you nowhere. On the other hand, a *charm offensive* usually brings about the desired results."

Abercorn winked at his daughter. "It is a good thing that D'Arcy doesn't know of his appointment yet. I shall take ruthless advantage of the fact."

"Just as a formality, Your Grace, I suppose I should read this marriage contract before I sign it." D'Arcy Lambton took the legal paper from Abercorn's desk and sat down in the brass-mounted armchair.

James Hamilton could not help contrasting D'Arcy's casual attitude with his own when he had negotiated the marriage contract with the Duke of Bedford before he wed his daughter Lady Louisa. Abercorn had used the services of his wily attorneys from both Ireland and Scotland. And before he signed the legal document, he had negotiated a dowry that was more than double what had been offered.

"I have no need of Lady Beatrix's dowry, Your Grace."

"Your generosity is commendable, my dear fellow. Since you don't need the money, may I suggest that you put it in trust for Beatrix? That's what I did when I married her mother."

"That's an excellent suggestion."

"Good. I'll just add that clause to the contract to clarify it."

D'Arcy was about to hand the document back when Abercorn shook his head. "Read the second page. It is of paramount importance."

D'Arcy turned to the second page and read: *If I predecease my wife, she will receive a lump sum of ten thousand pounds, and five thousand each year thereafter from my estate in Durham.*

"I don't like to contemplate my demise, but I understand that if anything befell me, my widow would need to be provided for."

"It is a relief to see that you have a good grasp of legal matters. If the contract is acceptable, I'll summon my secretary to witness both our signatures."

When the document was signed and sealed, Abercorn poured two glasses of Scotch whisky and handed one to his future son-in-law.

"Congratulations, my dear fellow. By the way, I have decided to recommend you for the appointment of lord lieutenant of Durham."

D'Arcy's face lit up. "Your Grace, how may I thank you?"

"I have every confidence that you will surpass your illustrious father in his many achievements."

"To be truthful, I barely remember my father. When I was seven, he became ambassador to Russia, and after that, he was appointed governor-general of Canada. I lived with my grandfather Lord Earl Grey."

"Your father was the member of Parliament representing Durham for sixteen years, long before he was sent overseas. He was nicknamed 'Radical Jack' because of his good work helping his constituents. The working-class people loved him. He did so much for Durham — that was the reason the Crown rewarded him with an earldom."

"Thank you for telling me, Your Grace. I had no idea."

"Your father was a man of the people, in spite of his great possessions. He helped my wife's brother Lord John to write and pass the Reform Bill. He was ever sympathetic to the Irish people, and a champion of the downtrodden. Everyone admired the first Earl of Durham, but I have confidence that the *second* Earl of Durham will achieve even greater admiration. It won't be easy to stand up to the greedy colliery owners who put profits before safety and the miners' welfare, but once you are appointed lord lieutenant, you will have the power and authority of the Crown behind you."

"You have given me much food for thought, Your Grace. I am most grateful that you recommended me to Prince Albert. If I am fortunate enough to be appointed lord lieutenant of Durham, I will strive to make you proud of me."

"Dearly beloved, we are gathered together here in the sight of God and this congregation to join together this man and this woman in holy matrimony." The reverend's voice echoed about the high-vaulted ceiling of St. George's Church.

The large stained-glass windows that rose above the altar mesmerized Harry. The August sunshine coming through the glass made the colors brilliant. Her glance traveled from the hand-clasped bride and groom to her mother and father, who were standing beside their daughter. *I hope Trixy has as long and happy a marriage as our parents.* Harry doubted that it would be, but here in the sight of God, she hoped her prayer would be answered.

When her glance passed over D'Arcy Lambton, she felt no pang of regret. For a moment she stared at her sister Jane. *She is gazing at Will Montagu with her heart in her eyes. She looks absolutely lovesick.*

Harry's eyes moved to Will Montagu, and she wondered why D'Arcy hadn't asked Thomas Anson to be his groomsman. *It's been three weeks since I've seen him.* Harry's thoughts flew back to her mother's birthday party. *Why the devil didn't I think of falling into the lake at Campden Hill?* Harry fantasized about being carried from the water in Anson's strong arms, and suddenly regret filled her heart.

Stop it, Harry. She glanced at Rachel, who was standing beside her. I must say something irreverent to banish my self-pity. She leaned close to Rachel and whispered, "Did you know that so many Mayfair debutantes have been married in this church, it's known as the London Temple of Hymen?"

Rachel had to cover her mouth to conceal her laughter.

When the newlyweds emerged from St. George's, the family followed them outside into Hanover Square, where they threw rice at the bride and groom. Almost immediately, it attracted strutting pigeons.

"Watch out for pigeon shyte!" Harry cried gaily.

Everyone laughed with the exception of Lady Montagu, who was clearly horrified.

D'Arcy helped Trixy into his phaeton for the ride to Hampden House, where the bridal supper would be held. The new Countess of Durham's wedding gown was so voluminous, there was room for no one else in the carriage.

Abercorn helped his wife and Jane into the family carriage. "Rachel, Harry, there's room for you two. Riley can come back for James and me."

"Rachel and I have decided to walk. It's such a lovely afternoon." The two young ladies linked arms and set off along Brook Street.

"Charlotte Montagu looked down her nose as if she smelled something putrid."

"It must have been pigeon shyte!" The two females roared with laughter.

Rachel sobered. "Was that difficult for you, Harry?"

"Not in the least. I feel like a condemned prisoner who has just been reprieved. And here's the best part. While Trixy is honeymooning at Lambton Castle, we are going to Ireland. Barons Court, here we come!"

"I'm so looking forward to it, Harry. Lord

Butler returned home only two days ago, and already I am pining for him."

"Well, if absence makes the captain's heart grow fonder, I predict an Irish wedding." Harry slanted her a wicked glance. "Or you could simply *jump over the brush!*"

The Hampden House ballroom was decorated with elegant vases filled with fragrant roses, lilies, spiky asters, and delicate meadowsweet. A long table had been placed at the center of the chamber for the adults, and a smaller round table had been set up for the younger Hamilton children and their nursemaids.

Separate buffet tables laden with food, desserts, and wine were set against the walls, and two liveried footmen were assigned to circulate, carrying silver trays holding glasses of champagne, the moment the wedding party arrived.

Harriet and Rachel were the last to arrive. The younger children, who hadn't been at the church, were dancing about the bride, eager to touch her voluminous wedding dress and floor-length lace veil.

While Harry conversed with Johnny and his wife, Fanny, she kept an eye on D'Arcy and Will Montagu. It wasn't long before they withdrew into the small antechamber that was being used as a cloakroom. She gave them a few minutes before she followed them.

"Ah, just the gentlemen I wanted to see." Harry looked from the groom to the best man and back again. "Allow me to welcome you to the family, D'Arcy. I warrant you will make an excellent brother, and I believe I will make a better sister than wife."

D'Arcy looked immensely relieved. Though it would take time to erase the awkwardness between them, Harry's friendly words helped to put them at ease. But if the young Earl of Durham thought he was going to get away scot-free, he was mistaken.

Harry glanced at Will Montagu. "D'Arcy lost the wager. Did he pay you yet?"

Montagu had the decency to flush. "Wager?"

"The one you both registered in White's betting book."

"I just gave him a bank draft," D'Arcy said stiffly.

Harry held out her hand. "May I see it, Will?"

Montagu, shamefaced, took the Bank of England draft from his pocket, and placed it on her open palm.

"Since what the pair of you did was *uncon-*

scionable, I shall relieve you of your shame by using this two hundred guineas to start a fund that will benefit the widows and orphans of Durham."

"Harry . . . I don't — ," D'Arcy began.

"Oh, I know. . . . You don't know how to thank me. I'm sure you wish you'd thought of it yourself. Never mind, D'Arcy; you'll be able to contribute on a regular basis." Harry tucked the bank draft into her décolletage. "Come, gentlemen, this calls for champagne."

CHAPTER THIRTEEN

"I much prefer comfort to speed," Lady Lu declared to her husband and son, who had suggested they take the train from London to Liverpool, where James Hamilton kept a small yacht to transport his family to Ireland.

"It would cut a day from our traveling time," James pointed out.

"Train travel is dirty, noisy, and uncomfortable. Sitting on wooden seats for hours on end would put my bum to sleep. On top of that, we would have to stop over in Birmingham. . . . *Birmingham,* for God's sake! A fate for more courageous souls than me."

Abercorn laughed and graciously conceded. "I shall go immediately and arrange for two Berlin coaches with post-horses we can exchange in Oxford and Stafford. Riley can drive one, and the coaching company will provide a professional driver for the second."

"I'll come with you, Father," young James offered. "I want to make sure the driver can spit through his front teeth, so he can teach me the skill."

"See? We will all be happier if we take the road. We'll spend the first night in Oxford, your old prowling grounds. Coach travel allows us to stop anytime to stretch our legs, dine at charming village inns, or do some sightseeing if the fancy takes us. Early August is the ideal time to enjoy England's lovely countryside."

Harry arose from the breakfast table. "I'll go and finish my packing." She hoped she sounded casual, though inside she was bubbling with excitement. *If Father changes the post-horses in Stafford, that's where we will stay overnight. I shall be able to visit Shugborough Hall and wander about the grounds to my heart's content.*

Upstairs, Harry found Jane doing her own packing. Her sister kept stealing glances at her and a strange silence stretched between them. "Is something bothering you, Jane?"

"I might as well confess, Harry. It's my fault that D'Arcy proposed to Trixy instead of you. She confided to me that she was in love with D'Arcy. So at Mother's birthday celebration I sang Trixy's praises to him,

272

and told him she had lost her heart to him. I revealed that Trixy was over the moon when you were being courted by Thomas Anson, because she thought that D'Arcy would pay court to her."

Harry hid her amusement. "The whole thing was a conspiracy against me. If you hadn't opened D'Arcy's eyes to Trixy's obsession with him, I would have been his bride."

"Can you ever forgive me, Harry?" Jane implored.

"Time heals all wounds," Harry said with a straight face. "Ask me again tomorrow." Unable to contain her amusement longer, she threw back her head and laughed.

"You're not heartbroken?"

"Jane, men are like hansom cabs. If you miss one, another will be along directly."

Jane looked puzzled. "Men remind you of hansom cabs?"

I'll never ride in a hansom cab again without remembering Thomas Anson's kisses.

"If females wore men's trousers when they were traveling, there would be much more room in carriages." Harry moved over to make room for her little sister Maud.

"It would cause a scandal. Queen Victoria would never approve," Rachel said.

"Mmm, I'm almost tempted," Lady Lu said irreverently. She lifted Maud onto her knee so she could look out the window.

"When we get to Barons Court, I shall purloin a pair of my brother's riding breeches," Harry said decisively. "The Irish are very accepting."

"Your father is Irish, but I doubt if he would accept it," her mother said.

"Where is Daddy?" Maud asked.

"He's riding in the other carriage this afternoon, so that your brothers will behave themselves. About now, he's likely cursing me for refusing to go by train."

Harry winked at Rachel. "He looked happy enough last night in Oxford when the two of you came back from your moonlight stroll."

The Duchess of Abercorn smiled her secret smile.

Harry glanced out the window at the lovely green meadows with their flower-filled hedgerows. "The countryside is so pretty, we must be in Staffordshire."

"Yes, thank heaven we have left the industrial Midlands behind. The manufacturing towns fill England's coffers, but they certainly detract from our country's beauty."

"Maud, would you like to come and sit on my knee? Let's see if we can spot any black-and-white sheepdogs in the fields," Harry suggested.

"I think we should have a day of leisure tomorrow, before proceeding on to Liverpool. Your father and the boys could go fishing in the River Trent, and I'd love to explore Lichfield. The shops are bound to have some lovely Staffordshire pottery, and the cathedral is reputed to be the most beautiful in all of England."

"That's a splendid idea," Harry agreed. "By the time we reach Stafford, there will only be time to have dinner at the posting inn and go to bed." *Tomorrow, I intend to take a look at Shugborough Hall. I fell in love with it a decade ago and I am curious to find out if I still feel the same way.*

Thomas Anson spent the day making the rounds of Shugborough's tenant farms. He had supped with the head steward, Ramsey, last night. The man had seemed anxious about the Earl of Lichfield's demise, and Thomas realized that keeping his position as steward was uppermost in his mind. Ramsey seemed like an honest, decent fellow, but Thomas had decided to question the tenant farmers about him. Today, he was relieved that he'd heard no complaints about the steward. If the farmers had been unhappy with the steward, Thomas would have sent him packing. *Tonight, I'll tell Ramsey that his job will be secure when I inherit Shugborough.*

After dinner, Thomas planned to go over the books. The spring sheep shearing had produced more wool than last year, and he hoped the profits would cover any repairs needed to the farmhouses and pay for the maintenance of Shugborough. The hall had eighty chimneys, and every year at least a few needed new bricks and mortar.

Tomorrow he intended to visit with some of his constituents and tell them that he had procured funding from Parliament to build another new school in the county, and also erect some additional wool-storage sheds along the Staffordshire canal.

As he rode toward the hall in the late afternoon, his thoughts returned to the dilemma his father had created. The old swine had demanded that he wed an heiress, but the only woman Thomas desired was Lady Harriet Hamilton. Now that she was beyond his reach, he would have to look elsewhere, no matter how unpalatable. He was well aware that many wealthy families were eager to exchange a large dowry for a title, but such a solution made his gorge rise.

As Shugborough came into view, he set aside his worries. He was determined to take pleasure in his beloved hall, while he had the chance. All too soon he would be back in London, trying to solve his problems. He thought of Fowler and cursed. *The first thing I shall do when I return to London is hire a personal attorney of my own.*

Thomas noticed a lady's saddle horse tied to a tree, cropping the grass on the lawn.

Then he saw a female standing before the house, looking up at it. As he rode closer, he thought his eyes were playing tricks on him. He dismounted and strode toward her.

"Harry! What the devil are you doing here?"

"Thomas!" Her gasp told him that she had not expected to see him. "I . . . We . . . are on our way to Ireland."

He could not control his emotions. Anger flared in him. He closed the distance between them and towered above her. "Why the hellfire did you marry D'Arcy Lambton? You know damn well you don't love him!"

He saw her pale green eyes widen. "I didn't marry D'Arcy. My sister Beatrix is his blushing bride."

For a moment he thought she was taunting him with a cruel jest. Then slowly the miraculous news that she was not married penetrated his brain. *She's not going to Ireland on her honeymoon; she's going with her family!*

His spirits soared. *This lovely creature before me is the answer to all my problems. The gods are giving me a second chance. All I have to do is woo her and win her.*

"We are staying at the Stafford inn, and I couldn't resist a visit to Shugborough when the opportunity presented itself. Early tomorrow we leave for Liverpool."

This is kismet. "Harry, it's a delightful co-incidence that we are here at the same time. Let me give you the grand tour." He reached out to take her hand, but rather than respond, she pulled away slightly. It was a protective gesture, as if she was fearful that he might hurt her. He was wildly curious about what had happened between her and D'Arcy. *If Lambton has caused her pain, I will take a horsewhip to the son of a bitch and thrash him within an inch of his life.* His instinct told him now was not the time to question her.

"May I visit the walled garden first, while it's bathed in sunlight?"

Her request sounds like a timid plea, as if she is apprehensive I won't grant her wish.

"That's a perfect place to start." *Where the devil is the audacious baggage that issued her imperious orders with the confidence of an empress?*

Thomas led the way around to the rear of Shugborough. As they crossed the velvet lawn, Harry stopped in her tracks. "It looks different without the lovely marble statues."

"Indeed it does."

"I remember Venus, and I particularly remember admiring Adonis. Though at the time I had no idea he was the *Grecian god of desire.*"

"Harry, you're blushing." *Judas, I never saw you blush before.*

Harriet's dark lashes swept down to her cheeks, and Thomas had an overwhelming urge to protect her. However, he knew that if he tried to put his arm about her, she would reject it. "I am determined to find out who owns the statues, and I have every intention of buying them back in the future."

"I hope you get them back, Thomas. This is where they rightfully belong."

When they arrived at the arched wooden door in the high wall, he turned the iron key and they stepped into the garden.

As he watched her, she suddenly became transformed. Her face suffused with joy and her self-consciousness vanished as if the sun had melted it.

"Oh, it's magic!" The brilliant sunlight shining through the cascading water of the fountain produced a dazzling rainbow. Harry ran forward and tried to capture the colorful mirage in her hands. She laughed with delight when the rainbow appeared on her arms.

She spun about to face Thomas. "I can smell jasmine and honeysuckle. But the garden is such a blaze of flowers, I can't see the honeysuckle."

"It's over there, climbing the wall. It usually blooms in the spring. It must be another fragrant flower you can smell. There are dozens of herbaceous plants that attract bees and butterflies."

"You are wrong. I know honeysuckle when I smell it." Harry ran to the wall, and to her amazement, the vines had no flowers because they had turned to berries. She ran back to Thomas. "When I was a child, this place enchanted me. All I have to do is picture this walled garden in my imagination and I can smell jasmine and honeysuckle."

"You can smell it now because it lingers in your memory."

Suddenly Harry felt mischievous. She pulled up her sleeve to display her tattoo, which had ignited his temper when he had discovered it. "The last time I was in this garden, a hawk swooped down and captured a little green snake. I screamed, and the raptor dropped it and flew off. The snake slithered away, and I was infused with happiness that I had saved its life." She waved her arm beneath his nose, much as she had done the day they had quarreled. "My little green snake is a memento of this lovely walled garden, one that I will carry with me forever."

"Then I offer you my sincere apology. I was wrong to object so furiously when it obviously brings you pleasure, Harry."

"I've kept it covered up all this time. But from now on, the world can go to the devil. I shall display it with pride."

"You are an incorrigible baggage, Harry Hamilton."

She laughed up at him. "Flattery, begod! Take me to the Tower of Winds."

The moment they entered the tower, with its diamond-shaped openings cut high into its walls, Harry stared in horror. "Where are the centaurs?"

"Sold, like every other Shugborough treasure."

"Oh, Thomas. That is desecration. You *must* get them back."

"I will. All it takes is money." He looked down at her ruefully. "If I had my way, I would have chosen to be born filthy rich, instead of devastatingly handsome."

Harry threw back her head and laughed. "You are always so staid and serious, and then out of nowhere you reveal that wicked sense of humor."

He threw her a speculative glance. "So, what made you decide against marrying Lambton?"

"Oh, it wasn't just D'Arcy. I've decided against marrying anyone. At least until I fall in love. I won't settle for anything less than a love match. My father loves my mother to distraction, and that's exactly what I want." She smiled with delight as she heard the music of the wind. "Rachel has waited until she is twenty-eight before finding a man who loves and adores her. And I'll wait that long too, if I have to."

Thomas felt his hopes floating out of his grasp on the summer breeze. *Harry may not be in love with me, but she feels passionate about Shugborough.* "Come, let me take you into the hall."

He led her to the front of the mansion, instinctively realizing that Harry would wish to make her entrance through the impressive grand portico. They went up the steps, and Harriet reached out her hand to reverently caress one of the massive Doric columns.

"The house is encased in slate. It has been sanded to look like stone."

"How unusual. I always sensed that Shugborough was unique."

He opened the heavy oak front door and they walked slowly through the vaulted reception hall. "Many of the rooms were designed by architect Thomas Wright. Both the dining room and the library boast his elaborate rococo plasterwork. But fifty years later, architect Sam Wyatt redesigned Shugborough in the elegant neoclassical style."

Harry's eyes shone with admiration. "I am familiar with Sam Wyatt's work. I have many books filled with drawings of houses that he designed."

"Some of which came from Shugborough's library," he teased.

"Yes. Now that you remind me, I believe they were yours before they were mine." She searched his face. "I'm sorry, Thomas. I know how you cherished Shugborough's treasures."

"It's less painful knowing they belong to someone who appreciates them. Here is the library. Though it has many empty book-shelves, it is a room where a few prized artifacts that were not sold at the auction are displayed."

Harry gazed at a huge glass cabinet. "Oh, it's the figurehead of a ship!" The carved wooden female had luscious breasts and long swirling hair. "She's magnificent."

"It's from the *Centurion*, Admiral George Anson's ship." He pointed to a weapon sheathed in an ornate scabbard. "That is the sword that the captain surrendered to my famous ancestor when he captured the Spanish treasure ship."

"How fascinating." She pointed to a gold coin that lay beside the sword. "Is that a Spanish doubloon?"

"Yes. It's the only one that's left. The largest amount of gold ever seized for the Crown of England came from the Spanish galleon Admiral Anson captured. Records say that it took thirty-two large wagons to transport all the treasure."

Harry heard a loud, plaintive *meow*. She looked down and saw a gray Persian cat rubbing itself against his ankles. Thomas bent down and scooped it up in his arms, and it immediately began to purr. "This is Kouli-Khan, thought to be bred from the admiral's cat that sailed around the world with him. There is a Cat's Monument dedicated to the first Kouli-Khan, on a small island beyond the Chinese pagoda."

"She's a beauty." She stroked the Persian cat's head and she purred even louder. "That's a charming story. Everything about Shugborough is warm and inviting."

Thomas led the way to an elegantly furnished drawing room. "I have managed to restore all the furnishings in this room that were sold at the auction a decade ago. I just hung those two paintings last night. They are landscapes by Claude. I had to twist the owner's arm a little, but he eventually succumbed to my persuasion."

Harry glanced at her companion. Though his words were spoken softly, his dark eyes and sharp cheekbones hinted that his methods of persuasion could be ruthless if he wanted something. In that moment she knew that if Thomas Anson set his mind to attain something, nothing would stop him. She had no doubt that he would restore Shugborough's treasures, no matter the cost.

She noticed a painting by the doorway that stood against the wall. "You forgot to hang this one."

"No, I just took it down. I don't want it staring at me. It's a portrait of my father."

Harry studied the portrait in disbelief. It showed a portly man who was fair, with a florid face. "Your father? You look nothing like him. . . . There is no resemblance whatsoever."

"I warrant that's the nicest thing you've ever said to me, Harry." He changed the subject. "This house has three stories. It would take a week to show you through every chamber. But since you like warm and inviting, why don't I take you to the kitchens?"

"Lead on, Macduff."

The kitchens were vast and spotlessly clean.

"This is my cook, Mrs. Stearn. This is a special friend, Lady Harriet Hamilton."

The cook bobbed Harry a curtsy. "Welcome to Shugborough Hall, my lady."

"You must be baking bread, Mrs. Stearn. It smells delicious."

"I've just taken it from the oven. It's on a cooling rack by the window."

Thomas saw the yearning look on Harry's face. "Are you hungry? That's a silly question — you are always hungry. Sit down, and we will break bread together." First he poured two mugs of ale from a stone jug. "We brew our own. You'll love it."

Next, Thomas cut two thick slices from a

freshly baked loaf of wheaten bread, spread them with homemade butter, then picked up a wooden honeypot.

Harry's eyes lit up. "Don't tell me. . . . Shugborough has its own beehives."

"How did you guess?" He set the ale and the bread before her and sat down across the table from her. "This calls for a toast."

She picked up her mug. "I'll give you an Irish toast:

Here's to yous, and here's to me,
And if someday we disagree,
Sod yous! Here's to me."

Harry took a long swig, then licked the foam from her top lip.

For once, Thomas allowed his amusement to show.

"What? No reprimand for my audacity, Lord Anson?"

"Not today, Harry. I welcome your irreverence."

The bread and honey tasted delicious, and she closed her eyes in ecstasy. When she swallowed the last morsel, she sighed with repletion and licked her fingers.

Before they left the kitchens, Harry saw a bucket of sand and asked its purpose.

"It's in case of fire. I have a mortal dread

of it." He led the way and pointed out the servants' quarters, then showed her the long gallery, the ballroom, reading rooms, sitting rooms, as well as a couple of guest suites with their private breakfast rooms and bathrooms. Many of the chambers were devoid of furniture, but the rooms he had restored were elegant and in exquisite taste.

Harry glanced from a window and saw the sun was much lower in the sky. "I hate to leave, but I must." *I could stay here forever.* "Thank you for the lovely tour."

"We have nine hundred acres out there to explore."

"And I long to see every one of them, but it is impossible today," she said wistfully.

"Come, I'll ride out to the gate with you."

When they got as far as the pillared portico, Harry stopped to admire the view. Formal terraces, framed by borders of lavender and roses, stretched out before her, filling her senses. "Shugborough is absolute perfection."

"It will be, before I'm finished."

Thomas lifted her into her saddle. He did not dare let his hands linger, or he would have swept her into his arms and carried her to his bed.

"You always ride a black hunter. What is this one's name?"

"Nemesis. He is from the same mare as Victorious."

"What a perfect name. *Nemesis* means a victorious rival!"

He mounted Nemesis, and they rode side by side along the river, where swans and other waterfowl made their home. "In spring, this riverside garden is a mass of daffodils." They arrived at the wrought iron gates and silence stretched between them.

"What really happened between you and D'Arcy?" He searched her face with dark eyes. "He didn't hurt you, did he, Harry?"

She saw the suppressed violence in his face.

"No, no," she denied quickly. "It was his wealth. I couldn't bear the thought of being supported by money that was earned on the back of Durham's coal miners."

"I'm glad that was the reason." Their eyes met. "Now I don't have to kill him."

As Harry rode away, her heart was singing. It wasn't only seeing Shugborough again that had made her happy; it was encountering Thomas. He was the most physically attractive male she had ever known, and he had made it clear he was still interested in wooing her. *When I return to London, I know he will call on me and try to take up where we left off. Is it possible that*

Thomas is in love with me? Harry shivered with excitement. *He'll have to give me proof before I accept his proposal of marriage.*

CHAPTER FOURTEEN

"Home at last," Lady Abercorn declared as she stepped down from the coach. "Barons Court is particularly inviting at sunset."

The younger Hamilton children tumbled from the second coach and ran to the house, where nursemaids Meg and Molly stood at the front door awaiting their arrival.

Harry knew her father and young James would help the grooms unharness the horses and put them in the paddock behind the stables. She hung back and waited until Rachel and Jane had followed the children into the house. Then, alone, she stood in front of Barons Court, assessing the mansion with critical eyes. She gazed at the portico with its four sturdy columns and realized for the first time that these features reminded her of Shugborough.

But Barons Court doesn't compare. Shugborough's portico, with its eight soaring columns, is magnificent. The pavilions on

either side are extremely graceful. The taste-
ful design gives Shugborough Hall a kind of
elegance Barons Court will never have.

Suddenly Harry felt guilty for thinking
their beloved Irish mansion inadequate. *I*
fell in love with Shugborough when I was a
child, and it became my ideal. In my heart, no
other house will ever be as beautiful. She
sighed deeply and entered Barons Court.

Sarah Kennedy, the head housekeeper,
bobbed a curtsy. "Lady Harriet, welcome
home. Yer chamber is plenished, and I'll
send the servants up with yer luggage the
minute they fetch it in."

Harry glanced about the oval rotunda.
Centered beneath its glass dome was a
polished table, holding a lead crystal vase
filled with flowers. "Delphiniums are Mother's favorite, Mrs. Kennedy."

"I know all yer likes and dislikes, as well
as all yer secrets." Sarah winked. "I told
Mrs. Pithers to prepare some oxtails especially for you."

"Thank you. I love food that sticks to the
ribs."

Harry joined the rest of the family gathered in the great hall. Though it was August,
a log was burning on the large open hearth
to welcome them.

"Barons Court is exactly as I remember

it," Rachel said.

"Did you write Lord Butler, letting him know when you'd arrive?"

Rachel's mouth curved in a smile. "I did. And your mother sent him an invitation to come and stay with us immediately."

"Then I predict he's already on his way. A guinea says he'll be here tomorrow." Harry corrected herself. "No, I've turned over a new leaf. I have decided that in the future I won't gamble or make any more wagers."

"That should be a relief to the stable-boys," her mother said dryly. "Rachel, let's go up and decide on a bedchamber for you."

Jane spoke up. "Rachel can have the room next to mine, now that Trixy won't be using it."

"Absolutely not," her mother said. "I shall put Rachel in the guest wing, in one of the suites, and assign Captain Butler adjoining chambers. Courting couples need their privacy."

Harry looked at Rachel and rolled her eyes suggestively.

"I can't believe you beat me to the stables this morning," young James declared.

Harry laughed. "I wolfed down my breakfast so I'd arrive before you." She and James both had their own Arabian horses, and the stables were the first place they visited when they came to Barons Court.

James saw that his sister had almost finished saddling her horse. "If you'll wait for me, Harry, I'll ride out with you."

"Hurry, then. I like to get out early so I'll see the otters, and perhaps a fox or two."

They left the stable side by side and headed toward the chain of lakes at a slow canter. "So, I take it that Will Montagu heads your list of suitors now that D'Arcy Lambton is out of the running."

"Whatever makes you think that?" Harry asked.

"Well, the wager, of course. They were rivals for your hand. It's no wonder Montagu was willing to take Lambton's bet. He knew D'Arcy wouldn't stand a chance with you."

Harry's brows drew together. "How did he know that?"

"Because Will knew he could make you a duchess someday. And what female would pass up a chance to become chatelaine of Dalkeith Palace?"

Harry was outraged. "You must think me a mercenary bitch, ready to sell myself to the highest bidder!"

"I don't think that at all, Harry. The purpose of having a Season is to secure a wealthy, titled husband. What female would wed an earl if she had a chance to marry a future duke of the realm?"

"You arrogant young devil! Because you are a future duke of the realm, do you assume you can have any woman you want? If you believe you are God's gift to women, you are deluding yourself. I want something far more precious than a title and wealth!"

"Whatever could that be?"

"*Love,* you idiot boy! Our parents have a happy, successful marriage because they are in love with each other. That's what I want. I will settle for nothing less!"

"You turned D'Arcy down because you didn't love him?"

"Exactly." *No, not exactly. I was going to turn him down, but didn't get the chance.*

"So if Will Montagu declares his love, you will fall into his arms?"

"Absolutely not! I'll have to be certain I love the man I marry, and I shall demand *proof* that a man loves me before I agree to marry him."

James laughed. "Will you send your suitor on a mythological quest and set him an epic task to prove his undying love for you?"

"Credit me with some intelligence. I shall be able to discern whether a man truly loves me or not." Harry touched her knees to her

Arabian mare and raced away from her inquisitive brother. *Tomorrow I shall ride alone.*

Riding lessons for her younger children were a priority for Lady Lu. They each had their own pony, and this year five-year-old Ronald and four-year-old Maud were provided with mounts. The duchess recruited Harry's help and happily took on the role of teacher, as she had done with her older son and daughters.

Harry led Maud's pony to the mounting block and showed her how to take a firm grip of the saddle to hoist herself to a sitting position. "That's very good."

"I want to ride astride like the boys," Maud declared.

"It takes far more skill to ride sidesaddle. Father will think you an accomplished rider if you can master it. Now, grasp the reins firmly, hold your head high, and keep your back straight. I'll lead you around the courtyard a couple of times, and then you can try it on your own." Harry knew that it would take pride as well as determination for her little sister to handle a pony.

As Maud rode past her five-year-old brother, she raised her chin and said, "I can ride much better than you, Ronald."

The duchess warned, "Pride goeth before a fall, Maud."

"Oh, I shan't fall, Mother. It takes far more skill to ride sidesaddle."

"You and Harry are like two peas from the same disdainful pod. Let's hope you are as skilled when you have your first swimming lesson this afternoon."

"I shall swim like a swan," Maud insisted.

Harry smiled. *Actually, Maud is the spitting image of Mother!*

An hour after they finished lunch, Harry provided Rachel with one of her bathing dresses. In actuality, they were sleeveless shifts made from colored linen. As the two young women joined the rest of the family at the lake closest to the house, Harry gathered her courage and braced herself for the uproar her tattoo would cause.

Her mother glanced at her bare arms and remarked casually, "I wondered if you were ever going to reveal your pet snake to us, darling."

"You knew about my tattoo?" Harry was amazed. "Didn't it shock you?"

"I've learned to anticipate and accept your unconventional behavior, darling. I put it down to the Irish blood you inherited from your father. And, truth be told, a tattoo is far less eccentric than turning down a marriage proposal that would have made you the wealthiest countess in England."

"I don't think it eccentric to hold out for a husband who loves me. I warrant you would have refused to marry Father if he hadn't been madly in love with you."

Lady Lu smiled at her vivid memories. "Your father first proposed to me when he was about nine years old. I turned him down many times, but he wouldn't take no for an answer. One thing is certain, however: I had proof that he loved me before I agreed to marry him."

"What was your proof?" Harry asked avidly.

"That is our secret. And I am secure in the knowledge that Abercorn loves me enough to never reveal it."

"Then I won't pry," Harry promised. "Every lady is entitled to her secrets."

Her mother smiled. "And her eccentricities."

The entire family spent the whole afternoon in the lake, and before the sun began to make its descent, Abercorn had successfully taught his younger children to swim and his older ones to dive to the bottom and retrieve heavy Indian clubs he tossed into the water.

They ate dinner in the great hall in front of the fire with their heads wrapped in towels, resembling nabobs from the Far East. After dinner, they helped themselves to nuts, figs, dates, and dried apricots, as they told stories of pixies, leprechauns, and Irish ghosts.

After Meg and Molly ushered the younger children up to the nursery wing, Abercorn took his wife for a romantic stroll through the night-scented gardens.

"We usually have a sett of badgers that make their burrow in the woods. Would you like to go and watch them play and romp about in the moonlight?" Harry asked Rachel.

"I'd love to see them. The number of wild creatures who inhabit Barons Court is amazing. The foxes and the otters seem almost tame."

"That's because Father doesn't allow shooting. The *cratures* feel safe. He delights in fishing, but draws the line at hunting."

On their way to the woods, the pair saw a hedgehog with her half-grown young, foraging for insects. "I had a pet hedgehog when I was a little girl. Whenever Trixy came on the scene, it curled up into a prickly little ball for protection."

"They are very sweet, but don't they have

fleas?" Rachel asked.

"Most *cratures* have. But Father is extremely knowledgeable about Irish wildlife. He explained that hedgehogs have their own fleas that won't live on anything else."

Inside the woods, Harry stopped at a clearing. She put her finger to her lips, and motioned for them to sit down. They waited for some time, before Harry heard some twigs snap. She squeezed Rachel's hand and pointed to the trees. They sat silent and motionless, and suddenly two badgers came gamboling across the clearing. In the moonlight they began to play and roll about like children. Three smaller badgers joined in the fun. *They dance by the light of the moon.*

On the way back to the house, they encountered young James coming from the stables. "You missed it, Harry. One of the Arabian mares foaled tonight!"

"Does Father know?"

"Yes, he and Mother are still in the stables. Father bred her to Sultan last summer. It's a little filly. . . . Longest legs you ever saw."

"How lovely. Let's go have a look."

As Harry watched the mare nuzzle her baby, it was brought home to her that motherhood was the primary role of a female.

"Lord Butler, what a lovely surprise. Welcome to Barons Court." The duchess summoned a manservant and asked him to take James Butler's luggage up to the guest wing. "You are in time for dinner. Come into the hall and meet the younger children before they go upstairs."

Rachel's face was wreathed in smiles as she greeted him. "James, I'm so glad you came." She lowered her voice. "I've been counting the hours."

Rather than kissing her hand, he gave her a quick embrace. "My darling Rachel, I've missed you every day."

He greeted Jane and Harry, who introduced him to the younger Hamiltons. He took Maud's hand and formally kissed it.

"Are you Aunt Rachel's special friend, my lord?"

"Indeed I am, Lady Maud."

"Ronald seems to be missing. Do you know where he is, Maud?" Harry asked.

"The baby of the family is upstairs, crying. He's afraid to come down!"

"You, little miss saucy-drawers, are the baby of the family," Harry informed her. "I'll go up and get him, and woe betide the one who made him cry."

Barons Court was a large house, and Harry had to climb two staircases and wind her way along a couple of twisting passages before she got to the nursery. She found her little brother sitting on his bed in the darkened room. When she lit the lamp and saw his cheeks were tearstained, her heart went out to him.

"My little love, why are you up here in the dark?"

He looked at her solemnly and whispered, "I'm afraid to walk through the Passage of Terrors all by myself, Harry."

She thought about the long passage and tried to see it through the eyes of a five-year-old. "Why do you call it that?"

"Because the crocodile lives there."

"But it's stuffed. It can't hurt you. . . . It's dead." The ancient reptile was part of a collection their grandfather had owned.

He shook his head. "It only pretends to be dead. We all know it comes to life when it starts to get dark. And grizzly bears live in the cricket-bat cupboard."

"Is this what your brothers have been telling you?"

He nodded his head. "And Maud."

"Oh yes, I can believe that." Harry poured water from the jug into the washbowl and dipped in a flannel. Then she wiped the tears from his face.

"The wicked devils have made up these tales to deliberately frighten you. I want you to stand up and shake your fist and shout, *I'm not afraid of a silly stuffed crocodile! I'm not afraid of bloody grizzly bears!*"

Ronald got off the bed and lifted his fist, pretending defiance.

"The more times you shout it, the less you will be afraid." Harry raised her fist. "Come on, I'll shout it with you."

The brother and sister lifted their voices together to banish the bogeymen. Then she took his hand. "Are we ready to defy the demons and go downstairs?"

"We are!"

He marched along bravely beside her until they got to the last staircase.

"What is it?"

"That's the Robbers' Passage."

"Robbers be damned! We'll face them together." Harry squeezed his hand. "You've been very brave. From now on, I'm going to make sure there are lights in all these passages to banish the darklings."

"I love you, Harry," he whispered.

His words brought a lump to her throat. Harry turned the knob and the door to the great hall swung open. The blazing lights and the logs burning on the open hearth brought a beatific smile of relief to her baby brother's face.

"Someday I want a little boy just like you, Ronald."

The Duke of Abercorn provided Rachel and James Butler with mounts, and the couple made plans to ride out alone together over the large estate the next day. Harry knew she would miss Rachel's company, yet at the same time she was determined to do all in her power to promote the love match.

"Barons Court is an ideal place for courting," Harry informed them. "The estate has great tracts of woodland and heather-clad hills to ride over. There are many rocky little bubbling burns that cascade over the stones to form swirling pools, and it also has a few wine-colored bogs that the Irish call flows."

"Your father tells me there is a salmon river with white rapids. Perhaps Rachel and I could go fishing one day," James Butler suggested.

"Father and my brothers haunt the place. You don't want to salmon fish with the rabble-rousers. You must choose a day when you can be alone."

James winked at Harry. "Thanks for your valuable advice."

"Why don't you take James into the woods tonight and show him the sett of badgers?" she urged Rachel, then rolled her eyes suggestively.

At the end of the week, the duke and duchess planned a visit to their flax mill that they leased to the Herdman brothers. The textile mill, which had now been in operation for twenty years, produced some of the finest spun linen and cambric in Ireland, and much of it was exported to England.

"May I come with you?" Jane asked her mother. "I've been looking forward to choosing a couple of bolts of linen for some new dresses."

"That's a splendid idea. I've noticed how tight your bodices have become lately. Why don't we all go?"

Rachel spoke up quickly. "James promised to take me rowing today. Your sparkling chain of fairy-tale lakes is irresistible."

"Oh, you will love it. Gliding up the lakes, watching Abercorn flex his muscles on the oars, is the most romantic thing I've ever done. He takes me every summer. You can visit the flax mill next week."

"I'll come to the mill with you next week, Rachel. The wild Irish roses are blooming and today I'm going to gather them and distill their fragrance so we can make some scented candles. Everything about Barons Court is steeped in romance at the moment."

Harry took her basket and knife out to the park and spent the next two hours cutting more than a hundred pale pink blooms. She carried them to the stillroom, and as she separated the petals from their stems, the air became saturated with the heady fragrance of wild Irish rose.

Harry inhaled deeply, savoring the romantic scent. She thought of the roses at Shugborough. *They are cultivated roses. I warrant their fragrance isn't nearly as intoxicating as these.* Her imagination took flight. *Perhaps I can plant some wild roses at Shugborough.* Suddenly her hands stilled. *What was I thinking? Shugborough doesn't belong to me.* As she crushed the rose petals, her lips curved into a smile. *It could belong to me, if I put my mind to it.*

The afternoon was uncommonly warm, and Harry took a favorite book of love poems with her as she walked out by the lake. Her senses were still drenched with perfume, and the solitude beckoned her. Thoughts of Thomas Anson stole to her, and for once she decided to welcome them rather than banish them. She walked past the boathouse, toward the shade of the ancient beech trees. The arching limbs of her favorite tree tempted her to climb it, as she had often done when she was a child. Since Harry seldom resisted her impulses, she slipped the book into her pocket and began her ascent.

Twelve feet in the air she found a secure, comfortable place to sit with her back against the sturdy trunk, and her legs stretched along a smooth gray limb. She took out her book and turned to a passionate sonnet by Elizabeth Barrett Browning:

. . . my thoughts do twine and bud,
About thee, as wild vines, about a tree

Harry stopped reading. She leaned her head back against the tree and thought of Thomas. She closed her eyes and saw his dark image on her closed eyelids. His animal magnetism invoked a longing inside her. *Is that what it would be like if I let him make love to me? A wild night of love?* Harry shuddered.

A woman's laugh out on the lake interrupted her forbidden reverie. She heard splashing, accompanied by more laughter, and realized it must be Rachel and James Butler. It sounded as if they were swimming, and she realized they were coming closer.

Harry felt slightly disappointed that her solitude would be disturbed. She peered through the leafy branches to the water's edge, and saw her aunt emerge from the lake and begin to run. *Rachel is naked!*

A nude James Butler, enjoying the playful game, began to chase her. James caught Rachel and they rolled together in the long green grass, directly beneath Harry's tree.

The couple's laughter ceased as they began to kiss.

I must sit absolutely still. They would die of shock if they knew I was here!

Harry watched, mesmerized as Butler caressed Rachel's breasts and belly. His lips followed wherever his hands touched her pale flesh, and she arched and writhed as her desire mounted.

Harry could hear their whispered love words — endearments that were so intimate they brought blushes to her cheeks. Yet at the same time, she envied Rachel. It was obvious that James Butler was in love with her.

When he mounted and thrust inside her, Rachel wrapped her legs about his back, and Harry realized that this was not the first time they had indulged in a sexual encounter. The lovely redhead was obviously enjoying her newfound sensuality as her fingers threaded through her lover's dark hair, and they moved together in the mating dance.

Harry drew in a swift breath as Rachel cried out her passion. James stopped thrusting and they lay motionless for long minutes. Then he clasped his arms about her and rolled with her until Rachel was in the dominant position.

"You are beautiful in your passion," James told her, as her glorious hair cascaded down onto his broad chest.

Harry held her breath. *If James glances up, he will discover me!* Luckily, he had eyes only for the beauty with whom he had just coupled.

"We had better get dressed," Rachel suggested as she caressed her lover's cheek.

Reluctantly, James agreed, and when they moved toward the boat, Harry sagged with relief. *Their act of love was so intimate and private; I should not have witnessed it.* But try as she might, Harry could not bring herself to regret seeing them.

CHAPTER FIFTEEN

"I have something to tell you." Rachel came downstairs shortly before dinner, wearing a cream gown, with her formerly disheveled hair now tamed and braided into a regal coronet.

Harry was surprised at the transformation of the naked hoyden into the elegant lady. "Are you sure you want to tell me your secrets, Rachel?"

"Oh, it's not a secret. It's a story I thought of for my next book."

Harry hid her amusement. "Ireland must have inspired you."

"Well, I'm thinking of setting it in the Scottish Highlands. It's a wild, rugged, romantic story, about a titled married lady who falls deeply in love with a young artist. They become lovers, and they have a child together. I shall call it *The Love Child.*"

Harry went still. *Good God, she's talking about my grandmother Georgina, Duchess of*

Bedford. Her heroine's lover is Edwin Land-seer, and their love child is Rachel. She licked her lips, which had suddenly gone dry, and made a suggestion. "Couldn't you write it without actually revealing who the father is? It could have an air of romantic mystery if you let the reader decide if the child was her husband's or her lover's."

"That could be rather titillating. The important thing is to write the story of a lady who makes the decision to take a lover. I want to make it wild and sensual. I intend to make it the most romantic story I've ever written."

Rachel is so enraptured over having a lover that she cannot wait to tell the world about how it feels to have a delicious, secret affair.

Lady Abercorn came downstairs with Lord Butler, who had also miraculously transformed himself into a respectable gentleman. He politely offered his arm to Rachel, and everyone went in to dinner.

"When did this happen?" Lord Butler demanded as he read the urgent letter from his brother's wife, Frances, Marchioness of Ormonde.

"Three days back, sor," the messenger from Kilkenny Castle replied. "I rode as swiftly as I could, m'lord."

"Whatever is amiss, James?" Rachel asked as she saw the look of grave apprehension on her lover's face.

"My brother John has had a riding accident. He is in a coma. Frances asks that I return immediately."

Rachel turned pale. "I'm so sorry, James. You must go home without delay. I hope John is recovered by the time you get there."

"Harry, take the messenger to the kitchen, and I'll have Mrs. Kennedy plenish a room for him. You cannot set out until morning, James," the duchess advised their guest.

Harry led the man to the kitchen and poured him a mug of ale as Mrs. Pithers made up a plate of food for him. Before he finished his ale, Butler arrived.

"Mick, this letter tells me next to nothing. You saw John after his accident. He will recover, won't he?"

Mick glanced at Harry. He wiped his mouth with the back of his hand. "I'm afraid I have me doubts, yer lordship." He shook his head gravely. "Doctor says Lord John fractured his skull, an' not likely to come out of his torpor. Lady Ormonde is beside herself."

James looked at Harry. "I need to talk with Rachel."

She accompanied him back to the great

hall. "Rachel, why don't you take James upstairs? He needs to talk to you in private."

Lord Butler paced across Rachel's suite. "I spoke with the messenger and he holds out little hope that my brother will survive. Since John's eldest son is only ten years old, I will have to take on the responsibility of running Kilkenny if my brother doesn't survive."

"James, I hope you don't have to suffer such a tragic loss, but your family could have none more capable of taking charge."

James took her hands and bent to kiss her brow. "Rachel, I want you to be my wife."

Rachel smiled up at him. "And I want you to be my husband."

James bit his lip. "If John does die, I'll have to observe a mourning period before I can marry."

"Darling, I understand perfectly."

"No, you don't understand. What I mean is that we should marry while he still lives. I want you to marry me tonight, so that you can come with me tomorrow."

Rachel caught her breath. "If Abercorn can arrange it, of course I will marry you tonight."

He held up his hand. "Before you make your decision, I want you to know what you're getting into, my love. John is only forty-six years old. He has seven young children who I will have to father if, God forbid, he doesn't survive."

Rachel stood on her toes to kiss him. "I don't mind sharing you, James. You have enough love to go around."

"You are very generous, Rachel. That's why I love you so much."

"Come, let's go and tell the family, and ask Abercorn to help us."

While Abercorn went into Omagh to get the priest from St. Peter and Paul's Church, Harry helped Rachel to pack. "In spite of the dreadful circumstances, I'm glad you are getting married tonight."

"James didn't want to wait. If his brother dies, he'd have to observe a long mourning period. It's strange how things we have no control over can change the course of our lives in an instant."

Harry thought about how her life had changed the day she found Trixy and D'Arcy together. "Perhaps the universe has a plan for us. Man proposes; God disposes."

"The Marquis of Ormonde is only forty-six, and his oldest child is only ten. If John dies, James will be head of the family, and will have the running of Kilkenny Castle.

His responsibilities will increase tenfold."

"I warrant it is fate that the two of you fell in love. James will need the help and comfort of a wife. You will bring him much happiness, Rachel."

The entire staff of Barons Court gathered with the family in the great hall to witness the hastily arranged marriage between Lady Rachel Evelyn Russell and Lord James Wandesford Butler. Abercorn had brought the priest from Omagh, and stood ready to give the bride away.

The wild Irish roses quickly gathered for the bride's bouquet filled the air with their heady fragrance, and Harry knew that from now on she would always associate the scent with weddings. As the priest intoned the solemnization of marriage, Harry's imagination took flight. *There is a superstition that weddings come in threes.*

When James and Rachel were pronounced man and wife, the groom kissed the bride, and Lady Lu directed a footman to bring champagne. The family and the servants drank a toast to the newlyweds and wished them a long, happy, and fruitful marriage.

"James, if you would like me to travel back to Kilkenny with you, I am at your service," Abercorn declared.

"Thank you for your kind offer, but I don't believe it will be necessary to disrupt you. Your time at Barons Court is limited this year. I'll apprise you of John's condition when we get to Kilkenny." He slipped his arm about his bride. "I truly appreciate your making it possible for Rachel and me to exchange our wedding vows on such short notice."

"On our return journey, I think we should go by way of Kilkenny," Louisa suggested. "Couldn't we sail back to England from the coast near Waterford?" she asked her husband.

"That's an excellent idea. I'll have my captain take his ship and anchor it in Waterford Bay, and then we can sail across to Bristol. From there, it will only take one day's coach ride to London."

I won't be able to visit Shugborough on our way back. Harry felt a pang of regret. *Still, Thomas won't be there. By September, he'll be back in London.*

Harry hung back until the newlyweds retired and then she climbed the stairs with Jane.

"That's the second rushed wedding," Jane murmured. "When I marry, I want to be formally betrothed, receive a ring, and have an engagement party. I want a beautiful gown, lots of bridesmaids, and a reception with a towering wedding cake. If I were Rachel, I would feel cheated."

"I can assure you Rachel doesn't feel cheated. She feels blessed that she has found a husband who loves and adores her. When all is said and done, that's the only thing that truly matters." She kissed her sister's cheek. "Good night, Jane. Sweet dreams."

Harry lay awake for a long time as she thought about the day's surprising events.

I'm so relieved that James asked Rachel to marry him. Once they became lovers, there was no guarantee that he would make her Lady Butler. His brother's accident spurred him to propose because he didn't want to leave her behind. I think Rachel was so taken with the romantic idea of becoming his mistress that she threw caution to the wind.

A full-blown picture of Rachel and James making love in the grass came into Harry's mind. *I know it wasn't their first time because Rachel felt no pain — only pleasure.* Harry could see Rachel's legs wrapped around her lover's body. *She knew exactly what to do.*

The encounter Harry had witnessed had taken *some* of the mystery out of the physical act that took place between a man and a woman, though certainly not *all* of it. She hadn't the faintest idea what it felt like. She could only imagine such passionate joy.

As she drifted off to sleep, the fragrance of flowers stole to her. *That's not wild rose — that's the scent of jasmine and honeysuckle,* she thought as her dream began.

Harry was swimming in the lake. She had transformed into a black otter, and a sleek, dark male began to chase her. To avoid him, or perhaps to lure him on, she dived deep, knowing he would follow. Not only did he catch up with her; he swam in circles and fancy patterns around her. He came so close that their bodies brushed against each other in what could be only a mating dance. His insistent male attention stirred her senses and called to the wild spirit that lay hidden deep within her. Her resistance to him gradually melted away and was replaced with an instinctive hunger for a soul mate.

When the male otter climbed from the water, he waited silently, hoping she would follow wherever he led. After an initial hesitation, she gathered her courage and emerged from the lake. He moved off into the long, green grass. Unable to resist his dark, dominant allure, she followed him.

He stretched his sleek body in the grass and she lay down beside him, admiring his male beauty. She felt the primal heat of arousal in her belly and rolled playfully onto her back, yielding to his dominance in feminine submission.

Slowly, she was transformed into a woman, and in the grass beside her lay dark and dominant Thomas Anson. The electricity between them was palpable. His animal magnetism was irresistible to Harry. She caught her breath as his fingers trailed across her cheek. She moved against him in invitation. She thrilled when his muscular arm swept about her, and when his mouth took possession of hers, she opened her lips. She gave in to temptation and threaded her fingers into his thick black curls. The heady fragrance of jasmine and honeysuckle saturated her senses.

Her dream changed once more. Suddenly before her eyes, Thomas was transformed into a magnificent black centaur. His glittering silver eyes flashed, demanding that she follow him into the forest. She was filled with an age-old knowledge that the adventure that awaited her promised to be glorious. She raised her head and pawed the ground impatiently. He towered above her; then he nuzzled her neck, and she accepted him.

Side by side, they loped through the long grass of the meadow and entered the woods.

They ran faster and faster, galloping hell for leather in a wild frenzy of joy, relishing their freedom, ecstatic that they had found each other. When they entered a clearing in the heart of the forest, she stopped and waited for him to claim her. He did not mount her as she expected, but knelt down before her in homage to her lithe beauty.

In that moment she knew that he loved her.

"Worrisome circumstances apart, Rachel's wedding is the second one we've celebrated recently. There is bound to be a *third*," Lady Lu predicted as she glanced at Harry. "When we return to London, I shall invite the Montagu family to a dinner party."

Mother is hoping for a match between William Montagu and me, Harry thought.

"I know that I am only seventeen, but if I receive a proposal of marriage, will you allow me to wed?" Jane asked.

"Darling, is this a fantasy or a real proposal you are speaking of?"

"Well, it's real enough to me," Jane declared.

"Since you'll soon be eighteen, I see no reason why you should turn down a proposal if it comes from a noble whose family is worthy of a duke's daughter."

Jane is hopelessly infatuated with Will Mon-

tagu, but Mother has marked him for me. 'Tis plain she does not consider Thomas Anson's family worthy in any way.* "The notion that marriages come in three is just silly Irish superstition."

"Harry, you believe in more Irish superstitions than anyone I know. Surely you are not dismissing the possibility that you could be the *third bride* in the family?"

"It's possible that *I* could be the third bride," Jane insisted. "You cannot deny that Trixy's wedding was a surprise, as well as Rachel's, so why couldn't my wedding be a surprise?"

Her mother cautioned, "Jane, it is decidedly unladylike to be so eager for a husband. My older sister Georgy earned a reputation for being man-hungry, and she was left on the shelf until she was thirty-two years of age."

"But the tarot cards say that it is the woman who leads, and the man who follows."

"Jane, darling, one cannot conduct one's life on what tarot cards say. They are a whimsical diversion used to entertain at parties. I'm off to give Maud and Ronald their riding lesson. It won't be long before we must leave for Kilkenny."

When her mother left the room, Jane

looked at Harry. "The tarot cards said that Trixy would get her wish in a *three,* and that's exactly what happened."

"What did your cards say, Jane?"

"I remember I got the *Temperance* card, but I'm not really sure what that means."

"*Temperance* is the Angel of Time. It means you must have patience. You are so young, Jane. You have all the time in the world before you need to think about marriage."

"But if I take my time, someone else is sure to grab him. Trixy stole D'Arcy right from under your nose. I don't want that to happen to me."

"I know you're speaking of Will Montagu. He's only twenty-two years old, so he too has all the time in the world to think about marriage. Jane, if it will stop you from worrying your guts to fiddle strings, I assure you I have not set my cap for Will."

"Truly, Harry? You won't try to steal him from me?"

"I promise."

Jane sighed. "He is the Earl of Dalkeith. There will be scores of other females eager to be his countess and live at Dalkeith Palace."

"That's true. But if you stay sweet and innocent, you will stand a far better chance of stealing his heart than all the others."

The corners of Jane's mouth lifted in a smile. "And here's the best part: Mother is going to invite the Montagu family to a dinner party when we get back to London."

"She's bent on matchmaking. Little does she know we will conspire against her."

At the end of August, the Hamilton family traveled to Kilkenny Castle to visit Lord Butler and Rachel. James Butler had sent Abercorn a letter telling them his brother John had died without ever regaining consciousness, so they knew the family was in mourning.

Abercorn sent a message that they would be arriving later in the day, so when the two coaches reached Kilkenny Castle, James and Rachel were waiting for them.

"Rachel, darling, you look radiant." Louisa embraced her youngest sister. "We are simply here to pay our respects. I won't subject you to my horrid horde longer than two days. Harry, Jane, and young James have promised to act as nursemaids to their younger siblings while we are at Kilkenny."

"That is extremely thoughtful of you, Lu. We are doing our best to take care of John's children in this sad time. The arrival of the young Hamiltons will be a welcome diversion for them."

The Hamiltons were accommodated in one wing, and then the two families had dinner in the castle's great hall. Widowed Frances still had a vacant look in her eyes, as if she hadn't fully comprehended her loss yet. She finally excused herself to feed her newly born baby girl.

Harry could sense that Rachel wanted to speak to her in private, so she asked if she would show her the garden.

Harry lowered her voice. "Any regrets, Rachel?"

"Oh, none whatsoever about marrying James. There is something I want to share with you, Harry. But I'd like you to keep it to yourself."

"I won't breathe a word."

"It wasn't just a riding accident. It was a *hunting* accident. John was shot and fractured his skull in the fall from his horse."

"Does your husband have any idea who shot his brother?"

Rachel nodded, and whispered, "It was his son Edward, who is now the Marquis of Ormonde. The child is drowning in guilt and clings to James as if he's a savior."

"That is so tragic. My heart goes out to the boy."

"Edward monopolizes James, so I am offering my comfort to the other children, especially eight-year-old Grace. Their mother is still stunned as a bird flown into a wall."

"With a new baby to look after, is it any wonder? You will surely have your hands full. It is such a sudden change for you, Rachel."

"After living alone, I find it gratifying to be surrounded by a husband and children."

Harry embraced her. "I shall miss you. I know it will be difficult, but you and James must come to London whenever it's possible. And in the meantime, promise me you won't give up your writing."

"I won't," Rachel vowed.

That night, Harry heard her parents discussing the tragic details of the hunting accident, and realized that James Butler must have confided in her father. She was relieved that her parents knew. It would make it easier for her to keep the secret.

Thomas Anson had a secret plan to return to London early. If everyone, including his family, thought he was still in Staffordshire, it would be his alibi if one should be needed. While he'd been at Shugborough, he had once again experienced his nightmare that his beloved home was on fire. He had been halfway down the stairs to fill buckets with water when he realized that his deep-seated fear was all in his head.

While at Shugborough, Thomas had made time to thoroughly examine the situation he was in. His resolve hardened and he concluded that it was time to take matters into his own hands.

Thomas timed his journey so that he arrived in the city after dark. He drove to Furnival's Inn, located in Ludgate, paid to have his carriage and horses stabled, and took a room for the night. After dinner in the taproom, he went upstairs and changed his clothes, donning black from head to foot.

At midnight, he picked up a small spanner and set off on foot to Fowler's law office, located on the first floor of a building off Chancery Lane. He made his way cautiously to the alley at the back of the building, and began the painstaking job of removing the iron bars that covered the window. He set the bars and the bolts he had removed on the ground and then with his fist, protected by his black leather glove, broke the window and crawled inside.

He moved about the law office slowly, feeling his way to familiarize himself with the layout, and did not strike a match until he had located the bank of heavy wooden filing drawers. He lit the lamp, turned it down low, and set it on the floor so its dim glow could not be seen through the front windows.

With rigid resolve, he removed the drawer marked *A*, sat down on the floor next to the lamp, and methodically went through all the files until he came to the one marked *Anson.* He read everything in the file including two signed wills. The first named Thomas Nathaniel Anson as his father's legal heir. The second will named his daughter Anne Frederica as his heir, with her husband, Lord Elcho, to hold the Staffordshire property in trust for her. A foul curse dropped from Thomas's lips. Next to the wills, he found his father's sworn affidavit that falsely claimed he was illegitimate, along with a letter of instructions that stated if Thomas married before his father died, Fowler was to burn the affidavit.

He carefully replaced everything in the file except the second will and the signed affidavit. He turned out the lamp and put it back where it belonged. Then he lifted the drawer from the floor and replaced it in the bank of wooden files. He put the papers inside his coat, climbed out the window, and carefully bolted the bars back in place.

Thomas picked up a few stones and

broken bricks from the alley. He tossed one through the bars of the broken window, then with the other stones proceeded to break the windows of other offices in the building. He didn't want Fowler to suspect that his office had been broken into, and fervently hoped it would appear that young hooligans had been on a window-smashing spree.

At least it should buy me some time before Fowler discovers that documents are missing from his files. The thought occurred to him, and not for the first time, that there could be other copies. There was little he could do about that, short of setting ablaze the building, and fire was anathema to Thomas. *Perhaps there are other copies in the safe that Father keeps in his bedchamber. The wily swine has always kept the combination secret, but perhaps there is a way of learning what it is.*

The following morning, Thomas left Furnival's Inn, drove north to Hampstead Heath, where he spent a few happy hours exploring the heath made famous by highwaymen. When the sun was at its zenith, he drove his phaeton west to the Brent river, and spent the afternoon fishing. Dusk was descending when Thomas drove south on the Circular Road and entered London as if he were returning from Stafford on the last day of August.

"It's the first day of September and it's still warm as summer, with not a hint of autumn in the air." For once Harry was glad to be back in England.

Abercorn's ship had made an overnight crossing to Bristol. Lady Hamilton leaned back against the velvet squabs of the coach. "We'll be in London tonight, and will be able to sleep in our own beds, for which I am truly thankful. Amen."

"Harry, I've never visited the House of Commons. How about taking me to the visitors' gallery one day this week?" Jane asked.

Harry hid her amusement. "I would be delighted. I'm so glad you are taking an interest in politics. Trixy wasn't the least inquisitive about the subject. Perhaps we'll be lucky enough to hear Uncle Johnny speak on the floor."

"You'll likely see Will Montagu. He's the member for Midlothian," her mother said.

Harry smiled. *And Thomas Anson is the member for Lichfield.*

CHAPTER SIXTEEN

Two days later, the Duke of Abercorn drove to his office in Westminster and dropped Harry and Jane off at Parliament. When the sisters climbed to the visitors' gallery, they were happy to find it empty.

"Since Parliament has just reconvened after the August break, visitors will be few and far between. The first week back is notorious for being slow and boring."

Jane fixed her eyes on William Montagu. "I'm not bored."

Harry spotted Thomas Anson immediately. His black curly hair made him stand out from the other members. She dragged her glance away from him when Lord John Russell stood and addressed Prime Minister Aberdeen. It took her a moment to realize the topic of discussion was the Crimean War that Britain and France were fighting against Russia. Her uncle John was advocating that Aberdeen should adopt a more aggressive policy in the war.

The minute John sat down, Lord Palmerston was on his feet, criticizing Aberdeen for his policy of appeasement. Palmerston was even more insistent than Lord John that Britain must be more aggressive in the war they were waging.

Harry lost focus on the talk of war, and her glance soon became riveted on Thomas Anson once again. Jane sneezed and Harry opened her reticule to find her a handkerchief. She was surprised that none of the men below even looked up.

Her mouth curved in a mischievous smile as she took an acorn from her fringed bag.

Harry hung over the railing, took careful aim, and let it fly.

When Anson looked to see what had just fallen from above, he spied an acorn sitting beside him on the green leather bench. He glanced up and saw a dark young lady with scarlet poppies in her hair.

The audacious Irish beauty is back! My prayers have been answered.

When Parliament recessed at five, both sisters were eager to go downstairs and wait for the members to leave the floor of the House and gather in the large foyer. They greeted Lord John, and Jane hoped Will

Montagu would stop to talk with them. If Harry hadn't given up betting, she would have wagered a guinea that Thomas Anson would be drawn to her.

"Hello, Thomas." Harry didn't offer him her hand to kiss. Instead she spoke to her uncle. "I was delighted to hear you give Aberdeen a hard time."

"My comments were mild compared to Palmerston's." Lord John kissed Harry and Jane on the cheek. "How was Ireland?"

"Eventful."

"Indeed. Your mother wrote to tell me our sister Rachel married Lord James Butler. She also shared the unfortunate circumstances. I approve the match, and hope she is happy."

Harry glanced at Thomas. "Rachel is exceedingly happy. Her husband loves her deeply. Jane, why don't you tell Johnny about our visit to Kilkenny Castle?"

She stepped closer to Thomas to explain the circumstances of Rachel's marriage.

"When James was with us at Barons Court, he received word that his brother John had had an accident and was in a coma. Before he left for Kilkenny, he and Rachel were married. He knew that if his brother died, they wouldn't be able to marry until the mourning period was over." *It would be wicked of me to ask after his father's health.*

"Yes, I heard that the Marquis of Ormonde had died suddenly." Her words brought home to Thomas his own dire predicament.

"You didn't speak on the floor today."

Thomas lowered his voice. "Lord John and Palmerston are playing a lethal game. They're trying to bring Aberdeen down. Palmerston has ambitions to become the next prime minister."

Will Montagu joined the group. "Lady Harriet, Lady Jane, how lovely to see you both. Were you watching from the gallery?"

"Oh yes, Will," Jane said fervently. "I was able to see your every move."

Montagu's brows shot up in amusement. "All I did was observe the machinations of Lord John and Palmerston."

His remark went over Jane's head, but Harry smiled knowingly. Her glance moved from Thomas to Will as she compared the two young nobles.

Montagu is a gentleman with everything to recommend him. He is already Earl of Dalkeith, and heir to the dukedom of Buccleuch. His family is not only aristocratic; they are extremely wealthy and own Dalkeith Palace to boot. Will is already half in love with me, and would propose marriage if I encouraged him.

Her glance moved back to Thomas. *On the other hand, Anson is not always a gentleman. He is heir to the earldom of Lichfield, though you could hardly call his father aristocratic. There is no wealth, but he will inherit Shugborough.*

Harry glanced at Montagu. *I'm very fond of Will — he will make someone an excellent husband, but not me, I'm afraid.*

Harry glanced at Anson. *Thomas sets my blood on fire.* She realized in that moment she had fallen in love with Thomas Anson. *He has stolen my heart!*

"Will you need a ride home?" John asked his nieces.

"No, thank you — Father's at his Westminster office today. If we show up, perhaps he'll come home for the night, rather than attend Prince Albert at the palace." As Harry bade the trio of males good-bye, Anson murmured, "Ride with me." Their eyes met, and without further words, Harry knew when and where. *Is that an invitation or a command?*

She gave no indication whether she would join him or not, because she pretended that she hadn't yet made up her mind.

■ ■ ■ ■

At dinner that night Lady Lu had an announcement. "I sent Hobson, the footman, to Montagu House with the dinner invitation for tomorrow evening, and Charlotte immediately accepted."

"Did you include Will in the invitation?"

"Jane, having Will Montagu come to dinner is the whole point of the invitation." She glanced at Harry. "Did you see Will when you visited the House today?"

"Yes, we had just greeted Uncle John when Will Montagu joined us."

"Wonderful. Now, Harry, don't think I'm being critical of you, but when Lady Charlotte is here, I would appreciate it if you refrained from vulgar Irish expressions, and stuck to Anglo-Saxon."

"Well, I assume the Irish expression you wish me to refrain from using is *shyte*. I believe the Anglo-Saxon noun would be *shit*. And there is a classic Anglo-Saxon verb that begins with the letter *f*. Would that be acceptable?"

"Depends on whether you're *saying* it or *doing* it," young James declared.

Lady Lu looked from her son to her daughter. "If the pair of you are trying to shock me, you will be sadly disappointed. I am thoroughly familiar with the classic Anglo-Saxon verb, both in expressing it and indulging in it. Please pass the salt."

Abercorn grinned. "You should know better than to try to spar with your mother. She was taught by an expert."

Lady Lu smiled. "Cocksure devil."

Harry was up before the lark. When Jane stirred, she told her to go back to sleep. "I have an assignation to go riding and it isn't with Will Montagu." She slipped a snood beaded with crystals over her long dark hair and pulled on a pair of green riding gloves. She had debated whether to wear the same riding dress she'd worn last time, or don the brighter burnt orange outfit. *Green is better; it won't show grass stains.*

In the stables, she assured Riley that she could saddle her own mount, and they exchanged a look that confirmed his trust that she would not indulge in foolish behavior. A thought tugged on her conscience. *You shouldn't trust me, Riley.* She thrust the thought away.

When Harry arrived at the Cumberland Gate of Hyde Park, it looked deserted, and for a moment she wondered if she had misinterpreted Thomas's words: *Ride with me.* Then Victorious emerged from the darkness, and she sighed with relief.

Without exchanging a word, they rode in tandem through the park, across the Serpentine Bridge, and past Kensington Palace.

"It is desecration to let the palace fall into decay," Harry declared.

"We think alike, at least about architecture. It is far less expensive to keep a building in good repair than to let it go to rack and ruin before it gets restored."

"For all we know, we could think alike on other matters. . . . We just haven't explored them yet," she said lightly.

"On the other hand, I've come to believe that opposites can attract to an amazing degree."

"Mm, that's certainly something we could explore."

They rode toward the river, crossed the Thames on Hammersmith Bridge, and followed the river toward Richmond Park.

"Today, we'll eat first before we take our wild gallop."

Harry gave him an appraising look. "You never ask. You make declarations."

"I am decisive by nature."

"Some might call it determined . . . even dominant."

"I am those things too."

"It is admirable to recognize one's faults."

"Those aren't my faults. They are my strengths."

Harry threw back her head and laughed, and it felt good.

When they got to the inn, they drew rein, and just as before, Thomas dismounted in one fluid motion and held up his arms. She looked into his eyes as he lifted her down. They stood with their bodies touching for long moments, enjoying the closeness, and rekindling the intimacy they had once shared.

After the hostler came to take their horses, they walked hand in hand behind the inn, and Thomas opened the door to the walled garden. Because the season had changed, the flowers were different. Bees and butterflies were busy among the anemones, the Michaelmas daisies, and the roses that climbed in profusion up the stone walls.

They sat down at the same rustic table, and when the mobcapped maid came, Thomas ordered them a full breakfast, including fried bread and a jug of ale. When it was served, he ate quickly so he could sit back and observe Harry enjoying her food.

"Can you cook, Harry?"

"In Ireland, I sometimes go to the kitchen and try. Why do you ask?"

"Because you enjoy food. I'd like to teach you to cook. Kitchens have a wonderful, warm atmosphere that panders to all the senses."

She remembered the smell and the taste of the freshly baked bread he'd fed her at Shugborough Hall. *Panders to all the senses . . . what a sensual phrase.* From there, her mind flew to the scene she'd witnessed in the long grass between Rachel and her lover. A sigh of longing escaped her lips, and she was brought back to the present only when Thomas captured her hand across the table.

"Marry me."

Her heart began to hammer. *He never requests; he simply declares: Ride with me. Marry me.*

"I would marry you, if I were certain that you loved me, Thomas." She held up her hand. "No, please don't make another declaration. Words cannot convince me."

"What will it take?"

"If . . . if you make love to me, I will know." *Your tenderness will show how much you love and cherish me.*

He controlled his features, masking the surprise and the shock he felt. "Harry, are you suggesting that I procure a room for us?"

"No." She was breathless. "Nature offers the most romantic setting for making love."

He looked into her eyes and smiled. He knew she was indulging a fantasy, and he was perfectly willing to go along with it, to a point. "Drink up, Harry."

She relished the strength of his arms as he lifted her into her saddle, and savored the power of his thighs as she watched him mount his own horse. Her excitement at what was to come made her pulse race wildly and her heart begin to sing.

Thomas led the way to one of his favorite places. He had always enjoyed it alone, but knew instinctively that Harry would be enchanted. When they came to water, they drew rein together. "This is Barn Elms wetlands. It attracts migrating wildfowl from across the world."

Harry pointed. "Swans."

"They are mute swans — they have black faces. This place has crested grebes, and tufted ducks, as well as teal and goldeneye." A spotted woodpecker flitted from the trunk of one elm to another, and the leafy branches were alive with buntings and warblers.

"This is a magical place. Just look at the butterflies!"

Thomas dismounted and lifted Harry

from her saddle. He pointed at some wild-flowers. "That's a golden skipper butterfly." He tied the reins of their horses to a tree and pointed to the ivy growing up the trunk. "This is a holly blue."

"How exotic. I've never seen a blue butterfly before. Oh, look, its legs are striped!"

"Dip your hand in the water and hold it out."

Harry did as he bade and was delighted when a butterfly came to her fingers to take a drink. "It's a purple hairstreak from Ireland, but I've never seen one in England before."

He took her hand and kissed it. The butterfly moved to her hair. Thomas reached up and removed the crystal-beaded snood, and her dark hair cascaded onto her shoulders in wild disarray. He cupped her face gently in the palms of his hands and dipped his head to capture her lips in a kiss designed to steal her senses. When he finally withdrew his mouth, she raised her lashes and he saw that her green eyes were dreamy.

Thomas took her hand and led her beneath a spreading elm. As lapwings cried overhead, he knelt in the lush grass and pulled her down before him. He removed his jacket, undid the buttons on the bodice of her riding dress, and laid her back in the grass. He came over her, brushed his lips across her temples, kissed her eyelids, and trailed the tip of his tongue across her cheekbones. When he took possession of her mouth, she opened her lips, inviting his ravishment.

He did not withdraw his mouth until she had been thoroughly kissed, and her lips were bee-stung. As he gazed down at her, her tattooed wrist reached out and she undid the buttons on his shirt. He found it amazingly erotic. Her palm stroked the hard muscles of his chest and she threaded her fingers through the black hair that furred his flesh.

"I once imagined what it must feel like to have my naked breasts pressed against your wide chest. . . . At last I'm about to find out."

He opened the bodice of her riding dress and then unfastened the ribbon on her chemise, freeing the luscious globes from their confinement. He caressed them with his eyes, then his hands. He bent slowly and anointed her breasts with his lips. Then he gathered her against him, rubbing his chest against her nipples until they stood erect with arousal.

"Undress me and make love to me," she gasped.

Thomas brushed the backs of his fingers across her cheek and shook his head. "No, Harry. I won't make love to you until you are my wife."

"Why not?" she cried.

"Because there will be pain."

"I don't care!" she cried passionately, thumping his chest with her fist. "I won't agree to marry you until I have irrefutable proof that you love me."

"How can giving you pain prove that I love you? You are being willful, Harry."

Her anger flared and she tried to sit up, but Thomas wouldn't allow it. "You dominant devil! You need to be in control — that's why you won't make love to me."

"Say you'll marry me."

"No!"

Her shout startled the wildfowl into taking wing.

"You've frightened the ducks off the pond, you tattooed little wanton."

The amusement in his eyes caused her anger to melt away, and she began to laugh.

"Marry me."

"Perhaps." Green eyes looked into silver. "But first I want proof that you love me."

"Why the hellfire would I saddle myself with an outrageous baggage who flies in the face of all my principles if I didn't love you?"

343

Harry gave him back his own words: "Perhaps because I am the daughter of wealthy nobility . . . and I am the most attractive, maddening female in London."

"And perhaps, *just perhaps,* it's because I love you."

Harry shook her head thoughtfully. "It may not be love. The attraction between us may be the *challenge* we symbolize to each other. *You want to tame me . . . and I want to make you wild!*"

"You once told me that if I laid a finger on you, Abercorn would have me thrashed within an inch of my miserable life." Thomas covered her breasts and retied the ribbon on her chemise. Then he buttoned the bodice of her riding dress. He donned his jacket and held out his hand. "We are at an impasse."

She took his hand and let him pull her to her feet. Her eyes sparkled with audacity.

"A duke's daughter trumps an earl's son any day of the year."

"I am about to make another declaration. You *will* marry me, Lady Harriet."

Thomas held out his mother's chair before the pair sat down for dinner together for the first time since he had returned from Staffordshire.

Barbara Anson glanced anxiously at her son and then confessed, "Before you returned, I was sorely tempted to give your father an overdose of laudanum."

Thomas almost choked on his soup. "For God's sake, don't do that, Mother. He can't live much longer, so don't blacken your immortal soul over him."

Barbara gave a mirthless laugh. "After being married to him for so many years, I have stopped believing that we have souls. In any case, if there is such a thing as a loving God, he would give me absolution for ridding the world of such vermin."

Thomas hadn't wanted to tell his mother of his father's vilest threats, but it was obvious he must now reveal at least a half-truth. "Father has signed an affidavit to disinherit me unless I marry an heiress before he dies. If and when I comply, Fowler has instructions to burn the affidavit."

"Surely it wouldn't hold up legally?"

"Attorneys know all sorts of devious methods to make things legal." He tried for a lighter note. "So please don't bump him off until I'm wed."

"Do you have someone in mind, Thomas?"

"As a matter of fact, I do. I am paying court to Lady Harriet Hamilton, the eldest

345

daughter of the Duke and Duchess of Abercorn."

His mother's eyes widened in surprise. "You are reaching high, Thomas."

"I will inherit no wealth. I must wed an heiress for the upkeep of Shugborough."

"Do you and Lady Harriet love each other, Thomas?"

Love means different things to different people. We both love Shugborough. "There is certainly a mutual physical attraction."

"Have you asked her to marry you?"

"I asked her this morning." He saw hope dawn in his mother's dark eyes. "She said *perhaps.* She is hesitant, but I have no doubt that I will be able to persuade her to marry me. The question is, will I be able to do so in the short amount of time that I have?"

"Welcome to Hampden House, Lady Buccleuch." The Duchess of Abercorn smiled warmly and gave her hand to Charlotte's husband, Walter.

"Louisa, please call me Charlotte." She gestured toward the window. "You are directly across from Hyde Park. . . . How very convenient."

Harry and Jane curtsied to the duchess, and then they flanked Will and led him into the drawing room. Though he was enamored with Harriet, he was far too polite to show favoritism in front of her young sister Jane.

"I take it you visited your constituents in Midlothian," Harry said. "August is usually a glorious month in Scotland."

"The weather was good. I'm sorry your family didn't get to visit Scotland this year."

"No, we went to Ireland, which I love and adore. Jane is the one who missed Scotland the most, I believe." Harry gave her sister a speaking glance. *I'll do my very best to make you irresistible in Will's eyes.*

Jane finally found her tongue. "Did you stay at Dalkeith Palace?"

"I did indeed, for the most part."

"Does it make you feel like a prince to live in a palace?" Jane asked ingenuously.

His eyes lit with amusement. "Scottish princes didn't fare too well in history."

"Well, certainly *Macbeth* didn't," Harry teased.

Young Hamilton joined them. "Hello, Will. Been to Hazard House lately?"

"That is not a fit subject for mixed company," Harry admonished.

"Just because you've sworn off gambling doesn't mean the rest of us are going to sit in the corner and eat pickled Bibles."

"Actually, James, your sister has a point.

347

The gaming house has an unsavory reputation. I'd stay clear if I were you."

"Oh well, I'm off to Oxford shortly. Just thought I might have one last fling before I'm submerged in academia."

"James, when you get there, start up a petition that they accept women scholars," Harry suggested.

"If I start a petition for females, it won't be for scholars," he jested.

Harry glanced at Will. "You'll have to excuse my brother. He's just discovered the opposite sex, and is rather obsessed at the moment."

When dinner was announced, Abercorn partnered Charlotte Montagu and led the way into the dining room. Louisa threaded her arm through Walter Montagu's and followed. Will, ever gallant, offered his arms to both Harriet and Jane and the trio went in to dinner, with James bringing up the rear.

When Harry saw that her mother had placed Will between her and her brother, she quickly moved the place cards so that he would be seated between her and Jane. The grateful look her sister gave her told Harry that she was the happiest person in the room.

The dinner conversation ran the gamut from Ireland to Scotland, from weddings to funerals, from politics to war, and finally to horses and racing. When the guests moved into the drawing room for after-dinner drinks, the conversation moved on to the royal family, then to art, literature, and finally opera.

"I'm taking Louisa to the ballet on Saturday. Marie Taglioni is performing *La Sylphide*," Abercorn declared.

"I always think the male dancers' costumes rather risqué," Charlotte Montagu said repressively. "Didn't you used to dance, Your Grace?"

"She still does," Abercorn said before Lady Lu eviscerated their guest with a rapierlike riposte. "When we were married, I had a stage built for her at Barons Court, Ireland."

"How extraordinary," Charlotte murmured. "Do you dance, Lady Harriet?"

"Only in the ballroom, Your Grace. My dancing is not proficient enough to perform onstage. My sister Jane is the one who has inherited my mother's graceful talent."

Will spoke to Harry quietly. "I'd like to escort you to the ballet on Saturday."

"Thank you so much, Will," Harry said softly. "In all fairness, and before I accept, I must tell you that Thomas Anson and I have made up our quarrel."

Will gave her a look that told her he understood how she felt about Thomas. "I'm glad that you are friends again, but I'd still like to take you to the theater."

"Then I accept your invitation whole-heartedly, Will."

When the Montagu family took their leave, Louisa, Harriet, and Jane escorted them downstairs to bid them good night.

"You behaved delightfully. I was proud of you, Harry. Jane, whatever happened to the lovely material we brought from Ireland? It is high time you had some new dresses."

Harry noticed an envelope on the floor underneath the table where the post was placed each morning. She bent down to pick it up. Her heart skipped a beat when she saw it was addressed to her, and that it was stamped with the Anson monogram.

She opened it quickly and scanned the letter. *It's not from Thomas; it's from his mother.*

My Dear Lady Harriet:

I hope you won't think me presumptuous if I invite you to supper on Friday evening.

My son will not be at home. It will be just the two of us. I hope you will accept. It will provide the opportunity for us to meet and become acquainted.

Barbara Philips Anson,
Countess of Lichfield

Harry went to the drawing room, sat down at the desk, and penned her acceptance. The thought of being invited to St. James's Square to meet Thomas's mother filled her with curious anticipation.

CHAPTER SEVENTEEN

"Harriet Hamilton to see the Countess of Lichfield." Harry stepped into the reception hall of the St. James's Square mansion. *I hadn't expected it to be so elegant.*

"This way, Lady Harriet; the countess is expecting you." The maid took her cloak, and led the way upstairs. By the time Harry reached the top step, Barbara Anson was there to greet her. "I'm so glad you accepted my invitation, Lady Harriet."

Harry curtsied. "I am delighted to meet you, Lady Lichfield."

"Oh, please, no curtsies. Let us be informal." She led the way to the drawing room. "Would you like a glass of wine?"

"I'd love one." *Bugger and balls, perhaps that was some sort of test. Oh well, too late now.* She watched the countess pour two glasses of sherry.

"Thank you." Harry took the glass and sat down facing her hostess. She wondered if Thomas had asked his mother to invite her.

As if Barbara Anson could read her mind, she said, "Thomas is unaware that I asked you to dinner. He's always absent on Friday evenings — that's why I chose it."

Harry tried not to stare at the attractive woman across from her. She was as dark as her son, with an olive complexion and black curly hair, streaked with silver, drawn back into a large bun. Harry detected a lilting accent that she couldn't quite place.

"You have a rare beauty, Lady Harriet. 'Tis easy to see why my son is drawn to you."

Harry smiled with delight. "You are Welsh!" she blurted as she recognized the lilt.

Barbara returned her smile. "Indeed I am. I was brought up in Pembrokeshire. If I tell the truth, and I invariably do, I much prefer Wales to England."

Harry raised her glass. "I have a great deal of respect for the truth, my lady."

"Good. I would like there to be truth between us, at all cost."

At all cost — whatever do you mean?

Again, as if she had read Harriet's mind, she said, "I shall be perfectly honest with you, and I ask no less of you in return."

Harry drained her glass to give her courage. "I pledge you the truth, my lady."

"London thrives on gossip. Have you heard the rumors about me?"

Ohmigod, do you really want the truth? Harry said hesitantly, "Yes . . . I have."

"My father, Nathaniel Philips, had a sugar plantation in the West Indies. Because of my extremely dark coloring, it is rumored that I am half-caste. Gossips insist my father had a mistress in the islands who gave birth to me."

Harriet's mouth went dry at the sheer bluntness of her words.

"Here is the truth. I haven't the faintest notion. My blood could be Celtic — Welsh — or it could very easily be West Indian."

Looking at you, it is impossible to tell. You could be either.

"My son has told me that he asked you to marry him. You told him *perhaps.* I would like you to tell me the truth. Is your hesitation because of my blood?"

Harry was shocked. "I swear on my life that it is not!"

Barbara Anson closed her eyes. Her relief was evident, but she wasn't finished.

"Then do you hesitate because your *family* disapproves of you marrying my son?"

Harry licked her lips as she searched for

the truth. "My father likes Thomas, and has made it clear that the choice of a husband is mine." After a moment she continued. "My mother hoped I would marry D'Arcy Lambton, Earl of Durham. I refused to become his wife because I didn't love him, and discovered that he didn't love me. Now my mother's fondest wish is that I'll marry William Montagu, Earl of Dalkeith. I am fond of Will, but I won't become his wife because I don't love him either."

Oh God, her next question will be, "Do you love Thomas?"

Harry said quickly, "The reason I hesitate to marry Thomas is quite simple. I need proof that he loves me."

Barbara nodded. "Marriage without love is abhorrent. I know firsthand, my dear."

"I am so sorry."

Barbara shook her head. "You need not be. My purgatory is about to end. I can literally smell the freedom of Wales beckoning."

"You won't remain in England when you are widowed?"

"I hate London, and though Shugborough is lovely, it holds too many unhappy memories for me. I shall return to Slebech Hall, Pembrokeshire. I have kept it secret from my husband that my father bequeathed it to me. It is held in trust, since the law says I cannot own it."

"That is a law that must be changed. I have joined the suffragists who campaign for women's rights. Once I marry, I shall become a member of the Married Women's Property Committee. Perhaps you would be willing to add your name to a petition?"

"I would be proud to sign a petition. What you are doing is most commendable. It won't just be an uphill battle, you know. It will be a *bloody* one. Men will wage a fierce war to keep women in their place."

Barbara looked up as a maid approached. "Dinner must be ready. The dining room is this way, Lady Harriet."

"What a lovely room." Harry gazed at the oversized Welsh dresser that held a display of china. "I've never seen a more beautiful dinner service."

"It is a prized collection of Chinese porcelain. The treasure was acquired by a renowned ancestor, Admiral George Anson, who sailed around the world on his ship, the *Centurion*."

"I saw the figurehead of the *Centurion* in the library at Shugborough this summer!"

Barbara was surprised. "You were at Shugborough this summer?"

"We were on our way to Ireland and our

family stayed overnight in Stafford. I couldn't resist revisiting Shugborough Hall. I attended the auction sale when I was a child, and the place enchanted me."

"Thomas was there in August."

Harry smiled. "Yes, he caught me trespassing and gave me a tour of the house."

"My son has a deep and abiding love for Shugborough. He treasures it above all else. It is meet and right that it will soon be his."

The maid wheeled in a tureen and ladled the first course into Harry's porcelain dish. Harry realized it was part of the prized Chinese collection. "You honor me."

"I have decided you are a lady of discerning taste, who can appreciate the aesthetic beauty of such a rare treasure."

"I appreciate the food as well. These prawns are delicious. I can taste curry, but I cannot name the other flavors."

"They are West Indian spices — red chili, cumin, ginger. I made this dish myself."

Harry smiled. "My compliments to the chef. Thomas claimed that he could cook. Now I'm inclined to believe him."

Before the meal was over, Harry knew she liked the Countess of Lichfield. She was direct and truthful, and appreciated those traits in others. *Now that I've met her, it is evident that Thomas takes after his mother.*

Though Barbara Anson had had an unhappy marriage, Harry could tell that she did not feel sorry for herself. *One thing is certain: She has no intention of becoming an intrusive mother-in-law to her son's wife.*

When the food was cleared away, they had one last drink together, and then Harry thanked the countess for her hospitality and bade her good-bye.

Later, as she lay abed, reliving the evening, she thought about how Barbara Anson had invited her to find out if her hesitation to marry Thomas was because his mother might be half-caste. It horrified Harry to think the countess could harbor such a suspicion. She thought of Thomas. *Lord God, I hope he doesn't think that's the reason I hesitate.*

Harry thumped her pillow. *If Barbara Anson had asked me if I loved Thomas, I would have had to admit the truth and tell her that I love and adore him.* Words that her uncle John had said, when she was contemplating marrying D'Arcy Lambton, floated in the air. *"If you are in love, you must let nothing stop you, Harry."* She smiled as she drifted into sleep.

Earlier that evening, Thomas had dined with

Solange.

He had known the young woman since she worked for his father at Ranton, the sporting estate where she helped lure the nobility to gamble away their fortunes.

When Thomas learned that the sixteen-year-old Solange was his father's mistress, he hated and detested her. Then his father was financially ruined, and ruthlessly abandoned the young girl. When Ranton was burned, Solange was left without even a roof over her head, and Thomas's hatred turned to pity. Like him, she was a victim of the brutish, profligate Earl of Lichfield.

Thomas took her to London, found her a job as a lady's maid, and occasionally checked on her while he was at Oxford. Solange hadn't lasted long as a lady's maid. Her beauty did not please the noblewoman who employed her.

Much to Anson's consternation, Solange took a job in a gambling hell utilizing the skills she possessed. When he realized her only alternative was prostitution, he had tempered his condemnation.

Today she was a self-sufficient woman, who leased her own town house near Shepherd Market. The fashionably dressed, elegant blond beauty, who had an air of mystery about her, turned the heads of males when she passed, and caused females to whisper about her behind their fans.

At Brown's Hotel on Albemarle Street, Thomas held a chair for Solange, then took his own seat across the table.

"We seldom dine together, m'lord. You must have an ulterior motive."

"I do." He ordered Dover sole for both of them, selecting an expensive wine for her and ale for himself.

"At Ranton, you often put money in the safe for my father. Do you happen to remember the combination, Solange?"

"Zounds! That must be twelve or thirteen years ago. Though I have a head for numbers, they are usually on playing cards."

"Yes, it seems a lifetime ago. But think hard; I need the combination to his safe."

"How do you know it's the same safe he had at Ranton?"

"Knowing him as I do, the safe would have been removed long before the place went up in flames."

"I remember the combination consisted of five numbers. Perhaps they will come back to me, if you give me a little time."

"I'd like to say take all the time you need, but I cannot."

Solange sipped her wine. "His death is imminent, then?"

"It is."

She smiled. "The curse I put on him is finally working."

He changed the distasteful subject. "Brown's serves the best Dover sole in London."

Solange sat pondering as she ate. When she was finished, she set down her knife and fork. "I remember the first two numbers were ten and twenty, but the other three numbers completely elude me." She shook her head. "I could sit here till doomsday and not recall them. They've vanished with the sands of time."

His brows drew together in concentration. After a few minutes of silence, he smiled a rare smile. "Thank you, Solange. I know what the other three numbers are."

"How on earth?"

"I know my father's egotistic way of thinking."

"Here's some more good news. I found out that the Duke of Devonshire just acquired some statues for Chatsworth that came from the Shugborough collection."

"Old Devonshire is a fanatic when it comes to acquiring neoclassical sculpture. I knew sooner or later, Shugborough's statues would end up at Chatsworth. Good work, Solange. I truly appreciate the information."

She pushed back her chair. "Thank you so much for dinner. Time to go back to work. There are some plump partridges to pluck tonight."

Will Montagu walked across the floor of the House of Commons to speak with his friend before the session opened. He was a Tory — or Conservative, as they were called these days — and Thomas was a member of the opposition Whigs, now known as Liberals. "Congratulations, Thomas."

"If congratulations are in order, I'm unaware of it, Will."

"I escorted Lady Harriet to the ballet on Saturday evening. She told me that you had made up your quarrel."

"Yes, I am wooing her. I have asked her to marry me, but as usual, Harry is being evasive. Unless she accepts, your congratulations may be misplaced."

"She may be evasive, but she made it crystal clear that you are the one she has set her heart on."

Thomas's hopes suddenly soared. "Thank you for passing that along, Will. I know you wanted to engage her affection."

"Well, it's no secret how I feel about her, but I am thoroughly convinced that I cannot compete with you, old man." His expression was rueful. "No man breathing can accept a woman's disinterest. She considers me a *good friend.*"

Thomas left the session early and made his way to 61 Green Street. He rang the bell and when Hobson, the footman, answered the door, he handed him his calling card. "Lord Thomas Anson to see Lady Harriet Hamilton."

"Please step inside, my lord, while I see if Lady Harriet is receiving."

The footman did not return. Instead, Harry appeared at the top of the stairs. "Come up, Thomas." Rather than take him to the drawing room, where their guests were usually entertained, she took him to her father's library and closed the door.

Before he sat down in the Regency brass-mounted armchair, he said, "These chairs came from Shugborough Hall."

"I didn't know that. No wonder I love them so much."

"I know you love Shugborough, but do you love me, Harry?"

"You expect me to confess my love for you, before you declare your undying love for me? *Bugger and balls,* you are an audacious devil, Lord Anson!"

"I am, and I have no intention of declaring my undying love. You don't care for my declarations, and you already informed me that *words* could not convince you."

"I also informed you that I needed proof that you loved me."

"Harry, you know how much Shugborough Hall means to me. By asking you to be my wife, I am offering to share it with you. I would not make that offer to any other lady. I warrant that is irrefutable proof of my love." His eyes glittered silver. "This is the last time I will ask you to marry me."

Her heart began to thud. *I do know how much Shugborough means to you. Offering to share it with me does prove that you love me.* Her resolve wavered, then disappeared completely. "Yes, I will marry you, Thomas!" He was so darkly handsome, her knees felt like wet linen at the thought that he would be her husband.

He did not sweep her into his arms. "There can be no delay. My father is dying."

If your father dies before we marry, you will be in mourning and the wedding will have to be delayed. This will be the third *rushed marriage. Mother won't be pleased.* "I will speak with my parents and explain the circumstances."

Thomas closed the distance between them and enfolded her in his arms. He looked into her eyes and brushed the backs of his fingers across her cheek. "I will try to make you happy, Harry. I'll make a formal call on your father tomorrow evening."

"Mother, may I speak with you in private?"

The duchess had just returned from taking the younger children for a drive in the park. The weather was still lovely and warm, but she knew that by the end of September, the leaves would turn color, and by mid-October, the winds usually denuded the trees.

"On Friday evening I was invited to dine with the Countess of Lichfield."

"You never mentioned it, Harry."

"No, I thought you might object."

"What made you think I would object?"

"You once told me people gossiped about Barbara Anson being half-caste."

"I was only informing you what people whispered — I didn't say I believed it."

"Well, I'm glad you don't believe it. She was born in Pembrokeshire. The lady is Welsh. It is Celtic blood that accounts for her dark coloring." *I don't give a fig if she has West Indian blood, but you might.* "Lady Lichfield was quite frank with me. She knows very well the rumors that circulate about London."

"Ah yes, an intelligent woman usually learns what the gossips have to say. My dear sister Rachel was devastated when she heard the rumors about her birth, and I'm sure Lady Lichfield was deeply hurt over the scandalous gossip as well."

"I was horrified that she might think that was the reason I hadn't accepted her son's proposal. I'm sure she believed me when I assured her otherwise, but then she asked if it was because my parents objected."

"So, Harry, you are telling me that Thomas Anson asked you to become his wife, and you turned him down?"

"Yes and no, Mother."

"Don't be cryptic, darling."

"Yes, Thomas asked me to become his wife, and *no,* I didn't turn him down. At first I said *perhaps.* I told him I wanted proof that he loved me. This afternoon he came and told me the irrefutable proof that he loved me was offering to share Shugborough with me. He swore that he would not make that offer to any other lady, and I believe him."

"So, you accepted his proposal?"

"Yes, I did. The only trouble is that it will be another rushed wedding. His father is dying, and his death would mean a mourning period."

Lady Lu sighed with resignation. "I suppose if you prefer Thomas Anson over Will Montagu, it must mean that you are in love with him. I hope the attraction is more than physical, Harry."

"I cannot deny that it's physical. But there is the added attraction of Shugborough."

Mother and daughter began to laugh. "You are an outrageous baggage, Harry."

"I warrant I take after you."

"Well, there's nothing for it but Jane must marry Will Montagu. I absolutely insist that one of you get to occupy Montagu House so that I can visit regularly and descend that magnificent staircase with the dramatic flair it deserves!"

"You too are an outrageous baggage!"

"Thomas will ask your father for your hand?"

"Yes, he said he would come tomorrow evening. He's giving me a chance to break the news gently."

"Then I'd better send Abercorn a note to make sure he will be home."

"Lady Harriet has agreed to marry me," Thomas told his mother.

"Oh, I'm so pleased. I like her very much."

"I wondered when you were going to let me know you had entertained her."

"There's not much that gets past you, Thomas. I don't know if you are clairvoyant or simply shrewd."

"Perhaps both, but as a boy, I learned to be vigilant. I dislike surprises, and I hate to be blindsided. I've trained myself to be one step ahead of my enemies and my friends. But it was Norton who told me Lady Harriet Hamilton came to dinner on Friday night. I told him to be sure to pass the information on to Father."

"Ah, there's method in your madness. Did you hope to put a stop to his badgering?"

"No, I don't expect pears of an elm tree. I simply didn't wish to discuss Harriet with him. Did the doctor come today?"

"Yes. He told me there is little time left. The doctor said he'd return tomorrow."

"Tomorrow evening I shall ask Abercorn for his daughter's hand. Until then, our betrothal isn't official."

"What is Abercorn like?"

He is everything that my father is not. He is trustworthy, moral, compassionate, noble, and his love for his wife and children is absolute. Thomas's lips formed a half smile. "Abercorn is magnificent."

Thomas retired, and as he waited for midnight, when the house would be in darkness and the last servant asleep, he jotted

368

down the combination to his father's safe. *If Solange is correct and the first two numbers are 10 and 20, I warrant they stand for October 20, the day he was born. Since the year was 1795, it follows that the next three numbers are 17, 9, and 5.*

Two hours later, he silently opened his father's bedchamber door and went inside. The smell of camphor assailed his nostrils, and he schooled himself to stop his gorge from rising. He shuddered when he picked up the lamp. Though it was turned down low, the fear of fire was always there, lurking beneath the surface. As he carried it to the iron safe, his ears were alert for any change in his father's labored breathing.

He turned the safe dial right to 10, then left to 20, and heard the tumblers fall into place. He turned it right again, almost a full circle, and stopped on 17. When he heard the tumbler, he knew he had guessed the combination correctly. He deftly turned it left to 9, right to 5, and slid open the heavy iron door. He took out all the papers inside, and sure enough, his instincts had been correct. As in the Anson file at Fowler's office, there were two wills, along with a signed affidavit declaring him bastard, and a letter stating the affidavit and the second will were to be destroyed if Thomas wed before the earl died.

He put the original Last Will and Testament, naming him heir and bequeathing him Shugborough Hall, back in the safe, firmly closed the door, and spun the dial back to where it had been before he touched it. He picked up the papers and put the lamp back on its table. Thomas silently looked down at his father, and his heart mourned for what might have been.

He returned to his own wing, locked the door of his bedchamber, and sat down to examine the items he had removed from the safe. He set aside the Last Will and the signed affidavit, and picked up the other papers. He was amazed to see that they were IOUs made out to his father for gambling debts incurred by some prominent men. A couple of the nobles were now deceased, but one of the two remaining was from none other than the immensely wealthy Duke of Devonshire. He concluded his father must have fallen ill before he could collect what was owed to him.

His eyes glittered silver. It was an unwritten law that gentlemen always paid their gambling debts. He anticipated with relish Devonshire's reaction when he presented the note for payment. Thomas locked the notes in his desk drawer.

He dropped the will and the signed affidavit into his metal wastebasket and burned them, as he had done with the documents he had taken from Fowler's files. When the papers turned to black ash, he felt as if the weight of an anvil had been removed from his shoulders. He strode to the window, threw it open, and took several deep breaths of clean, fresh air. He had successfully removed his father's ruinous threat, and the feeling of freedom that surged through him was euphoric.

Thomas reveled in the knowledge that he would inherit Shugborough along with the title Earl of Lichfield without impediment. The decision to marry would be entirely his. *I am free to exercise my own will, and swear to do so for the rest of my life!*

CHAPTER EIGHTEEN

"Harriet has informed me that she wishes to become your wife, Thomas. Since her happiness is important to me, I gladly consent to the marriage."

"Thank you, Your Grace. Has she explained the circumstances?"

"Yes. Since you don't want the wedding postponed because of a mourning period, you would like the ceremony to take place without delay."

"We will have to be married tomorrow."

"That's short notice. Have you made arrangements?"

"I took out a special license that will dispense with the banns, and I have arranged with the reverend of St. George's to marry us. It will be in the Mayfair Chapel, rather than the church, since there will be so few of us in attendance."

Abercorn's eyes twinkled. "You anticipated that I would give you my blessing."

"I did, Your Grace."

"All that's left is the marriage contract. I've taken the liberty of setting down some of the details. Harriet's dowry is five thousand pounds. I will give you a draft on the Bank of England."

"That is most generous, Your Grace, but I prefer that you put the money in Harriet's name. My father drained away all the money he received when he wed my mother, and I refuse to follow in his footsteps."

"That is very commendable, Thomas. I will make the arrangements."

"Before you start praising me, you had better hear what I want in lieu of her dowry money."

Thomas Anson reminded Abercorn of himself. "Say on."

"I ask that you return everything you bought from Shugborough Hall in 1842 . . . the entire library, the paintings, and the furniture."

Abercorn steepled his fingers, coolly contemplating the audacious request. Silence stretched between the two men, as they took each other's measure.

"I am convinced it would make Harriet happy to have the things restored. Of course, it goes without saying how greatly I would benefit from such generosity."

Finally, Abercorn assented. "With one caveat — Lady Lu is particularly fond of Rousseau's first edition of *Émile*."

Thomas nodded. "I would not dream of depriving her of it, Your Grace."

Abercorn turned to the second page of the marriage contract. "If you should predecease your wife, Harriet is to receive a lump sum of ten thousand pounds, and five thousand per annum from the Shugborough estate."

Thomas drew his brows together. "To provide her with that kind of money may necessitate the estate being sold. I cannot agree to ever selling Shugborough. What I will agree to, in the event that I predecease her, is that on my death Shugborough will be put in Harriet's name and held in trust for her and my heir, should I be fortunate enough to have a son."

Abercorn smiled. "That is even better than my proposal." He meticulously wrote everything into the contract. "Well, all that's left is to have Harriet in so you may both sign, and we can have my wife act as witness."

"There's just one thing before they come in, Your Grace. Since you have been generous enough to give me your daughter, I would like to give you something in return."

Thomas took a paper from his pocket and placed it on Abercorn's desk. "This is an IOU made out to my father for three thousand pounds. It is a gambling debt incurred two years ago by Arthur Hamilton-Gordon, your youngest half brother."

"Goddam the young devil, I can't believe it! He was little more than a baby when my mother died. In memory of her, I created a trust fund for him, and this is how he squanders the money I provide. Thank you for confiding this to me. I will pay off his IOU immediately, Thomas."

"I have no intention of collecting on this, Your Grace. I give you this evidence in hope that you will confront him and stop him from ruining his life with gambling. Since his father is the prime minister, and Arthur acts as his father's secretary, if this or other IOUs fell into the wrong hands, he could be blackmailed."

"It is no secret that I have nothing but contempt for the Earl of Aberdeen. I don't give a rap what his older sons do, but I don't want young Arthur to turn out like his father. I feel a responsibility for him, because my mother died when he was only three. I even allow him to live at Bentley Priory in Stanmore. Believe me, Thomas, I will put the fear of God into the irresponsible young devil."

Abercorn strode to the library door and spied his daughter hovering in the hall.

"Harry, get your mother, then come and sign the marriage contract."

In a few moments, his daughter and his wife came into the library. Thomas Anson stood so that the ladies could be seated in the brassbound Regency armchairs that would soon be restored to Shugborough.

Abercorn signed the contract, then handed it to Harriet. "I don't think I need to caution you to read the document carefully before you put your signature on it."

Harry dutifully began to read and when she got to the part where Thomas was to receive the books, paintings, and furniture that had once belonged to Shugborough, she raised her eyes to her groom. Her look of surprise quickly turned to admiration that he had negotiated so astutely.

Harry lowered her eyes and turned to the second page. When she read the part where her husband was to bequeath Shugborough to her in his will, she gave him a beatific smile, and a lump came into her throat at his touching generosity. *Thomas is proving beyond a doubt that he loves me.*

She signed the document and handed it to Thomas so he could affix his signature.

He signed his name with a flourish and passed it to the duchess.

Abercorn declared, "You are only witnessing that you saw them sign the contract, Lu. You are not approving its contents."

The duchess quickly scanned the terms, and though she was shocked at Thomas Anson's shrewdness, she kept it to herself. She affixed her signature and smiled graciously. "Thank you for allowing me to keep *Émile,* though I think it beyond the pale to snatch away my library chairs."

Everyone laughed, though they knew she was being perfectly honest.

While Abercorn called for champagne, Thomas took Harry's hand. "I've made arrangements for us to be married at St. George's Chapel tomorrow at five o'clock."

He looked at the duke and duchess. "I'm sorry everything has to be rushed."

"We understand perfectly, Thomas," Louisa assured him. "Harry has been packing all day. Let us hope that the warm weather stays with us so you can enjoy a couple of weeks at Shugborough."

Abercorn poured the champagne and they toasted the happy couple. "Why don't the two of you spend the night at Campden Hill before you set off for Staffordshire? The place has been sitting empty since Rachel left for Ireland."

"Thank you, Your Grace. That is most generous of you."

"Rubbish! Unbend a little, Thomas. From now on, you must call me Lu."

Abercorn took the empty champagne glass from his wife's hand and led her to the door. "I think the young people would appreciate a little privacy, Lady Lu."

When they were alone, Harry suddenly felt shy and absurdly tongue-tied, though she was breathless with excitement.

Thomas drew her into his arms and when he kissed her, she opened her lips in eager invitation. She went weak at the mastery of his mouth, and clung to him for support when the kiss ended. "Oh, it's true — opposites do attract!"

The following day at four, Thomas, dressed in his best gray suit, stood before his mirror and attached a white rosebud to his lapel. He was about to leave for St. George's when his mother came to his bedchamber door and silently beckoned him.

She led the way to her husband's bedchamber, opened the door, and closed it firmly behind them once they were inside.

Thomas approached the bed and looked down. He covered his father's hand with his own, and though it was still warm, he knew that his father was dead. Thomas closed his eyes. "I can't believe it." He removed his hand. "Why did it have to happen now?"

"It is a fateful day, Thomas," Barbara Anson murmured.

The wedding will be canceled. He clenched his fists and vowed, "I will not allow his death to spoil Harriet's wedding day." He turned to face his mother. "Will you help me to keep this quiet until tomorrow? Can you stay here and keep it from Norton until after midnight? First thing in the morning, send word to me at Campden Hill, Kensington. I will return immediately so we can carry out the necessary arrangements."

"I think that's a wise plan, Thomas." She looked over at the bed. "He can't do any more harm to us now."

Let us fervently hope not.

He enfolded his mother in his arms and held her against his heart. "I'm sorry you'll miss the wedding, but the nuptial ceremony will be short. Just a formal exchange of vows to make it a legal marriage." He kissed her brow. "Remember that I love you."

Thomas awaited the Hamiltons in the vestry of the chapel. When they arrived, he took Harriet's hands in his and lifted them to his lips, one at a time. "My mother deeply regrets that she cannot join us for the ceremony. My father's condition has deteriorated and she feels it is her duty to stay with him."

Harry squeezed his hands, telling him she understood.

"That is most admirable of her, Thomas," the duchess declared.

Hand in hand, the bride and groom approached the small chapel altar. Jane and James, who was leaving for Oxford shortly, followed them. Harry's sister was maid of honor and her brother was acting as groomsman. Beatrix and D'Arcy were not yet in London. The Duke and Duchess of Abercorn stood a short distance behind their children.

Harry was wearing her presentation gown. *I'm so thankful it is all white. Perhaps Fate knew it would be my wedding gown.*

The reverend entered the chapel through the adjoining door of St. George's Church.

He greeted the noble family with great deference and opened his prayer book.

"Dearly beloved, we are gathered together here in the sight of God, to join together this man and this woman in holy matrimony."

Harry gazed at the small window above

the altar and decided she liked the chapel far better than the vaulted, cavernous church where Trixy had been married.

"Thomas Nathaniel Anson, wilt thou have this woman to thy wedded wife? Wilt thou love her, comfort her, honor and keep her, in sickness and in health, and forsaking all others keep thee only unto her, so long as ye both shall live?"

"I will."

His deep voice sent a shiver through her. *I didn't know his middle name was Nathaniel. That's a lovely name. Mine is horrible.*

"Harriet Georgina Hamilton, wilt thou have this man to thy wedded husband? Wilt thou obey him, and serve him, love, honor, and keep him, in sickness and in health, and forsaking all others keep thee only unto him, so long as ye both shall live?"

"I will." *Before God, I pledge that I love him with all my heart.* She glanced up at his dark hair and eyes, in marked contrast with his gray suit. His features were solemn. *I promised to obey him. I warrant it would take a great deal of courage to disobey him.*

"Who giveth this woman to be married to this man?"

James Hamilton, Duke of Abercorn, stepped forward and said firmly, "I do."

Harry's eyes met her father's. She fervently hoped that Thomas would come to love her as much as her father did.

The couple pledged their troths, and then Thomas produced a small gold ring and slid it onto her finger.

"For as much as Thomas and Harriet have consented together in holy wedlock, I pronounce that they be man and wife together, in the name of the Father, and of the Son, and of the Holy Ghost. Amen."

Thomas dipped his head and placed a chaste kiss on his bride's lips. Harry lifted her bouquet of roses and breathed in deeply. Her eyes shone like stars. *I smell jasmine and honeysuckle!*

As the newlywed couple moved to a side table to sign the register, organ music piped in from the church filled the air. When they reached the vestry, Abercorn kissed his daughter and shook hands with his new son-in-law.

Louisa kissed her daughter and hugged Thomas. "I sent word ahead to Campden Hill to prepare a wedding supper for around eight o'clock. You should be there just after seven if you leave right away."

When they moved outside, Lady Lu showered them with rose petals.

Harry looked at Jane. "Did you bring the rice?"

Her sister nodded and scattered the rice.

Harry laughed up at Thomas. "It's a treat for the pigeons."

They all made their way behind St. George's Church, where Riley had transferred Harry's baggage to Anson's phaeton. Abercorn wrapped a fur cloak about his daughter's shoulders, and Thomas took up the reins. "Thank you for everything."

"Good-bye, darling. Enjoy your honeymoon," her mother cried.

As everyone waved the newlyweds on their way, Harry tossed Jane her bridal bouquet. Then she turned around to see what the thudding was. She began to laugh. "They've tied a string of old boots to the carriage!"

"We have your brother James to thank, I believe."

"In a conspiracy with Riley, no doubt. It's an old Irish tradition."

He slipped his arm about her and drew her close. "I think it's rather touching." He saw her fingers twist her wedding ring. "I promise to buy you a diamond soon."

"I'd much rather you spent your money on restoring Shugborough's treasures."

His arm tightened. "That's precisely why I married you, Harry."

It took just over an hour to get to Kensington, and when they arrived, it was starting to go dark. Thomas drove up to the stables, and when the head groom came out, he helped the man to unharness his matched pair of carriage horses.

"I'll rub them down and feed them, Lord Anson. Yer not dressed for mucking about the stables." The man's broad grin told them he knew they had just been married.

Harry was impressed when Thomas carried her luggage to the house, when there were plenty of servants willing to do it. He set her bags down and went to get his own.

Campden Hill's housekeeper, who'd known Harry since she was a baby, hugged her and wished her every happiness. "Since Lady Rachel's been gone, we've been rattling about the place looking for things to occupy us. Cook and I enjoyed making you a special wedding supper. I'll let you know when it's ready." She glanced up the staircase. "I thought you'd like the yellow room. It's got such a nice, big bed."

Harry blushed. "Thank you, Mrs. Bailey." *Bugger and balls, I'm all aflutter.*

Thomas brought his own bag, then picked up one of Harry's and headed to the stairs.

"I'll show you which room we are in," she said breathlessly, and ran up the steps. She led the way to the east wing. "This is the master bedchamber. It gets the morning sun; that's why it's called the yellow room. The windows overlook the lake."

"I'll fetch the rest of your bags."

When Thomas returned, Harry was standing looking out the window. "It's such a pretty view, but you can't enjoy it tonight. It's completely dark outside."

"You are the only pretty view I wish to enjoy tonight."

Harry laughed. "You are not usually given to flowery speeches."

"I've hidden depths you've yet to discover. Perhaps you bring out the *gallant* in me."

He took the fur from her shoulders and laid it on the window seat. "You are a very beautiful bride, Harriet. I'm a lucky man." He brushed his lips across her brow.

"Oh, don't start kissing me," she said breathlessly. "We have to get through dinner."

"In that case," he said solemnly, "I think we'd better go downstairs."

A small table was set for two, side by side. Thomas held her chair and lightly caressed her shoulders when she took her seat. Then he moved his chair and his place setting so that he could sit across from Harry, because he enjoyed watching her eat.

He lifted the bottle of chilled champagne

and poured them each a glass. "I toast the lovely Lady Anson." *Tomorrow you will learn that you are the Countess of Lichfield.*

Harry raised her glass. "And I toast the *gallant* Lord Anson."

The first dish was sautéed shrimp and tiny scallops in a heavenly lemon sauce. Harry dipped in her finger and was about to taste it when Thomas captured her hand, drew her finger to his mouth, and licked it. "Sinful."

When her lips curved into a smile, he knew the teasing gesture had pleased her. When she put the last scallop in her mouth, she closed her eyes. "Mmm. If I weren't on my best behavior tonight, I'd pick up the dish and lick it clean."

His eyes danced. "I wasn't aware you were capable of restraint."

"I warrant one of the reasons you married me was to bring mayhem and madness into your sober, *strait*laced existence."

She's losing her shyness. He hid his amusement. *That certainly didn't take long!*

Mrs. Bailey wheeled in a tray and lifted the silver cover to reveal a brace of roasted game birds stuffed with chestnuts. There was also a salad made from greens grown in Campden Hill's kitchen garden. "I made the special wine and honey dressing you like."

"Thank you. . . . That's so thoughtful."

"Nonsense! Everything should be special on your wedding day."

"Mrs. Bailey is right." *I'll do my damndest to make everything special for you.* He watched with delight as Harry picked up the breast of roast game with her fingers, and devoured it with relish. She held up the wishbone. "Pull it with me?"

He reached across the small table, took hold of one end, and pressed down his thumb. He was left holding the smaller half.

"Oh, I get my wish! I'm sorry you didn't win, Thomas."

"I already have my wish," he said gallantly.

Her mouth curved with mischief. "Whatever happened to that dark, dominant devil who wanted to tan my arse?"

"The night isn't over yet," he teased.

She wiped her fingers on her napkin and sighed with repletion. "I couldn't eat another thing."

When Mrs. Bailey and the cook wheeled in the dessert, Harry was so moved it brought a lump to her throat. "You baked us a wedding cake! Thank you both from the bottom of my heart." She looked at her husband. "We have to cut it together."

They got up from the table and stood together before the two-tiered cake, decorated with candied violets, and real white roses. He picked up the silver knife and handed it to Harry; then he placed his hand over hers and they made the first cut.

Thomas gifted the two women with a rare smile. "You must share it with us."

Harry brought two glasses from a side table. "Wedding cake must be accompanied by champagne. It's the law!"

"She's a law unto herself," he told the women, as he poured them wine.

"She is that, Lord Anson," they both agreed, and lifted their glasses.

He watched Harry pick off the candied violets, one by one, and eat them.

"Is that your favorite part?"

"Oh no, my favorite is the almond paste. I have a voracious appetite for it."

Once I get a taste of you, Harry, I warrant my appetite will be voracious.

Up in the master bedchamber, Harry said the first thing that came into her head. "You carried up all this luggage and I won't need any of it except a nightgown. In the morning, you'll have to carry it all back down. I can't wait to see Shugborough again."

"I carried it up to impress you." He felt

regretful that she wouldn't see Shugborough tomorrow.

Harry opened her case and took out a white silk nightgown. Thomas removed his jacket and waistcoat. Then he took off his silk neckcloth and unbuttoned his shirt. "Let me help you." He moved behind her and unfastened the back of her gown. She stepped out of it, and stood before him in her frilled white petticoat, which she removed herself.

She took both to the wardrobe. "I think I'll leave these here. No point in packing them and taking them with me." She was now clad in her white satin corset and stockings.

"You must take the corset." It was a declaration. He stepped close and took the pins from her hair. The dark silken curls cascaded into his hands and he shuddered with desire. His fingers unfastened the strings at her waist, the corset fell away, and her breasts spilled into his cupped palms. "You are sinfully lovely," he whispered.

She stood on tiptoe and wound her arms about his neck. He put his hands beneath her bum, and carried her to the bed. He sat her on the edge and slowly removed her stockings. When he saw her toes curl, he raised her foot to his lips and kissed her instep.

Harry wanted to scream with excitement. Her nightgown was forgotten as she reclined naked against the pillows and watched as Thomas undressed. When he was nude, she went weak at the sight of him. "Would you draw back the curtains and open the window? In the morning, I want the room to be bathed in sunlight." *I want us to be bathed in sunlight.*

He raised the window and glanced at her over his shoulder.

"Thank you." Then she confessed, "I wanted to see you walk across the room naked. And walk back again," she added as her glance swept over him from his dark eyes to his glorious manhood. *If I narrow my eyes, you look like a centaur.* A shiver ran down her back at the thought of his body touching hers.

Thomas lay down and drew her into his arms. His kisses began at her temple; his lips touched her eyelid, then brushed across her cheekbone. He blew warm breath on the tiny spirals of dark curls that clustered about her ear and whispered, "I smell roses."

"I smell jasmine and honeysuckle," she murmured breathlessly.

He captured her lips in a long, slow kiss.

"You taste delicious."

"Like champagne?"

"Yes, like wine . . . and *woman*."

Impulsively, she set her tongue to his throat and licked his skin. "You taste like more." Her tongue moved up to the cleft in his chin. "And more." With the tip of her tongue, she traced his bottom lip. "And more, and more, and more."

He moved over her and kissed her deeply. "My audacious Irish beauty."

She laughed up into his dark face, falling more in love with him every minute.

He knelt, his thighs straddling her hips, and gazed down at her. His palms cupped her breasts, and his thumbs toyed with her nipples until they ruched like rubies.

She reached up and threaded her fingers through the thick black pelt that covered the powerful muscles of his chest. When she touched him, she felt the muscles in his thighs tighten and his cock became rigid. "Everything about you is hard."

Her provocative words inflamed him. He knew that with one hot, driving thrust he could be inside her, but with iron control he schooled himself to patience. He gently rolled with her so that she was above him, her knees now straddling his hips.

She leaned forward and her dark tresses

trailed against his throat as she dipped her head and captured his mouth in a sensual kiss. When she felt him shudder with need, she suddenly wanted to arouse him to madness. She pressed her breasts against his chest, and gasped with pleasure. The feel of naked skin against bare flesh was so exciting she wanted to scream. She could feel his erection against her soft belly and moaned with longing. She writhed against him and bit his shoulder in a frenzy of need.

"Softly, my beauty." He rolled with her until he was in the dominant position. His fingers caressed her mons. After long moments of play, he separated her curls, and slid a finger into her dew-moist sheath. When he felt she was ready, he murmured, "Open for me, sweetheart." He positioned the tip of his cock at the opening of her cleft and thrust deeply inside her.

She cried out at the pain and he held absolutely still until the hurt subsided and she got used to the fullness. "It's done, sweetheart — no more pain." She was so hot and so tight around his throbbing cock that it took all his willpower to keep from ravishing her.

Slowly, he began to thrust and withdraw, inching deeper and deeper into her woman's center. His whispered love words, hot and dark, poured over her.

She wrapped her legs about his back, matching her body to his rhythmic, mesmerizing thrusts. She found the act of love so intimate and intoxicating, she willingly yielded all control to him, and within seconds she was crying out her pleasure, as she dissolved in shuddering tremors.

Not until he felt her last pulsation did he allow himself to spend. Then he gathered her close and held her against his wildly beating heart. He knew he would never have enough of her. Her effervescent, passionate nature made him realize she was a rare treasure. The desire she aroused in him was so passionate, he could have made love to her all night, and he vowed that in the not too distant future, he would. This was not the night, however. He had given her pleasure and would not spoil it with uncontrolled lust.

Thomas felt her body soften with surfeit as he held her close. They whispered softly between kisses, until finally her eyelids drooped and her lashes brushed her cheeks as she drifted off into slumber. He knew sleep would be impossible. He wished he could stop time and keep tomorrow away indefinitely. Then he laughed at his own folly. He had no choice but to face life head-on.

When Harry opened her eyes, the lovely autumn sunshine was streaming through the windows. Her heart skipped a beat when she saw that she was alone in bed. But she sighed with happiness when the door opened and Thomas carried in a breakfast tray. She gave him a radiant smile. "Tonight we'll be in Shugborough. I can't wait."

He set the tray before her. "I want you to enjoy every mouthful."

"Won't you join me?" she tempted.

He shook his head solemnly. "I've already eaten."

She picked up the bacon with her fingers and didn't speak again until she had eaten everything the cook had made her for breakfast. Then she pushed away the tray and threw back the covers. "I must hurry."

He sat down on the bed, a somber expression on his face. "Harry, I'm afraid something terrible has happened. A messenger has brought the news that my father has died. I have to return to London."

Her hand went to her throat. "Oh, Thomas, I'm so sorry. I'll get dressed right away."

"No, Harry, I want you to stay here. We've

been expecting it for so long, the arrangements have been made for a private burial. I have to return to be with Mother for the reading of the Last Will. No matter how late it is, I'll return tonight, and we can travel to Shugborough tomorrow."

"Surely, it's a wife's duty to be beside you at such a time."

"Harry, I don't want my father's demise to touch you or shadow your happiness in any way. His death is a blessing, not only for him, but for my beloved mother."

"I understand, Thomas," she said softly.

"It would please me if you would spend the day with Fanny and the children. Take Fanny and your uncle John some wedding cake." He tucked the covers around her and dipped his head to kiss her brow. "The rest of our life starts tomorrow."

CHAPTER NINETEEN

"It was selfless of you to miss the ceremony, Mother. It was short, and went off very well. Harriet had a happy wedding day. Did you encounter any difficulties?"

"None at all. I called Norton to your father's bedchamber just after midnight. He summoned the doctor, who pronounced him dead and made out the death certificate.

"At six this morning, the undertaker removed his corpse, and I dispatched a messenger to Campden Hill to bring you the news."

Thomas checked his pocket watch. "It's eight o'clock — time to summon Fowler."

Barbara Anson closed her eyes and pressed her lips together.

"Don't be afraid, Mother. I hold the whip hand."

Thomas went up to his own chamber and changed into a black suit. As he checked his image in the mirror, his thoughts were reflective. *His death has not brought me the overwhelming relief I expected. Perhaps because all hope of reconciliation between us died with him.* He laughed at his own folly. *Thomas, never look back and never think twice.* He realized that all he could do was look to the future, and once again he vowed to give his own children the love he had never received.

An hour later, when attorney Martin Fowler knocked on the door of 15 St. James's Square, it was Thomas who opened it. "Fowler," he acknowledged curtly.

Fowler pierced him with a glare from behind his spectacles. "I understand the Earl of Lichfield has died?" He sounded as if he couldn't quite believe it.

"You understand correctly." When the attorney stepped over the threshold, Thomas closed the door. "Follow me up to the library."

As he ascended the stairs, Thomas could feel the animosity radiating from the man of law, and he wondered just when Fowler had discovered there was only one Last Will and Testament in the Anson file. *It must have been recently, or he would have flown here like a homing pigeon.*

When they arrived in the library, Thomas's mother, garbed in traditional widows' weeds, was already present.

Fowler nodded. "Lady Lichfield."

"Thank you for answering the summons so promptly, Mr. Fowler."

The attorney set his leather portfolio down on the desk.

"Feel free to use my desk, Fowler," Thomas said graciously.

"The Earl of Lichfield made his last wishes exceedingly clear to me during the last few weeks of his life. He stipulated —"

"I am fully aware that my father frequently consulted you about changing his will. We are quite prepared to have you read it, Fowler." Thomas held a chair for his mother, then took the seat behind his desk. There was no other chair in the room.

Fowler opened his case and took out a sheaf of papers. Then he hesitated for a moment and shoved them back into the case. "The Earl of Lichfield kept his Last Will and Testament in the iron safe in his bedchamber."

"Alas, we will not be able to retrieve it. My father never gave me the combination to his safe."

"He entrusted the combination to me," Fowler said with grim satisfaction.

"Are you sure?" Thomas asked in disbelief.

"Quite sure. If you would accompany me to the safe, I shall be happy to retrieve the earl's Last Will and Testament and read it to you."

Thomas bowed his head in acquiescence. "Lead on. I'm sure you remember the well-traveled path to his bedchamber."

Fowler picked up his case and headed from the library. Thomas offered his hand to his mother, and they followed the attorney to the late earl's chamber. Fowler opened the bedroom door and paused when he saw the empty bed. Then he walked to the safe, set his case down on top of it, and searched until he found a folded sheet of paper.

He knelt before the safe, dialed the first two numbers, then consulted the paper, and dialed the last three numbers. He opened the safe door, reached inside, and drew out the will. When he found only one document, he peered inside, and felt around with futile determination.

He stood up and whirled about to face Anson with a piercing look that was so accusatory, it would have intimidated a less dominant man. Bristling with outrage, he opened the document, and saw that it was the earl's original will. "This safe has been tampered with. Your father's Last Will and his signed affidavit have been removed!"

Thomas demanded in outrage, "Are you accusing my mother of duplicity?"

"Of course not. It is you —"

"I believe you knew my father well enough to know he would never trust me with the combination to his private safe."

"The earl stipulated that if he died before you wed, you were to be disinherited."

"I was married yesterday to the eldest daughter of the Duke of Abercorn," Thomas said smoothly. "You are here for the sole purpose of reading my father's will. I suggest you get on with it."

Fowler held up the document. "You know exactly what it says. There is no need for me to read it."

"Nonetheless, I would ask that you do so. As the deceased's attorney, it is your legal obligation and duty."

Fowler stared down at the document he held. His hand shook with thwarted anger as he read the words in a droning tone bequeathing Shugborough Hall, Staffordshire, to Thomas Anson, the late Earl of Lichfield's legal heir.

When the attorney was finished, Thomas held out his hand for the document. "Thank you, Fowler. Your legal services are no longer required."

Fowler's face turned dark with fury. "The Earl of Lichfield stipulated —"

"*I* am the Earl of Lichfield. You are dismissed."

Fowler grabbed his case and scurried from the room like a cockroach.

"Thank you, Thomas. The affront to the vile swine was almost too much for him to bear. It was he who had to swallow the bitter pill of humiliation for a change."

"What time is the burial?"

"I explained to the undertaker that we would like him buried today. He was aware that Hanwell Cemetery in Ealing was for the exclusive use of St. George's parishioners. He told me that he could not have the coffin there until five o'clock."

Thomas nodded. "Did you send word to my sisters?"

"Yes. They will be as relieved as we are, and their husbands even more so. I will finally be able to visit my daughters." Barbara Anson shuddered and walked to the door. "I cannot bear to be in this room one more minute."

Thomas summoned Norton and the rest of the servants. "I want this room emptied today. Give the furniture to a poor family in need. I want even the carpet and drapes stripped from the room. Norton, while I'm away at Shugborough, have the room painted."

Harry stood at the window that overlooked the driveway long after it was too dark to see anything. All her thoughts were focused on Thomas. *He always had a difficult relationship with his father, though he never spoke of it.* Her uncle John had told her Thomas was the antithesis of his father, and she believed that the earl had had a profound influence on his son. *The reason Thomas has such rigid morals and is so honorable and straitlaced is due to his father's disreputable character.*

"Standing at the window won't make him come any sooner, my dear. Can I make you a cup of tea?"

"No, thank you, Mrs. Bailey. You needn't wait up with me. I won't require anything else tonight."

"I'm off, then. There's brandy on the sideboard, should you feel the need."

"Thank you. Good night."

Harry rearranged all the pillows on the sofa and thought of Barbara Anson. *She is free at last. I wonder how many years she has endured an unhappy marriage. It's been a dozen years since everything at Shug-*

borough was sold at auction, but when I went to dinner, she confided that it held too many unhappy memories for her. *She could have been in purgatory long before everything had to be sold to settle her husband's gambling debts.*

Harry went to the window again. *Perhaps Thomas won't return tonight. It must have been a stressful day, both for him and for his mother. Perhaps she needs his company tonight. I think I'll go up to bed. There is no point in my sitting here alone, worrying and wondering.* She picked up the brandy, turned out the lamp, and went upstairs to the lovely yellow bedchamber.

She undressed and put on the white silk nightgown that had lain forgotten last night. Then she turned out the lamp and got into bed. *This bed is so wide, it feels strange to lie here alone.* She stroked the pillow where her husband's head had lain, and her cheeks felt warm when she thought of the way he had made love to her. *Thomas gave me absolute proof that he loves me.* She closed her eyes and saw his dark image on her closed eyelids. Harry curled over onto her side and imagined she could feel the warmth of his powerful body behind her.

Some time later, a noise made her open her eyes. She did not know if she had been asleep or not. When she sat up, she realized that Thomas was there. She slipped from bed and relit the lamp. It revealed his face, taut and unsmiling. "I missed you fiercely."

He enfolded her in his arms and kissed her hair. "It's over and done."

"Would you like some brandy?" she asked softly.

He nodded. "Have some with me."

Harry poured the brandy and Thomas undressed. She handed him his glass, and together they downed the fiery liquor. They kissed and when they tasted the brandy on their lips, they smiled into each other's eyes. Harry got back into bed, and then Thomas turned out the lamp and followed her. When he gathered her against his heart, Harry put her arms around him and held him tightly. They clung together for more than an hour as the warmth of their bodies seeped into each other. Then they drifted off to sleep, safe in each other's arms.

Harry awoke to a room filled with sunshine. When she opened her eyes, she found her husband watching her. His eyes shone with silver this morning and she instantly realized that the dark mood of yesterday had lifted, and in its place was an atmosphere of love, happiness, and anticipation.

"Good morning, my beauty."

"Yes, it is a good morning, Lord Lichfield."

His arms swept about her, and his mouth captured hers in a long, slow kiss. When their lips parted, she said breathlessly, "If the kissing starts, we'll never get to Shugborough today. I want both desperately, so you must decide which it is to be."

Thomas made no effort to hide his amusement. "I'm guessing Shugborough is your first choice, Lady Lichfield. You'd better get dressed before you tempt me to dalliance."

She lifted her mouth to his. "Hurry and dress. Don't take time to shave. I want to see you haul all this luggage again just to impress me." *Every time you do something to please me, you are proving your love. In church, you vowed to love and cherish me, and I truly believe you do.* Harry sighed with happiness. *I'm the luckiest bride in the world.*

"Shugborough Hall. We are home!" Harry grabbed his arm and dug in her fingers. "Oh, Thomas, those are the loveliest words I've ever uttered. It's still dusk, and there's just enough light left to see the hall in all its glory."

"It's a good thing we stopped only once to water the horses and enjoy the food that

Mrs. Bailey so thoughtfully packed for us, or it would be full dark."

When they drove up to the stables, a groom came out to greet him. "Welcome home, Lord Anson." His appreciative glance went to the lady who accompanied Thomas.

"I'm the Earl of Lichfield now, Toby, and this is my countess, Lady Harriet. Would you send your boy up to the house to let Mrs. Stearn know what to expect? I'll unharness the horses and get them into stalls. You can give them a rubdown and feed them."

Toby grinned. "That I will, Lord Lichfield. Welcome to Shugborough, my lady."

"Thank you, Toby. I've been enamored with Shugborough since I was a child." Harry waited until Thomas unharnessed the pair of carriage horses; then she took the bridle of one. "I'll take him to his stall. You lead and I'll follow."

Thomas teased, "I'm extremely flattered that you are bowing to my authority."

She flashed him a mischievous smile. "Enjoy it while you can — it won't last long."

Toby gaped at the lovely young countess, who handled the carriage horse with skill.

The black hunter, Nemesis, whickered a greeting when he heard his master's voice, and Thomas rubbed his nose and spoke affectionate words to him. Then he hauled Harry's trunk to his shoulder and picked up one of the traveling bags. "I'll send Vickerstaff for the rest of the luggage," he told Toby.

As they walked from the stable, they met the young boy returning from the house, and Harry said, "Hello, there. What's your name?"

"My name is Toby too," he informed her.

"Well, Tobytoo, was Mrs. Stearn surprised?"

The boy grinned. "She were that, lady. She's in a fair tizzy."

Harry glanced up at her bridegroom. "Me too," she whispered.

When the newlyweds stepped onto the elegant, columned portico, the front door swung open. Thomas set down the luggage, and picked up his bride. Harry slid her arms about his neck, thoroughly delighted that her husband was carrying her over Shugborough's threshold. He set her down before the staff that had been hastily assembled by Mrs. Stearn.

Thomas said solemnly, "It gives me great pleasure to present my wife, the Countess of Lichfield. I know you will serve her as faithfully as you have served me."

The housekeeper-cook bobbed a curtsy. "Welcome to your new home, Lady Lichfield."

"I'm sure she would prefer that you call her Lady Harry," Thomas said.

"Then Lady Harry it is." Mrs. Stearn began her introductions with the two males. "This is Mr. Ramsey, Shugborough's steward, and John Vickerstaff, our footman."

Harry held out her hand to the steward. "How do you do, Mr. Ramsey?" Then she shook Vickerstaff's hand. "I am promoting you to *butler,* John."

Vickerstaff glanced swiftly at the new earl. When he saw no dark look of disapproval, he straightened his shoulders. "Thank you, my lady. It will be my pleasure to serve you."

Mrs. Stearn moved on to the female servants. "This is Dorothy Nicklin, my kitchen maid, and Sally Willis, the scullery maid. MollyAnn Hooper is the laundry maid, and this is Mary Trudgett, the stillroom maid." The housekeeper-cook looked apologetic. "I'm sorry we don't have a lady's maid for you, but it's been donkey years since Shugborough has had a mistress."

Harry greeted them all by name, and then smiled at the stillroom maid. "I think Mary would make a lovely lady's maid." She took her husband's hand and winked suggestively. "I won't need you tonight, but tomorrow you can help me unpack."

Mrs. Stearn threw the master an accusing glance. "If you'd let me know you were coming, I'd have prepared a grand dinner for you."

"Whatever you have cooked will be delicious, as always, Mrs. Stearn."

There was a loud meow, and the gray Persian cat came running into the entrance hall. It rubbed itself against Thomas's ankles.

"Here's Kouli-Kahn to welcome you. How lovely." Harry bent down and picked up Thomas's feline. "Who's a beauty? That's right, Kouli is a beauty." She was rewarded with a loud purr.

John Vickerstaff was dispatched for the rest of the luggage, and once again Thomas lifted Harry's trunk to his shoulder and headed for the stairs.

"May I choose our bedchamber?" Harry asked breathlessly.

"No."

"Why not?"

"My room, the master bedchamber, is the only one that's furnished, sweetheart."

Harry was aghast. "Thomas, I'm so sorry. I'm extremely thoughtless at times."

He led the way to his chamber, set down

her trunk, and watched her face.

"Oh, it is a splendid room, and furnished so elegantly."

He could tell she was surprised. "It took a great deal of time and effort to restore this master chamber to its original grandeur."

She twirled about the spacious room. "It was worth it." The tall windows that faced east had gold brocade drapes with black tassels. A huge four-poster bed was hung with matching curtains, and the black velvet cover was embroidered with golden lilies and dragonflies. The thick-piled Oriental carpet boasted a pattern of brilliant blues, gold, and jade green. On the wall that faced the bed, there was a fireplace with jade green tiles. The andirons were fashioned into brass monkeys, and the pokers and coal tongs had matching monkey handles. A double wardrobe covered one wall with polished silver mirrors mounted on the doors. The final wall was lined with black and gold lacquered cabinets. A games table held a chess set whose chessmen were carved animals.

"Oh, the kings are stags, and the pawns are dear little hares. I love it!"

Thomas joined her before the games table. He raised her chin with his fingers.

"Stags *rampant*," he emphasized.

"You have a wicked humor."

"I warrant you can match me in that department."

"You mean I give as good as I get."

He waggled his eyebrows. "That remains to be seen."

Harry blushed at his innuendo. "Let's go and eat — then we can come back up to this glorious chamber and shut out the world."

Mrs. Stearn had set the table with the few Spode china pieces that Shugborough possessed. She served the earl and countess with a humble dish of lamb shanks cooked with barley, along with a dish of salad greens from the kitchen garden.

Thomas couldn't stop watching Harry eat because she enjoyed her food with relish. "You do everything with passion, and I find that not only admirable but stimulating."

Harry licked her lips. "I love this sort of food. While we are here, let's spend some time in the kitchens, and you can give me some cooking lessons."

"Instructing you, in all things, will give me great pleasure," he promised.

She felt Kouli rub against her ankles and selected a morsel of lamb for her.

"You shouldn't feed her at the table."

Harry laughed. "I shouldn't, but I shall!"

Their dessert was pears poached in wine, served with a dish of clotted cream. Harry accompanied her last mouthful with a drawn-out "Mmmm!" Then she dipped her finger in the cream and let the Persian cat lick it off.

Thomas opened his mouth to protest, and in a flash, she dipped in a finger and held out the cream for him to lick. Without hesitation, he took her finger into his mouth and sucked off the cream. "You revel in audacity. You want me to think it is the same finger you offered Kouli, but I know better. The thing is, I don't really care."

"Hell and Furies, you're catching on to my tricks. I'll have to invent some new ones."

Mrs. Stearn apologized when she brought in a jug of ale.

"Home-brewed ale is perfect, Mrs. Stearn. Thomas is taking me to the brewhouse tomorrow to show me how it's made."

His lips twitched. "Lady Lichfield, you have taken to making declarations."

Harry smiled into his eyes. "Yes, I know. I caught the habit from you."

"How in the name of hellfire will two such strong-willed people survive?"

"Love conquers all! I warrant we'll rub along together very well."

"Come to think of it, you did vow to *obey* me," he teased.

"Dream on, Lord Bloody Lichfield." Harry jumped up from the table and began to run. Thomas was after her in a flash and caught her before she left the dining room. He lifted her into his arms and captured her mouth in a sensual kiss.

"Ooh," she said languidly, "do give me some orders, darling."

"I'm taking you to the moonlit walled garden. Do not resist."

"I am incapable of resisting either you or the garden."

The huge harvest moon bathed them in light as he carried her through the gate in the wall. He set her feet to the grass, then took her hand so they could stroll through the garden that was so special to Harry. The night-scented stocks and heliotrope perfumed the warm air, and the sounds of the splashing fountain lured them from beneath the shadowed trees. The call of a nightingale echoed hauntingly, and they stood still so they could listen to the cricket chirps and the rustle of small animals.

"Cratures," she murmured softly. *Absolute perfection.*

He drew her to the bench and pulled her into his lap. They whispered love words between kisses, and Harry sighed blissfully. "I hope we are always as happy as we are tonight." She caressed his cheek and found it rough. Desire flared in her. "Don't shave."

He captured her hand and dropped a kiss into her palm. "Let's go up."

She kissed his ear and whispered, "Yes . . . let's."

Halfway up the staircase, he lifted her into his arms and carried her to the master bedchamber. He kicked the door closed with his foot and set her down on the edge of the wide, curtained bed. Then he knelt before her and removed her shoes. "Since you nominated me to be your lady's maid tonight, I intend to enjoy the role." His hands went beneath her skirt, and his palms stroked up her legs. His fingers slid past her garters to caress the soft, bare flesh where her stockings ended. When he felt her shiver with pleasure, he slowly drew off her garters and stockings. "Prettiest things I've ever seen."

"The blue garters belonged to Mother."

"I don't mean the garters — I mean your delicate feet and ankles." He lifted one to his lips, kissed it, then trailed the tip of his tongue across her high instep. When he set her foot to the thick-piled carpet, he watched her toes curl.

Harry lifted her other foot. "Now this one." She smiled into his eyes when he repeated the pretty gesture.

He pulled her up from the bed and turned her around. He unfastened the long line of buttons on the back of her dress, lifted her dark curls, and kissed the nape of her neck.

"I love the feel of your lips on my skin."

"That's good. I intend to kiss every delicious inch of you."

She stepped from her gown and stood before him. "You have to undo the strings," she said breathlessly.

"You wore the corset just for me."

"I did. Tonight, I will allow you to pull my strings."

"But not every night?"

"That depends on how much pleasure it brings."

"To you, or to me?" he teased.

As he took the strings into his hands, she stood on tiptoe, raised her chin, and looked into his eyes. "I hope I give you as much pleasure as you give me, Thomas." *I'm mad in love with you, my dark centaur.* As her corset fell away, he cupped her full breasts, and Harry reached out to unfasten his shirt.

When they were both naked, she said, "Help me to fold this exquisite velvet cover.

I imagine the bedsheets will be in a terrible tangle before we are done."

The golden lily and dragonfly cover was safely set aside. "Any more orders, m'lady?"

"Perhaps a game of chess?" she teased.

"I do have a game in mind, but I assure you it isn't chess." He scooped her up and rolled onto the bed with her. His kisses began at her dainty feet, and his lips made their slow ascent from ankles, to calves, to knees, and on up the delicate flesh on the insides of her thighs. Though he had vowed to kiss every inch of her skin, he was suddenly diverted from his intent when his lips arrived at her high mound of Venus. He blew warm breath on the tiny black spiral curls, and heard Harry's swift intake of breath.

His thumbs brushed aside her curls and the tip of his tongue explored her sensitive woman's center. When he plunged his tongue inside her sugared cleft, she cried out with both surprise and pleasure. "Thomas, you make me feel wicked as sin."

His mouth made her writhe with delight and she threaded her fingers into his coal black curls, loving the crisp texture of his hair and the roughness of his tongue. The hot, sliding friction built up inside her and spilled over in delicious quivers as her pulsations began. When he withdrew his tongue, she lay sprawled before him in silken splendor.

He moved over her and she gazed up at him. "You make me feel beautiful."

He kissed her over and over. Tiny kisses, quick kisses, slow melting kisses, and urgent kisses that aroused her desire to madness. "Now, Thomas. Love me now!"

Harry wrapped her legs about his back and gasped when he thrust his marble-hard erection inside her scalding sheath. She closed sleekly around him, and as he began to move, she opened her mouth, loving the satin slide of his tongue as it matched the throbbing rhythm of his demanding cock. She felt as if she would go up in smoke as her burning desire turned to flame. His man-scented skin provoked a sensuality she didn't know she possessed. Suddenly the night exploded into a million tremors as he impaled her with a driving thrust that sent them both over the edge into shuddering ecstasy.

He lay still so that he could enjoy every exquisite pulsation of her lush body. Then he whispered words of adoration that made her heart melt. *With my body I thee worship.*

The words floated through her mind as she clung to him, and her mouth curved in a contented smile as she drifted off to sleep, secure in the knowledge that her husband truly loved and adored her.

CHAPTER TWENTY

"This home brew is rather potent. You should stop at one tankard," Thomas warned.

"I love the aroma inside this brewhouse." Harry handed her empty tankard to her husband. "Fill it up. If I become legless, you'll have to carry me."

"Try to behave yourself, Harry. I suspect you are already tipsy."

"I am! But it isn't the ale that intoxicates me, Thomas — it's *you*. You make my senses reel."

He picked her up, swung her around, and kissed her soundly before he set her back on her feet. Then he refilled her tankard from a huge barrel of ale.

She drank half of it and pretended to stagger. When his arms reached out to steady her, she roared with laughter and gave him a push. "I'm teasing you."

He rolled his eyes. "You most certainly

are, madam." He ran his fingers over the swell of her breast. "I'd take you to see the water mill if I wasn't afraid you'd fall in."

"You are very good at diving into water to save damsels in distress."

"That was the day I convinced D'Arcy Lambton that Trixy was mad about him."

Harry suddenly became still. "Why did you do that?"

"Because I couldn't let him marry *you,* of course."

"Is that true, Thomas?"

"Absolutely."

She was flattered, but also surprised that he had done such a thing. "I would like you to always tell me the absolute truth. I don't want there to be any secrets between us. I won't make you promise, though. I want you to know that I trust you. Implicitly."

He took her tankard away and drank the rest of her ale.

"You dark-eyed devil, I trusted you!"

"I want to introduce you to our Shugborough tenant farmers. I don't want them to think my bride can't hold her ale."

"Perhaps they will be delighted that the serious and sober Thomas Anson has chosen a mate who is impulsive and imprudent."

"Come on. Fresh air will banish your giddiness." He took her hand and led her from the brewhouse. "Here comes a wagon. I wonder what it brings."

When the wagon drew up in the court-yard, Harry could see a ducal crest. "It belongs to the Duke of Devonshire!" She drew closer. "I think it holds statues."

"I had no idea who purchased our statues at Shugborough's infamous auction. But recently I learned that William Cavendish bought them a short time ago for Chats-worth. I managed to reacquire them."

"Oh, Thomas, how clever of you. Was his asking price very high?"

"Higher than I was willing to pay." His eyes flashed silver. "After a fierce negotia-tion, we came to a gentleman's agreement."

Thomas greeted the two men on the wagon. "If you will follow me, I'll show you where I want the statues unloaded."

He and Harry made their way across the lawns to where the statues had originally stood, and she watched avidly as the men lifted the statues from the wagon, removed the protective sacking in which they were wrapped, and set them up where Thomas directed. "Oh, it's Venus and Adonis! How lovely and white the marble is." She watched as two more male statues were unloaded. "I don't know the name of these gods."

"They are Castor and Pollux. Twin sons

of Leda and Zeus."

"Oh, I know the myth. Zeus disguised himself as a swan and seduced Leda."

"You're educated as well as beautiful, a rare and dangerous combination," he teased.

"There are two small statues in the bottom of the cart, Lord Lichfield."

Thomas climbed on the wagon to inspect them. "Yes, this one is Flora. She belongs in the greenhouse. The other goddess is Thalia, the Muse of comedy."

"Flora is the goddess of flowers and springtime. Why don't we put her in the walled garden?" Harry suggested.

Thomas smiled at her. "If that would please you." He gave the men directions, but told them to leave it outside the small gate. Harry realized that he didn't want the workmen in their private garden, and upon reflection neither did she.

When the men returned, he had them carry Thalia into the house and directed them to the library. He thanked them, tipping them generously, and he and Harry followed them back outside. As the cart disappeared down the long drive, Thomas took her hand. "Let's find a spot for Flora."

When they arrived at the gate of the walled garden, Thomas directed Harry to open it. He then proceeded to lift the heavy marble statue and carry it inside.

"Your strength always amazes me. Let's put it where I saw the little green snake."

He set the statue in the flower bed, and stood back to admire it. "Flora is a fertility goddess. She represents springtime, fruit-bearing flowers, and *sex*."

"I prefer to think of her as a *love* goddess."

"Little puritan," he teased.

Her eyes glittered with mischief. "Untrue! When I look at you, my thoughts are decidedly impure."

"You may regret sharing that secret with me." He removed his jacket, laid it on the grass, and pulled her down into his arms.

They rolled on the ground, kissing and laughing. Harry's hands caressed his arms and shoulders; she thrilled at his powerful physique. "Your muscles are huge."

"Feel this muscle," he invited, taking her hand to his cock.

"Now who is being impulsive and imprudent?"

"It must be catching. I feel an urgency to make love in our garden, since this could be the last warm day of autumn."

"You want me nude as the goddess?"

"I'll let you keep on your stockings and garters," he whispered.

"You have persuaded me. Your negotiating

skills are formidable indeed."

"And then some." He lifted her skirts and removed her drawers.

That night, as she watched him undress for bed, she recalled the first time she had seen the statues in Shugborough's grounds. "I was familiar with Venus, but it was the statue beside her that drew my eyes. The name carved on the pedestal was Adonis, and as I gazed at him, I wondered if all males looked like that when they were naked."

"And what did you conclude?"

"I decided that only gods could be that perfect. Of course, I hadn't seen you then."

"Flattery will get you everything you desire, my darling."

"I want to see if I can make you as hard as a marble statue."

He turned to face her. "I'm already there."

"Oh, bugger and balls, so you are!"

He made a dive for her, and his arms clasped her close. He rolled with her until she was above him in the dominant position, and took possession of her mouth.

When the kiss ended, Harry knelt above him. "I want to explore you tonight. Your body fascinates and enthralls me."

He raised his arms above his head and

grinned up at her. "Do your worst."

Her fingers immediately began to explore his exposed armpits. The texture of the black hair was soft and silky. "You don't seem to be ticklish."

"Things aren't always what they seem. I am indeed ticklish, but I exercise control over my response."

"You like to be in control. It makes you feel safe. Aren't you ever tempted to abandon your control and revel in being unconstrained?"

"Tempted, yes. But I seldom give in to temptation."

I want to know what will make you frenzied and wild, and moaning with hunger. She stroked her fingertips across his wide shoulders. She toyed with his male nipples that were flat as copper pennies and felt delight when they became erect. She dipped her head and drew circles around them with the tip of her tongue. Her lips trailed down his rib cage; then she dropped a kiss on his navel and dipped in her tongue.

When his hands cupped her bum cheeks, she felt a flame of arousal, and guessed that his passion was ready to explode. Slowly, and deliberately, she began to lick the swollen head of his cock. When she took him into her mouth, he cried out and arched his body off the bed in a wild frenzy of need. "Harry! Don't ever stop!"

Hours later, after he'd made love to her twice, they lay entwined, their bodies warm and soft with surfeit. Thomas was happy over his marriage. He had needed someone to share things with for a long time, and he felt he had chosen the right woman. But sharing physical intimacy was far easier than sharing other facets of his life. He stared into the darkness for long minutes and then his lips brushed her temple. *For now this will suffice.*

The following day, Thomas took Harry across the bridge to the small island behind the Chinese pagoda to view the "Cat's Monument" where the original Kouli-Khan was buried. She read the inscription and traced the feline's name with her fingers. "I admire your ancestor George Anson very much. In spite of his fame and fortune, his pet obviously came high on his list of priorities. I warrant you have inherited his qualities."

"I have inherited his love for Shugborough at any rate. Come — let me show you our more famous 'Shepherd's Monument.' The marble relief is copied from the Nicolas

Poussin in the drawing room. The carved letters form a cipher that's never been solved."

"How fascinating." Harry took his hand and he led her past the Tower of Winds.

"There it is. Since the Ansons had a connection with the Knights Templar, legend has it that the cipher refers to the whereabouts of the Holy Grail."

Harry knelt in the grass and traced the letters. Then she placed her hand on the sun-warmed marble and closed her eyes. "I'm only guessing, but I believe it is a secret message between lovers. An ancient Anson ancestor lost his beloved and this inscription tells her how much he adored her. The letters probably represent some beautiful Latin phrase or line of poetry that was known to the two of them."

Thomas held out his hand to raise her. "Harry, you are a true romantic. A secret message between lovers is such a lovely thought." He enfolded her in his arms, and his lips captured hers in a tender kiss.

"I think I hear another wagon." He led her toward the courtyard.

"Why, it's Riley, my father's coachman." Harry ran to the wagon and greeted Riley.

He jumped down and handed Thomas a letter from Abercorn.

Thomas broke the seal and read the letter. He looked at Harry and smiled. "Your father wasted no time gathering the books, paintings, and furniture he agreed to return to Shugborough. He says that the only books missing are the ones at Barons Court in Ireland. He says that when he and your mother go over there in the spring, he'll crate up the books himself. He also says he will bring one of his prized Arabians as a wedding gift for you, Harry."

"Oh, I never expected anything so generous," she cried.

"Your father loves you very much, sweetheart."

Harry dashed away a tear. "Riley, come to the kitchen and meet Mrs. Stearn. She will fill your belly with some rib-sticking grub, and you can wash it down with a jug of our home-brewed ale."

"I'd better unload this lot first, Lady Lichfield. There's quite a haul here."

"First you will eat, drink, and be merry. Then I'll get the staff to help, and we will all unload Shugborough's treasures."

After the servants brought everything into the vaulted entrance hall, Harry ordered Riley to stay for a couple of days, rather than return to London the following morning.

That evening, after an early dinner, Thomas and Harry took the paintings up to the long gallery and hung them back in the spaces they had originally occupied. Altogether, there were six paintings, so it took three trips up the curved staircase to the gallery.

She could see how important the ritual of restoration was to her husband, and she took her joy from his satisfaction. They laughed as she insisted the paintings were far more beautiful displayed here than they had ever been in the Hamilton residences.

"Your father was extremely generous to return these paintings in the marriage contract. This one, *Sleeping Venus and Cupid,* is extremely valuable."

"Venus and Cupid?" She stood back and looked at it. "I thought it was a painting of a nude mother and her child."

Thomas was amused. "I shouldn't laugh at you. Venus *is* the mother of Cupid."

"My education in art is lacking. Since you are an expert, you will have to give me lessons. How did you become an associate of Whitfield Cox?"

"He came into possession of a painting from Shugborough and offered to sell it to me. I couldn't afford to buy it, so I told him I'd earn it by selling paintings to wealthy art collectors. I was so successful at authenticating and selling art that we decided a permanent business association would be beneficial to both of us."

Her glance moved about the long gallery, assessing all the paintings. "I still love the horse paintings best. I am glad you secreted them away from the vultures who bought up Shugborough's treasures at the auction all those years ago."

"Do you feel up to sorting books tonight?"

"Oh absolutely! I can't wait to put them back in their rightful place."

They went downstairs and carried the books, a few at a time, into Shugborough's library. They both took deep pleasure arranging them on the almost empty shelves. Almost two hours passed as they sorted the books into their various categories. When they were done, they looked at each other and declared in the same breath, "The brass-mounted library chairs!"

They raced to the entrance hall and separated the pair of chairs from the other items of furniture that Riley had brought. Working in tandem, they carried them to the library, one at a time. Then they each sat down in one and laughed with delight that another of Shugborough's rooms had been miraculously restored.

Thomas held out his arms and Harry immediately abandoned her own chair to sit on her husband's lap. He tenderly cupped her face. "I am immensely grateful to you, sweetheart. Sharing things with you fills my being with deep, warm satisfaction."

She wound her arms about his neck. "I wish I could wave a magic wand and magically restore everything to Shugborough, and make it exactly as it used to be."

"You won't need a magic wand, sweetheart. I will restore everything," he promised. "I am a ruthless businessman."

"I love this house as much as you do. I'm so glad you seduced me into marrying you, Lord Lichfield."

"Tell the truth and shame the devil. Was it me who seduced you, or Shugborough?"

"Since we have agreed there will be absolute truth between us, I freely admit that it was both."

"You are a shameless baggage. Some secrets are better left unspoken," he teased.

She rubbed her bum against his cock. "Since you invited me to shame the devil, if you'll take me up to bed, I'll see what I can do."

The following day, Thomas hitched up the carriage horses and took Harry to visit all

Shugborough's tenants. Some of the farmers bred sheep and others grew crops, and it was obvious that they all respected Thomas. Most of the crops were in for the year and as Thomas and the farmers discussed which fields to plant in the spring, Harry made friends with their wives. She took an interest in their children and was pleased to learn that they all went to school.

As they drove back to the hall in the late afternoon, she told Thomas that Shugborough's tenant farmers seemed happy and contented. "The women told me how much you had done, not just for your tenants, but for the area in general."

"I regret that I will no longer be the member of Parliament for Lichfield. It gave me a great deal of satisfaction. Now that I'm the Earl of Lichfield, I will have to take my seat in the House of Lords. In my opinion, the work isn't nearly as important."

"Then you won't need to attend every session, and we can spend more time here at Shugborough. I'd love to return in the spring and stay through the autumn."

"Perhaps we could breed your Arabian mare with my hunter. Shugborough's stables lack riding horses. I'm sorry I haven't got a mount for you, Harry."

"You are right to spend your money on

Shugborough, rather than horses. Breeding our own horseflesh is a good idea. Tomorrow you can take me up before you, when we explore Cannock Chase."

He winked. "Perhaps we can ride hell for leather again."

She laughed. "We did that last night. You are insatiable, my lord."

"Did you notice the splendid Staffordshire workhorses on some of our farms?" he said as they pulled up to the stables. "Next year perhaps we could start a breeding program. It may prove profitable."

"Thomas, that's a wonderful idea. They are magnificent animals."

When they entered the hall, Harry took his hand. "I forgot to tell you. I informed Mrs. Stearn that we would feed ourselves tonight. It is high time you gave me the cooking lesson you promised."

He leered at her. "Kitchens have a wonderful warm atmosphere that panders to all the senses."

When Mrs. Stearn saw them, she ushered her maids from the area. "Lord and Lady Lichfield wish to be alone, I warrant."

"You are very perceptive, Mrs. Stearn." Harry said. "Thank you."

Thomas lifted his wife onto the wood chopping block. "What does the count

fancy for her dinner?"

"Since this is my first culinary lesson, let's have something simple."

"Mmm, how about Spanish omelettes?"

"Sounds good. What will we need?"

"A potato, an onion, a couple of mushrooms, some bacon, some hot red pepper, and eggs of course."

"Where will I find red pepper?"

"Look in the pantry. You should find a package of dried hot peppers."

When Harry returned with the dried hot pepper, he had gathered all the ingredients and was frying bacon in a pan on top of the iron woodstove. "Mmm, that smells good."

"Melt some butter in that other pan, and slice the potato very thin. Add some chopped onion, and cook them together on a low heat so the butter doesn't burn."

"Low heat?"

"Place the pan to the front of the range. The back gives off higher heat than the front, for safety reasons of course."

When the bacon was cooked, Thomas cut it up and told Harry to add it to her pan along with the mushrooms and the red pepper. "Crack six eggs, and whip them with a fork."

When she cracked the first egg rather gingerly, he grimaced. "Do it with passion."

Her eyes sparkled. "I shall do it with the flourish of a countess!"

"That's better," he approved. "Now pour in the eggs and brown the omelettes on both sides." He handed her a wooden spatula and stepped back.

Thomas brought two plates, and she successfully lifted the delicious-smelling omelette from the pan and divided it. "I'm so clever."

"Absolutely brilliant." He pulled out a chair for her at the kitchen table and they both sat down to eat. When he had devoured the last mouthful, he declared, "Not bad for an amateur. What shall we make for dessert?"

"I enjoyed the pears we had the other night."

"That's good, since they are in season now. I'll teach you to make pears flambé."

"French dessert sounds sinful."

"Then it should be right up your alley. Back to the pantry and find some preserved berries. I'll get the brandy."

Harry came back with a jar of preserved black cherries. "These look good."

"First you have to core the pears." He handed her a paring knife. "You needn't peel them if you enjoy the skin." He unscrewed the metal cap on the jar and removed the plug of preservative wax. "Spoon some cherries and juice into the pan, add sugar, and heat it to a simmer. When it bubbles, pop in the pear halves, and pour on some brandy. I'll whip some cream."

Harry followed his instructions. Then Thomas lit a taper from the stove and handed it to her. "I won't deprive you of the fun part. Set the brandy alight and jump back."

Her eyes were bright as the flame she wielded. "Keep that bucket of sand handy!" She set the pan aflame and hopped back. When the blue flame stopped burning, she divided the concoction into two dessert bowls and anointed them with a dollop of cream.

This time Thomas sat down at the table and pulled her into his lap. "This is the way dessert à deux must be eaten." Laughing like children, they fed each other and licked their lips between kisses.

The next day, Thomas took his wife before him on his black hunter. Shugborough estate was on the edge of Cannock Chase, an area of outstanding natural beauty. He spoke softly with his lips close to her ear. "We'll go easy at first. This is the largest swath of heathland in all the Midland counties and it teems with wildlife. This place has it all — woodland, grassland, and wetland habitat."

Harry was enthralled at the abundance of small animals that made their home in the different sections of the chase. They entered a coppice of oak and birch trees.

"Cannock Forest is mentioned in the Domesday Book. Some of these trees are five hundred years old. Richard the First granted the chase to the bishop of Lichfield."

"What a pity you don't still own it. Oh, look, a herd of deer! But they are white."

"They are fallow deer, first brought here and released by the Normans. But there are also herds of red deer, and muntjac that bark like dogs."

Harry slid her arms around his neck and kissed him. "Thomas Anson, I love you! I know of no other man who would not hunt these creatures."

"Think of it as our own private wildlife preserve."

When they emerged into the grassland, they startled a covey of game birds.

"What are they?"

"Gray nightjars. See their black bills and white-tipped tail feathers? Now that we've disturbed them, we can ride hell for leather.

Are you ready?"

Harry nodded eagerly. "Ready when you are, my lord."

When they arrived back at the hall in the late afternoon, they learned that yet another delivery had been made. A huge wooden crate with bits of straw falling from it awaited them in the kitchens.

Mrs. Stearn handed Harry a letter addressed to Harriet Anson, Countess of Lichfield.

When Thomas glanced at it, he recognized his mother's handwriting. "Read it."

Harry obeyed his declaration, and gasped with delight. "Oh, Thomas, your mother has made us a wedding gift of her prized Chinese porcelain collection. She says its rightful place is Shugborough."

He opened the crate, and they both carefully lifted out the exquisite pieces and set them on a long kitchen table.

"After dinner, will you help me wash them so we can put them on display in the dining room?"

He enfolded her in his arms and kissed her. "I never heard of a countess who washed her own porcelain. It thrills me that you treasure this collection, Harry."

Hours later, when they retired, she stood

at the bedchamber window. An autumn wind had come up suddenly and was blowing the leaves from the trees. "I'm sorry that our fortnight is up, and our honeymoon must end."

He came up behind her and nuzzled the nape of her neck. "Our honeymoon will never end." He wrapped his arms around her. "Don't be sad, Harry."

"Oh, I'm not sad, darling. This was one of the most glorious days of my life."

His arms tightened and he murmured suggestively, "And it isn't over yet."

She sighed with happiness. "Our time at Shugborough has been absolute perfection."

CHAPTER TWENTY-ONE

The door at 15 St. James's Square swung open, and Thomas carried Harry over the threshold and set her down in the elegant reception hall.

"This is Norton, who proved indispensable to my mother and me during the last difficult year. As reward," Thomas declared, "I've promoted him to butler."

"I am delighted to meet you, Norton."

"This is Mrs. Simpson, our housekeeper and cook."

Harry smiled and held out her hand. "I met you before when I came to dinner."

"Please call me Clara, Lady Lichfield."

"I will call you Clara, if you will call me Lady Harry."

Thomas lifted a bag from the doorstep. "You can meet the rest of the staff later. I know you want to go upstairs and change your traveling clothes."

"Lady Lichfield . . . I mean the Dowager

Lady Lichfield left a letter for you." Clara handed it to Harry. "She took her lady's maid with her on her travels."

"That's all right. I can manage without a maid."

As they ascended the staircase, Thomas explained, "The layout is much the same as Hampden House, though we don't have a ballroom. The kitchen and servants' quarters are on the main floor, the drawing room, dining room, library, etcetera are on the second floor, and the bedchambers and bathroom are up on the third."

They stopped on the second floor so Harry could view the rooms. "Oh, lovely, there is a cozy breakfast room that lets in the morning sun."

"And this chamber is a private sitting room. It's less formal than the drawing room."

Thomas led the way to the third floor and opened his bedchamber door.

She stepped inside and gazed about. "Because there is no ballroom, the bedchambers are spacious. You have marvelous taste, Thomas."

He set down the bag and cupped her face. "In women as well as furnishings. I want you to feel free to change anything you like. Not just in here, but in the whole place. It is your house now."

"I won't change anything in here. I like it just the way it is." The curtains and bed hangings were royal blue velvet. The wardrobe and tall bureaus were polished red mahogany. The deep-piled Turkish carpet was patterned in vivid red, gold, and blue. "We even have a fireplace to keep us warm on winter nights."

"I'll keep you warm on winter nights."

"I shall hold you to that promise, you wicked devil."

"There's a small dressing room through that door that will accommodate your substantial wardrobe. It has an adjoining door that leads to the bathroom."

"How convenient. This is such a lovely big house for just the two of us. I'm used to sharing with a horde of brothers and sisters. I shall enjoy our privacy." Harry opened the letter from her husband's mother. "She's gone to visit your sisters before she travels to Wales. She apologizes for taking her maid, but thinks it best I choose my own. She wishes us every happiness." She handed the letter to Thomas.

"She's very generous and selfless. The house is now mine, though the furnishings are hers. But she prefers to leave it intact for our convenience."

"I'm amazed she took nothing with her except her maid. I shall pay a visit on Mother tomorrow and steal away one of her servants."

"I should take my seat in the Lords tomorrow. I'll have a lot of catching up to do."

"If you have no objection, I shall attend the women's rights meeting at Langham Place on Friday. Since I'm now a married woman, I can go in the evening."

He hid his amusement. "I have no objection, but even if I did, I warrant you would do exactly as you wished."

"After only a fortnight of marriage, you know me so well."

"I've *known* you since we met at the opening of the Crystal Palace in June."

"Not in the *biblical* sense," she teased.

"Think of all the months I wasted."

His words thrilled her, and she sighed happily. "I can't believe it's October. The winter social Season is upon us, and Christmas will be here before we know it."

"Harry, there will be times you'll have to attend social functions without me. I am not a member of the idle rich. I have to earn my money."

"That's the price I have to pay for marrying a ruthless businessman." She laughed. "We'll be kept so busy until the year ends;

then suddenly it will be spring and we can return to our beloved Shugborough." She turned her back so that he could unfasten her traveling dress. "Do you suppose I have time to take a bath before dinner?"

"There might be time if you allow me to help."

"I wouldn't have it any other way," she purred. Then her eyes sparkled with mischief. "You can start by running my water."

He swung her up into his arms and bit her ear. "You need your arse tanned."

"Harry, darling, you look so happy." Her mother embraced her. "I don't need to ask if you enjoyed being at Shugborough. You've coveted the place since you were a child."

"Being there was a dream come true. When Riley arrived with the books and paintings, Thomas and I had the time of our lives restoring them to their rightful places. It was extremely generous of you and Father."

Beatrix, with their sister Jane in tow, arrived in the drawing room. "Oh, Harry, it is so good to see you. D'Arcy and I just returned to London. Congratulations on your marriage! Did you thoroughly enjoy your honeymoon?"

"It was wonderful. Thomas managed to

restore almost all of Shugborough's classic statues. Now if we could just learn who owns the pair of black marble centaurs so we could get them back, it would be perfect."

"What on earth are centaurs?" Trixy asked.

"Mythical creatures that are half man and half horse."

"They sound hideous to me. My honeymoon at Lambton Castle was divine. We hosted the annual pheasant shoot, and in return we received so many invitations we couldn't keep up with them. Then D'Arcy got the official news that he had been appointed lord lieutenant of Durham. We threw a huge party to celebrate, and I was the belle of the ball. I absolutely adore being the Countess of Durham!"

"The role suits you well, Trixy. Congratulations on your husband's appointment. Being the wife of the lord lieutenant carries a great deal of prestige and responsibility. Why don't you come with me to Langham Place Friday night to the women's rights meeting?" Harry invited. "I'm going to join the Married Women's Property Committee, and I think you should join too."

"Why would I want to do that?" Trixy asked.

"We want to get a law passed that married women can own property. You may be a wealthy countess and live in a castle, but you cannot own a stick or a stone in your own right. Even if your husband were generous enough to give you property, it would have to be held in trust for you. For the sake of any daughters you may have, you should help us get the law changed." Harry added an incentive. "As the Countess of Durham and the lord lieutenant's wife, your name will carry a great deal of weight and have a profound influence."

"I'll think on it. If I have no social obligations on Friday evening, I may join you."

Harry hid her satisfaction, but she saw the knowing look on her mother's face. *Not much escapes the shrewd Duchess of Abercorn.*

"I must dash," Trixy declared. "I have an appointment to be fitted for some new gowns this afternoon. The winter Season is upon us, and I intend to be a lady of fashion. It's so much fun having a great deal of money to spend."

When Beatrix left, the duchess glanced at Harry with speculation. "I warrant the first thing you'll do is manipulate her into donating an obscene amount of money to the Widows and Orphans Fund of Durham."

"Persuade her, perhaps." Harry's eyes sparkled. "Never *manipulate.*"

Jane laughed. "I've missed you. With you and Trixy married, and James away at Oxford, I have no one to amuse me. Will you invite me to dinner one evening and give me the grand tour of St. James's Square?"

"You are most welcome anytime." She gave Jane a knowing wink. "Perhaps I'll persuade Thomas to invite one of his bachelor friends. That should amuse you."

"Oh, thank you, Harry. Your powers of persuasion are formidable."

"Next Wednesday," the duchess decided, "we'll have a family dinner with my married daughters and their charming husbands. Perhaps that will persuade Abercorn to spend the night at home rather than the palace."

"Your powers of manipulation are far superior to mine," Harry teased. "Oh, while we are on the subject of manipulation, Mother, I have a favor to ask. You have such a large staff; could you let me have one of your maids?"

"That depends on who you have in mind."

"It's Rose, of course. We get along so well."

"You may ask her, but the decision must

be Rose's."

"Thank you. I'll go and ask her now."

Harry found Rose in the nursery, helping Mary, one of the nursemaids. She was sewing on buttons that had come off the children's winter clothes.

"Hello, Rose. How would you feel about moving to St. James's Square as my personal lady's maid?"

She jumped up and curtsied. "Lady Harriet — I mean Lady Lichfield — I've no training as a lady's maid."

"Call me Harry. You are perfectly capable of looking after my clothes, helping me dress, and going about London with me, but if you'd rather stay at Hampden House, I will understand."

"I'd love to come, Lady Harry," she said breathlessly. "It's just that Lady Abercorn gives my family the clothes that her children outgrow, and she gives me food to take home on Saturdays."

"I promise you'll still get the clothes, and you can go home every Saturday, and not empty-handed. Is there anything else that concerns you?"

"Well . . . Lord Anson — I mean the Earl of Lichfield — is . . ." Rose hesitated.

"Dark, dominant, and rather intimidating?"

"Well, yes."

Harry laughed. "He can be sober and straitlaced. That's why I need you as an ally, Rose. He wouldn't dare beat me with you there to defend me."

Rose giggled, and then she sobered. "What will your mother say?"

"I already asked her. Though she will be loath to lose you, she said that the decision is yours."

"Then yes, I'd love to come and be lady's maid to the Countess of Lichfield."

"Wonderful! Put those buttons down and I'll help you to pack."

October and November flew by, filled with family dinners, social invitations, and visits to the theater. Harry went with her family on the nights her husband was occupied with business, and she cherished the evenings they spent at home together.

After dinner, Thomas usually spent time at his desk in the library working on accounts connected with Shugborough and his business ventures. He often had piles of letters and paperwork to attend to. But at precisely ten o'clock, Harry always took a jug of ale and joined him in the library. Before she had poured his drink, his full attention was riveted on his beautiful wife and the paperwork was forgotten.

"I love this nightly ritual where you lure me from my work and lead me into temptation."

"I like to share your ale." She drank from his mug, and between mouthfuls she lifted her lips for his kisses.

"You intoxicate me," he whispered. "I can't wait to carry you upstairs."

"You wouldn't have to wait if your desk wasn't always so cluttered," she teased.

He slanted a dark eyebrow. "There's always the floor."

"You have no shame. Besides, I much prefer the carpet in our bedroom."

He didn't give her time to finish the ale. He swept her into his arms, held her high against his heart, and carried her up to their private sanctuary.

As promised, Harry took Trixy to the Langham Place women's rights meeting, and when they learned that she was the Countess of Durham, they shrewdly put her in charge of the Widows and Orphans Fund. The suffragists were masters of manipulation, and by means of flattery and deference soon had Beatrix Lambton doing their bidding. To Harry's delight, Trixy was convinced the committees couldn't manage without her, and she attended the Friday night meetings regularly.

Harry and Thomas dined early on the last Friday in November. "I'm amazed D'Arcy approves of his wife's visits to Langham Place."

Harry laughed. "Don't be silly, darling. Trixy doesn't tell him where she goes — he only knows she's with me. They don't live in each other's pocket. She says D'Arcy is out late most nights."

"I'm guilty in that respect too, lately, but at least I'm out on business. I'm happy you are occupied on Fridays. It gives me the opportunity to meet with various nobles who own furnishings and artifacts that once belonged to Shugborough. It's amazing how many of them are in the Lords. Word is out that I'm restoring the hall and I get tips every week. Tonight I'm meeting with Fritz, Earl Spencer. He bought some of our furniture for Althorp. Don't wait up for me, darling."

"Wouldn't it be wonderful if you could trace who bought the black marble centaurs?"

"I'll find out one of these days. You can rely on it."

His dark features were so deadly serious and his tone so resolute, she shivered.

■ ■ ■ ■

The first week of December was taken up with plans for Christmas. The Duke and Duchess of Abercorn decided they would invite the whole family to their Campden Hill estate in Kensington, and Harry was looking forward to seeing Uncle John and Fanny.

The post brought many social invitations to St. James's Square, and Harry was sorting through a dozen envelopes that had just been delivered. A letter addressed to Harriet Anson, Countess of Lichfield, that displayed no return address caught her attention and she carried it up to her private sitting room. She sat down, opened it, and read:

I have information that the late Earl of Lichfield had his attorney change his Last Will and Testament to disinherit his son and heir unless certain conditions were met with regard to marriage.

I would advise you to keep this letter confidential. If you do so, another will follow, indicating a time and place where this information may be passed on to you.

Harry's brows drew together, and a frisson of apprehension made her shudder. The letter itself was highly disturbing. *I'll show it to Thomas when he comes home. He must know what this is all about and will explain it to me.*

She read the letter again, carefully, and the warning to keep it confidential jumped out at her. *It has something to do with our marriage. If I want to learn more, I must keep quiet.* She decided not to say anything to Thomas until she received the next letter. She put the note back in the envelope and secreted it in her sitting room's writing desk.

That night at dinner, she waited until dessert was served, then asked casually, "What is the name of your attorney, Thomas?"

"You met him when we returned to London. Have you already forgotten? His name is Simon Kendall."

"Yes, now I remember. Was he your father's attorney?"

"Absolutely not. I cut all ties with the last law firm. Why do you ask?"

"Frances Cobbe at Langham Place asked if anyone could recommend an attorney."

Harry was immediately covered with guilt at the deliberate lie and changed the subject.

Some time after dinner, she made her way to the kitchen to tell Cook which nights they would be out and which they would be dining at home.

"Clara, do you know the name of the Ansons' last attorney?"

Clara rolled her eyes. "Martin Fowler. He was a dreadful man — spent more time here than the doctor. Her ladyship couldn't abide him."

"Then thank goodness we are well rid of him," she declared. "We'll only be dining at home on Thursday next week. You can have some time off if you like."

"Thank you, Lady Harry. I shall go and visit my sister."

The following morning, after a restless night plagued with worry, Harry retrieved the envelope from the writing desk and read it again. She was convinced that it came from Martin Fowler's law office, and was determined to learn the address and beard the lion in his den. She weighed whether to take Rose along and then decided against it.

"Rose, we are invited to Montagu House tonight and everyone will be dressed to the nines. I've decided to wear my jade velvet. Will you lay out my corset and a starched petticoat? I have matching shoes and fan somewhere in the dressing room."

"Don't worry, Lady Harry. I'll find everything you need."

"I have to go out. I should be back by early afternoon."

Harry took a hackney to the law district and got out at Chancery Lane. She entered the first law office she came to and made inquiries. She learned that Martin Fowler's office was in a building on Cursitor Street.

After much searching, she found a soot-blackened building bearing a sign that read fowler, attorney-at-law. Harry gathered her courage, raised her chin, and entered the offices. The smell of musty books assailed her nostrils. She assumed the thin young fellow with ink-stained hands, wearing wire-rimmed spectacles, was a clerk.

He looked at her agog. "Can I help you, my lady?"

"Yes. Kindly inform Martin Fowler that there is a lady here to see him."

The fellow disappeared through a door and after a few minutes that seemed like an hour to Harry, he returned. "I will make an appointment for you, my lady."

She tossed her head. "Appointment indeed!" She swept past the clerk, threw open the inner door, and entered the office. She stared at the man behind the desk. *He is malevolent — I mustn't underestimate him.* "I'm here to see Martin Fowler." She reached into her reticule, pulled out the letter, and slapped it down before him.

He read the name on the envelope. "Lady Lichfield?"

"You know who I am, and you know what the letter says, since you wrote it."

"Won't you have a seat, Lady Lichfield?"

She picked up the letter and sat down, covering her apprehension with an air of assumed confidence. She composed her features and braced herself to hear the revelation. *No matter what the wretched man says, I must not let him see my reaction.*

"Since your intelligence is obvious, I will dispense with subterfuge. When the Earl of Lichfield engaged me as his attorney-at-law, I enjoyed his full confidence and became privy to his wishes regarding his estate."

"You mean the *late* Earl of Lichfield."

His eyes hardened. "In May, I prepared the Last Will and Testament for the late Earl of Lichfield and at that time he confided that he was urging his son to marry. The cost of the upkeep and restoration of Shugborough weighed heavily on his mind. Since the earl had no wealth, he pressed his son to contract marriage with an heiress."

Harry felt her mouth go dry.

"Anson refused his father's advice and it became a bone of contention between them.

In June, Lichfield changed his Last Will to read that if his son wished to inherit Shugborough, he must wed an heiress before his father died."

Thomas and I met in June at the Crystal Palace. Her throat tightened.

"Anson was determined to control his father, whose health was deteriorating rapidly. They fought on a daily basis and by July, Lichfield had no choice but to prepare a signed affidavit stating that his son would be disinherited unless he wed a wealthy wife."

It was July when Thomas told D'Arcy that Trixy was mad about him. Harry had difficulty swallowing. "I warrant you cannot wait to show me the signed affidavit."

"It was stolen from my files along with the Earl of Lichfield's rightful Last Will and Testament."

Harry's lip curled in contempt. "A likely tale." *Why would he tell me this unless it was true?* Cold fingers squeezed her heart.

"I have every reason to believe Thomas Anson broke into my office."

Harry raised a defiant chin. "What is your purpose in telling me these things?"

"I wanted you to know what sort of a man you married, Lady Lichfield."

She gave him a pitying glance. "My husband and I have no secrets. He made it quite plain that we must marry before his father died. Thomas legally inherited the Lichfield title and Shugborough Hall and that is all that matters, Mr. Fowler. I bid you good day."

The carriage jolted and Harry came out of her trance. She realized she was riding in a hackney cab. She didn't recall leaving the attorney's dank office or what address she'd given the driver. She wished she didn't remember the things Fowler had said, but unfortunately every syllable he had uttered was indelibly etched in her mind.

She wanted to scream her denial, but she was suddenly remembering things that made denial difficult. When she'd asked Thomas why he'd told D'Arcy that Trixy was mad about him, he had replied: *"Because I couldn't let him marry you, of course."*

Harry's thoughts flew back to the time she'd asked Thomas why he was courting her. His answer echoed in her head: *"You are the daughter of wealthy nobility."*

She remembered the night they signed the marriage contract, and how surprised she was at his astuteness in negotiating that everything from Shugborough be returned. Then he had declared: *"I've made arrange-*

ments for us to be married at St. George's Chapel tomorrow at five o'clock. I'm sorry everything has to be rushed."

Harry thought about the night he came to Hampden House to propose marriage.

"I have no intention of declaring my undying love."

Her hand went to her throat. *I truly believed that Thomas loved me.* She was devastated to learn that he did not. *He married me to secure his inheritance. Shugborough means more to him than anything or anyone in the world. How could I have been so gullible?*

As Harry sat in the swaying carriage, she could feel her heart breaking.

When the hackney stopped at 15 St. James's Square, Harry paid the driver and walked listlessly into the house. She climbed the stairs slowly to her private sitting room, put the letter back in her writing desk, and sank into a chair. Her thoughts were in turmoil, her emotions were in chaos, and her happiness was shattered. For the first time in her life, Harry did not know what to do or say. She was so overwhelmed with sadness and disappointment, and so afraid of what she might learn, that she knew she could not bring herself to confront her husband.

"Are you cold, Lady Harry?"

She blinked. "Rose, I didn't hear you come in."

"Let me take your hat and coat."

Harry stood up and allowed Rose to remove them.

"Since dinner at Montagu House will be hours away, I'll get Clara to prepare you a substantial afternoon tea."

She shook her head. "No, thank you. I have no appetite today."

Rose gave her an odd look, and put some coal on the fire. "I'll let you rest."

Hours later, Rose found Harry sitting in the same chair. "I laid out your jade velvet gown and everything else you'll need."

"There's no hurry." Harry glanced at the window and saw it was dark outside. *How long have I been sitting here? Thomas could be home any minute. I must get ready now. I don't want him to find me half-dressed.* "I want you to help me, Rose. We must hurry."

Harry sat before her mirror in her corset and petticoat, absently brushing her hair.

"I believe you have some lovely hair ornaments that match your gown."

"Never mind, Rose. I can't be bothered with such things." She heard a footfall on the stairs. "Quick! Help me into this dress."

460

on their way to spend the festivities with Harry's family at Campden Hill. He thought that his wife looked unusually pale today. "Are you feeling all right, darling?"

"I never felt better." She tucked her fur against her throat and gazed out the window.

"Is something wrong, Harry?"

"Of course not. It's Christmas, the most exciting time of the year. My family loves and adores me, and I'm married to an earl of the realm. What could possibly be wrong?"

"When we're alone, you seem distant and withdrawn."

"Nonsense; it's simply fatigue from all the season's festivities. Please, don't concern yourself with some imagined problem."

There was a problem, and it wasn't imagined, but Thomas bit his tongue. He didn't want to upset her at Christmas. In spite of the fact that she said she felt well, her paleness disturbed him, and his common sense told him that something was ailing her. If she wouldn't confide in him, he hoped she would discuss it with her mother.

At Campden Hill, all the men went out to cut the Christmas tree. Thomas joined Abercorn, Lord John, D'Arcy, and young James, home from Oxford. After they set up the tree, the ladies and the younger children had great fun decorating it, and Thomas saw that Harry joined in. She seemed to be enjoying herself, though she was a bit subdued.

Harry spent her time with the children, reading to them and then putting them to bed. Thomas took her mother aside. "Have you noticed how pale Harry is? She insists she feels well, but I'm worried about her."

"She's spent hours with the children today. Perhaps she is practicing."

When Thomas took her meaning, his heart soared. "Perhaps you are right, but she hasn't said anything."

"A woman usually keeps her secret until she is sure. Don't worry, Thomas; she'll tell you in her own good time. I'm speculating about Trixy — she's plump as a partridge."

Harry sat in the darkened nursery long after the excited children hung up their stockings and had at last fallen asleep. She had avoided her husband's company by surrounding herself with the little ones. Their obvious love made her feel less vulnerable.

Knowing that Thomas had married her to secure his inheritance was deeply humiliating. Harry's pride had been dealt a mortal blow, and her self-confidence had deserted her. When she looked in the mirror, she found the image that looked back at her unattractive. She appeared pale and listless, and her eyes had a haunted look. Harry lived in dread of her family learning the truth of why Thomas had married her. The last thing she wanted was pity, so she had put on a false face of gaiety and laughter when she was in their company.

What a naive fool I was to go about telling everyone I needed proof that Thomas loved me before I would accept a proposal of marriage. She closed her eyes. *Perhaps there's no such thing as love.* She shook her head sadly. She knew that wasn't true, because regardless of how her husband felt, she loved Thomas with all her heart.

She had avoided intimacy as often as she could because she was terrified of her wanton response to him. She often pretended sleep when he came to bed, because his touch set off a wildfire of desire. If he knew how much she hungered and longed for his love, she would be mortified.

Music from downstairs floated up to her, and she knew the Yuletide carols had begun. She straightened her shoulders and went below to join in the festivities. Harry was relieved when the ladies decided to retire and the men stayed up to talk politics and enjoy a couple of drinks together, without reproachful looks from their spouses.

Christmas Day was taken up with presents, a huge feast, and sleigh rides around the lake. The entire family joined in the merriment and Harry was never alone with Thomas.

The next morning when it was time to leave, the duchess invited her married daughters to stay at Campden Hill until New Year's, while their husbands returned to London. Thomas encouraged Harry to stay. A few days apart might be just what his wife needed, and he thought she would benefit from time spent with her mother and sisters. He kissed her good-bye and promised to return for the New Year's Eve fireworks.

The following day, when Louisa and her three oldest daughters were alone, Trixy confided that she might be having a child. Harry was relieved that all the attention was focused on her sister. All the talk was centered on symptoms, cravings, weight gain, and babies, babies, babies.

Trixy explained that she had no intention of telling D'Arcy until she was sure. She was uncertain of his reaction and needed her mother's assurance that he would be happy about becoming a father.

"All men look forward to begetting an heir, and if it turns out to be a girl, they welcome the chance to try again," Louisa told her daughters. "How about you, Harry? Any secrets to confide?"

Her hand went to her throat. "Secrets?" Then she realized they were still talking about babies. "No, no, I'm not having a child."

"Good!" Trixy declared. "I don't want you to steal my thunder."

On New Year's Eve, D'Arcy arrived, but Thomas did not. Harry found her emotions were between the devil and the deep. She was relieved that business must have prevented him from joining them, yet wistful that he did not rush from London so they could celebrate their first New Year together. He showed up the next day with profound apologies, and on the ride home, Harry lapsed back into silence.

Thomas gave his wife time to unpack and refresh herself from the journey. Then he joined her in her private sitting room. He schooled himself to patience, but knew he was dangerously close to the end of his rope.

"Are you feeling all right, darling? Please tell me what's wrong."

"There is nothing wrong."

Thomas exploded. "Damn it all, Harry, there is something terribly wrong! It is a brand-new year, and I intend to start it with a clean sweep. If you think I'm going to carry on allowing you to withdraw from me, you are deluding yourself. What the hellfire happened to that audacious, outspoken baggage that gave as good as she got? I married an impulsive, reckless creature with a voracious appetite for life. I want her back!"

She jumped to her feet, goaded by his words. At last her anger ignited, and her temper flared, turning her pale cheeks to bright pink. "I *deluded* myself, all right! I actually believed you married me because you loved me!" She rushed to her writing desk, pulled out the letter, and thrust it at him. "I had no idea you married me to secure your inheritance. I was blissfully ignorant!"

He tore the letter from the envelope and read it. "Fowler!" He laughed bitterly. "Knowing human nature as I do, I should have expected the vindictive bastard would need to slake his revenge for being dismissed. Where's the other letter?"

"I didn't wait for another letter. I suspected it was from your father's attorney. I found out his name was Martin Fowler and went to see him."

"Why the hell didn't you come to me?" he demanded.

"I wanted to hear for myself what he had to say," she said defiantly. "He informed me that your father swore out a signed affidavit to disinherit you unless you married an heiress before he died. It was like a knife in my heart to learn the real reason for the rushed wedding."

"Oh, Harry, no wonder you've been so unhappy." He wanted to enfold her in his arms and take away her pain, but he feared she would recoil from him. "Sit down, and I will explain everything."

She sat, desperately wanting to hear him refute Fowler's accusations.

"My father never stopped hounding me to marry an heiress, as he had done, for the upkeep of Shugborough. He wed my mother, went through her fortune, and brought her nothing but unhappiness. I vowed I wouldn't follow in his footsteps, and told him so.

"Then I met you, Harry, and you stole my heart. I didn't want him to know anything about you, so when he ordered me to find a wealthy wife, I told him to go to the devil. It infuriated him when he couldn't control me, and as a way to force me to his will, he signed an affidavit to disinherit me."

"Why didn't you confide in me?" She raised her chin. "I trusted you, implicitly."

"Confide that I was being coerced to marry an heiress? I think not! When your father offered me your dowry, I refused it, and told him to put the money in your name."

"I didn't realize that." She was momentarily disarmed. "But you cannot deny you negotiated that my father return everything he bought from Shugborough."

"I don't deny it. I freely admit how significantly I benefited from that, but I knew how much you loved Shugborough, and believed it would make you happy if the books and paintings were restored."

"You should have taken me into your confidence. If I'd known you had to marry before he died to secure Shugborough, I would have agreed."

"Harry, I didn't need to marry to secure my inheritance. The laws of primogeniture would have prevailed. The choice to marry you was mine alone."

"Then why did you have to break into Fowler's office and steal the signed affidavit?"

"I refuse to be blackmailed!" His face was hard, dark, carved in stone.

"Tell me the truth, the *whole* truth, Thomas. I don't want secrets between us."

His dark eyes searched her face as he calculated how much he could tell her. He decided to take a chance and reveal some of the truth.

"My father died an hour before we were married. I vowed that I would not allow his death to ruin your wedding day. Your happiness meant everything to me, so I kept it from you until the next morning."

Harry was astounded by the revelation. Even if he had done it to protect her, it was still an act of deception. "Thomas, I am not a child who needs to be shielded from reality. I am a woman and want to be treated like one." She was still unsure whether he was being completely honest with her. He said he'd lost his heart to her and had wed her from free choice, but could she believe him? "I want no more secrets between us. From now on, I want the truth."

"More than anything, I want you to believe that I married you because I love you. That is the truth, Harry, and I will do my utmost to prove it to you from this moment forward."

"I lost my trust in you." She raised her chin and said coolly, "Don't expect me to fall into your arms until it is restored."

I will woo you relentlessly and win back your heart.

Harry awoke late the next morning. She felt disheartened when she saw that the bed was empty. But a moment later, Thomas arrived with a breakfast tray, and her spirits lifted.

He set the food before her and drew her hand to his lips. He placed a kiss on each finger, then opened her palm and dropped a kiss inside it. He folded her fingers upon it to catch and hold it. "Enjoy your breakfast. I'll see you tonight."

As she was brushing her hair, she found a note on her dressing table. She picked it up and read it. The words astonished her:

My only love, you enthrall me. Your image is before me day and night. Your loveliness haunts me. I have an unquenchable thirst for you. When I hear your voice, it fills me with joy. When I see you across a room, I have to draw close to you. When I am close to you, I have an uncontrollable need to touch you. When I touch you, I become wild with desire. From the hour that we met at the Crystal Palace, I loved you. And today I love you more than yesterday.

The love words warmed her heart, and she knew she would keep the note so that she could read it again when doubts assailed her.

When Thomas returned from Parliament that evening, he brought her flowers. "These daffodils, grown in a hothouse, are to remind you of the riverside garden at Shugborough. They are a promise of spring."

When she thanked him, his eyes told her how attractive he found her. "Come with me to the kitchen. I want to cook for you."

"A clever ploy! You know I cannot resist food." *He knows my appetite has been nonexistent lately.* She followed him, determined to eat something.

He picked her up and sat her on the wooden chopping block. "What do you fancy?"

"Something spicy, perhaps with curry. I think Clara bought prawns today."

He returned from the larder with two small enamel pails. "Scallops too — we'll have both." He put rice on to steam, while he cleaned the shellfish, and cut up shallots, mushrooms, gingerroot, and cilantro. He melted a generous amount of butter in a pan, threw in the prawns, scallops, and the other ingredients, sprinkled on a generous

amount of spicy curry, and sautéed everything until it was bubbling, golden, and
fragrant. He served it over the rice, brought
it to the chopping block, and hopped up
beside her.

"This smells good enough to eat."

"It's sinfully good. Take care, lest it lure
you into temptation."

"Thank you for the warning," she said
lightly.

Hours later, when they retired, Harry
expected Thomas to make advances, but
after he built up the fire, he invited her to
join him in a game of Fox and Geese. It
was played on a checkerboard; the fox tried
to eat the geese, while the player with the
geese tried to trap the fox. Thomas won easily, and when she challenged him to a re-
match, she was gratified to beat him. Then
she suspected he'd let her win on purpose.
She decided not to accuse him. Perhaps he
was merely being gallant.

When she undressed, she tried not to
think about the times he had eagerly helped
her, and when she lay beside him in bed,
she made sure there was a space between
them. She wasn't yet ready to forgive him,
though she was pleased at the special attention he had shown that day. When he kissed

her hair and bade her good night, she didn't know if she was relieved or disappointed.

Bringing her breakfast in bed and penning her love notes became a ritual. On a warm day at the end of January, Thomas left for Parliament, but returned within a half hour. "It's far too lovely a day to waste, and I'm sure the Lords won't even notice my absence. Would you join me on a ride to Richmond?"

His eyes were filled with hope, and she bit back the excuse that sprang to her lips. If she was being truthful, she'd like nothing better than to go for a long ride. She was fully aware that Thomas was trying to woo her, but what woman didn't enjoy being wooed?

"Richmond sounds delightful."

He entered her dressing room and came out with her green riding dress. "Wear this."

"You are back to making declarations."

"Am I?" Their eyes met, and she vividly remembered lying in the grass, half-naked, urging him to make love to her. The green habit had obviously lingered in his memory.

She suddenly felt shy. "Go and get the horses saddled. I'll be right down."

His hands did not linger as he helped her mount Amber. She tried not to gaze at him astride Victorious, though he made her pulse race whenever she saw him on the black hunter. Side by side, they cantered through St. James's Park and headed toward the river.

Then they rode along the Thames embankment, enjoying the myriad watercraft carrying produce from the country up to London. They crossed Putney Bridge, rode over Putney Heath, and headed into Richmond Park.

"It's such a lovely day, I'm glad you persuaded me to join you. Look! The crocuses are up. I hope I see some snowdrops."

"There may be some in the walled garden at the inn. We are too late for breakfast, but could I tempt you to join me for lunch?"

"Since you are *inviting* me rather than *commanding* me, I accept with pleasure."

"First, we'll ride hell for leather," he declared, and knew she'd be unable to resist.

"You devil!" She urged Amber to a wild gallop, determined to win the race through the park. The last stretch, their mounts were neck and neck, and Harry threw back her head and laughed. She had forgotten how good it felt to drink the cup of life to the dregs.

"You look radiant."

You said that the first time you brought me to Richmond. She remembered how he had

476

taken her up before him to ride hell for leather. She could still feel his hard cock against her bum, and the grip of his muscled thighs. The wooing had been delicious.

Was it love or lust? her suspicious mind questioned. *Surely, if it had been lust, you would have taken me when I offered myself to you.*

Harry dismounted before he could help her. They turned their horses over to the hostler and went through the gate into the garden. Because it was enclosed by the stone wall that protected it from the wind, birds had made their winter home here, and white snowdrops and purple and yellow crocuses were lifting their faces to the pale sun.

They enjoyed lamb and barley broth with chunks of crusty baked bread, warm from the oven, followed by treacle tart, and hot mulled cider. When Harry was done, she scattered her crumbs for the birds, watching with delight as they fluttered down from the branches as hunger overcame their timidity.

Thomas reached across the rustic table and covered her hand. "Because of you, I find walled gardens unbelievably romantic. This one has happy memories for me. Thank you for coming today."

"Thank you for inviting me." The romantic atmosphere had disarmed her and made her more conducive to closing the distance between them.

On the ride home they followed the river until they came to Chelsea. They rode through a wooded area of cedars and elm trees that were just coming into bud. Beneath the shelter of the branches, a patch of bluebells had sprung up through the moss.

"I love bluebells. Their intense fragrance is heady and overpowering."

Thomas drew rein and jumped from the saddle. He picked a solitary bluebell and brought it to her. "Like attracts like — heady and overpowering."

With sparkling eyes, she lifted it to her nose and breathed in its intoxicating scent, beguiled by his romantic gesture.

That night when she got into bed, Thomas drew the side bed-curtains, but left the foot open to let in the warmth of the fire. He lay on his side facing Harry with his head propped on his hand. The drawn curtains turned their bed into an intimate cocoon that shut out the world. "Bathed in the fire glow, you look like an enchantress from a mythic tale. . . . *Circe* perhaps."

Her lips curved into a smile. "Circe could

turn men into animals with her magic. If I had her power, I would turn you into a black centaur."

"So you could ride me," he murmured suggestively.

His words evoked such a sensual picture in her mind, she went weak with desire. "You look dark and dangerous tonight."

"Perhaps I am. Does *dark and dangerous* attract or repel you?"

"Both." She shuddered.

"You have the most wondrous hair. I ache to caress it and play with it." His hand reached out. "Like this." He threaded his fingers through her curls possessively, feeling their silky texture. His hand moved down to her shoulder. "Your skin feels like creamy, smooth velvet." He traced her clavicle with a finger. Then he cupped her right breast in the palm of his hand and caressed its pink tip through her sheer nightgown gently with his thumb.

You have the most seductive hands in the world. She thought of pulling away, but she was enjoying his caresses too much to deny herself the exquisite pleasure.

"Harry, tonight I'm going to show you how much I adore you. I intend to prove beyond a shadow of a doubt that I am passionately in love with you." He pulled down the covers, slipped off her nightgown, and drew her into his arms.

He began with quick kisses to her temples, eyelids, and the corners of her mouth. His lips kissed her hair, traced along her cheekbone to her ear, and then slid down against her throat. He whispered love words against her sensitive skin, inhaling her woman's scent, as his tongue licked over her delicate flesh.

She could not wait for his mouth to claim hers. She opened her lips in sensual invitation and for a whole hour they lost themselves in the bliss of slow, melting kisses.

His manly scent made her senses reel. The feel of his powerful hands caressing her body aroused her until her pulse quickened and her blood ached hot and wild. When she felt his hard erection seeking against her soft belly, she wanted to scream. Her nails dug into his shoulders as she tried to stop herself from moaning with excitement.

He came over her in the dominant position and slowly thrust inside her. He felt her sheath close sleekly around his cock, and his breath swept her neck as his lips sought hers, and he drank from her honeyed mouth that was hot and sweet with desire.

"I love you, sweetheart. I love everything about you. I love the way you feel; I love your scent; I love your taste." He began to move with a slow, tantalizing rhythm, wanting to draw out her pleasure and make it last. "When I see you flushed with passion, excitement stabs through me and makes me long to make you lose control."

She gasped as his plunging heat made its relentless demands upon her to yield up everything to him. She loved his animal maleness. Everything about him was hard. His chest and shoulders, even his thighs, were corded with muscle. Tonight he took her to the edge, and she found it impossible to hold back physically. She matched his thrusts by arching her body, and his throbbing fullness inside her made her cry out with pleasure.

He became aware of a pulse point deep within. It fluttered erratically and her sheath tightened, inflaming him to unleash the fierce passion that would bring her to her final surrender. When he felt her climax begin, his thrusts slowed to an undulating rhythm. When he heard her shattering cry, he took his own release.

He gathered her close. "I've never felt this way before. I love you deeply from the bottom of my heart. I pledge my love to you now and forever."

She reveled in his vows of adoration, and

longed to believe that he loved her. She had long ago lost her heart to him, and now she willingly admitted that her body was his to command. But some small protective part of her being made her hold back the words.

She feared that declaring her undying love for Thomas at this moment would make her too vulnerable. He was dominant by nature, and if she told him how much she loved him, he would be in complete control of her. *I must be absolutely sure that he is in love with me.*

He kissed her tenderly and she sighed and drifted off to sleep with her head tucked beneath his chin.

Hours later something woke her. She lay quietly, wondering what had disturbed her.

Suddenly she felt her husband's legs begin to thrash and he shouted something.

"What is it?" she asked softly.

Thomas sat bolt upright. He threw back the covers and shouted, "Fire!"

Fear rushed over her. "Where is the fire?"

He jumped from the bed and ran to the window. "Everything's ablaze."

Harry rushed to his side, but all she saw outside was darkness. "Where is it?"

"Shugborough. I must save Shugborough!"

Harry grabbed his arms. "Thomas, we are

in London."

He stared at her until he realized where he was. "Thank God. It was my recurring nightmare."

Harry lit the lamp, and she watched him walk back to the bed, pull back the curtains, and sit down.

"I'm sorry to frighten you. It was just a dream."

"You said it was a recurring nightmare. You've obviously had it before."

"No, no, they don't happen often. I haven't had the nightmare since we've been married," he reassured her.

She could see that he was shaking. "Get back into bed."

"No, it will come back."

She heard the apprehension in his voice. It was the first time she had seen his vulnerability and her heart turned over in her breast. She went to him and cupped his face in her hands. "Darling, I will hold you — I won't let it come back."

His dark eyes stared up at her. He did not dare to show her his weakness.

"Thomas, if you love me, you will trust me enough to share the truth." She turned down the lamp, got back into bed, and waited.

Finally, he slipped into bed and pulled up

the covers.

When Harry enfolded him in her arms, he was still shaking. Gradually, as the warmth of her body seeped into his, his limbs grew still. "Tell me," she whispered.

Eventually he spoke. "I have a deep-seated fear that Shugborough will be destroyed by fire. I try to suppress it, but it manifests itself in dreams."

"How long have you had these dreams?"

He remained silent.

"Don't you remember?"

When he didn't answer, her arms tightened.

"I remember exactly."

She waited patiently, willing him to confide in her.

Finally, he told her. "It began when I was seventeen. It was right after my father burned down his sporting estate, Ranton Abbey, for the insurance money."

She was shocked beyond belief at Lichfield's perfidy, but she remained silent, and in a low, confiding voice he told her everything that happened that day. When he was done, he slid his arms around her and they held each other close.

Harry was finally convinced that her husband loved her enough to trust her, and the last barrier was swept away. "Thomas, I love you with all my heart."

CHAPTER TWENTY-THREE

"I shall be glad when February is over. I've never known such rain." The Duchess of Abercorn greeted her two married daughters, and led the way into the drawing room, where Jane was eagerly awaiting her sisters.

"Harry, you are absolutely blooming," Jane declared. "You were so thin and pale at Christmastime, I was worried about you."

Louisa glanced at her daughters. "In my experience, the best beauty tonic is love."

Harry laughed. "I take a spoonful every night when I go to bed." She winked mischievously. "Sometimes I take two."

Jane blushed, her mother laughed, and Trixy, not to be outdone, said, "I'm the one who is *blooming!* I'm absolutely sure. My breasts have enlarged so much, I'm having a new wardrobe made."

"I'm very happy for you, Beatrix." Harry hugged her sister.

"Congratulations, darling. D'Arcy must

be proud as Punch. When is it to be?"

"I'm not exactly sure — sometime in the month of August, I believe."

The duchess opened her planning book and wrote it down. "I invited you to afternoon tea to discuss our plans. Your father and I intend to go to Ireland early this year. We will need more than a month, because we want to visit Rachel and James at Kilkenny before we go to Barons Court. We plan to be away for March and April, so we can be back at the beginning of May for Jane's Season." Louisa gave her daughters a speaking look. "There will be no rushed weddings this time." She turned to Trixy. "August will be the perfect time for the arrival of my first grandchild."

"I miss Rachel." Harry set down her teacup. "Jane, ask her to come to your debut ball. Talk her into coming back with you for a visit."

Her mother gave Harry a speculative look. "You could come to Ireland with us."

"Thank you for the lovely invitation, but Thomas and I are looking forward to Shugborough in April. Spring can't come fast enough for me."

"D'Arcy and I are dining with the Marlboroughs tonight at Spencer House. That must be close by your house, Harry."

"It's not far. Spencer House is closer to Green Park."

"George Churchill, the Duke of Marlborough, is on his third wife. He's a grasping sort of man," the duchess said. "His father gambled and left terrible debts, so it's no wonder he's avaricious. I heard he charges for shooting parties at Blenheim Palace. I hope he doesn't have his eye on D'Arcy's coffers."

"Marlborough is the lord lieutenant for Oxfordshire. That's how he and D'Arcy know each other. I'd best be off. I have to go through my wardrobe and find a gown that still fits me." Trixy kissed her mother and sisters and bade them good-bye.

"Speaking of wardrobes, the children are growing like weeds. I have to go through their clothes before we go to Ireland. I know they'll need lots of bigger things."

"That's good," Harry declared. "Leave whatever they have outgrown in a neat pile and Rose and I will take it round to Soho."

"How is Rose doing? Did she learn the ropes of becoming a lady's maid?"

Harry laughed. "She doesn't have a lot to do. I do the dressing and Thomas takes care of the undressing."

"Well, lucky Rose." Her mother winked suggestively. "And lucky you!"

■ ■ ■ ■

As Harry was about to leave, her father arrived home.

"I'm highly flattered you came home early, darling." Louisa kissed her husband.

"I have portentous news. Because of the war losses, Aberdeen was forced to set up a parliamentary inquiry of his policies, and his failure to appoint Lord Palmerston as secretary at war. Today he lost a confidence vote in the Commons and had to resign as prime minister."

"I believe Uncle Johnny and Palmerston were working in tandem against Aberdeen," Harry declared.

"Yes, John is coming to dinner tonight. He's backing Palmerston for prime minister, but I'm afraid there is a fly in the ointment. Prince Albert informed me an hour ago that Victoria doesn't care for Palmerston and doesn't want to ask him to be her PM."

"Well, you and John must do your best to get it settled before the month is out. I don't want it to interfere with our trip to Ireland," Louisa said firmly.

"Wouldn't it be wonderful if Uncle John became prime minister again?" Harry said.

When Thomas came home, he told her the news.

"I was visiting Mother when Father arrived. I warrant he wasn't too unhappy to learn that Aberdeen had to resign. You were right, Thomas. That day when I visited Parliament, you told me that Uncle John and Lord Palmerston were trying to bring Aberdeen down."

"Palmerston has ambitions to be the next prime minister."

"How do you know him so well?"

"I've known him for many years."

"Father said the queen doesn't care for him. What do you know about him?"

Thomas hesitated. "This is confidential, Harry. Members of Parliament have a gentleman's agreement not to divulge secrets about each other's private lives. Palmerston is an inveterate gambler. I met him years ago when he frequented Ranton, my father's sporting estate."

"That explains why Victoria doesn't care for him."

"I doubt she knows. These things are kept private."

I warrant she knows more than you think.

Women thrive on gossip.

"Mother says they are going to Ireland for March and April, so before I forget, will you invite Will Montagu for dinner one night next week? I promised Jane an evening with an eligible bachelor, and it goes without saying that Jane assumes I meant the *braw Scots laddie*."

"I shall willingly aid and abet you in your matchmaking. I wouldn't mind having Will for a brother-in-law."

On Friday evening, Trixy arrived early to take Harry to the women's meeting in Langham Place. When Thomas greeted Trixy and kissed her brow, she never mentioned the baby to him, so Harry kept her mouth closed.

"Harry, you wouldn't believe it, but last night at Spencer House, the subject of centaurs came up and Jane Frances, the young Duchess of Marlborough, said they had a pair at Blenheim Palace."

"Oh, what a coincidence." Harry looked at Thomas. "I wonder if they could be the ones from Shugborough."

"It's a possibility." His brows drew together. "I know Marlborough. I'll check into it." He kissed Harry. "Don't wait up for me, darling."

When the two sisters left the house, it had started to rain again and they hurried into the carriage. Before they got to Piccadilly, Trixy experienced a wave of nausea.

"Oh dear, I feel sick again. I felt wretched this morning, but it passed off."

"Having a baby and nausea go hand in hand, Trixy. You need something to settle your stomach. There's an apothecary shop in Shepherd Market. We'll stop and I'll get you something."

Harry signaled the driver and told him to go left to Shepherd Market instead of right to Regent Street. When the carriage stopped, she hurried across to the apothecary shop. Farther down the street, she noticed a striking woman leave a house and climb into a carriage. For a fleeting moment, Harry thought it looked like Thomas's carriage. She dismissed the notion. *In the rain all black carriages look alike.* A trickle of rain ran down inside her collar, and she hurried into the shop. A few minutes later she was back with Trixy.

"I asked the apothecary's advice. He assured me that powdered bistort and mint would take away your nausea. He recommended it for morning sickness."

"I suppose it is morning sickness, even though it's evening."

"Trixy, I don't think you should go to Langham Place tonight."

Trixy sighed. "I was looking forward to announcing my news to the ladies, but you are right. I'm feeling quite poorly."

"Why don't we go back to my house and I'll mix you some bistort and mint?"

"Can I stay with you tonight, Harry? I don't want to be alone, and D'Arcy will be out until all hours."

"Of course you can stay with me." She stepped out of the carriage and spoke to the driver. "We've changed our minds. Please take us back to St. James's Square. Then you can take the carriage home. Lady Durham is staying with me tonight."

The sisters went upstairs and Harry mixed the powdered bistort. Within a half hour of drinking it, Trixy's nausea began to abate. Rose plenished the guest room, and Harry provided her sister with a nightgown. They helped Trixy undress and get into bed.

"I don't want to be alone. Won't you share the guest room with me?"

"Of course. I'll leave a note for Thomas, and be right back."

In the morning, Harry arose and drew back the curtains. "The sun is out. Thank heaven it's stopped raining. How do you feel, Trixy?"

"My nausea has gone. I feel quite normal. That stomach powder did the trick."

"If you feel up to breakfast, I can bring you a tray."

"Nonsense. We'll go down to the breakfast room."

"Good. You know where the bathroom is. I'll send Rose to help you dress."

Harry went to her room to get dressed. Thomas had left her a note, and she was disappointed that he'd already gone out.

At breakfast Trixy talked about her visit to Spencer House.

"What's George Churchill like? Mother said he was avaricious."

"She's probably right. After dinner, he and D'Arcy went off to play cards, while the young duchess and I talked. She has a baby not quite two. I quite like Jane Frances. I feel sorry for her, married to a man in his sixties. I warrant she's lonely."

"I can't stop thinking about the centaurs at Blenheim. I wonder if they are the ones that were sold from Shugborough."

"I have an idea. Why don't we pay Jane Frances a morning visit? I know you'll like her, and you can ask her about them. We can walk over to Spencer House."

"We could — it's only five minutes away, but I've never met her."

"Now is your chance, while I'm here to make the introductions."

Harry thought about the centaurs, and on impulse agreed.

At Spencer House, a footman took their cloaks and showed them to the young duchess's private sitting room, where Jane Frances greeted Trixy warmly.

"Your Grace, I brought my sister the Countess of Lichfield to meet you. Harriet is a neighbor of yours from St. James's Square."

"I'm delighted to meet you, Lady Lichfield."

"Please, my friends call me Harry."

"My sister is curious about the centaurs you were telling me about."

Harry bit her lip. Trixy got straight to the point with no subtlety whatsoever. She smiled at Jane Frances. "Could you describe them? Centaurs are unusual and I wondered if they came from my husband's Shugborough estate."

"They are a pair — black marble, about six feet tall."

Bugger and balls, you've described them to a T.

"The *late* Duke of Marlborough must

have acquired them for Blenheim, so I have no idea where they came from."

"I thought I heard voices." A florid-faced man strode into the sitting room. "Lady Durham, how nice to see you again." He glanced with curiosity at Harriet, boldly assessing her figure.

"Your Grace, this is my sister Lady Lichfield."

Harry held out her hand and he took it to fleshy lips. "I know your husband very well." He lowered an eyelid. "Very well indeed."

Marlborough made Harry feel uncomfortable. She stood up. "We really must be going. My sister and I were just out for a walk and dropped in to say hello." She bade good-bye to Jane Frances and politely invited her to drop in for a visit.

On the way back to St. James's Square, Harry remarked, "There's something about Marlborough I don't like. I don't envy Jane Frances being married to him. It's not his age; it is his manner that offends."

"We are particularly fortunate in our husbands, Harry. We are very lucky."

She thought about Thomas and smiled. "Exceptionally lucky."

Harry was bubbling with excitement. She was almost certain that the centaurs at

Blenheim were from Shugborough. She wanted to share the news with Thomas, but at the same time, she didn't want him to think she had interfered. After all, he had promised that he would look into the matter.

When they were eating dinner, she broached the subject in a roundabout way. "Trixy had a bout of nausea last night because she's having a baby."

"Yes, I know. D'Arcy told me. He was like a dog with two tails."

"This morning she was feeling so well that we went for a walk. When we got to Spencer House, she insisted we pay a visit on the young duchess. While I was there, I asked her to describe the centaurs at Blenheim. Thomas, I think they are ours!"

"You shouldn't have done that," he said sharply.

"I'm sorry. I know it was impulsive, but I couldn't resist."

"When I heard there were centaurs at Blenheim, I was pretty certain they were the ones from Shugborough. The late Duke of Marlborough gambled away half his fortune at Ranton. If George Churchill knows I'm interested in them, the price will go sky-high."

"I didn't say we were interested in buying

them. I just asked her to describe them."

"Is that all?" He couldn't keep the sarcasm from his voice. He saw the look of dismay on her face. "I'm sorry, sweetheart. I'll handle Marlborough. It won't be the first time we've dealt together."

"Of course . . . you know him from the Lords."

"The Lords and elsewhere," he said cryptically.

On Thursday, the following week, Harry was expecting Jane. Will Montagu had accepted the dinner invitation, and she'd told her sister to come early so they could spend the afternoon together.

When she heard Norton answer the door, she came to the top of the stairs. Instead of Jane, Harry was surprised to see the Duke of Marlborough in the reception hall. "It's all right, Norton." She hurried down the stairs. *Thomas must have contacted him about the centaurs.* "I'm sorry, Your Grace. My husband isn't at home this afternoon."

Marlborough looked annoyed. "I gave Solange the price I had in mind for the centaurs, and expected Lichfield to contact me."

"Solange?"

His mouth quirked. "Solange is Lichfield's . . . *associate.*"

She hesitated only a moment. "Yes, of course. I'll tell my husband you dropped by. I'm sure he will be in touch with you, Lord Marlborough."

"I'll no doubt see him tomorrow night." He put his hat back on and departed.

Harry walked toward the stairs. *Solange must be connected with Whitfield Cox. The way Marlborough spoke of her was positively suggestive. What a vile man. It's too bad he owns our magnificent centaurs.*

Harry was halfway up the stairs when she heard the door knocker. *This must be Jane.* She hurried back down and greeted her sister eagerly. "I'm very happy to see you."

"I'm so excited, I can hardly breathe!"

"You'll have lots of time to compose yourself. He won't be here for hours." She took Jane's cloak and led her upstairs to her private sitting room. "Shall we have some tea, or would you rather have sherry?"

"Perhaps I will have a little."

Harry laughed. "I'd better get Rose to bring us some biscuits if we are going to start drinking this early."

The sisters chatted about everything from courtship to marriage and babies. When the conversation turned to fashion, Jane voiced her frustration. "My clothes are all so childish. I don't even own a dinner gown." She smoothed the collar of her cream dress, and said wistfully, "I wish I had something more sophisticated to wear tonight."

"You are welcome to choose something from my wardrobe, if you like."

"Oh, Harry, that's a wonderful suggestion. You wouldn't mind?"

"Of course not. Let's go and take a look."

Harry took Jane into her dressing room and refrained from making suggestions.

"I *love* this sapphire blue. Do you think I dare wear such a vivid shade?"

"Absolutely! It will emphasize the blue of your eyes, and your pearls will go beautifully with it." Harry carried it from the dressing room and put it on the bed.

"Why don't we put up your hair? It will transform you from a girl into a lady of fashion."

Harry called in Rose and they spent the next hour with the hot tongs, fashioning Jane's brunette tresses into large curls that they pinned on top of her head. Then they sat her down at the dressing table and applied powder and lip rouge to her face.

While Harry changed into a dinner gown, Jane sat before the mirror, mesmerized by her own reflection. When Harry was ready, she took her sister's hand. "We will await the gentlemen in the drawing room. Thomas is bringing Will home with him."

"Lady Jane, is it really you?" Montagu looked at her as if he were seeing her for the first time. "You've grown up since the last time we met." He took possession of her hand and gallantly raised it to his lips.

From behind him, Thomas looked at Harry and waggled his eyebrows.

She smiled innocently. "Darling, why don't you pour us some wine?"

The conversation flowed effortlessly as they discussed the political situation and then moved on to the new inventions on display at the Crystal Palace. During dinner they talked about Scotland, Ireland, and Harry's favorite subject, Shugborough Hall.

After dinner they reminisced about various entertainments they'd attended together, and had a good laugh about Mademoiselle Rachelle's Mystical Tarot Card Reading.

"Jane is off to Ireland for the next two months. The family will be visiting Rachel before they go to Barons Court. When Father took Mother there for her honeymoon, he had a stage built for her so she could dance for him. Jane has inherited Mother's talent."

Will Montagu's attention was focused on Jane, and Harry was delighted with her matchmaking efforts.

When the hour grew late, Will offered to escort Jane home.

"I planned to take Jane home." Thomas felt his wife kick him, so he added, "But I know you'll give her safe escort to Hampden House."

They bade their guests good night, and Will and Jane departed. "Perhaps I shouldn't have permitted Jane to be alone with Will in his carriage. Whatever will Mother say?"

"Your mother will thoroughly approve. She would like nothing better than a match between her daughter and the Montagu family." He touched her cheek. "Will was in love with you, you know."

She looked up into her husband's eyes. "My heart was already taken."

Thomas slipped his arm around her and they went upstairs together.

It had been such a happy evening that Harry was reluctant to bring up Marlborough. She slipped off her shoes and began to undress. "George Churchill came to see you this afternoon."

"Marlborough came *here?*" he asked sharply.

"Yes. He seemed annoyed that you were not at home." For some inexplicable reason Harry could not bring herself to say the name *Solange.* "He said he'd given your associate a price for the centaurs, and had expected you to contact him by now."

His eyes searched her face. "I'm not so gullible. He's asking the ridiculous price of two thousand apiece for them, so I'm ignoring him." He closed the distance between them. "Let me do that." He unfastened the back of her gown and dropped a kiss on the nape of her neck. When she stepped out of her gown, he untied her corset strings.

"That price is outrageous! He said he'd likely see you tomorrow night."

He swept her up into his arms and carried her to the bed. "Promise me you won't even think about the rapacious swine."

She watched him undress. "I promise."

He slipped into bed and enfolded her against his heart. Once the kissing began, it was easy for Harry to forget everything else.

In the middle of the night, however, as she lay awake against her sleeping husband, it was not so easy to keep her promise. In her mind's eye, she relived Marlborough's visit, and examined every word he had said. Like a silent whisper, she heard the name *Solange.*

■ ■ ■ ■

When morning arrived, it completely banished the darklings, and Harry laughed at her foolish fancies. She made a decision to keep the unsavory Duke of Marlborough out of her thoughts. From now on she would trust Thomas to deal with him, and was confident that her husband would find a way to acquire the beloved centaurs.

After breakfast, she got a note from Trixy letting her know that she'd had no more bouts of nausea and would pick her up and take her to Langham Place this evening. Harry looked forward to the meeting. The topic of conversation would be politics, and she would be able to voice her opinions on who would be the next prime minister. If it was her uncle Lord John Russell, she was sure he would present their petitions to Parliament regarding married women's property rights.

At the end of the month the Abercorns held a family dinner at Hampden House before they left for Ireland. Trixy and D'Arcy, who were returning to Durham shortly, arrived at the same time as Harry and Thomas. John Russell and his wife,

Fanny, were also invited.

At the dinner table the primary conversation was politics. "I understand that the queen asked the leader of the opposition, Lord Derby, to become her prime minister and form a government." Abercorn looked at John for confirmation.

"True, but when Derby asked Palmerston to become secretary at war, he politely declined, making it impossible for Derby to form a government."

Harry's eyes lit with excitement. "Then did the queen invite *you* to become her prime minister?"

"As a matter of fact, she did. However, when I asked Palmerston to become my secretary at war, he once more respectfully declined. So I thanked Her Majesty profusely for the great honor, and told her it was impossible for me to become the next prime minister."

Harry's face fell. "Why didn't Palmerston cooperate?"

"My dear, we had a gentleman's agreement. Lord Palmerston deserves to be prime minister, and I back him wholeheartedly. This morning the queen asked him to form a government. Though reluctant, she had no choice."

"A pox on *gentleman's agreements!* It's

outrageous how easily men can manipulate a woman — even the queen." Harry looked pointedly at all the males at the table.

"Since you backed Palmerston, what are you getting in return?" the duchess asked shrewdly.

"I shall be going to Vienna for the peace talks to end the war."

"Well, I'll be damned!" Harry declared, and they all had a good laugh.

After dinner, Harry took Jane aside and gave her an envelope. "I've written Rachel a long letter. Be sure to give her my love, and find out if she's finished the story about the lady who was given in marriage to settle a gambling debt."

"What a scandalous thing to do. How could her story have a happy ending if the bride was no more than a pawn?"

Harry smiled knowingly. "Love conquers all."

CHAPTER TWENTY-FOUR

"I'm keeping my fingers crossed that spring will come early. I know it's only the middle of March, but the sparrows are already building their nests." Harry was in her dressing room, deciding which clothes she would take with her to Shugborough. "I'd like you to come with me, Rose. Staffordshire is so lovely."

"I'd like to come, Lady Harry, but if you stay all summer, my family would sorely miss my visits."

"We have to come back to London at the beginning of May for my sister Jane's debutante ball, so we'll only stay for April. Hopefully Thomas and I can go back later. You don't have to decide right away." She handed Rose her jade velvet evening gown, then began to sort through her riding dresses.

"Will one gown be enough, Lady Harry?"

"I think so. We are not formal at Shugborough. I need country clothes and day dresses, sturdy walking shoes and riding boots. There are a few books in the library I'm taking. They can go at the bottom of my trunk. While I'm thinking of it, I'll get Norton to bring it from the attic."

Harry went downstairs and heard voices coming from the library. She remembered Thomas had mentioned his attorney was coming. *I should say hello to Simon Kendall.* Her footsteps slowed. *Perhaps I shouldn't disturb them.* As she hesitated, she heard Kendall say, "I have renewed the lease on the Shepherd Market house."

I didn't know Thomas had any leased property. A picture of the striking-looking woman she had seen in Shepherd Market flashed into her mind. Then she heard Kendall say, "The lease on the other property comes due May first. Do you wish me to renew it?"

Thomas replied, "I'm not sure. I'm seriously considering giving it up, but it will depend on what Solange decides to do."

Solange. The name filled Harry with disquiet. She hurried past the library and went in search of Norton. When she found him in the dining room polishing silver, she looked at him blankly. "Ah, now I remember. Would you please find my traveling trunk and take it to my dressing room?"

Clara appeared at the door carrying a tray. "Will you take your afternoon tea in your sitting room, Lady Harry?"

"Tea?" She made an effort to gather her thoughts. "Yes, thank you, Clara."

As she sipped her tea absently, her thoughts chased one another in circles. *I believed Thomas put any money he had into Shugborough. I didn't know he leased properties in London. What else don't I know?* Harry shook her head. *Stop being ridiculous!*

But the silent whisper grew louder: *Solange.* She tried to dismiss her suspicious thoughts. *She is his associate.* Harry thought of her husband's affiliation with Whitfield Cox. *Solange must be an associate in the art dealership.*

She put her cup and saucer back on the tray, and examined her emotions. *Could it be jealousy? Is that what I'm feeling?* She dismissed the idea as nonsense. She could not possibly be jealous of someone she didn't know and had never met. *I'm simply curious.*

That night, and many nights following, Thomas was particularly attentive and tender with her. After making love, they talked about Shugborough. He told her that he had bought two suites of bedroom furnishings from Althorp that had come from Shugborough, and that he'd arranged to have them shipped from Northampton at the end of April.

In the last few days, Harry had successfully pushed away all thoughts of jealousy. She smiled into the darkness. "I can't wait to see the daffodils in the riverside garden."

The next morning, Harry went to the library to gather the books she intended to take to Shugborough. As she passed her husband's desk, she paused to read a notation he'd made on his calendar: *Lease renewal.*

Her thoughts came flooding back. Thomas and his attorney had spoken of the lease renewals in connection with Solange. *I'm not jealous of his associate — I'm simply curious.* A picture of the woman she'd seen in Shepherd Market came unbidden. *My imagination is playing tricks on me. Because I don't know what Solange looks like, I picture the woman I saw in Shepherd Market.*

By lunchtime, the silent whispers had magnified. Questions to which she had no answers taunted her. In the early afternoon, Harry decided there was only one way to satisfy her curiosity. She put on her hat and coat, and took a hackney to Oxford Street.

Her mind conjured the conversation she'd overheard between Simon Kendall and Thomas. *"I have renewed the lease on the Shepherd Market house."* A vivid picture of the woman she'd seen in Shepherd Market filled her head. She saw the striking woman step up into a coach. Harry could deny the truth no longer. *It was Thomas's coach I saw in the rain that night.*

At lunchtime, the knot in her stomach made it impossible for her to eat. She pushed her plate aside and left the table. *Perhaps if I lie down for a while, I will feel better.* But as she reclined quietly on the wide four-poster, she found it impossible to relax. She grew tenser by the minute as doubts and questions swirled about in her mind. After a half hour, she left the bed and decided that a long, warm bath would soothe and calm her nerves.

By three o'clock, Harry knew she must find out the truth or she would never again enjoy a peaceful moment. She went into her dressing room and carefully chose an outfit she knew was flattering. The amethyst wool dress had a matching cloak. She donned a smart gray hat adorned with violets.

On her way downstairs she encountered Clara, who looked surprised that she was going out. Then she remembered that it was Friday and that she didn't usually leave for Langham Place until after dinner.

"I'll be out for the rest of the day, Clara."

"Very good, Lady Harry. Have a nice meeting."

At Pall Mall she hailed a hackney. "Shepherd Market, please." She saw that the traffic was busy. She sat back against the squabs and folded her hands. Harry dreaded what lay ahead. She was in no great hurry to arrive at her destination. From Piccadilly, the driver turned into White Horse Street and stopped at the corner of Shepherd Market.

She stepped out of the carriage and paid the driver. Then with measured but determined steps, she walked past the apothecary shop and stopped before the house farther down the street. She approached the door and hesitated. She still had the hard knot in her belly, but now, in addition, her heart was fluttering like a wild bird trying to escape from its cage.

She straightened her shoulders, took a deep breath, and raised her hand to the knocker. *There's no one home. I should leave.* But she forced herself to stand there stoically until the door swung open.

The woman's eyes widened. "Lady Lichfield!"

You know who I am. She stared at the beautiful female in the elegant gown, whose blond hair was fashioned into a smooth chignon. "Your name is Solange, I believe."

"Yes, I am Solange." After a moment she said, "Won't you come in?"

Harry stepped over the threshold, and followed the woman. The house was narrow, the stairs steep, but the drawing room was furnished in good taste. She ignored the chair she was offered and remained standing. "What is your relationship with my husband?"

"We are associates."

"What sort of associates?"

"Lord Lichfield and I are partners — business partners."

"What sort of business?"

Solange stiffened. "I suggest you ask your husband, my lady."

And I suggest you are my husband's mistress. Harry pressed her lips together, before she blurted the accusation. "My husband's attorney, Simon Kendall, renewed the lease on this house. Why would Thomas pay your lease?"

"I assure you that I pay my own lease, Lady Lichfield. Your husband had his attorney handle it as a courtesy."

Harry saw that the woman was offended

515

at the suggestion that Thomas paid her lease. *Either you are telling me the truth or you are a good actress.* She remembered that the Duke of Marlborough said he had given Solange a price for the centaurs.

"It is no secret that my husband has been trying to restore Shugborough's furniture and artifacts for some time. Am I to understand you help him in this by acting as go-between to negotiate a price?" *Please, please, let this be the nature of your relationship.*

"I do act in that capacity sometimes." Solange raised her chin. "If you have any more questions regarding your husband's affairs, I respectfully suggest that you ask *him,* Lady Lichfield."

Harry knew she would get no more out of her. Solange was both discreet and loyal.

Harry inclined her head gracefully. "I bid you good afternoon."

When she got outside, the light was already leaving the sky, and she knew it must be past five o'clock. As she walked toward the apothecary shop, her thoughts were in turmoil. *It was Friday night that he picked her up in his carriage. Thomas always goes out on Friday, and gets home very late.* The thought that he spent every Friday night with Solange was hard to bear. *Will he call for her tonight?*

Harry went into the apothecary shop and pretended a great interest in the bottles and jars displayed on the shelves that held herbs, roots, seeds, powders, and electuaries. She kept glancing through the shop window, dreading yet expecting to see a coach.

After dawdling for a half hour, she realized she must buy something and approached the man behind the counter. "Last time I was here, you were kind enough to recommend a cure for morning sickness. I've quite forgotten what it was."

"I remember you, my lady. There's nothing better for nausea than powdered bistort and mint. It must have done the trick, if you are back for more."

Harry glanced through the window and drew in a swift breath as she saw Solange walk past the shop. She turned back to the apothecary. "Yes, yes, that's the stuff."

She watched as he carefully measured out the bistort; then he crushed some dried mint leaves, mixed them together, and handed her the package.

"The dose is a half teaspoon."

"Thank you so much." She paid him and left the shop, determined to follow Solange. The woman was nowhere in sight, and Harry knew she must have turned the corner onto Curzon Street. She reached the corner in time to see her turn onto the next street. Harry walked slowly; she didn't want Solange to know she was following her.

It was getting dark, and when she reached the next street, she peered quickly along the pavement to make sure she could still see her. Harry glanced up to read the name of the street. *Half Moon Street.*

She stopped as memories came flooding back to her. *The last time I was on this street, I was with Rachel and the Montagu brothers.* Suddenly Harry began to suspect where Solange was going. She peered down the street but could no longer see her. As if being drawn against her will, Harry put one foot in front of the other, until she was standing before Hazard House.

She gazed up at the dark facade, indistinguishable from its neighbors. The exact same thought she'd had last time she was here ran through her head: *It looks like a respectable home, not a gaming hell.*

She stood for a long time as if she was dazed. *This cannot be where they meet.* Her mind flatly denied that such a thing was possible.

A carriage stopped and two men got out. Harry was completely oblivious until one of them spoke to her.

"It looks closed, but it's past opening time. Are you coming in, my dear?"

She did not reply, but when they opened the door and walked inside, she slowly followed. The men put something in the porter's hand, and he welcomed all three of them with a bow.

She hung back until the men went upstairs before she slowly followed. The gaming rooms were brilliantly lit, but due to the early hour, there were few customers about. As if she were in a trance, Harry walked through the rooms. She moved past the one with the roulette wheel and dice table, and entered the cardroom where Montagu had played faro.

She stared at the staircase at the end of the room, and she heard the echo of Will Montagu's words: *I've seen his ravishing female partner who runs the place. Her fatal beauty lures men to wager deep.* Harry knew it was a perfect description of Solange.

As she moved inexorably toward the staircase, her mind screamed its denial. *The owner has a rather black reputation.* She recoiled from her dark thoughts. *It cannot be. It must not be. It is unthinkable.*

She stood there, as fear warred with courage. *I refuse to be a coward.* She raised her hand, rapped sharply on the door, and waited.

Solange opened the door, and the two females stared at each other. After a long hesitation, Solange moved aside.

Harry stepped over the threshold, and the hair on the back of her neck stood on end as she stared with incredulity at the scene before her. The Duke of Marlborough sat at a gaming table. She saw Thomas jump to his feet when she entered the room, and she watched the card he had taken from the dealing box flutter to the floor.

"Harriet! What the hellfire are you doing here?" He came toward her.

She put up both hands to stay him. "Don't come any closer!"

He stopped and stared at her with dark, burning eyes.

She shook her head in disbelief. "I don't even know you."

Harry jumped out of the hackney cab in St. James's Square. "Wait for me," she instructed the driver. The front door banged closed behind her as Norton hurried to see who had arrived. "I need your help." She rushed up the stairs and called, "Rose, Rose, where are you?"

By the time Norton and Rose followed

her into the bedchamber, Harry was in her dressing room, filling her half-packed trunk with clothes.

"Rose, are you packed and ready to go?"

"Yes, Lady Harry."

"Good. We are leaving." She spoke to Norton. "Take this trunk to the carriage outside, and then come back for Rose's luggage."

"Are we going to Shugborough tonight?" Rose asked in amazement.

"No, we are going to Hampden House. Get your coat."

Harry hurried down the stairs to the front door, with Rose following breathlessly.

When Harry got outside, she was livid to see her husband's coach pull up. Norton moved toward Thomas's carriage with her trunk.

"Not in there, you idiot! Put it in the hackney."

Thomas jumped from his carriage. "Harry, stop this!"

She looked through him as if he were invisible. "Rose, get in the cab. Norton, go up and fetch Rose's luggage." She spoke to the driver, who was looking most skeptical. "We are going to 61 Green Street."

Thomas took firm hold of the horse's bridle. "You are going nowhere. Get back in the house."

Harry reached up and grabbed the driver's whip from its holder. She brought her arm down with a wild flourish, and the whipcrack made the horse rear its head in fear.

Thomas had his hands full, calming the horse, as Norton emerged with the luggage.

Harry grabbed the bag from him, thrust the whip into his hand, climbed into the cab, and banged the door shut.

Norton handed the whip back to the driver, who spoke to Thomas. "Kindly stand aside, yer lordship."

As Thomas loosened his grip on the horse's bridle, he was filled with impotent fury.

"Go and be damned to you!"

CHAPTER TWENTY-FIVE

"We need some help with our luggage, Hobson," Harry told the Hampden House footman when he opened the door.

Hobson hauled in the heavy trunk. "How long will you be staying, Lady Harry?"

"Indefinitely. You can get Rose's bag. She'll be staying indefinitely too."

Harry removed her cloak and made her way to the kitchen, where she found Mrs. Foster, the housekeeper, and Mrs. Gilbert, the cook, entertaining Riley. "Since I'm back to stay, I'd like a front-door key, Mrs. Foster."

The two female servants exchanged a speaking glance before the housekeeper took a key off her ring and presented it to Harry.

"I brought Rose with me, so she'll need her old room back." Harry glanced at Riley. "I'm surprised they didn't take you to Ireland with them."

"Lord and Lady Abercorn trusted their persons to the Great Western Railway line that runs from London to Bristol. They had no need of me this time."

"Well, I have need of you, Riley. It will be most convenient to have my own carriage and driver, after being transported in shabby hackney cabs by cockeyed drivers."

The footman came to the kitchen door. "Pardon, Lady Harry, but will the Earl of Lichfield be joining you?"

"No, Hobson, he will not. And if he has the bloody effrontery to show his face, you will inform him that I am not receiving." She glanced at the footman and, in spite of the width of his shoulders, gravely doubted he could keep Thomas Anson at bay.

Harry filled the kettle and swung it over the kitchen fire to boil. "Since our beds haven't been slept in for some time, Rose and I will need hot-water bottles." She sniffed the air with appreciation. "Something smells good. I've had no lunch or supper, so you can rustle me up some grub, Mrs. Gilbert."

A half hour later, Harry sat at the kitchen table finishing off a hearty portion of steak and kidney pie. She hoped the hot food would help to fill the gaping, empty void inside her. When Mrs. Gilbert poured her a

524

cup of tea, Harry turned to Riley. "I warrant it would go down better with a dollop of fine Irish whiskey in it."

Riley grinned and reached for his flask. "A nod's as good as a wink to a blind horse."

When Harry retired to the bedroom she had shared with her sisters, her cheeky bravado fell away. She shoved the stone hot-water bottles between the sheets of two beds. "You might as well stay in here with me tonight." Then she helped Rose finish unpacking her trunk and hung her clothes in the wardrobe.

When she got into bed, Harry resolved that she would not weep and wail and gnash her teeth. Nor would she cry softly into her pillow. Though the revelation about Thomas had stunned her, she adamantly refused to feel sorry for herself. She knew that the anger that had begun to simmer inside her would banish all self-pity. She was furious that this wasn't the first breach of trust in their relationship. After the misunderstanding about his father's will, they had agreed there would be no more secrets between them. *How could Thomas do this?*

During the next few days, Harry kept busy. In April, the weather turned warm and sunny as she had predicted, and each afternoon Riley took her and Rose for a carriage ride in Hyde Park. She thought about Shugborough every day, and was devastated that her planned visit, which she had been looking forward to for months, was now ruined.

At the end of the week, she began to realize that she was waiting for something. It didn't take much soul-searching to realize she was waiting for Thomas to come and beg her forgiveness for blatantly deceiving her. Though she had forbidden his entrance to Hampden House, she fully expected him to come and demand that she return to him.

Harry was anticipating a flaming argument and knock-down fight in which she would fling at his head accusations of his towering hypocrisy and vile deception.

When he did not come, she was filled with self-righteous indignation.

Each successive day of April was more beautiful than the previous one, and Harry seethed with frustration that she was stuck in London when she should have been enjoying Shugborough. She laid the blame for this injustice at Thomas Anson's door.

The dark, dominant, dangerous, and deceitful devil should be horsewhipped!

Harry was filled with restless energy. "Rose, let's pack up all the clothes that my brothers and sisters have outgrown and deliver them to your family this afternoon."

"That would be grand, Lady Harry."

"You look in the clothespress, and I'll go up to the nursery."

In the next half hour, Harry made three trips from the nursery, her arms piled with outgrown garments. "Whew, this is hot work. I'll get Hobson to find us some bags." When she and Rose were done packing, they had five bagfuls.

"I'll just go down to the kitchen and ask Mrs. Gilbert what food we can take."

When Harry explained they were going to visit Rose's family in Soho, the cook suggested she take the ham. "We had it last night for dinner, but there's still so much left on the bone, we'll be eating it for a sennight."

"Good idea. Wrap it up, and I'll take the loaves you baked yesterday, and some of those turnips from Campden Hill. We'll never eat a whole bushel."

Riley slowed down the carriage when they got to Soho's cobbled streets. He turned into Broad Street and stopped just down from the corner because it was filled with playing children and barking dogs. "I don't dare leave the horses, Lady Harry. These young buggers will spook my cattle if I so much as turn my back."

"That's all right, Riley. Rose and I can manage. We'll just carry one at a time."

Harry took the ham and the loaves, while Rose lifted the basket of turnips. When they went into the house, Mrs. Ferguson greeted the pair as if they were angels of mercy, and Rose's sisters and brothers surrounded them, dancing with joy.

When the ham was unwrapped, their eyes were like saucers, and they sat down at the table ready to sample the huge smoked hindquarter of pig. Harry handed Mrs. Ferguson a package of tea, knowing such a luxury would be a rare treat. She smiled with satisfaction when Rose's mother immediately put the kettle on to boil.

"We've brought some clothes too," Harry announced, and the youngsters shouted hooray and clapped their hands. "Rose, why don't you sit down and visit with your family? I can manage the bags."

She walked down the street to the carriage, lifted out one of the bags of clothing, and carried it back to the Fergusons' house. Harry repeated the exercise and by the time she struggled down the street with the fifth bag, she was both hot and out of wind.

Rose took the bag from Harry. "Sit down,

my lady; you're exhausted."

She took Rose's chair. "No, I'm just hot . . . and thirsty."

"Billy, fetch Lady Harriet a cup of water." Mrs. Ferguson smiled at her guest. "He's just brought it fresh from the pump. It's nice and cold."

Young Billy brought the water and Harry took a few gulps. "Thank you. That's better. I shouldn't complain — I'm glad the weather has turned warm."

After a short visit, Rose bade her family good-bye. "Riley is waiting for us down the street. We shouldn't keep the horses standing any longer." She kissed her mother and sisters. Billy walked to the carriage with them so he could look at the horses.

Harry felt a small sense of accomplishment. It was good to think of others. Her problems paled in comparison with those of the less fortunate. She promised herself that the visits to Broad Street would be more frequent from now on.

Thomas paced across his bedchamber with a restlessness and anger he couldn't quell. The anger was directed at himself, of course. *I should have given up the lease on Hazard House before we were married. That way Harry wouldn't have found out about it.*

529

Now it is too late for anything but regrets. She knows the dark secret I was so careful to conceal, and I doubt she will ever forgive me.

Thomas had been extremely busy in the past week. As he had surmised, Solange had jumped at the chance to take over Hazard House and run the business herself. Simon Kendall had arranged to take Thomas's name off the lease of the house on Half Moon Street, and register it in the name of Solange Samson. Thomas had also called in all the markers owed to him, and done an audit of the books, so Solange would have a clean slate to start her business.

He had held a meeting with the people he employed at Hazard House from the porter and the barman to the croupiers and the maintenance staff. Some refused to have a female boss, but most were amenable to staying on at the Half Moon Street gaming house.

It was the nights without Harry that Thomas found almost unendurable. The endless hours crawled by, and often in the middle of the night it felt as if time had stopped completely. A half dozen times he had sat down at his desk to pen a letter to Harry explaining his reasons for opening a gaming house, but each time he'd crumpled it up. What he put down on paper sounded like futile, even pathetic, excuses and he was convinced he could make a better case if he could talk to her face-to-face. Yet still he hesitated to go and explain himself. *She will think me nothing more than a hypocrite and a liar.*

As he stood at the window, trying to suppress the ache in his heart, he thought back over the years that had brought him to this pass. By the time he was twelve, Thomas had learned all there was to know about cards, dice, betting on horses, and games of chance at his father's sporting estate of Ranton. He had also learned to defend himself against the beatings his father administered in the drunken rages brought on by Lichfield's losses.

As Thomas grew older, he came to despise gambling and all it stood for. He was seventeen when his father's profligate excesses brought about his financial collapse.

During the years Thomas was at Oxford, he had vowed that once he finished university and came of age, he would do everything in his power to restore Shugborough Hall. But the years from twenty-one to twenty-five had clearly shown him that the task he had set for himself was impossible to achieve without money.

Thomas then decided to try for a seat in

Parliament. He campaigned hard and became the Whig member for Lichfield, and then he worked even harder for his constituents. Though he enjoyed representing his own people, he soon realized the money he earned as a member was nowhere near enough to restore Shugborough in the way he had always dreamed. He augmented his income by selling fine art, and by authenticating paintings, but even the commissions from Whitfield Cox fell far short of what he needed.

Three years ago, when his father became ill, Thomas's resolve hardened. He knew gambling was the only way he could make the kind of money it would take to refurbish Shugborough. It was the means to an end. And to Thomas, at this point in his quest, the end justified the means. Running a gaming house could be a profitable enterprise, especially if it was run as a business and the man who made the bets was not addicted. The odds were always in favor of the house. It had not damaged his reputation among the nobility because he had kept it secret. Though running a gaming house clashed with his stern morals, he resolutely ignored his conscience.

With cold calculation, resolve, and determination, he leased the Mayfair house on

Half Moon Street, talked Solange into coming to work for him, and set up the fashionable establishment with a private room for wealthy nobles who had a secret addiction to gambling. At long last, Thomas was able to start buying back Shugborough's treasures.

He thought about Marlborough. *How bloody ironic that the duke's losses over the past fortnight were greater than the price he was asking for the centaurs.*

Thomas drew the velvet curtains across the window and turned to face the empty room. *What the hellfire is the point of restoring Shugborough if I don't have Harry to share it with me?*

"I see no reason why I should stay in London, when I am longing to be at Shugborough. I don't need Thomas Anson's permission to travel to Staffordshire and visit my beloved house. When I married the decadent devil, he endowed me with all his worldly goods."

"Shall I pack your trunk, Lady Harry?"

"Yes, and pack your things too, Rose. I'll ask Riley to have the coach ready first thing in the morning." It had been three days since they had visited the Fergusons, and Harry was at loose ends at Hampden House with her family away in Ireland. The only antidote to thinking about her husband and cataloguing her grievances against the dark devil was to keep busy. She also told herself it would be a good idea to put distance between them. Then when he came to beg her pardon and ask her on bended knee to forgive him, the *Knave of Clubs* would find that the bird had flown.

Harry took the books from her bedside table and put them in the bottom of her trunk. Rose brought her afternoon tea up to the bedchamber and Harry insisted they share it. They put their empty cups back on the tray, and then with Rose's help, she began to pack all the clothes she had brought from St. James's Square.

Suddenly without warning, Harry realized she was going to be sick. She bolted for the bathroom, hung her head over the lavatory, and threw up the tea. When her retching stopped, she sat back on her heels, and took a shuddering breath.

Oh, no, this cannot be happening. My timing is impossible. The minute I am estranged from my husband and we are living apart, Fate steps in to give me a child.

Harry tied back her hair, washed her face, and returned to the bedchamber to search for the powdered bistort and mint she'd bought at the apothecary. She found it in her reticule and hurried back to the bathroom to mix a dose. "He recommended a half teaspoon."

The minute she drank it, she knew it would come back up. Strangely, she experienced no nausea; her stomach simply ejected the bistort as it had the tea. Harry wrapped protective arms about her midsection as a painful cramp in her belly almost cut her in half. Her cry of anguish brought Rose.

"Lady Harry, you're ill. You must have eaten something bad."

Harry got up from her knees and sat down on the lavatory just in time. "Get me a bowl, Rose. I'm going to be sick again."

True to her word, Harry vomited the minute Rose held the bowl in front of her.

"It's just water. . . . It looks like rice water, Lady Harry."

"I have water coming out both ends, Rose," she managed between gasps of pain. "I feel so ill. You'd better send Hobson for the doctor."

Rose flew down two sets of stairs until she reached the kitchen, where the servants were having early supper. "Lady Harry is spewing her guts up, and she has the flux too! She's bad — she wants Hobson to fetch the doctor."

The footman went out immediately to summon the Abercorns' physician. Mrs. Foster and the cook rushed upstairs to aid Lady Harriet. They found her rolling on the floor in agony.

"Please . . . please," Harry said weakly, "lift me up. It's happening again."

The housekeeper and the cook picked her up and sat her on the toilet. Harry pointed at the bowl, and Mrs. Gilbert held it in front of her barely in time to catch more rice water. Cook handed the bowl to Rose to empty, but one glance told her Harry was pale as a ghost and so weak that she could no longer sit upright unaided.

Rose was alarmed. She'd seen this sort of ailment before. A year ago in Soho, the poor souls who caught this contagion had died. Her family had been saved because they moved to Aunt Lizzy's in St. Giles until people stopped dying. She ran back downstairs.

"Riley, Riley, can you ready the coach? We must go and tell Lord Lichfield that his wife is poorly. If we don't take him the news, and something bad happens to Harry, our lives won't be worth tuppence. Lady Harry is his whole life."

"That's a sensible suggestion, Rose. If

aught happens to her while the Abercorns are in Ireland, the family will never forgive us. I'll put the horses in the shafts."

Rose banged on the door at St. James's Square, and when Norton opened it, she ran past him, asking over her shoulder if his lordship was at home.

"You'll find him in the library. Is aught amiss, young Rose?"

"Yes, Norton, I'm afraid there is." She tapped on the library door, but didn't wait for Thomas to answer. "My lord, my lord, your wife has come down with a terrible contagion. Riley's got the coach outside. Will you come, sir?"

Thomas dropped the pen he was holding, and came around his desk. "Of course I'll come." His black brows drew together with concern. "What sort of contagion?"

"She's rolling about in agony. She can't keep anything down and she's got the flux."

"Has a doctor been summoned?" Thomas flung on his coat.

"Hobson went to get a doctor while Riley brought me here."

"There's a physician called Hardcastle, lives in St. James's Place. He's often called on by the royal family." Thomas gave Riley the address, and when he alighted from the coach and banged on the door, he had already thought of persuasive words that would compel the physician to accompany him.

Hardcastle was just finishing his dinner when his butler announced the Earl of Lichfield. He came out to the reception hall, where Thomas stood waiting.

"My wife is the eldest daughter of the Duke of Abercorn, Prince Albert's groom of the stole. She has contracted a contagion and I would be most grateful for your help. The Abercorns undoubtedly have their own worthy physician, but they are away in Ireland at the moment."

"All right, Lichfield, I'll come." His butler helped him into his caped greatcoat and handed him his black leather physician's case.

Thomas climbed in the coach after Hardcastle and pulled the door shut.

"I believe the Abercorns live by Hyde Park?"

"Yes. Hampden House is on Green Street."

"Two days ago there was an outbreak of cholera in Soho, but that is a world apart from Green Street."

"Cholera?" Thomas's gut knotted. People died like flies from cholera.

Rose gasped, "Oh, no!"

"What is it?" Thomas demanded.

"Lady Harriet visited my family in Soho three days ago." Rose began to sob.

When the carriage arrived at Hampden House, Hobson met them at the door. "Lord Lichfield, thank God you've come. Abercorn's doctor was not at home."

"It's all right. I've brought Dr. Hardcastle. This way, sir." Thomas took the stairs two at a time. The sight that met his eyes was not encouraging. Harry lay on the bathroom floor. Her knees were pulled up to her chest to try to alleviate the agonizing pain in her belly. She was retching, but nothing was coming up.

Thomas went down before her on his knees. "Harry, I'm here, love. I'm so sorry I let this happen to you. I've brought Dr. Hardcastle. We will soon have you feeling better."

She cried out and as if it were a signal, the housekeeper and the cook picked her up and sat her on the lavatory.

Hardcastle didn't need to examine the patient. He knew immediately by the water coming from both ends that Lichfield's wife had cholera. "Strip her and bathe her. It's the only way you'll keep her clean. Her strength has gone. Put her to bed on a bedpan, and put a bucket beside the bed."

As Mrs. Gilbert began to fill the tub, Thomas said, "I'll do it."

Hardcastle beckoned him into the hall. "First I must give you instructions."

Thomas was torn, but common sense told him to follow the physician from the room.

"It is indeed cholera. The only patients who have even a chance of surviving have round-the-clock nursing. Once the body purges itself of all fluid, the organs shut down, and death follows. So you must get as much fluid back into her as her body loses. She must drink continuously — she must not be allowed to stop."

Thomas nodded grimly. "I understand."

"Servants are deathly afraid of contagion, so tell them I will speak to them downstairs."

When Thomas returned to the bathroom, he was in time to lift Harry from the tub, and wrap her in a towel. Rose followed him with a bedpan and a bucket as he carried her to her bed. He gently pushed the bedpan underneath his wife and covered her nakedness with the sheet. He called to the servants and told them the doctor wanted to speak to them. Rose hovered at the door.

"Go down and listen to what Hardcastle says. Then come back and tell me."

When all the servants were gathered into

the kitchen, including Riley, Hardcastle explained the facts. "You must not fear that this disease is passed from person to person. There is no contagious fever — in fact, the skin becomes cold and clammy. It is not spread through breathing foul air. It is spread by drinking contaminated water. Last year there was an outbreak in Soho. My colleague Dr. John Snow discovered that drinking contaminated water pumped from the Thames is what spread the cholera. When the pump handle in Broad Street was removed, the outbreak stopped.

"Some ignorant fool recently reattached the pump handle, and three days ago, another outbreak of cholera began. I want to assure you that you cannot catch it by tending Lady Harriet. She must drink constantly to replace the fluid her body loses, or she will certainly die."

Cook spoke up. "What can she drink, doctor?"

"Any fluid at all — water, tea, anything so long as it is liquid. Don't give her food." He put on his coat. "Tell Lichfield I'll return tomorrow."

Rose flew up the stairs and found Thomas holding the bucket while Harry retched.

She beckoned him outside and told him everything Hardcastle had said. "I'll go down for a jug of water, and Mrs. Gilbert is making a big pot of tea."

Thomas returned to Harry's bedside. Her skin was clammy and pale as death. She had dark circles beneath her eyes, and she didn't have enough strength to lift her head from the pillow. She licked dry lips. "What is it?" she whispered.

Thomas knelt down beside the bed. He was terrified of frightening her, and searched his mind for words that would put her fear to rest. But his conscience balked. He'd kept secrets from her, with the excuse that he didn't want to hurt her, but in the end, secrets had harmed her far more than the truth. "I won't ever lie to you again, Harry. You have cholera from drinking contaminated water from the Broad Street pump."

She gripped her belly in agony, and Thomas gently pried away her hands and rubbed it to soothe away the pain. "I'm . . . so . . . thirsty."

"That's good, Harry. You are going to get well, but we have to replace all the fluids that your body is losing."

She tried to smile but didn't have the strength, and Thomas's heart turned over in his breast. When Rose brought the jug of water, Thomas poured a glass and held it to her lips. "Drink, sweetheart. Quench your raging thirst."

She obeyed him and sipped the water, but a minute after it went down, it came back up again. Thomas was ready with the bucket, and as soon as she stopped retching, he put the glass back to her lips and encouraged her to drink again.

He was amazed at her courage. She sipped and retched, over and over, until she didn't have the strength left to even move her lips and swallow.

Fear for her was like knotted ropes in his gut, but he smiled into her eyes and told her how courageous she was.

When she closed her eyes, he told her that Rose would stay with her until he returned. He slid out the bedpan from under her, emptied it in the bathroom, scoured it clean, and put it back with gentle hands. Then he brought a bowl of warm water and a flannel and bathed her face and mouth, which were befouled.

Thomas again held a cup of water to her lips, but she closed her eyes as if she couldn't face it. "Go down and get the tea, Rose. I have to keep her drinking."

A maid appeared in the doorway. "There's

a little lad asking for you at the back door, Rose."

The young servant rushed to the door, knowing it would be her brother Billy.

"Rose, you mustn't come to Broad Street. There's a cholera outbreak. We've moved to Aunt Lizzy's in St. Giles until it's all over."

"Oh, I know, Billy. Lady Harry has come down with it. She drank the water you got from the pump. I've been so worried that you'd all have the cholera by now."

"Lucky for us, we didn't drink the water. Lady Harry brought our mam some tea. When she boiled the water to make tea, it must have made it safe to drink."

"Thank God, Billy. Don't drink water in St. Giles until you boil it. Tell the others."

Thomas propped up his wife with pillows so she could drink more easily. He poured weak tea into a cup, and patiently held it to her lips as he implored, begged, and cajoled her to take a few mouthfuls. He did it over and over, never tiring, never losing patience, and yet never forcing her. His powers of persuasion were formidable, his dedication was unwavering, and his persistence dogged.

Twice in the long night, he gave her a warm sponge bath and changed the befouled sheets. Once, when he thought she had fallen into a blessed sleep, his anxious gaze examined her face. Her eyes were sunken with dark circles beneath them. Her face was pale as death. He prayed silently that she would not be taken from him, and made endless promises to a higher power that he would never again indulge the sin of gambling.

When morning arrived, Thomas could see no improvement and knew she would not get better overnight. He sent Riley to St. James's Square for some clean shirts and undergarments. When they arrived, he quickly bathed, put on fresh garments, and returned to Harry's bedside with a hardened resolve to get more liquid into her.

In the late afternoon, Hardcastle arrived and after he examined the patient, he bluntly told Thomas there was no improvement in her condition. "Her skin is very cold, but it is no longer clammy. Her body hasn't enough moisture to even dampen her skin. If she continues to expel more fluids than she retains, there is no chance of recovery."

"Is there not something — *anything* — you can give me that will bind the bowels and stop the flux?"

"Well, some apothecary shops sell bismuth or medicinal chalk, but these folk remedies are highly dangerous."

"They are more than dangerous. They are poisonous," Thomas protested.

"You are right. In conscience, I would not personally recommend them, Lichfield." Hardcastle cleared his throat. "I shall come again tomorrow, but you must prepare yourself for the worst, your lordship."

"Thank you, Doctor." *I won't let her die. My will is far too strong.*

Mrs. Gilbert recommended chamomile, and Thomas, at his wit's end, eagerly agreed.

He patiently and unwearyingly held the cup of chamomile tea to Harry's lips, tempting, enticing, cajoling, and finally ordering her to swallow the tepid fluid. When her face contorted with pain, he placed his hands on her abdomen, willing the warmth from his body to seep into her flesh and ease her pain.

The following day, she began to suffer from leg cramps. Each time, he rubbed them away, but by evening, he began to suspect she was losing the feeling in her limbs. When Hardcastle came, he confirmed that the problem was caused by the body's dehydration. He gave Thomas a solemn look and told him that paralysis was the next stage.

After the doctor left, Thomas redoubled his efforts to get liquid into his wife, and he refused to take no for an answer. He got into her bed, cradled her in his lap, and held the chamomile tea to her bloodless lips for two full hours until drop by drop she swallowed the whole cupful. Then he replenished the chamomile and did it all again.

In the middle of the night, Thomas could see she was trying to speak. He put his ear close to her lips so he could hear her faint whisper.

"I'm dying. . . . Please take me . . . to Shugborough."

He masked the dread in his eyes, and gently touched her cheek with the backs of his fingers. "My precious love, you are not going to die. *I won't allow it.* But the moment this flux subsides a bit, I promise to put you in the carriage and take you to Shugborough."

Thomas clutched her hand, fearing that if he let go, Harry would slip away. Though his words to Harry were strong and reassuring, his thoughts were filled with doubts. For the first time he admitted to himself that his wife's chance of recovery was almost nonexistent. *Her life hangs by a thread. I must fulfill her wish to take her to Shugborough.*

Chapter Twenty-Six

Early the next morning, a knock came on the bedchamber door. Thomas's eyes flew open as he realized he must have dozed off. Fear stabbed its fangs into his throat as he gazed down at the small, still figure in the bed. "Harry, Harry, open your eyes!"

My God, don't let her have slipped away. Thomas held his breath for what seemed like endless minutes, and then finally he saw the flicker of an eyelash. Relief washed over him. He heard the knock again and called, "Come in."

The door swung open and Riley stood there holding a paper packet. "Beggin' yer pardon, m'lord, but in Ireland we put a lot of faith in alkanet. I took the liberty of getting some from the apothecary. In the old country, we put it in wine. Will ye try it, sor?"

"I will indeed, Riley." Thomas took the packet and mixed the powered alkanet in some watered wine. He moved his wife up against the pillows, gently opened her dry lips with his thumb, and poured a few drops into her mouth.

Harry choked and coughed. She raised her lashes and gave her husband a beseeching look that implored him to make it stop.

She looks to me for strength. I would give my life to make her better. "My love, at last we've found the cure." If he was lying, he was beyond caring. "Alkanet is an Irish remedy to cure the flux, and the wine will give you strength."

For answer Harry closed her eyes and opened her lips. He put a few drops into her mouth. "Swallow for me, sweetheart. Swallow the wine."

Little by little, as the hours crawled by, Harry was able to keep the herbal concoction down without retching it back up. And no one was more surprised or thankful than Thomas when her flux stopped. In the afternoon, she fell asleep. He reasoned the wine probably induced it, but he didn't have the heart to awaken her.

While she slept, Thomas bathed, and ate the first meal he'd had in days. He dispatched Riley with a note to Norton at St. James's Square asking him to pack enough clothes for a trip to Shugborough.

When Harry awoke, he made her drink another cup of alkanet in wine. Then he gave her a sponge bath and changed her bed linen. She was far from recovered, but at least she was no longer losing her vital body fluid, and Thomas believed the very best medicine would be to get her to Shugborough, in spite of the long carriage ride.

He sat down on the edge of the bed and took her small hand in his. "Your condition is greatly improved, Harry. Tomorrow, if I wrap you up and put you in the carriage, will you let me take you to Shugborough?"

He saw the light of hope in her eyes for the first time since she had come down with the contagion. "Please," she whispered softly.

True to his word, the next morning Thomas had Riley ready the coach. He loaded his own and Harry's trunks, as well as Rose's baggage. He dressed his wife in a warm flannel nightgown and knit slippers, then wrapped her in an eiderdown and carried her down to the carriage. Rose brought a bucket and a bedpan, just in case.

Though Thomas showed great enthusiasm that Harry was able to undertake the journey, on the inside he was racked with silent worry. His wife's legs were paralyzed, and he agonized over whether she would ever regain the ability to walk. He hoped against hope that once Harry got to Shugborough, her happy spirits would miraculously make her whole again.

They set off from London, and when they reached the countryside, Thomas was tempted to bare his conscience and confess to the reasons why he had leased a house on Half Moon Street and turned it into a gambling establishment. More than anything, he wanted to assure Harry that he'd sold the lease and was no longer involved. He longed to apologize to his wife, beg her forgiveness, and assure her it would never happen again.

But he could clearly see the fatigue written on her face. She was being extremely brave just tolerating the rigors of the carriage ride and summoning the strength it would take to reach Shugborough. Thomas decided he could not salve his conscience at Harry's expense. It would sap her strength and leave her in a state of utter exhaustion.

It was after dark when Riley drove through the gates of Shugborough Hall, and Thomas saw that both Rose and his wife were asleep. His heart overflowed with relief that she had not been taken from him. Before he disturbed her, he whispered, "I love you, Harry."

When he picked her up and carried her up the steps of the grand portico, through the elegant columns to the front door, Harry opened her eyes and breathed a sigh of pleasure.

"Mrs. Stearn, you remember Riley, the Abercorns' coachman. He will need a room plenished. And this is Rose, my wife's personal maid. She'll need a room close to our bedchamber." He sat down on an oak settle in the reception hall, holding his wife in his lap. "Please call the household servants. I need to explain something to them."

Thomas waited until the butler and all the maids were gathered. "Lady Harry has been extremely ill, and is still not well, so I have brought her to Shugborough to recover. What she has is not contagious, so you need have no fear. She cannot walk at the moment, but with time, that will be remedied." He stood up. "I'll take her upstairs now and Riley will carry up the luggage. Thank you all for your understanding."

When Thomas carried Harry into their gold and black master bedchamber, he watched her glance lovingly linger on the brass-monkey andirons and the chess set with its carved animal pieces. He set her down on the edge of the bed, and went down on his knees to remove her knit slippers. Then he massaged the muscles of her legs, and didn't stop until he saw her pale flesh turn pink. "Are you happy, Harry?"

For the first time since she'd been ill, Thomas saw her eyes smile.

When the luggage was brought up, Rose found Harry a clean nightgown. She helped Thomas fold up the beautiful bedcover with its golden dragonflies, and then he lifted Harry into the wide bed. "I know you're exhausted, sweetheart, but I still need to get a cup of alkanet wine into you."

Just then, there was a loud *meow.* "Here's Kouli come to see you. Would you like me to put her up on the bed?" The Persian cat rubbed her head against Harry's shoulder a few times and then cuddled down beside her.

The following day, Harry overcame her biggest hurdle. Mrs. Stearn made her some barley water, and not only did the patient keep it down; her retching disappeared and her flux did not return. The barley water quenched her raging thirst, and Mrs. Stearn set the kitchen maid to preparing a beef broth that would bring back Lady Harry's strength.

By afternoon she was restored enough to talk. "I want to see the daffodils."

"And so you shall." Thomas directed Rose to bring a day dress and stockings. The dress fit Harry loosely because she had lost so much weight. He brushed her hair and covered her head with a sun hat. He wrapped her in a cloak, picked her up in his arms, and carried her downstairs. Kouli trotted after them.

He strode outside and did not slow down until he reached the water. The riverside garden was a mass of yellow, and beyond the flowers, the swans and waterfowl glided.

"Thomas, the daffodils are breathtaking, and look! The cygnets have hatched."

He sat her down on the river wall so she could look her fill. "Breathe deeply and fill your lungs with the unique scent of daffodils."

Harry lifted her face to the sun and inhaled deeply. "I won't just fill my lungs; I shall fill my soul." She closed her eyes and smiled. "Thank you for bringing me."

"Nay, I thank you for sharing Shugborough with me. It makes the enjoyment a thousand times sweeter. Are you ready to go to your walled garden?"

"It is *our* garden, Thomas." She slid her

arms about his neck and he lifted her.

He carried her through the wooden gate, and sat her on the rustic bench so she could watch the birds flutter about the cascading fountain.

"I can smell jasmine and honeysuckle. It is the most romantic scent in the whole world. Shugborough is absolute perfection. I just wish I could walk."

"You will walk. Never doubt it for a moment. Your muscles have to regain their strength." He thrust away his doubts. *I have to completely believe what I'm saying, so that Harry will believe.* "If the weather stays hot, I'll take you in the water and hold you while you swim. Little by little, you will regain the use of your legs. In a few days, I warrant you'll be strong enough to sit a horse, and we'll take a ride into Cannock Chase."

She undid the ribbons of her sun hat and removed it. "That would be so lovely."

Thomas sat down beside her and took her hand. "Harry, when you discovered I was running a gaming house, I know you were shocked and hurt. I offer no defense or excuse because that would be rationalizing my mistakes. I want you to know my connection with Hazard House is over and done. I am ready to change. More than anything in the world, I want your trust."

She lifted his hand to her cheek. "Thomas, I thought all that was important. But it wasn't. When I became deathly ill, the only thing I wanted was you. And you came because you loved me. Without you, I would have surely died. You saved my life. You have earned my trust a thousand times over. I will never doubt you again."

Kouli jumped into the flower bed chasing a butterfly. Harry laughed and Thomas thought it was the loveliest sound he'd ever heard. "Aren't you going to scold her?"

"She's far too fat to jump high enough to catch it." His arm went around her to draw her close. "You could use a little fat on your bones. I live for the day when your voracious appetite returns and you are hungry again."

"As a matter of fact, I am hungry right now. No more broth for me." She gave him a saucy, sideways glance. "A guinea says I can eat something solid tonight."

"If I were a gambling man, I'd double that bet."

During the next week, Thomas carried her to visit the pale blue Chinese pagoda, as well as the brewhouse, where he poured her half a tankard of Shugborough's home-brewed ale.

"Fill it up. If I become legless, you'll simply have to carry me."

He grinned. "I'm delighted that your audacious sense of humor has returned. I could have no greater sign that your health is almost fully recovered."

He carried her to her walled garden for an hour every afternoon. He massaged her legs twice each day and was rewarded by the fact that she could now stand, though not yet walk. The dark circles beneath her eyes disappeared, and her lovely black hair became lustrous again. His apprehension began to ease slightly.

Every night in their four-poster, Thomas gathered her close against his heart. He whispered words of adoration to let her know how lovely she was, and how lucky he was to be her husband. Above all else, he wanted her to trust him implicitly, and wanted her to feel safe and secure in the knowledge that he loved and adored her. She clung to him trustingly and he kept his desire under control, sensing that when she was strong enough to make love, she would let him know.

Early one morning, Thomas carried her out to the beehives so she could watch him gather the honeycombs. Mary Trudgett, the stillroom maid, accompanied them, toting a big earthenware crock.

Harry laughed when she saw him light up a cigar. "Another secret vice!" she teased.

"Most of the bees have already left the hives to gather the day's pollen, but this smoke will lull any that remain and make them drowsy so they won't get angry." Thomas removed only one honeycomb from each of the dozen hives and put it into the crock. "This way, the theory goes, they don't even know one honeycomb is missing. But I think bees are far smarter than that. I prefer to think of them as being generous."

"I love honey. What do you do when you get these to the stillroom, Mary?"

"I put them in a press to extract the honey. Then later today, I will melt the beeswax combs to make candles, Lady Harry."

When they returned to the house, the post had been delivered. Thomas received a note from the coaching inn in Stafford informing him that they had received delivery of a pair of statues from Woodstock, Oxfordshire. The note said that they could transport the items to Shugborough the following week, or if Lord Lichfield preferred, he could make his own arrangements.

The centaurs! Thomas knew that the Duke of Marlborough had made good on his gambling losses, and had the marble statues shipped from Blenheim Palace. *I'll go and get them this afternoon. I want it to be a surprise for Harry.*

He summoned Ramsey and asked the steward to accompany him to the stables, where the head groom was currying the carriage horses. "I have a task for you, Toby. Go with Ramsey and borrow one of the farm wagons and a couple of Staffordshire workhorses. We are going into town to pick up a delivery of statues. They are extremely heavy, so I'll get Riley and Vickerstaff to come with us."

Thomas returned to the house, where he was in time to join Harry for lunch. He was encouraged to see her eat a whole breast of partridge and a half dozen spears of asparagus dipped in butter. Then she devoured a large serving of strawberries and cream, and stole half of his. "You are insatiable." He picked her up and kissed her nose.

He carried her upstairs, put her down on their wide bed, and propped pillows behind her. "I have to go into Stafford on business, and while I'm gone, I want you to have a rest. I'll be back in a couple of hours. Here's Kouli to keep you company."

"Darling, hand me a couple of the books I brought from London."

He ran his fingers over the titles. "Which would you like?"

"Any two will do, so long as one of them is *Tom Jones.*"

He raised his eyebrows, pretending to be shocked.

Harry giggled. "I find that men christened Thomas are the very devil!"

He brought her the books and dipped his head for a lingering kiss. *Oh, Harry, you are going to be over the moon when you see the centaurs are back in the Tower of Winds.*

When the farm wagon got to the Stafford coaching inn, it took all five men to lift and load the black marble centaurs. On the way back, Riley sat next to Toby, who was driving the wagon. He was itching to drive the big Staffordshire workhorses, but decided he'd better leave it to someone with experience.

Thomas sat in the bed of the wagon with Ramsey and Vickerstaff. The trio kept a firm grip on the treasured statues to keep them steady. Thomas couldn't keep the grin from his face. It had taken many years of searching and, once he learned their location, an enormous amount of dealing before he regained possession of the centaurs. *At long last they are returning to Shugborough where they belong.*

Before the wagon drove through the gate, Thomas thought he could smell something burning. The horses slowly clopped past the daffodils in the riverside garden, and the house came into view. Black smoke billowed up from the mansion. All the men saw it at the same time and cried out their alarm. "My God, Shugborough's afire. We have to save the house!"

Thomas was off the wagon in a flash. "To hell with Shugborough. Harry can't walk!" He ran as if all the demons in Hades were after him. He dashed between the columns on the portico and when he opened the front door, a cloud of black smoke met him. He could hear the high-pitched sounds of women's voices — panicking and shouting that seemed to come from the kitchen area. He could not take the time to investigate, but as he bolted toward the stairs, he bellowed, "Get out! Everybody get out!"

He took the stairs two at a time. The higher he went, the thicker the smoke seemed to be. In the hall outside the master bedchamber, the smoke was drifting in menacing gray swirls. It caught in his throat, and it was difficult to take a deep breath, which did nothing to keep his fear for Harry at bay.

He flung open the bedroom door, and was gripped by panic when he saw the bed was empty. Then he heard her cough, and saw that she was on the floor. Her legs prevented her from crawling, but she was pulling herself toward the door using only her hands.

He swooped her up in his arms and began to run.

"Thomas, I knew you'd come for me. Set me down outside and go and fight the fire. We cannot lose Shugborough!"

When he reached the ground floor, he could now hear men's voices mixed in with the women's. He could hear someone issuing orders. He was totally focused on getting Harry to safety and didn't stop running until he reached the stables, where he set her down on a pile of hay in one of the stalls. The only person there was Toby's young son.

"I want to go and fight the fire, m'lord."

"I forbid it," Thomas declared. "Shugborough's people are what matters, not the hall. I charge you to look after my wife until I return."

"Go around the back, Thomas, I think it

must have started in the kitchen."

"No time for that," he explained. "I have to find Kouli." He was off and running before she could reply.

Back inside the house, Thomas thought the smoke was not quite as thick, but he reasoned that was because it would now be dispersed over a wider area, and a greater number of rooms. He retraced his steps to the master bedchamber. The Persian cat had been with Harry when he had left for Stafford.

He entered the bedroom, calling the cat's name, but there was no response, and though Thomas circled the entire chamber, there was no sign of Kouli-Khan. He knew that Harry would be distraught if the cat perished, so he searched the bedchambers in the same wing. His heart sank when he came up empty. He knew he should abandon the search and join Shugborough's people, who he guessed were doing their best to fight the fire and keep it from destroying the entire house.

At the last minute, an idea occurred to him. *Kouli may be hiding under the bed.*

Thomas tied his neckcloth around his nose and mouth, went down on all fours, and crawled beneath the bed. He saw the cat huddled in a corner in abject terror. He grabbed it by the scruff of the neck and dragged it toward him. Kouli dug her claws into his hand, but when Thomas did not let go, the cat transferred her claws to his coat and clung tightly.

He ran downstairs and did not stop until he reached the stables. He pried Kouli from his jacket and dropped her into Harry's lap. "If you stay here in the stables, you'll be safe." He was panting heavily. "I'll go and see what I can do."

When Thomas arrived at the back of the hall, he found that the entire house staff, plus Ramsey, the stable grooms, and Riley, had formed a bucket brigade from the outside pump to the kitchen. He saw that the stillroom had burned away completely, and the fire had spread to the kitchen. But because the house was covered in slate, the flames had taken much longer to get inside and do irreparable damage.

The fire had managed to burn through two large window frames and the kitchen door. The iron stove and the immense cooking range were still intact, along with the cast-iron cooking pots and pans. Though the oak table and butcher blocks were on fire and the kitchen chairs were now piles of ash, Thomas was surprised to see that the slate floor was unmarred, the porcelain sinks — though black with soot — were undamaged, and though the walls were smoldering, they were still standing. Thomas was extremely relieved that the fire had not burned through the ceiling to their bedchamber above. There was an abundance of smoke upstairs because it had risen through the chimney of the kitchen fireplace.

Thomas wielded the buckets of water alongside his staff until every last lick of flame was out and nothing was left smoldering. Everyone sank down on the floor to catch his or her breath.

"I thank all of you from the bottom of my heart," he panted. "You have saved Shugborough. Your loyalty and devotion to me and to the house are beyond belief. The sensible thing would have been to save yourselves. I owe every single one of you a deep debt of gratitude." His gaze traveled about the kitchen. "This can all be restored. The damage looks far worse at the moment than it really is."

He gazed around the room and began to laugh as relief set in. "If any of you have strength left to climb stairs, we'd better throw open all the windows and doors to rid the rooms of smoke. We'll be smelling the stuff for weeks."

Riley, Ramsey, and Vickerstaff followed him from the kitchen, while the women stayed behind to clean up the mess.

Early the next morning, Harry gazed at her sleeping husband. Her heart overflowed with tenderness for him. *He loves me far more than he loves Shugborough.*

She prodded him awake. "Come on, slugabed, I refuse to wait any longer to see the damage. I let you put me off last night with the excuse that you were tired, but the real reason you wouldn't carry me to the kitchen was that you didn't want me to be upset."

"That is exactly the reason, my shrewd, tattooed beauty."

"Thomas, I am not a delicate flower who wilts in the face of adversity. In any case, Rose told me what to expect. I know the stillroom is completely gone. Apparently, Mary Trudgett had pressed the honey from the wax combs, and was in the process of melting the beeswax to pour into the candle molds.

"She accidentally knocked over the crock of honey and it covered everything. In her agitation, the flame she had lit to melt the beeswax spread to a keg of brandy and set it ablaze. It was like a river of fire, and Mary did the right thing to flee from the wooden stillroom and cry the alarm."

Thomas dressed himself and then brought Harry her petticoat and stockings.

She took them from his hands. "I can do this," she insisted.

"Yes, I know. But it deprives me of a great deal of pleasure."

The corners of her mouth went up. "You are full of blarney. Sometimes I suspect you have Irish blood."

He grinned. "It's Welsh — Celtic; same thing, really." He helped her into her dress, fastened the buttons up the back, and kissed the nape of her neck.

"I suppose it is. You share many similarities with my father. Another dark, dominant, dangerous devil, according to my mother."

"And then some," he said with a wink.

Thomas stoically carried Harry into the kitchen. The burned-out windows and door had been boarded up, and all the ash and soot had been cleared away. He watched her face with trepidation, and saw her eyes flood with tears. "Not a delicate flower, indeed!"

Harry tried to smile through her tears. "I think of Shugborough as a living, breathing thing. I can feel the house's pain."

He kissed her ear. "That's because you've

been in a lot of pain yourself recently. You are sensitive at the moment, and I wouldn't have you any other way." He set her feet to the floor and stood behind her to hold her steady. "Actually, we were extremely lucky. If Shugborough hadn't been encased in slate, the whole place would have gone up like an inferno. We will have it repaired in no time."

"But, Thomas, what will we use for money?"

"The sheep shearing produced more wool than last year, and I hear the price of wool has gone up." He lifted her and carried her to the breakfast room.

Before the food arrived, Harry put her hand over her husband's. "How are *you* feeling, Thomas? Your great fear of Shugborough catching fire has been realized. It must have been extremely traumatic for you, darling."

"When I saw the house was on fire, my priorities immediately fell into their rightful order. Saving you was all that mattered. Shugborough took second place."

"Nay, Kouli took second place. Shugborough came last."

"Perhaps my deep-seated fears of Shugborough burning have been laid to rest."

Harry picked up her fork and waved it like

a magic wand. "I hereby decree all bad dreams are in the past. From now on, we will only dream about the future."

Mrs. Stearn brought in their breakfast, and Harry immediately reached under the table and fed Kouli a piece of bacon.

"When your father returns from Ireland, I intend to swallow my damnable pride and ask him to advise me about investments and stocks, although truth to tell, that is the riskiest form of gambling that exists."

"I warrant there is a great deal of money to be made if you are shrewd. If your *damnable* pride will allow you to take a woman's advice, I would recommend *iron.* Thousands of items in this modern day and age are made from cast iron. Woodstoves, kitchen ranges, pots and pans, park railings, fire grates, and locomotives. Just promise me you won't put your money in coal?"

"You are the most audacious female I have ever met. Now, begod, you fancy yourself as my financial adviser."

"Oh, I don't just limit myself to finances. I'm willing to advise you on any subject you fancy, Lord Bloody Lichfield."

"Well, in that case, I would value your opinion on something I brought from Stafford. If you don't like it, we'll get rid of it."

Thomas picked her up and carried her

outside. He crossed the velvet lawn and headed toward the Tower of Winds. He set her down just inside the entrance.

"Thomas! Oh my God, it's the *centaurs!*" She raised her arms and took five steps toward them.

"Harry, you are walking!" He ran to her, swooped her up in his arms, and twirled her about. "The minute you saw the centaurs, you forgot about your legs."

"I did. Isn't that amazing?" She laughed with relief. Then she took a few more steps, and placed a loving hand on the black marble.

"Oh, you are my magic man. How did you ever get Marlborough to give them up?"

"I won the damn things, of course."

Harry reached up and kissed him. "Bugger and balls, you are a wicked devil."

CHAPTER TWENTY-SEVEN

"Thomas, put me down."

"But, Harry, I enjoy carrying you."

"I want to walk into Shugborough un-aided."

"You just want to show off to the servants. You love being the center of attention."

"Of course I do! So let's come to a compromise. I will walk on my own until I want to go upstairs. Then you can pick me up and carry me."

"You win, my beauty." He put her feet to the ground. "I was just teasing you. I think you know just how thrilled I am that you can walk again." He stepped back and allowed her to go into the house unaided.

"Lady Harry, you are walking!" Rose ran to get Mrs. Stearn, and the rest of the staff followed the housekeeper to the reception hall to see with their own eyes.

"It's a miracle!" Mrs. Stearn declared. "We should celebrate this occasion. I shall cook something special for dinner. What do you fancy, Lady Harry?"

The females of the household spent the next half hour focusing on the Countess of Lichfield, naming their favorite food, and planning the dinner menu.

Finally, Thomas interrupted. "Harry, I know you've been looking forward to a ride through Cannock Chase. If we leave now, we can be back in time for this fancy dinner."

She looked at him with sparkling eyes. "Do you truly think I can manage to ride?"

He bent his head to whisper in her ear. "I plan to take you up before me."

"That would be perfect. What are we waiting for?"

Thomas lifted his wife into the saddle, and then mounted Nemesis behind her.

"I love to watch you mount. When you throw your leg across your horse, you become one with it."

He bent his head and nipped her ear. "That sounds like a fantasy to me. What other secret fantasies do you have, my wild little wanton?"

"The last time I was in Ireland, I dreamed that I was a black otter, and a sleek dark male began to chase me. He kept brushing his body against mine and we did a mating dance in the water."

"That sounds like me." He slowed his mount as they entered the forest.

"He lured me from the water to lie in the long grass, and then the otter transformed into you. Your kisses were more intoxicating than wine."

"Were we naked?"

"Yes."

"You outrageous baggage — that was before we were married."

"It gets better."

He flexed the saddle muscles of his thighs as he felt her soft bum against his hardening erection.

"You were transformed into a black centaur, and your gleaming silver eyes demanded that I follow you into the forest."

"Were you also a centaur?"

"I was. I remember pawing the ground, impatient to follow you. We entered the forest and ran faster and faster on a wild hell-for-leather gallop. When we came to a clearing, I waited for you to claim me. Instead of mounting me, as I expected, you went down before me in homage."

"Sweetheart, in your innocent dreams I was the perfect gallant. Can you ever forgive me for disillusioning you?"

"Thomas, I wouldn't change anything about you. I love you exactly as you are. The terrible illness that brought me close to death gave me new perspective. I truly understand why you did what you did — you kept it from me because you love me."

He reined in and put a finger to his lips. "Did you hear that bark? There must be muntjac deer close by. There they go!"

"Oh, the herd has babies. Look how tiny the fawns are," Harry said in awe.

"Let's follow them." They emerged from the trees into grassland, and as the deer loped through the lush pasture, they disturbed myriad flocks of game birds that filled the sky with beating wings and shrill cries.

When they arrived at the marshland, they spotted two pairs of otters and a pair of muskrat. "They all have young. It's so thrilling to see them."

"It's breeding season. Let's make plans to ride through the chase every week so we can watch their progress. I don't think we should ride hell for leather today. I don't want to take the chance of injuring the baby hares and rabbits that hide in the grass."

"Your love of *cratures* is such an endearing quality, it melts my heart."

"I have come to realize that we are very

much alike, Harry. We are kindred spirits, as the poets say. We are lucky to have found each other. Not many married couples are so fortunate."

"Hell and Furies, your opinion of me has undergone an amazing transformation. Don't you remember your accusations? *You revel in audacity! You have no shame! You deliberately hurl yourself against my principles! You are impulsive and reckless, and need a firm hand to protect you from yourself!*"

"I applied the firm hand and turned you into a paragon." His hand came up and cupped her breast.

"I much prefer being reckless to being a paragon. Let's go and wade in the stream."

"Done!" He dismounted, raised his arms, and lifted her down to him. Before he let her go, he warned, "I think it would be prudent to walk slowly."

She pushed him playfully and danced away from him. "I don't know how to be prudent. It isn't in my nature!" She kicked off her shoes, raised her skirts, and peeled off her stockings. She stepped into the stream and laughed as the water swirled about her knees.

Thomas removed his shoes and rolled up his pants. "Wait for me. I want to play."

He joined her in the stream, and hand in

hand, they waded about, laughing like children as frogs jumped out of their way and hatchlings swam between their toes.

When they tired of their game, they climbed out and lay in the sun on the bank of the stream. They kissed away the rest of the afternoon, reveling in their solitude. When at last they reluctantly knew it was time to join the rest of the world, he lifted her into the saddle and swung up behind her.

On the ride back he held her possessively, and the feel of his hard cock against her bum was so arousing to both of them that by the time they entered Shugborough, all they could think of was the wide, inviting bed that awaited them.

The delicious smell of food that assailed their nostrils brought them out of their sensual reverie, and they looked at each other with comical dismay as they realized they would have to sit through the special dinner that had been planned.

His dark eyes brimmed with laughter. "I want all of you to join us in the dining room for dinner. This is your celebration as much as ours."

The meal began with mushroom bisque, laced with wine and cream.

"This is heavenly, Mrs. Stearn. You must

teach me how to make this." Harry was perfectly sincere. She licked her spoon with relish, trying not to think of licking the cleft in her husband's chin.

Next came a spring artichoke salad, and the spiny leaves of the olive green flower reminded Harry of the exciting feel of her husband's abrasive jaw before he shaved.

"Artichokes are an aphrodisiac," Mrs. Stearn confided.

Thomas and Harry glanced at each other, and could not mask their amusement at the irony of their cook's words. Harry winked at Mrs. Stearn. "I'll tell you if they work."

"You have no shame," Thomas said solemnly.

The main course was lamb chops with mint sauce, roasted potatoes, and new green peas fresh from the garden.

The lovers caressed each other with their eyes, no longer able to hide their longing.

When Dorothy, the kitchen maid, carried in a luscious trifle, Thomas got to his feet. "I want all of you to stay and enjoy yourselves, but I beg you to excuse us. It is Lady Harry's bedtime."

As Thomas swung his wife into his arms, Riley stood up and raised his glass. "Three cheers for Lady Harry!"

As everyone cheered and whooped with

laughter, Harry threw them a kiss.

"Thank you so much. You know I love being the center of attention."

Thomas kicked the bedchamber door closed with his foot. "Only the thought of the reward to come enabled me to climb two flights of stairs with this erection."

He sat her down on the edge of the bed and knelt before her to remove her shoes and stockings. "I have a dilemma. I cannot possibly give your legs their nightly massage. My need is too great."

"Mine too," she gasped. "Hurry with the undressing."

Their fingers touched and became entangled as she helped him remove her clothes. Then by mutual consent, they made short work of his garments.

They needed no foreplay. It seemed an eternity since they had last made love and she hungered for his hard body. When he came over her, she arched up to meet his thrusts. As her tight sheath stretched to accommodate his great size, the pleasure became too intense to sustain for long. He gripped her with his thighs and plunged deeply. Their release came hard and fast, and at exactly the same moment.

They lay entwined, catching their breath,

each wishing it had lasted longer. "I was in an indecent hurry," he confessed. "How do your legs feel?"

"Weak as wet linen."

"I couldn't massage them before, but I can now, sweetheart."

With his strong hands rubbing her limbs, Harry was becoming aroused again before he was finished. Thomas lay down beside her and with the backs of his fingers brushed her shoulders, her throat, and her cheeks as lightly as thistledown. His gesture was so infinitely tender, her eyes flooded with tears.

His lips grazed her eyelashes, tasting her tears; then he captured her lips in the gentlest kiss he'd ever given her. Every inch of her body anticipated the caress of his hands and his mouth. She watched his dark, handsome face and her breath caught in her throat as he reverently showed her how much he loved her.

She traced his lips with her fingertips and he kissed them gently. When his hands caressed her breasts, he used a delicate touch, as if they were made of precious porcelain.

He drew her beneath him. "I love you so much," he whispered. "Yield to me, darling."

She opened her silken thighs, and he

sheathed himself gently, sweetly. She had never imagined making love could be so poignant and beautiful. His mouth never left hers. Their warm lips fused over and over until her mouth tingled from an abundance of kisses. His lovemaking was tender and unhurried, and with closed eyes, she drifted on soft, billowy clouds, smiling dreamily as he filled her with his love. Her pleasure grew intense until she thought she might faint. Then at just the right moment, they melted into each other.

Harry sighed. "I love you with all my heart, Thomas Nathaniel."

During the first week of May, Harry's parents and her sister arrived. Thomas had sent word to Ireland that Harry was deathly ill, then sent another letter as soon as her health improved to ease their alarm. The moment they returned from Ireland, they rushed to Shugborough.

Abercorn brought the treasured books from Barons Court and, as he had promised, one of his prized Arabian mares for his daughter.

Harry was greatly relieved that the fire damage in the kitchen had been skillfully repaired and that the two suites of bedroom furniture had arrived from Althorp in

Northampton before her family arrived.

Harry gave her mother and Jane the grand tour of Shugborough. "I know it is wretched of me, but I don't look forward to returning to London for your debutante ball. I long to stay at Shugborough for the entire summer."

"I am so relieved to see you recovered," Jane declared. "I think you should stay here for an extended honeymoon."

"Jane is right, darling," her mother agreed. "Besides, I think she is looking forward to being the center of attention. You and Trixy did have a way of stealing Jane's thunder."

"But surely Trixy will attend your ball?"

Jane laughed. "Yes, she will. The beauteous Countess of Durham is in London to see her doctor. But I'm afraid Trixy won't be doing much dancing."

"She's as big as a pig full of figs," Lady Lu confided. "We are delighted that she is blooming with health, but there is no denying that she is truly swollen with child!"

"And what about Rachel?" Harry asked.

"I've brought you her letters, Harry. She and James will be in London in a few days, and as soon as they've attended my debutante ball, they are planning on visiting you here at Shugborough. She's put it all in her letters."

"That's wonderful. I knew she married the right man to make her happy."

Thomas and Abercorn were in the stables, introducing the young Arabian mare to Nemesis. "I think your suggestion of breeding these two is excellent. The best time to have him cover her is June. Daylight stimulates estrus, so she should be in heat by then," Abercorn advised.

Thomas ran an appreciative hand along the Arabian's glossy neck. "Yes, June would be good. Then she'll foal next May, when there's plenty of grass to help her milk supply."

Abercorn put his hand on his son-in-law's shoulder. "I deeply appreciate you nursing Harriet through her dreaded bout of cholera. We could have easily lost her if you hadn't taken over and tended her day and night."

"She had a bad time of it. It truly was touch and go for many days. She became paralyzed and lost the use of her legs. I've never been so deathly worried in my life."

"Bringing her to Shugborough has done her a world of good."

"Yes, I agree. Would you mind terribly if we didn't come back to London right away? Harry is longing to stay the entire summer."

"I think that's a splendid idea. Stay and breed your horses and enjoy your estate. You've done an amazing job restoring Shugborough's treasures and furnishings. I know that money has been a problem for some time."

"I promised Harry that I would swallow my pride and ask you for financial advice."

"Nothing would please me more, my boy. There's money to be made in English manufacturing. We produce the best-quality goods in the entire world at the moment."

"Thank you. Come to the library after dinner. You provide the advice and I'll supply the home-brewed ale."

When the two men returned to the house, Abercorn made a suggestion. "You know, I think it advisable if you stay at Shugborough for the entire summer, Harry. London is an unhealthy place at the best of times, and contagions are rife in the hot weather."

"Thomas has likely been painting you graphic pictures of my illness. But thanks to him, I am completely recovered. My reasons for wanting to stay at Shugborough for the summer are totally selfish, so I thank you for indulging me, Father."

Abercorn winked at his daughter. "We all have selfish reasons for doing things. For instance, the reason I came rushing to

Shugborough the moment we returned from Ireland, quite apart from seeing how you were, Harry, was to make sure Riley and my best carriage are returned to London. I can't manage without them."

"Hell and Furies, Father, I was hoping to keep them," Harry teased. "Next thing, you'll be wanting Rose back at Hampden House!"

"This has been the most wonderful summer of my life!" Thomas was driving Harry back to Shugborough from a day of shopping in Stafford. She had bought material for new curtains in the kitchen, and some lovely Staffordshire pottery for the new stillroom they had built. Then they had enjoyed dinner at the posting inn.

As they drove through the gates and the lights from the house came into view, Harry said, "I don't know which season is my favorite. Spring was delightful with all the daffodils in bloom, and Cannock Chase filled with newly born wildlife, but the summer months also have been splendid. I have truly enjoyed the warm, lazy days and my walled garden overflowing with jasmine and honeysuckle." She sighed happily. "I can't believe it is August. Where has the time gone?"

"It has been the happiest summer of my life, because I've spent it here with you."

"Let's do it again next year. What is to stop us from coming in the spring and staying until autumn? We could possibly even do some entertaining. Perhaps by next year, our honeymoon will be over and we can bear to let others into our lives."

"I very much doubt our honeymoon will be over."

She glanced at him as they drove up to the stables. "You have an enigmatic look on your face, as if you know something that I am unaware of."

Thomas smiled. "I do have a surprise for you, but I intend to keep my secret just a little longer."

"You take inordinate pleasure in keeping secrets, you dark devil."

As they walked from the stables to the house, Harry pointed with delight. "Do you see the glow flies in the darkness?"

"Did you know that when their luminescent glow goes on and off, the fiery signal is a mating invitation?"

"Oh, how lovely. I never thought about it, but I warrant you are right."

When they went into the house, Harry saw that there was a letter from her mother on the table in the entrance hall. "Good! We have news from London. I'll take it with me and read it upstairs."

She paused when she got to the foot of the staircase. She could now climb stairs faster than anyone at Shugborough, but it was far more pleasurable to have Thomas carry her, especially when it was bedtime.

Harry undressed quickly and slipped on her nightgown. Then she sat on the edge of the bed and opened her letter.

"Oh, Thomas, you'll never guess. Trixy and D'Arcy have twin sons! Bless her heart, no wonder her tummy was so huge. Mother and babies are doing very well."

"That's wonderful. I'm very happy for them. But when you have babies, I hope they come one at a time. I'd die of worry if you were having twins, Harry."

"There's more amazing news. Jane is engaged to Will Montagu! My sister has been in love with the braw Scot for years."

Thomas grinned. "Your mother will be over the moon. She's always wanted Will Montagu for a son-in-law."

"Jane will be the Countess of Dalkeith and the future Duchess of Buccleuch. Mother always insisted that one of us should marry Will so that she could visit Montagu House on a regular basis and descend its glorious staircase with the dramatic flair it deserves."

Harry was distracted from her letter the moment Thomas began to undress. If truth were told, it was the highlight of her day to see the lithe body of her naked husband. Tonight, for some reason, he removed his trousers and left on his shirt. Her eyes followed his fingers as he began to undo the buttons. Then he deliberately turned his back before he took off the linen shirt.

When he turned to face her, Harry's eyes went wide with delight. "You got a tattoo today!" She ran to him and traced the indelible image on the left side of his chest, above his heart, with her fingertips. Then she kissed it and went weak with desire. "A centaur was the perfect choice." She slipped off her silk nightgown, lifted her arms about his neck, and rubbed herself against his body. "Oh, I was right. Our attraction *is* physical!"

AUTHOR'S NOTE

In *The Dark Earl* I refer to the Marquis and Marchioness of Abercorn as the Duke and Duchess of Abercorn, though James Hamilton did not receive his dukedom from Queen Victoria until 1866.

Harriet and Thomas Anson, the Earl and Countess of Lichfield, had thirteen children. Thomas became the lord lieutenant of Staffordshire from 1863 to 1871.

Beatrix and D'Arcy Lambton, the Earl and Countess of Durham, had twin sons, followed by eleven other children.

Jane Hamilton married William Montagu, the Earl of Dalkeith, in 1859, and they had eight children.

Shugborough Hall, Staffordshire, is open to the public.

ABOUT THE AUTHOR

Virginia Henley is a *New York Times* best-selling author and the recipient of numerous awards, including the *Romantic Times* Lifetime Achievement Award. Her novels have been translated into fourteen languages. A grandmother of three, she lives in St. Petersburg, Florida, with her husband.